the
geek girl
and
the
scandalous
earl

the geek girl and the scandalous earl

GINA LAMM

sourcebooks
casablanca

Published by Sourcebooks Casablanca, an imprint of Sourcebooks, Inc.
P.O. Box 4410, Naperville, Illinois 60567-4410
(630) 961-3900
Fax: (630) 961-2168
www.sourcebooks.com

Printed and bound in the United States of America.
VP 10 9 8 7 6 5 4 3 2 1

Even though he'll probably never read it, this is for my Daddy. Thanks for never ever giving up on your "knee baby." I love you.

One

HER SWORD GLITTERED AS IT SWUNG IN A WIDE ARC, whistling as it cleaved the air. She smiled as the goblin bolted.

"Jamie, I need heals."

Ignoring the call for help, she advanced on another goblin. The tide was turning now. Her allies had almost annihilated the threat.

"Jamie?"

With a wild cry, she loosed a spell on the disgusting creature. It staggered backward before recovering and charging on her in a berserk rage, eyes wild and fangs extended. Her next swing missed, and she took a critical hit.

"Jamie, for chrissakes, we're dying here!"

Some quick spellwork took care of the goblin, and Jamie reluctantly turned her attention back to her allies. Whoops. Three of the guild's portraits were glaring red, signaling their imminent deaths.

"Hang on, guys. I'm here."

Targeting the leader, she cast her most powerful healing spell. The computer screen flashed: OUT OF MANA.

"Eeep!"

She fumbled in her bags for her mana-restoring potions. She'd just managed to find one, clicking to

activate it when the screen went gray. YOU HAVE
DIED. RESURRECT NOW?

The guild's groans sounded through her headset as she
slumped back in her seat.

"Jamie, where the hell were you?"

"Worst. Healer. Ever."

"I wouldn't use your heals for a paper cut, Jamie. That
was pathetic. Haven't you ever run this level?"

She shoved her long highlighted brown hair over her
shoulder, glaring at the computer screen. "Of course I
have. I can heal this run in my sleep. I just got a little
carried away with the mobs. It won't happen again."

Kurt, the guild leader, let out an audible sigh over the
chat channel. "Fine. One more run. Everyone ready?"

Jamie readied her character's potions and spell rota-
tion. *Typical.* They figured since she was the only girl
in the guild, she should be the healer. She didn't mind
healing, especially in the more difficult dungeons, but she
wanted to do her part to take down the bad guys too. It
wasn't fair. Men never took her seriously. That's why she
played these games. It was supposed to be a level field.
But the game, like her life, was rarely ever exactly what
she thought it should be.

The Lords of Discord guild cleared the dungeon run
easily that time, with Jamie focusing on healing alone.
She picked at the chipping mauve polish on her finger-
nails between fights, only needing to keep half an eye on
the large computer screen.

"Great job, Lords." Kurt's voice held a ton of relief as
he divvied up the loot.

After securing her share of the rewards, Jamie said her
good-byes to her guild-mates, logged out, and switched
to her other character, Killaz. A hulking Amazon melee
class in a chain-mail dress with a huge two-handed

sword, Killaz was how Jamie saw herself in her mind's eye—kick-ass, tough, and more than a little bit intimidating. As she cut a swath through the forest full of giant spiders, she wished that she was anything like that in real life. *If I was as tough as Killaz, then that jerk Logan wouldn't have broken my heart and walked all over me like a dollar store welcome mat.*

After an hour of grinding out daily quests, a vibration in the front pocket of her shorts made her jump. Her groan echoed through her junky living room when she saw the text: "Go help Pawpaw Milton with the antiques or I'll sell your Comic-Con pass. Love, Leah."

Jamie slogged up the stairs with a huge sigh, studiously ignoring the piano with half-written songs strewn across the bench. The last thing she wanted was to move dusty furniture and knickknacks in the triple-digit heat. But her best friend, Leah, had had enough of Jamie's post-breakup isolation and had put her foot down where it hurt—right on the pop-culture fan's trip to the Holy City.

As she drove downtown to the storage unit she was helping Pawpaw Milton clear out, she tried to believe that everything would go back to normal. Well, before-Logan normal. With Leah's help and this part-time job, maybe she could get there. Maybe even start writing music again. And besides, she'd grown up a lot since the last time she'd worked at the antiques store. Her first summer job there had ended after only three days. The antiques were probably way less fragile now.

❦

"Damn!"

The resounding crack of glass echoed through the storage unit, making Jamie flinch. Pawpaw Milton had left her alone in the unit to go to an estate auction. The hundred-degree heat had her dripping with sweat—not the best condition for handling two-hundred-year-old crystal.

Jamie hoped that Pawpaw hadn't noticed the pretty bowl tucked away in the corner. She carefully shoved the evidence of her klutziness into a large black garbage bag. *What he doesn't know won't get me fired,* she figured, though she couldn't exactly shake the guilt.

Holding the end of her ponytail atop her head, she gulped from the giant bottle of water like a frantic desert survivor. This was hell.

Jamie pulled her phone from her pocket: 2:00 p.m. Another three hours to go before she could escape to her cave and take a shower. Oh well. It would be worth it in two months when she got to Comic-Con. Hopefully.

She unknotted the bottom of her tank top and dried her face and hands with the tail of it. Even in her thinnest tank top and shortest shorts, she still felt overdressed for this weather.

After carting out and cataloging a number of fragile items without incident, all that remained was the large furniture on the opposite side of the unit. Well, other than the big sheet-covered monstrosity behind the table. *What is that, anyway?*

Reaching up, she stood on tiptoes to toss back the corner of the dust cover for a quick peek. But she tugged just a little too hard, and the white fabric billowed as it floated down on top of her, dust and cobwebs coating her sweat-slicked skin. Arms flailing, she fought free of the cover, stomping it in a fit of frustration when it lay on the concrete at her flip-flopped feet.

"What the hell is your problem?" Jamie yelled at the innocent-looking mound of fabric. It said nothing, just laid there looking smug.

She turned her back on it to see what it had been covering.

The piece was a tall bureau, made of a rich mahogany that almost glowed gold from deep within the wood. It sloped outward in the middle, wider at its drawer-filled base than the top. Mirrored doors covered the upper portion.

She touched the wood lovingly. It was beautiful, cool to her skin even in the sweltering heat. When she'd reached up as high as she could, she sighed and trailed her thumb down the center of the shiny mirror on one door.

Her thumb dipped into the center of the glass.

With a gasp, she pulled, trying to free her hand. It wouldn't move. She was stuck.

She yanked backward with all her strength. The mirror pulled on her hand, drawing her farther into the glass. She braced against the bottom of the bureau, using her legs to give her leverage. She was in up to her wrist now.

"Help!" she yelled, frantically scrabbling against the mirror's hold. "Somebody, please!"

Using all her weight, she jerked backward, nearly dislocating her shoulder in the process. The mirror refused to release its hold. She whacked the slanted middle with the flat of her free hand in frustration.

With one last effort, she braced her feet against the bottom drawer and pulled with all her might. Without loosing its grip on her, the furniture tilted dangerously, almost tipping before she hit the floor to right it again.

Well, this sucks, she thought, slumping against the bureau. Her right ear was traveling through the mirror now.

So much for Comic-Con. So much for her place in the Lords of Discord guild. So much for showing Logan she could be fine without him. She hadn't really been doing a good job of that anyway, but dammit, she deserved better than being consumed by antique furniture!

Once she gave up fighting, the pull went much

faster. Within moments, the glass had swallowed her
entire head.

☙

Jamie blinked. And blinked again. A large, very masculine
bedroom was spread out before her, filled with luxurious
furniture and dark fabrics. In front of the huge four-poster
bed, a greyhound sat slumped on one hip, legs sprawled
open like an old bald man watching Skinemax.

She leapt off the cold wooden floor and turned. The
bureau was behind her. At least, it looked like the same
bureau. The wood was brighter, the mirrored doors even
shinier. It looked like a brand-new piece of furniture.

She tapped the glass. Solid. She pressed her hand flat
against it, pushing. Nothing. *Crap.*

She put her hands on her hips, turned, and glared at
the dog.

"What the hell just happened?"

Claws scrabbling against the wooden floor, the dog
barreled straight for her. She barely had time to put
her hands out to ward him away before the tall animal
plowed into her, tail wagging and tongue lolling. Caught
off-balance by the force, she went down like a rock.
The slanted corner of the bureau caught her temple, and
everything went black.

Two

LORD MICAH AXELBY, EARL OF DUNNINGTON, WAS having an unusually fine day. He had just returned from calling on Miss Felicity Lyons, a most amiable young lady. After a turn in the park in his phaeton, in which he had spoken civilly to no less than three members of society's elite, he'd returned her and her chaperone to her home. He had asked her to accompany him to the theatre the next evening. She had agreed in a most well-bred manner. He was becoming quite sure that she would do well as a countess—now that his difficulties seemed to be over.

He tossed the reins to a waiting footman and descended from the phaeton. The chill of the air turned his breath to frosty smoke as the sun fell lower in the sky. The pleasant afternoon was a mere memory now, giving way to the cold March evening.

"Welcome home, my lord," his butler said as he assisted the earl in removing his hat and coat.

"Thank you, Thornton."

"Will you be dining at your club this evening, my lord?"

Micah rubbed his hands together. "No, it's too cold to be gadding about. I'll dine here."

With a nod and a bow, Thornton disappeared into the kitchens.

Micah sighed, content to his bones for the first time in many a fortnight. He headed up the stairs to his bed-chamber, intending to dress for dinner.

"What the bloody hell?"

∽∾

"Baron, to me," Micah ordered the dog. With one last lick on the woman's nose, Baron rose and trotted to his master's side.

Micah knelt beside the girl, pressing his fingers to her throat. A pulse beat there, underneath her clammy skin. At his touch, a shiver went through her body and she moaned softly.

Well, Micah thought as he sat back on his heels, *she's alive at least.*

She needed care, and as a gentleman, he couldn't ignore that, despite the fact that she was in his home uninvited. With a gentle hand, he pushed back the hank of hair on her temple. The knot was faintly bruised, and he frowned.

"Yes, m'lord?" asked a maid timidly from the doorway.

"Fetch Mrs. Knightsbridge. This, ahem, person requires attention."

She bobbed a curtsy and disappeared in a flash of wide eyes and frilly mobcap.

"Damn and blast," he muttered to himself as he picked up the courtesan and deposited her on his bed. He must be mad.

Micah paced at the end of the bed, wondering what the devil he was going to do with this chit.

The last thing he needed was a stranger's death on his own damned bed. Baron hopped on the bed and resumed his position curled protectively near the female. The jostling of his hound settling next to her drew another moan from the woman, just as Mrs. Knightsbridge entered the room, followed by the still surprised maid.

"Yes, your lordship? Muriel said you needed my… Good heavens!" The round housekeeper splayed a palm on her ample bosom.

"Yes, good heavens indeed. It seems that my home has been invaded by a young woman in a shocking state of undress. However, she has been injured, and she requires attention. I will leave her in your capable hands. Please alert me when she wakes."

Jamie's head swam, visions and voices swirling around her like a tornado. A drummer beat in her skull, sounding suspiciously like the bass line to a Puddle of Mudd song. Each thump of the drums brought a spear of pain into her brain. What the hell had just happened?

She was cold now. She hadn't been cold before. She'd thought she would melt in that storage building. Pawpaw Milton's storage building. The one full of antiques. The antique bureau that had eaten her.

Then a dog, then a deep voice with an absolutely scrumptious accent. She really had to stop playing online games. They were giving her freaky visions.

"Ooh, Mrs. Knightsbridge, she's coming 'round."

"Quiet, Muriel. Let me see to her. Hello? Can you hear me, dearie?"

Well, crap. Everyone in my dream has a British accent. Jamie opened her eyes and screamed aloud at the two strange female faces only inches in front of her.

The younger one wore a frilly white cap and a high-necked, drab brown dress. Her pale face was surrounded by wisps of unremarkable brown hair. She couldn't have been more than sixteen or seventeen. The other woman, much closer to her sixties, had gray-streaked hair that was pulled back severely from her face. Her dress was as old-fashioned and conservative as the teenager's was, but there were laugh lines at the corners of her clear gray eyes.

Jamie looked around, panicked. She was lying in that huge bed she'd seen from across the room. The dog that had knocked her down was nowhere to be seen. How had she gotten into the bed? She'd passed out by the bureau, hadn't she? *Oh shit. I need to get out of here.* A panicked squeak escaped her as she tried to throw the covers back and rise from the bed. The older woman grabbed her hands, stopping her.

"Let me go!" Jamie struggled against the woman's surprisingly strong grip, but she wouldn't let go.

"Oh dear, hysterics. Pass the smelling salts, Muriel."

Jamie thrashed and kicked as the young maid held her against the pillows. Mrs. Knightsbridge shoved a vile-smelling vial under Jamie's nose. The pungent odor brought tears to her eyes and she coughed as she pushed the older lady's hands away. The maid released her captive's shoulders as Jamie grimaced at the odor and covered her nose with her hand. *Ugh, that smell.*

"Oh God, what the hell is that stuff?"

"Language, miss!" Mrs. Knightsbridge's eyebrows climbed nearly to her hairline.

Jamie stopped her struggles immediately at Mrs. Knightsbridge's tone. "Um, I'm sorry?" How confusing. Had she really offended a dream lady? "Where am I exactly?"

"You really do not know? Oh dear. And what an odd way of speaking you have. This is more complicated than I had imagined. Muriel, please fetch his lordship."

"Yes, Mrs. Knightsbridge." After bobbing a quick curtsy, Muriel disappeared through the door.

Mrs. Knightsbridge gave a small smile. "Now then, you mustn't fret. You are safe here in Lord Dunnington's home."

Jamie shook her head, sure she hadn't heard right. "Lord Dunnington?"

"Yes, his lordship Micah Axelby, Earl of Dunnington."

"You're kidding."

"I beg your pardon?"

"You're joking. This isn't real. I'm going to wake up in front of that god-awful storage building after a huge case of heat stroke."

"I am sorry, miss, but I am most definitely not jesting. Lord Dunnington found you here in his chamber in a sorry state indeed. Have you lost your protector?" She patted Jamie's hand sympathetically.

Jamie sat upright, slack-jawed as she stared at the woman. Protector?

"I don't need a protector. I'm completely capable of taking care of myself."

Mrs. Knightsbridge shook her head. "You poor dear. You must have gone through such a trauma."

"I'm sorry." Jamie threw the covers off and swung her legs over the side of the bed. *Where the hell did this robe come from?* "I need to get home." Her knees wobbled as she took two steps toward the bureau. Her head swam and her stomach roiled, but she paid them no attention. She needed to wake up fast. This was too damn weird for words.

"You cannot go, miss. His lordship…"

"Is here and would like an explanation for your presence in his home."

Jamie turned on her heel at the deep, masculine voice and was completely gobsmacked at the sight of the man in the doorway.

He looked like Colin Firth from that A&E miniseries Leah had forced her to watch over and over again when they were twelve. He was tall, dark-haired, and his chocolate-brown eyes pierced Jamie from beneath low brows. He wore an old-fashioned kind of outfit, the ones with sinfully tight pants, a waistcoat, a jacket, and that kind of frothy looking lace beneath his dimpled chin. His face wasn't perfect, but it was stunningly handsome, and the sight of him sucker-punched Jamie in her already-churning guts.

"Holy crap," she whispered, staggering backward and sitting on the bed.

"Your lordship, she seems to have lost her wits." Mrs. Knightsbridge wrung her hands. "She has no recollection of entering your chamber."

"Is that so?" Colin's twin drew himself up even taller, that imperious look fitting his masculine face so well. His clean-shaven jaw tightened as he looked down his nose at Jamie. "Perhaps the watch will be able to assist her in remembering how she came to be lying in front of my new bureau."

"Bureau," Jamie said, echoing the unfamiliarly accented pronunciation. "Bureau! That's it! The bureau!"

"Completely queer in the attic." Mrs. Knightsbridge shook her head, the corners of her mouth drawn down. A strange twinkle in her eye made Jamie wonder if the older lady honestly thought she was crazy.

"No, the bureau! That's how I got in. I was in the storage unit, and it was a billion degrees, and the dust cover fell on my head, and I touched the mirror on the door and I got eaten by that damn bureau!" Jamie stood and pointed at the offending furniture, wishing she could hack it to pieces for the weirdness of this dream. Of course, if it were only her and Mr. Firth, then that would have been okay. But he'd have to get over the proud grumpiness. Not sexy.

"Saints preserve us," Mrs. Knightsbridge said. Did she sound excited, or was that just Jamie's screwed up brain?

The earl addressed the housekeeper, ignoring Jamie completely. "Leave us, Mrs. Knightsbridge. I have some questions to ask of this…person."

Jamie wanted to be offended at his pointed pause, but she was too busy swallowing convulsively. Damn smelling salts.

"My lord." The rotund woman drew herself up to her full height, which wasn't especially impressive next to the towering earl. "It is not at all proper. Are you sure you wish to be alone with her, especially after…"

He waved a hand to stop her. "I am quite capable of guarding my own virtue, and I doubt she is in a position to have any virtues of her own."

"Hey!" Jamie's ire rose at the thinly veiled put down. "I'm very virtuous!"

Mrs. Knightsbridge curtsied and left the room. Jamie could have sworn that the little round lady winked at her before the door clicked shut.

When he turned his attention back to Jamie, she clutched the neck of the robe closed at her throat, suddenly feeling vulnerable. The earl was tall and handsome, and really, really pissed. He stepped toward her, his shiny boots thunking solidly on the patterned carpet.

When he was only two feet from her, his brows lowered, a nervous thrill went through Jamie as his deep voice rang out. "Who are you?"

She sucked in a breath. "Who are you?" she countered, rankling a little at his tone.

He tapped his fingers lightly against the side of his thigh, the only sign that he wasn't as cool as he appeared.

"Madam, I can assure you, if your intention is to acquire a new protector, I am hardly likely…"

"What is it with everybody assuming I need protection? I'm completely capable of taking care of myself."

His nostrils flared, and he stood up even straighter. She hadn't realized that was possible. She was face-to-buttons with a very nice waistcoat until she tilted her chin upward to look him in the eye.

He looked down at her, disapproval clear in the corners of his downturned mouth. "You may have heard that I gave Collette her *congé*, but I assure you I am not in need of a mistress at the moment. And breaking into my home is not the best way to garner my favors."

"Mistress?" Her jaw went slack. "You think I'm a hooker?"

He shook his head, a perplexed expression on his face. "I do not take your meaning."

Jamie crossed her arms in exasperation. "Listen, who are you?"

"I am Micah Axelby, Earl of Dunnington, as you well know since you managed to infiltrate my home without my servants' knowledge."

"I didn't know whose home this was. How could I know where that fricking mahogany monstrosity would spit me out? And seriously, who has servants?"

He looked over his shoulder when she pointed at the bureau again. When he looked back at her, the disbelief on his autocratic features was almost comedic. "Are you daft?"

"No, I'm not daft. I'm pissed. I don't want to be here, and it's cold, and I don't know why you're giving me the fifth degree about every damn thing! Ugh, I really need to wake up soon."

The earl sighed and looked at the ceiling. She couldn't

stop the little thrill in her chest at the sight of his lean throat. Why'd he have to be so damn good-looking?

"Let us begin again. Your name, please?"

"I'm Jamie. Jamie Marten." She stuck out her hand.

Instead of shaking it, as she anticipated, he turned it and bowed over it. His hand was warm, his long fingers strong but gentle as they gripped hers. The courtly gesture left her feeling warmer inside, but her uneasiness grew. *This* is *a dream, right? Then why does he feel so damn real?*

He released her hand and clasped both of his behind his back. "Well, Miss Marten, it is quite odd for a young lady to have the name of a man, and odder still for her to appear in my bedchamber."

"Mike, do you mind telling me where I am exactly?"

He arched a supercilious brow at her. "I beg your pardon?"

"Where are we? It's not a hard question."

He raked a hand through his dark hair, a delicious chaos taking the place of the formerly ordered strands. "We are in my townhouse, in Grosvenor Square, in London. I trust you know where London is?"

Her knees turned to Jell-O again, and she sank back down onto his bed. Whoo boy. London? England London? As dreams went, this was the most vivid she'd had. It was making her feel ill.

"Okay, so I guess your accent is legit. What's with the costumes, though? Do you do historical reenactments or something?"

"Costumes?" He shook his head in exasperation.

"So those are what you wear every day?" A chill ran through her, one that had nothing to do with the temperature of the room. "Mike, what year is it?"

He blew out an angry breath. "Have your wits indeed

gone begging? As you well know, it is the year of our Lord 1816."

"Oh shit."

She bent over and threw up on his extremely shiny boots.

Three

EDGARS, MICAH'S VALET, WOULD HAVE AN APOPLEXY when he saw the state of those boots. Edgars prided himself on his abilities, spending no less than a half hour polishing each boot every morning of his employment. Micah was no dandy, but he loved these damn boots, and the wench had just ruined some very expensive Corinthian leather. Besides, since Edgars had buggered off to avoid the scandal last season, the task of cleaning the boots would fall to his poor elderly butler.

Being a gentleman, however, he couldn't curse at her. She drew a hand across her mouth and sat back on the edge of his coverlet, her arms wrapped across her middle.

"Oh God, I'm so sorry. I didn't mean, I just, that smell from that thing she shoved under my nose before and it's cold in here and…you must think I'm a total bitch."

He looked skyward, begging for patience. "Madam, I cannot speak as to your character. I cannot deny that your, ahem, ill health has just caused irreparable harm to my boots, but at the moment, I'm more concerned with getting to the truth of the matter at hand. Now, are you well?"

The wench nodded her head, setting her streaked hair to trembling.

"Excellent." He drew the word out. "So, now, please tell me how you came to be in my home. I want the complete truth and no nonsense."

"This is going to sound crazy, and I'm sorry, but it's the God's honest truth. I'm from Concord, North Carolina, and the year 2012. That stupid bureau sucked me in through one of the mirrored doors and spit me out right over there. Your dog jumped on me, and I fell and got knocked out. I know it sounds insane, but I promise you, that's what happened."

She looked up at him with the clearest blue-green eyes he'd ever seen. She was an odd creature, with an odder way of speaking in a flat, drawn-out voice, but he couldn't help remembering the way her lean body had felt against him when he deposited her on his bed. "I am to believe that you came to be in my bedroom by traveling through a mirror?"

She nodded.

"And you are from nearly two hundred years in the future."

She nodded again, twisting the robe in her hands.

"Impossible." He crossed his arms and skewered her with his best lord-of-the-manor stare. "You are either an escaped Bedlamite or a witch. I will know which I am dealing with, if you please."

The chit's brows lifted in desperation. "I know it sounds crazy, but it's true."

Micah shook his head. He'd never been susceptible to the megrims that had afflicted his mother throughout her life, but he was certain that the pounding at his temples heralded something very similar. He closed his eyes and took three deep breaths before responding.

"Madam, I have listened to your tale, and since you do not have a reasonable explanation for how you came to be lying in my bedchamber, I'm afraid I must call the watch and have them deal with you."

"Wait, is that like the cops?" She bit her lip, and Micah felt a twinge of guilt at the worry in her expression. She must be simple—or mad. That was the only logical explanation for her oddly accented words that made no sense.

"I cannot help you."

Micah gave her a curt bow, turned on his heel, and winced at the wet, sucking sound his boot made as it traveled through the gunk on the carpet. Mrs. Knightsbridge would also have a fit of the vapors at the state of the Aubusson carpet. In a spate of sympathy for the beautiful but daft woman in his bed, he decided to blame the carpet incident on Baron. Mrs. Knightsbridge had a fondness for his blue greyhound, and he'd not suffer under her wrath.

"Please, wait."

At the plaintive sound, Micah turned. "Yes?"

"I can prove it."

She stood, untying the robe at her waist. She let it fall to the bed. Micah averted his gaze, all too aware of the vision of her nearly nude form. She might be daft, but she was a beautiful female, and he was a young, healthy man with a healthier sexual appetite. Control. He must maintain control. He held out a hand to stop her.

"Madam, please remain clothed. It is not at all seemly for you to be standing there in such a state of un—What the bloody hell?"

She'd shoved a smallish, heavy thing into his hand. Bright colors danced across the front of the object and a tinny sounding music sounded in the room. Words appeared on the object. ANGRY BIRDS.

"What the devil is this?" He thrust it back at her,

more than a bit unnerved. She backed away, forcing him
to keep hold of the strange thing.

"It's a phone. A smartphone. I can make phone calls,
play games, and get on the Internet with it."

"Trickery and deceit," he roared. "Take this device
away." He shoved it at her again as the tune tinkled, birds
still angrily flying across the screen.

The wench crossed her arms and stepped back again.
"Don't be stupid. It's not magical, and I'm not lying.
Look at it."

"I will do nothing of the sort." His jaw worked as he
glared at her, and he held the phone as far away from his
body as he could get it. He would throw it at the wench
if she did not take it back soon.

She blew a breath upward. "Fine." She snatched it
back from him. "Then watch over my shoulder."

She backed up against him, pressing her bottom
against his thighs. He'd have to have been a monk or
a eunuch not to enjoy the soft feel of her body as she
pressed it so carelessly against him. Micah was neither,
so to distract his lustful thoughts, he stared at the device
in her hand. It was so vivid! Funny looking birds with
cross faces flew across the words, the lively music playing
all the while. She shifted slightly, brushing against the
front of his trousers. He ceased to breathe and screwed
his eyes shut.

"Okay, so these pigs stole the birds' eggs, right? That's
why the birds are angry. So we're going to launch them
from this slingshot…"

The chit stopped speaking. Micah fisted his hands at
his sides. "I shall never harm a female, but you try my
patience, madam. Please move away."

"For chrissakes, just try it. Please?"

He opened one eye. She held the object out to him.

"I should not be moved by your pleas. I should call the watch immediately." He realized that talking to himself aloud made him sound daft, so he quieted as he gingerly accepted the small box from her hand.

"Okay, so touch the bird in the slingshot. Keep your finger on it; don't let go. Good. Now slide it back, and you can kind of aim it." She maneuvered his finger on the glass, helping him aim, then lifted it straight upward.

A little gasp blew from him as the red bird went sailing through the air and crashed into the pig's wooden and glass tower.

"See? Here. Now you have to shoot the rest of the birds to get the pig."

The next few moments were incredible. Might she be telling the truth?

❧

Jamie smiled. The earl was completely transfixed by the little animated birds as they flew across the screen. It was almost funny how excited he looked, as if he were a kid with a brand-new toy on Christmas. She remembered her first video game system, and it sort of tickled her to see similar feelings flit across his face. He stared at the brightly lit object in his hand, dark eyes bright with interest as he played through the rest of the level.

"Here, go on to the next one." She reached out and took his hand in her own and used his fingers to touch the little white arrow.

They spent several moments laughing together while the green pigs exploded. Some of her tension eased at Mike's delight. He clearly enjoyed the game, laughing and smiling easily. He'd even seemed to forget that she'd yakked on his boots. *Bully for me.*

While he tried to explode the pigs with helmets,

she put the robe back on. Even with the roaring fire in the room, it was still chillier than she was used to. She looked at that damn bureau again. Why the hell had it sucked her in? And why had it dumped her here of all places? She knew approximately bupkes about this place and time, but she did know she was going to need help and a lot of it.

When the earl grew frustrated at the pigs laughing at another failed attempt, he handed the phone back to Jamie.

"That was quite diverting."

"So, you believe me? There are lots of things like this back where I come from."

He straightened his waistcoat and assumed a thoughtful face. Her guts twisted nervously. What if he kicked her out? That stupid piece of furniture was the only way back home, as far as she knew. She had to stay close to it, to figure out how to return.

"I am not prepared to toss logic to the winds quite yet. That object was certainly different, but how am I to know that it is not some sort of trickery on your part? You did appear in my bedchamber unexplained and uninvited."

"Look, I want to leave even more than you want me to leave, but I don't have anywhere to go at the moment. Can I stay for a little while? I'm sure that stupid bureau is the key to getting back, but I need some time to figure out how it works. Let me stay, and I promise I'll be out of your hair in no time." She looked up at him, desperate and disgusted with the way she was begging. He wouldn't kick her out, would he? God, she sounded so pathetic.

"Out of my hair?" Mike looked at her, clearly confused, before he sighed and shook his head. "Even if your tale is true, it would be difficult to conceal your presence. Servants talk, and the gossip would spread—"

"You would kick me into the streets because of gossip? I didn't figure you for an ass."

He set his jaw then, and his eyes bored a hole in her. She gulped. She'd forgotten to be intimidated by him. Not a smart move.

"Miss, choose your words carefully. I shall have to think upon this matter, but if you wish to intrude upon my hospitality…"

"You're going to let me stay? Oh thank you, thank you, thank you! I won't be any trouble, and I'll figure out how to go home and everything will be fine. You're the best, Mike." In an excess of relief, she threw her arms around him and hugged him tightly. *Whaddaya know,* she thought as she pressed close to him. *That fancy-pants costume covers some pretty nice muscles.*

He stood rigid, arms at his sides. After a moment, she began to get the idea that maybe she'd committed a giant faux pas. She stepped back, cheeks burning.

"Thanks," she mumbled again, and tucked a loose strand of hair behind her ear. She wasn't normally so impulsive.

He bowed to her sharply and left the room without another word. Baron the dog, who'd apparently been waiting outside the bedroom for his master, wagged his tail, thumping it against the door as Mike shut it behind him. His voice came muffled through the door as he talked softly to the hound and they walked away.

Jamie flopped backward onto the bed and stared at the beamed ceiling. This was incredible. This was impossible. This was *not* how she'd planned to spend her day. What the heck did she do to deserve it? How was she going to fix such a godforsaken mess?

First things first. Before Mike decided he really should

kick her out, she should see how the hell that mirror had gotten her here in the first place. Then she'd find a rag and a bucket to try to fix the poor, abused rug. She got off the bed and went over to the giant bureau in the corner. Starting with the left door, she tapped and touched each part of the glass, searching for the hidden trigger that would suck her back into her own time.

"It does not work that way, you know. Good heavens, I must have Muriel clean this frightful mess on the carpet."

Jamie whirled around at the sound of the voice behind her. It was Mrs. Knightsbridge with a tray full of stuff. She set the tray on a side table and briskly pulled a velvet rope that hung by the bed.

"Sorry about the rug," Jamie said awkwardly. The tips of her ears burned with embarrassment.

"Do not fret about that, dear. All will soon be set to rights. Here. You must be famished."

The housekeeper gestured to an ornately carved wooden chair beside the table. The smell of the pastries on the tray suddenly hit Jamie's nostrils, and she realized Mrs. Knightsbridge was right. Her stomach felt completely normal again, the rumbling sounds of hunger confirming it. The table was situated close to the fire, and Jamie was grateful for the warmth as she sank onto the cushioned chair's seat.

Mrs. Knightsbridge poured Jamie a steaming cup of…tea?

"How do you take it?"

"Cold and sweet, preferably." Jamie eyed the cup. She was a Southern girl. She'd never had tea above fifty degrees before.

Mrs. Knightsbridge laughed. "The warmth will do you good." She spooned some sugar into the cup and gave it a brisk stir. "There. Drink up, and we shall have a little coze."

"What's a coze?" Jamie warily picked up the teacup and gave it a sniff.

"A conversation." Mrs. Knightsbridge settled into the chair across the table and smiled kindly. Jamie was really beginning to like this lady, vile-smelling medicine notwithstanding. *She'd done that to help anyway*, Jamie thought.

"What did you mean when you came in and said it doesn't work that way?" Jamie took a sip of the tea. The warmth was extremely disconcerting, but the taste was pretty good.

"The portal. It was spelled one way."

Jamie's jaw hit the floor and she stared at the smiling woman. "What the hell?"

Mrs. Knightsbridge's pleasant expression slipped. "Language, miss. Ladies do not use that sort of coarse talk."

"Ladies? What are you talking about? I'm not a lady. I'm a regular woman. Female. You know what I mean. All liberated and stuff."

The housekeeper sighed and smoothed her skirts before reaching onto the tray. "Scone?"

Jamie took the golden-brown crumbly goodness from the outstretched hand and munched, all the while looking across the table distrustfully.

"My sister, Wilhelmina, is an expert in the Old Ways." Mrs. Knightsbridge whispered the last words, as if afraid someone would hear. "She agreed to help me search for the perfect match for his lordship."

"Mike?" Jamie nearly sprayed scone crumbs across the table, but she clapped a hand to her mouth just in time. Mrs. Knightsbridge looked at Jamie like her first grade teacher used to. Like she'd screamed out the F-word in church.

Jamie used the fabric napkin from the tray to wipe her face before speaking again. "Mike? Why does he need help finding a match? He's completely delicious; he should be able to get any woman he wants."

Mrs. Knightsbridge shook her head sadly. "Lord Dunnington is a fine man, a good man. That whole business with his dead mistress was not at all what the gossips made it out to be…"

"Wait a minute. Dead mistress? Dead as in, 'call the cops there's a body on the floor' dead mistress?" Jamie's voice came out in a strangled whisper as she stared at the closed door. "Did he kill her?"

"Not at all," the housekeeper assured her. "'Tis only that Louisa died in such an odd manner. In any case, he has finally broken it off with that tart who snagged him next, Collette. I was quite relieved when he released her from his protection."

"Well, good for him. Gotta jump back on the bike, after all." Jamie wasn't sure if the sarcasm in her voice had been detected. The housekeeper continued as if she hadn't even spoken.

"That is not the worst of it. He is courting a young lady now. It would not disappoint me so were I not certain that she will disappoint him and break his heart. Miss Felicity Lyons is all wrong for his lordship, a spineless, simpering miss." The housekeeper's pinched lips and tight eyes confirmed her opinion of the unfortunate Miss Lyons. "She only desires the wealth and position that comes with the earldom."

"So, where do I fit into all this? Wrong place, wrong time kind of thing?" Jamie gestured with the remnants of her scone.

The housekeeper shook her head at Jamie, and her smile brightened. "Not at all. You are the one that is perfect for him. Wilhelmina said so. You are going to be his bride, and the Countess of Dunnington."

Four

JAMIE HAD ALWAYS PRIDED HERSELF ON HER LEVEL-headedness. When Bobby Gillespie drew on her Wonder Woman comics in the first grade, she didn't lose her cool; she simply stuffed his Spider-Man books in the girls' toilet. When her first guild wiped out sixteen times in a row on one of the easiest bosses in the game, she said a polite good-bye and then quit the guild. But when that nice old lady told her she was going to be a countess, Jamie couldn't help but laugh straight in her face.

"Countess? You've got to be kidding." She shook her head.

"Oh no, it is quite certain." Mrs. Knightsbridge's face was the picture of sincere conviction. "I saw your face myself in her scrying bowl. It is meant to be, or you would not have been able to pass through the portal."

Jamie dropped the rest of her scone and splayed her hands on the table. "Let me get this straight. So, your sister the witch—"

"Sssssshh." Mrs. Knightsbridge stood quickly as the door opened. "Ah, there you are, Muriel. See to this mess on the carpet and then remove the tea tray. I shall take Miss Marten to see her new chambers. Now remember, we must be circumspect. No one is to know that she is staying here, do you understand?"

The girl nodded, giving Jamie a curious look. She bobbed a quick curtsy and disappeared.

Mrs. Knightsbridge turned to Jamie. "Please, mind your speech. Do not use that word aloud in any circumstances. People fear the Old Ways, and we mustn't harm Wilhelmina." She walked to the door of the bedroom.

"Yeah, because Wilhelmina's been so awesome to me, dumping me in a foreign country a couple hundred years in the past," Jamie muttered. Mrs. Knightsbridge must not have heard because she simply beckoned for Jamie to follow her.

Jamie knotted the robe at her waist and regretfully left the warm tea and comforting fire to follow the meddling housekeeper. She needed some answers, and it looked like Mrs. Knightsbridge was her only lead.

The hallway was much gloomier than the bedroom had been, lit by sconces set into the walls. Massive painted portraits dominated the corridor, severe looking men in historical dress scowling down at Jamie. *God, no wonder Mike had been so grumpy. If I had these guys staring at me every day of my life, I'd be pissy too.*

"Why can't anybody know that I'm here? That seems kind of odd. And anyway, I'm not staying," Jamie said as she hurried along behind her. She stuck close, worried that those portraits might start following her with their eyes. She'd seen way too many creepy movies to trust the dark, heavy paintings.

"Because it is simply not done. You are an unwed woman, and his lordship is also unmarried. It would be a scandal the likes of which London has not seen in quite a time. A man in his lordship's position must be above reproach. Circumspection on your part is of the highest import. Ah, here we are."

They turned the corner into another corridor. "I told Clara to prepare the yellow room for you." Mrs. Knightsbridge stepped aside and motioned Jamie into a lemony dream.

Jamie had never been what you'd call a girly-girl. She liked to dress up every now and then, and she put on makeup about once a month or so for shits and giggles. But when she saw the softly lit bedroom done in sunshine, buttercream, and canary lace, she almost melted into a puddle of princess-flavored bubblegum.

"Oh my God, this is so beautiful." Jamie turned in a slow circle, trying to take in everything. The furniture in Mike's room had been dark, ornate, and forbidding. This furniture was lighter, simpler, and much more feminine. There were chairs upholstered in white with little yellow throw pillows, and lacy white curtains hung at the large window. A cheerful blaze burned in the fireplace, and the smaller room was much warmer than the big drafty room the earl slept in. She wanted to throw herself onto the cozy bed, snuggle into the pillows, and not get up for a week.

"The late countess tatted all the lace in this room." Mrs. Knightsbridge's voice held a hint of sadness. She smoothed a corner of the bed covers. "She dearly loved lace."

"I'm sorry, was that Mike's mother?"

Mrs. Knightsbridge crooked a brow at the nickname for Mr. High-and-Mighty but let it slide. "No, she was his aunt. His uncle was the earl before him. When he died without a son, Lord Dunnington was next in line to inherit."

"Oh," Jamie said, biting her lip in thought.

"I worked for the late earl and his wife for many years

before their passing." Mrs. Knightsbridge sounded a little choked up but buried it in straightening the already perfect bedspread.

"I'm sorry," Jamie said lamely.

"The past is best left to the past." Mrs. Knightsbridge sniffed and matter-of-factly plumped the pillows. "Now, I trust you have convinced his lordship to allow you to stay for the nonce?"

"Sort of, but I'm not staying. You have to get Wilhelmina to send me—"

"Excellent. It will be much more convenient to have you under my tutelage here. Now, let me see what I have to work with. Stand up straight."

"No, you don't understand. I don't need tutelage; I need to go home. I really—"

"Come, child, quick! Do not lag about. Stand up, chin up now, do not slouch. Hmm. Your posture leaves much to be desired. It will have to do for the moment, but we shall improve it with time."

She'd put a hand under Jamie's chin, forcing her up ramrod-straight. Jamie spoke through gritted teeth, since the housekeeper wasn't moving her hand away from Jamie's lower jaw.

"Listen, Mrs. Knightsbridge. There's been a mistake. I'm not the woman you need."

Mrs. Knightsbridge removed her hand, but Jamie wasn't allowed to slouch because the woman then spread her fingers across the small of Jamie's back, ignoring her question and muttering to herself—something about modistes? She measured the breadth of Jamie's shoulders with another span of her hands. When she turned Jamie around and started to use the same splayed-finger method to measure her chest, Jamie grabbed the woman's hands and forced her to look into her eyes.

"If you would just tell me where Wilhelmina is, then I'll explain everything to her and get her to send me home. I'm sorry this didn't work out the way you two planned, but I'm not the one you were looking for. So, I'll ask again. Where is Wilhelmina?"

"She is in hiding." The housekeeper looked up at Jamie, the innocence in her expression almost too much to swallow.

Jamie dropped her plump hands, afraid that she might squeeze too hard to get a straight answer from the woman. "Hiding where? Like in the broom closet or in darkest Africa?"

"I cannot say."

Jamie glared at her, the already thin pieces of her patience disappearing completely. "Look. You've dragged me from my home into a time and place that I know absolutely nothing about. I have no clothes, no food, and I'm pretty sure that my host would like nothing better than to never see my face again." She ticked the points off on her fingers, her volume increasing with each one. "I need to see Wilhelmina. Now."

Mrs. Knightsbridge's face crumpled like used tissue paper. "I am so sorry, Miss Jamie, but I do not know where she is. It is safer for us all that way. As soon as she contacts me, I will request that she send you home. Is that acceptable?"

Jamie deflated. *If her own sister doesn't know where the witch is, then what chance do I have in this foreign time and place?* "I guess I don't have any choice."

Mrs. Knightsbridge clapped her hands together delightedly. "Excellent. Now, walk. We may as well make the most of your time here."

Jamie trudged from one end of the room to the other, her bare toes curling when she stepped off of the cream-colored rug onto the floor. What had happened to her flip-flops, anyway? The least comfort she could ask for was her shoes, right? And they were gone too. What a miserable day this was turning out to be.

Mrs. Knightsbridge clucked her tongue disapprovingly. Her eyes filled with despair when Jamie turned to walk back the way she'd come.

"What?"

"We've a lot of work to do."

An hour later, Jamie was exhausted, starving, and itchy from the fine layer of dust still coating her body under the robe. Mrs. Knightsbridge had given her walking lessons straight out of a historical movie, book-on-the-head-for-balance and everything. Since Jamie's main form of exercise for most of the last year had been her hands on the computer keyboard, it was damned trying.

Jamie had tried to talk her out of it, but the round little woman was pitiless. She eventually gave up. As the only connection Jamie had to this Wilhelmina of the Old Ways witchy woman, she figured she should do her best to make Mrs. Knightsbridge happy. It sure wasn't easy, though.

"A lady never stomps like a horse. She floats gracefully."

"Floating…gracefully…" Jamie hissed through gritted teeth. The book was slipping again. She lifted her chin to keep it balanced, staring upward as hard as she could without moving her head.

"She is serene and pleasant and always composed."

"Composed…" Jamie parroted without moving her jaw. She rounded the chair in the corner for the sixteenth time and serenely, pleasantly, and gracefully glided back to the door. She was about as sick as she could be of this. She was not cut out for this ladylike shit.

"A lady is beauty and kindness and—oh gracious, Miss Jamie, this will never do!"

Jamie let the book of sonnets fall from her head as she collapsed in a heap on the carpet. "What, what now?"

"Your fingers! That horrid chipping paint simply will not do. It is not at all in fashion. Now, we will…"

Jamie pulled her legs close to her body, sitting Indian style on the plush carpet. "Mrs. Knightsbridge, listen. I'm tired, I'm hungry, and I'd give my tier-twelve gear to feel clean right now. Can we pick up the lessons tomorrow?"

Mrs. Knightsbridge clucked her tongue sympathetically. "Of course, dear. I shall send the footmen with a bath."

"Huh? I can't just use the…" *Oh crap.* When did they invent indoor plumbing? Jamie's blood froze inside her veins.

"They will only be a moment. Then I shall bring a tray for you." Mrs. Knightsbridge patted her fondly on the head and sailed out of the room like the mother ship.

Jamie was so screwed.

She moved to sit on the chair by the window and watched in horror as the uniformed footmen brought in a copper tub. They set it in front of the fire and filled it with water brought up in buckets. Homely, plain, actual buckets. When the tub was about three quarters full, they left her alone.

A quiet knock on the door interrupted her bleak stare at the stingy, tiny tub.

"Miss?" A pale, thin face poked through the crack in the door. "I'm Muriel. I'm to see to your bath."

"No, they already brought what I guess they think is a bath." Jamie sighed heavily. "Thanks anyway."

"No, miss." The girl giggled as she came through the door and shut it behind her. She held a length of cloth folded up, a towel Jamie presumed, and a basket with bottles and things. "I am to help you bathe."

Jamie stared at the girl. What was wrong with these people? Grown-ass women weren't expected to wash themselves? They needed someone to do it for them? What kind of jacked-up farce had she stepped into, anyway?

"I've been pretty much responsible for my own personal hygiene since I was six, but thanks anyway."

Muriel crossed her arms and made a knowing face. "How do you rinse your hair, then? You can hold the bucket over your head by yourself? How do you reach it?"

"Oh." Jamie stared at the two buckets sitting on the hearth. They did still have water in them. "Good point."

"Come now, miss. Before the water cools."

As Jamie stood, she realized that she couldn't delay certain needs forever. As embarrassing and as terrifying as it was, she had to face the music.

"Um, Muriel? What do I do if I need to, um, go?"

"Go?" The maid looked up from arranging the bottles on the table beside the tub.

"You know." Jamie mimed the potty dance. "Go."

"Oh. Behind the screen there, miss." She pointed to the far corner.

"Okay."

Jamie took a deep breath, marshaled her courage, and went to face her fate.

"Ho. Ly. Shit."

It was a pot. A literal pot. Not a toilet but an actual, honest-to-God pot. What was she supposed to do? Squat over it? Sit on it? It'd be damn uncomfortable. And what was she supposed to wipe with? *Ugh. Just…ugh.*

She decided she'd hold it forever. No way in hell could she go in something like that.

"Are you well, miss?"

"Uh, yeah. Fine and dandy. Just frickin' incredible."

The pot seemed to mock Jamie as it sat there. Smug porcelain bastard. *You know what? I am not going to let it beat me. I am tough. I was strong enough to survive being dumped, being alone, and then being sucked into a time I know nothing about, so I can conquer my fear of, well, going.*

"Hey, Muriel?"

"Yes, miss?"

Jamie poked her head around the screen to find the maid. "I'm not used to doing things this way. Any tips?"

A confused look crossed the thin face. "To relieve yourself?"

Jamie nodded, feeling like a complete dumbass.

Without any comment, Muriel rounded the screen, showed Jamie the neatly folded pile of cloths beside the pot, and mimed the proper technique. Jamie was deeply grateful that the maid didn't treat her like she was stupid, even though she was acting like a clueless idiot.

After quite possibly the most embarrassing two minutes of Jamie's life, Muriel left her alone to take care of business. Jamie was successful in her efforts and left the hideous pot to mock her behind the screen some more.

After the toileting issue, it seemed stupid to feel self-conscious about getting help bathing, but Jamie couldn't help asking Muriel to turn around while she undressed. Hey, she used to be one of those girls that changed in the stall during high school gym class.

Muriel shook her head but turned her back anyway.

The bath, while not Jamie's preferred method of getting clean, was okay once she got used to it. The water was nice and warm, and the tub's position in front of the fire kept it from cooling too quickly. The bottles that Muriel sat beside the tub were filled with soaps, oils, and other scented goodies. Washing her hair was sort of harrowing, since she had to slip down beneath the water to get her hair wet, and it didn't really feel rinsed even after Muriel dumped two whole buckets of water on her head, but it was better than feeling gritty all night.

Muriel handed Jamie a towel, and while she dried, the maid opened a trunk at the foot of the bed.

"Here, miss. Mrs. Knightsbridge said for you to use the late countess's clothing. This night rail is quite soft."

Jamie swallowed. She didn't love the idea of wearing some dead woman's clothes, but what choice did she have? The only things she had with her were filthy, skimpy, and completely inappropriate for both the weather and the company. She remembered enough about history to know that exposing that much skin was a no-no.

"Okay."

The maid helped Jamie pull the gown on over her head. The swaths of fabric billowed around Jamie, choking her. She hadn't worn this much clothing since they'd gotten that freak snowstorm two years ago. She thanked the maid anyway, though. A dead person's too-voluminous nightgown was better than being naked in Mike's house. Although seeing Mr. Firth's twin naked would certainly make this trip much more interesting. If, that is, Mrs. K was right and he wasn't a murderer.

"Shall I fetch you a supper tray, miss?"

"Shouldn't I go get it myself?"

Muriel's eyes went wide and Jamie could swear she saw horror written on the maid's features. "Oh, no, miss! You are his lordship's guest. It would not be at all proper. Besides, you are not attired!"

Jamie looked down at seventy billion yards of white cotton that seemed to indicate otherwise.

"I will only be a moment, miss. Stay here." Muriel held her hand out almost like you would a dog that you've asked to sit and you're not exactly sure if they understood you or not. Jamie sighed and watched her back out of the room.

Jamie spied a hairbrush on a side table and sat on the rug in front of the fire to brush out her hair. It was going to look like crap, but at least it was cleaner than it had been.

As the fire crackled at her back and the smooth strokes of the bristles massaged her scalp, she couldn't help but feel bewildered. She'd spent the last few hours in a time and place very far from home. After Logan had left her, she'd thought that she could never be happy again. She'd been convinced that her life was over. The brush caught on a knot, and she pulled the length of her hair over her shoulder to work it out. Short, firm strokes of the brush pulled at the strands, causing tiny pains along her scalp. But with perseverance, the stubborn tangle disappeared.

Maybe this forced vacation from reality was exactly what she needed to get un-stuck. She wasn't on board with Mrs. Knightsbridge's plan to hitch her up with the earl, and she'd still like to hang Wilhelmina up by her pointy-toed shoes, but maybe she could enjoy herself just a little bit while she was here. But for that to happen, she should probably go thank her host for letting her stay and try to get on his good side a little bit. Maybe once he got over the grumpies, he would be okay. And he was freaking gorgeous, which never hurts. She and Mike might enjoy spending time together once he was certain that Jamie wasn't a witch and she'd convinced herself that he wasn't an axe murderer.

Five

ACCORDING TO THE DEEP BONGING SOUND COMING from somewhere downstairs, it was nine o'clock. Jamie hoped Mike was still at home. He might have gone to a party or out to dinner or something. *They do have restaurants now, don't they?* Then again, they didn't have toilets, so maybe restaurants were too much to assume.

She poked her head through his bedroom door, but it was empty. The other doors along the hallway revealed similarly empty rooms. *What does a single guy need six bedrooms for, anyway?* she wondered. From what Mrs. K had said, Jamie didn't think his many lady friends had lived here.

The gloomy corridor and the forbidding portraits made her nervous, so she hurried down the stairs as quick as she could. She didn't really believe in ghosts, but something about the place gave her the heebie-jeebies.

A white-haired old guy that she assumed was the butler passed by the front door. Jamie smiled at him, but he looked too stunned to return the expression. *Weird. I guess maybe Mrs. Knightsbridge hasn't told everyone they have company.* He gave Jamie a tight nod as she passed.

A parlor type room was located off the main entryway.

It was dark and empty. It appeared to be done in a deep rose color, but the flickering candlelight from the hall-way made it tough to judge.

The next door was locked.

The next was a dining room, in which several maids were clearing dishes from the long table. They took them to a doorway in the back of the room which Jamie assumed led to the kitchen.

She rounded another corner, and irritation chafed her. This was a huge house, and she didn't know where she was going. It was uncomfortably cold, and despite the yards of fabric in her nightgown, it still wasn't a pair of long johns. Drafts from the chilly house swirled around her legs beneath the gown. She'd almost decided to abandon her Mike search and head back upstairs to her warm and toasty bedroom when she saw it.

The door stood open. A piano stood alone in the center of the room, dark wood glinting in the bluish moonlight that poured through the large window. The music room.

She let the door click shut behind her and crossed over to the piano. It was beautiful, a square grand pianoforte, the likes of which she'd only seen in Pawpaw Milton's shop. The wood glowed from deep within, genuine ivory keys stark in the dim light. This piano would probably cost a bundle in her time, but for now, it was only a showpiece in a rich man's house. Her fingers trailed lightly over the keys, the perfectly tuned high notes dancing through the chilly darkness of the room.

Feeling like a thief, Jamie couldn't deny herself the familiar pleasure of sinking down on the bench. She indulged the itch in her fingertips by placing them lightly on the keys. "You shouldn't do this," she whispered, but then she got lost in the music.

She played like she hadn't played since before Logan left her. The music poured from deep within her, through her suddenly strong fingers and across the keys. It must have been the unfamiliar surroundings, the forbidden feeling of playing an instrument that didn't belong to her. For months, she'd been unable to play. But now, in this strange room, on this strange instrument, she lost herself in the comfortable sensation of song. The bewilderment she'd felt, the depression that had ruled her life, all of it stained the music that she created. The only constant in this new world she'd been thrust into was music, and she clung to it as desperately as a kid with a favorite toy.

The final notes hung in the air, shimmering softly before disappearing forever. She opened her eyes and a smile spread across her face.

"That was incredible," a masculine voice said from behind her.

Jamie started and turned quickly. It was Mike, a dark curl of hair falling over his forehead now, and he had the oddest expression on his face. His brows were lifted, his eyes bright, and the corners of his mouth had turned upward the slightest bit.

"Thanks," Jamie replied. "I'm sorry, I should have asked before I played, but the room was empty. I hope you don't mind." She stood, and Mike—wait, was that a blush beginning around his high collar?

"Miss Marten…"

She smiled at him. "Jamie. Call me Jamie."

The softness she'd seen around his edges disappeared as if it had never been there. His brows lowered.

"That is a man's name, and you should not be walking through the house in such dishabille."

Her smile melted quickly at his curt tone. "Such what? English, for cripe's sake."

"Undressed in such a fashion. It is not at all seemly. And mind your tongue. You sound like a trollop." He glowered down at her, his entire body screaming disapproval.

She looked down at herself. She wasn't exactly the most buxom of women, and the nightgown was plenty thick. There was no way anyone could see anything. *I sound like a trollop?*

"Listen, I'm sorry for playing your piano without permission. I'm sorry if the way I'm dressed offends you. I'm sorry you don't like the way I talk. I didn't ask to be dumped here, two hundred years in the past. I've had sort of a crap day, and you just pissed on the only five minutes that I've been happy. So thanks for that, Mike. I really, really appreciate it." Tears stung her tired eyes and she swiped at them, furious at the emotional betrayal of their appearance. "I wanted to find you before I went to bed to thank you for letting me stay here. So thanks. And good night." She withheld the "asshole" she wanted to tag at the end of that sentence, but it was a very near thing.

She tried to move past him, but he grabbed her arm before she could leave. She turned to him, ready to give him another taste of her trollopy tongue, but a flash of something in his eyes stopped her.

"Wait," he said, then took a deep breath and released her arm as if it were aflame.

She didn't give him much slack. "What is it? Any other insults you want to throw at me before I hit the hay? Maybe something about my loose morals or lack of respect for your lofty station?"

"No," he said, and she might have actually seen a genuine tinge of regret cross his all-too-masculine face. "I only wonder, is it so different where you come from? Are the ladies not conscious of their state of undress? Are sensibilities a relic of the past?"

She sighed and shoved a hank of hair from her forehead. "It's just not really a big deal. I mean, women do run around wearing a whole lot less than I am." She fluffed out the sides of her nightgown to illustrate that Mrs. Knightsbridge could fit in this garment with her if she wanted to. "The way you saw me dressed earlier, when I first got here? That's a lot more like women dress where I'm from. As long as you've got the chest and the bum covered, people don't so much care about anything else."

"The sight of a woman's stockinged ankle as she enters a carriage is enough to make a callow boy salivate. To think that men are so jaded elsewhere…" He shook his head incredulously.

"It's not just a geography thing. From my calculations, it's been about two hundred years since ankles were a big deal." She shrugged. "Anyway, I'm sorry."

His throat worked for a moment before he spoke again. "Miss Marten, it is I who should apologize. You are a guest in my home, and I have behaved abominably. I should not have expected you to be familiar with the courtesies of my time. Can you extend your forgiveness to me?"

He took her hand, and his palm was hot in hers. She looked up at him and could find nothing more than sincerity written in his features. His appeal was undeniable, despite the high-handed way he'd treated her. Without thinking, she stepped closer to him, wanting to be nearer to the person she saw in those eyes. She tilted her chin up to him, and her tongue darted out to wet her lips.

Mike's eyes grew darker, and his nostrils flared slightly. He hadn't let go of her hand. A shadow lined his jaw now, the whisper of a beard appearing. A tingle started in her belly, one she hadn't felt in quite a while. It

streamed into her through his contact on her hand, swirling through her blood, heating it as it flowed through
her body. The delicate lace of his neck-cloth contrasted
so much with his purely male features that it was hard
to look away. He was so gorgeous. She took advantage
of their continued physical contact and leaned closer to
him. Her gaze traveled back up to his face, and she let
herself drown in his eyes. Drawn as if magnetized, she
reached up on her toes to be nearer.

I want him to kiss me. Mike, or Micah, or his lordship
the earl, or whatever he was called. Somewhere deep
underneath that bossy exterior was a person that she
wanted to get to know much, much better.

A heartbeat passed, then two. He was still standing
there, still staring at her, still holding her hand gently.
But he didn't bend down to kiss her. His strong jaw
was tight; his eyes were intense, almost anguished. The
realization that he had no intention of doing so doused
her like a bucket of icy liquid. The delicious tingle in her
belly died a quick, cold death.

"Sorry," she whispered. Backing away from him
slowly, she watched as he gave a sharp bow and left the
room. She followed, turning the opposite direction and
carrying the tattered shards of her pride with her.

She headed up the stairs as quickly as she could.
Halfway to the second floor, she caught up to Mrs.
Knightsbridge, who held a tray full of delicious smelling
food. When the housekeeper reached the landing, she
turned to see who was following her.

"Oh dear! Whatever are you doing about in a night
rail? Oh, come with me, back to your room. Ladies do
not wander about in their nightclothes, you must realize."

"I'm beginning to get the picture," Jamie said wryly as
she followed the housekeeper back into the Lemon Room.

Mrs. K set the tray down on the table and gestured to the chair. Jamie sank down into it with a sigh, stretching her bare feet toward the fire. She didn't say anything, watching the flicker of the fire's light against the white nightgown.

Mrs. Knightsbridge stepped behind the chair and began to braid Jamie's hair. Though the motion startled Jamie at first, the smooth motions calmed her, and she let the housekeeper maneuver the parts into a tail halfway down her back.

Mrs. K tied the end with a ribbon she pulled from her apron pocket. "There. Now, eat, dearie. You will need your strength for the morrow."

Jamie looked over her shoulder. "What's tomorrow?"

"More lessons on becoming a countess, of course."

Jamie wanted to slap her forehead with her palm. She wanted to scream, "Oh HELL no!" and run out of there. She wanted to tell the nice old lady that she was ape-shit, monkey-nuts crazy, and that she was not going to be a part of her schemes.

What did she do?

She grabbed a fork and shoved a bite of chicken into her mouth. She had to play along just enough to convince Mrs. K and Wilhelmina to send her home. Once they saw how not into her Mike was, she'd be on the express train back to the future. Or the present. Whatever. Just, home. She wanted to go home.

❧

After a surprisingly tasty supper that Jamie washed down with wine—and boy, did she need that alcohol—Mrs. Knightsbridge left her to sleep.

Jamie blew out the candle by the bedside and watched the light from the fireplace make odd shadows in the room. What a weird day. What a handsome, incredibly arrogant, and sort of an asshole guy. What a nice, if really meddling, housekeeper. A gigantic yawn escaped her, and she turned onto her side, ready to go to sleep.

Scritch scritch scritch, whiiiiiiiiine.

Jamie rolled her eyes and stuffed a pillow over her ears.

Scritch, scritch, scritch, scritch, whiiiiiiiiiiiine. Whiiiiiiiiiine. Whiiiiiiiii…

"Oh shut up and get in here already." As soon as she opened the door, Baron bolted into the room, tail wagging and tongue lolling. He jumped up on the bed and curled up on the pillow she'd been using.

She climbed into bed behind him and was oddly grateful for the bony dog's comforting presence. He licked her hand, and together they went to sleep.

Firelight reflected through his glass of brandy, making the amber-gold liquor glow as if alive. Micah took a large swallow, grimacing at the sweet burn in his throat. Too close. That had been much too close. Draining the rest of his drink, he crossed to the sideboard to pour another. His estate room, usually a place of peace and solitude, held none of its usual tranquility tonight.

His hand trembled as he lifted the decanter. In disgust, he set it down and crossed to the window. Looking out into the blackness of night, he gripped his knuckles behind his back.

His peace had disappeared when *she* had entered his home. Miss Marten. Her speech was immoderate, her appearance disconcerting, and her manner altogether quarrelsome. She should be repugnant to him. All striped hair and foul mouth and wide eyes and soft lips…How close he'd come to kissing her.

He paced from the window, agitation bubbling in his gut. Despite his title of earl, his position in society was precarious at best. The *ton*, while capricious and flighty, had long, vindictive memories. No one had forgotten poor Louisa's death, Micah least of all. While the thought of pandering to society's matrons galled him, he could ill afford a scandal the likes of which Miss Marten could cause. Not if he wished to wed Miss Lyons. And he did, he told himself. He did wish to wed the delicate beauty. She would make an excellent countess.

His decision firmly set, he splashed another dollop of brandy into his glass and sprawled in his chair before the fire. Miss Marten could bait him all she wished. He'd not quarrel with her. *Too much passion,* he mused, *is roused in a verbal joust. That's why I nearly kissed her. That and nothing more.*

He drained the rest of the brandy and left his estate room, carrying a candle with him. Snapping his fingers at the foot of the stairs as he usually did, he waited for his hound to appear. The darkened hallways were empty. Baron was nowhere to be seen. Bemused, Micah walked up the stairs. Could the dog have been shut in his bedchamber all evening?

Micah entered his room. The light in the hearth flitted lazily, illuminating the empty rug that Baron usually inhabited each night.

"Baron," Micah commanded in a low voice. "To me."

No answering click of toenails on polished floors sounded. With a sigh of exasperation, Micah journeyed down the corridor. Occasionally, the hound would bed down in one of the empty chambers if one of the maids left a door ajar. *But that is only in the summer months*, his subconscious objected. Shaking his head, he peered into each room.

Rounding the corner of the hallway, a faint glint of light caught his eye. It was coming from beneath the door of the yellow bedchamber. *What the devil?*

His hand closed on the cool brass doorknob. The door opened with a soft squeak, and his blood stirred at the sight of Miss Marten lying across the cream and yellow bedding, asleep. Her hair, now bound in a braid, lay like a velvet rope across the pillows. And there, beside her, lay the traitorous greyhound, the thin skin over his ribs moving like a bellows as he dreamed.

If Micah called to Baron, she'd surely wake. For a long moment, Micah stood in the doorway, watching her sleep. Her forehead delicately wrinkled as she dreamed, a heavy sigh blowing from her lips. *So beautiful*, he thought. It would be no onerous task to take her as his mistress. It would be quite pleasant for the both of them.

She turned then, snuggling into her pillow, and Micah felt like a lecherous bastard. She'd made it quite clear that she was no loose-moraled Cyprian, despite her odd manner of undress. Even though he desired her, he'd made her a guest in his household, and he'd not take advantage of the young lady. Leaving Baron to watch over the sleeping maid, he shut the door softly and headed back to his lonely bedchamber. All the while, he wondered what to do about his damned inconvenient sense of honor. And also, what had she done with that small device with the cross birds?

Six

JAMIE STRETCHED AND YAWNED. THE WARM BODY next to her adjusted slightly, and she rolled over to wrap her arms around Logan. When she encountered smooth fur instead of skin, her eyes flew open.

Baron lapped at her nose.

"Hey, dog." She sighed and wiped the slobber from her face. She'd forgotten where and when she was. Unfortunately, she hadn't been sucked back into her own time during the middle of the night, as she was half hoping she would. She'd have to keep up the countess lessons for a while longer, until she could convince Mrs. Knightsbridge to have Wilhelmina send her home.

A soft knock came at the door.

"Yes?"

The hinges squeaked softly as Muriel entered the room. Baron saw the open door and bolted. Guess it was time for his morning constitutional. "Good morning, miss. I have your chocolate here."

Jamie's ears perked up. "Chocolate?"

"Yes, miss. Hot chocolate. 'Tis just the thing for the morning. And Cook's is delightful."

Muriel set the tray on the bedside table and handed

Jamie a steaming cup. She took a wary sip. What if chocolate meant something different than she was used to? Fortunately, Muriel was right. It was damn tasty.

"Ah, that hits the spot. Thanks, Mur."

The maid giggled. What, did nobody have nicknames in the past? "My pleasure. Now, Mrs. Knightsbridge said I am to help you dress."

Jamie looked down at her nightgown. "Well, I don't really have anything other than the tank top and shorts I showed up in yesterday."

Muriel's pale face was clueless, light blue eyes blank. "Tank...top?"

Jamie waved her hand in the air. "Never mind. I don't have anything you people will let me wear."

"Oh, his lordship instructed Mrs. Knightsbridge to garb you however she saw fit. You are to wear the late countess's clothes."

Jamie threw back the covers. "Oh, okay. I don't know what size the countess was, but I'm about an eight. Or a ten, depending on how it's...cut." Shit. They didn't have sizes. Jamie rubbed hard at her temples. This was going to take a lot of adjustment. She hoped Wilhelmina wouldn't take too long to send her back. Things were way too weird here.

Muriel nodded and ignored Jamie. She opened the trunk again and pulled out a long dress.

"Oh, this sprigged muslin should do. Are you ready to dress now, miss?"

Jamie stared at the maid. She hadn't had a shower yet today. She hadn't brushed her teeth. She hadn't shaved her legs or her underarms, and she certainly hadn't applied deodorant. She was supposed to hop straight from jammies to dresses without cleaning up first? The thought gave her the creeps.

Jamie crossed her arms, almost getting tangled in the generous yards of fabric. "We're going to have to have a discussion."

With several comments about her peculiarities, Muriel finally agreed to help. Once she'd talked Jamie out of a full bath (it seemed the footmen weren't too keen on lugging all that water up the stairs again so soon after her last bath), she used a basin and a sliver of soap. It was hardly adequate, but she couldn't really argue.

Her request for a toothbrush only got her another blank stare from the maid. A clean rag dampened with water had to do. Her teeth still felt coated with furries. *Blecch.*

After she'd made the best of a bad situation, it was time to get dressed. She'd hidden behind the potty screen to do her washing, so she wouldn't be parading around naked in front of Muriel. The maid passed a plain white cotton garment behind the screen. Jamie held it up in the air, trying to figure it out.

"What's this?"

Muriel's exasperated sigh was loud, even from the other side of the screen. "It is your shift, miss."

Jamie made faces in the maid's direction, but she pulled on the dress anyway. It reminded her of a slip that she'd worn the few times her family had attended church when she was little.

Jamie poked her head around the corner. "Hey, I can't go out in this, can I? It's more see-through than that nightgown was."

Muriel shook her head. "Miss, these are your under-garments. The dress goes over them. Mrs. Knightsbridge swore that you were not simple, but I wonder…"

"She is not simple, Muriel, she is unfamiliar." Mrs. Knightsbridge bustled into the room. Her round face held its usual cheerful expression, chubby pink cheeks contrasting with the drab brown of her serviceable gown. "She was brought up very oddly, so it is up to us to help fill in the stops. Good morning, Miss Jamie. Are you well?"

"I'm great. Trying to figure this clothes thing out." Jamie fluffed the sides of the cotton gown out from her body. "It kind of swallows me whole."

"We will put it to rights. Come now. Muriel, the pantalettes?"

They put her in bloomers. They put her in stays, which was apparently an English word for hellish death-trap of boning and laces. By the time they'd stuffed her into the petticoats and long-sleeved gown, stabbed her skull with thousands of hairpins, and tied a perky green ribbon in her hair, she was planning ways to murder Wilhelmina in her sleep. And Mrs. Knightsbridge. And that grumpy-ass earl for trying to marry some fortune-hunting bitch in the first place.

"Oh, she looks a treat, Mrs. Knightsbridge." Muriel beamed, clapping her bony little hands. Jamie wanted to murder her too. All of them. With a double-handed axe. With plus-fifty pain. And then she'd resurrect them so she could kill them again. She couldn't breathe.

"She does indeed. Now, should you like to come down to breakfast?"

Jamie stared at Mrs. Knightsbridge. The morning light revealed more of the lady's face than the firelight had the night before. She was nice looking, for an older woman. Her dark brown hair held streaks of gray at the temples, and her eyes smiled even when the rest of her face didn't. Who'd have known that such an innocent face could hide such a pitiless, evil monster?

"How am I supposed to eat in this getup? I can't even

take a good breath. There's no way I could make room for food. There's not even room for my boobs." Jamie poked at one of the pale mounds that peeked above the neckline of the dress. It jiggled in response. Much as she hated to admit it, that corset thing was doing pretty impressive stuff with her cleavage. Too bad Logan couldn't see her now. He might rethink things.

A shocked giggle escaped Muriel before she could stifle it with a hand. Mrs. Knightsbridge glared at the maid before turning her stink eye to Jamie.

"Ladies never refer to their, ahem, bosoms in such a manner. In fact, endeavor to forget that they even exist."

"It's going to be hard, since my chin is basically going to be resting on them all day." Jamie hunched her shoulders and demonstrated. Muriel got a good squawk out that time.

"Miss Marten..." Ooh, that tone was never a good thing. Apparently "I'm going to kick your ass" sounded about the same in 1816 as it did in her time.

"All right, sorry. I won't talk about my boobs."

Muriel fled the room. The door hadn't clicked shut behind her before her giggles escaped. That girl really needed to get out more.

Mrs. Knightsbridge led Jamie down the stairs to the dining room she'd seen last night. As they walked, the housekeeper lectured.

"Be polite, be engaging, and most of all, please, no coarse language. His lordship is a fairly patient man, but you must not try him." She pointed to the open doorway and left Jamie.

Jamie would try him as much as she could and then some. He'd been a jerk last night, and she wasn't about to let him think he could treat her that way without a fight. She was done being any man's doormat, and that included Mr. High-and-Mighty-Oh-Holy-Crap-She-Forgot-He-Was-That-Frickin'-Gorgeous.

The slippers that Muriel had shoved on her feet stuck to the floor at the doorway of the dining room. He sat at the head of the table, his dark hair shining in the sunlight that poured into the window. He leaned back in his chair, reading a letter. The dark blue of his jacket contrasted nicely with the crisp white of his collar and neck cloth thing. He studied the paper in his hand intently, eyes never leaving it even when he brought the steaming cup of tea to his lips. Full, beautiful lips that she'd come very close to kissing last night.

But he'd rejected her.

Remembering that little fact acted like a stun gun on her fluttering heart, and she set her jaw and marched over to the table.

Her first step raised his eyes from the paper. The second had him shoving his chair back to stand. The third lowered his brows into that now-familiar glower.

She flopped down into a chair, grabbed a piece of ham from the platter in the center of the table, and shoved it into her mouth with a grin.

"Mornin', Mikey!" Her nauseatingly cheerful greeting was spoken around a mouthful of food. She smacked as loudly as she could, inwardly wincing at the sound. It had to be good if she was that annoying to herself.

If he hadn't been born with that silver spoon lodged up his ass, she thought he would have gone slack-jawed. But she had to give it to him; he really played it cool. He sat back down in his chair, took another sip of his tea, and resumed reading his letter as if she hadn't pissed all over his cornflakes.

The lack of reaction did disappoint her a bit.

Jamie helped herself to the platters of food in front of

her. Although she was used to either a bagel or a bowl of cereal in the morning, the more substantial, if a little odd, fare was sort of tasty. Eggs, toast, ham, and tea took priority in her brain once she figured out it was possible to eat with the deathtrap, er, stays, compressing her middle.

She munched in silence for several minutes while trying to wrap her brain around a game plan. It was fairly obvious to her that Mrs. Knightsbridge's conviction that she and Mike would fall desperately in love was a load of animal dung.

After several moments of quiet eating, Jamie looked over at Mike. He'd set the letter down and was looking straight at her.

"What?" she asked around a mouthful of buttered toast.

"You are looking quite fine this morning," he said. She gasped and nearly choked.

"What?" she sputtered, tears welling as she coughed.

He gestured toward her, a bemused expression on his face. "You look, well, almost a lady. I did not expect that. After your appearance yesterday, I thought I would find you looking fit for Newgate prison again."

She lowered her brows as she finished swallowing the wayward bite of toast. She took a sip of tea, mainly to cool her rage. She'd been working yesterday. Wor-king. Something she suspected Lord Dunnington hadn't ever had to do in his lifetime. She hadn't exactly had the time or the means to put on her evening gown and stilettos before meeting his worshipfulness. She set her teacup down with a clink and gave him her best death-to-earls scowl.

"Oh, really? Well, thank you. You look, well, just as snotty and conceited as you did yesterday. Is that a new stick up your ass, or do you use the same one every day?"

Her heart warmed as his nostrils flared. God, why did pissing him off make her so happy? *Oh yeah, maybe because he tosses insults at every opportunity.* She smiled at him sweetly as she took another sip of hot tea. She was really getting to like the stuff.

He groomed his face into an impenetrable mask, sitting up even straighter in his chair. "I spoke too soon, miss. Your waspish tongue would make an angel look haggard."

She nearly spit her mouthful of tea back into the cup. She almost strangled when she swallowed it instead. "Waspish? You stuck-up, arrogant son of a bitch!"

"I assure you, my mother was a saint."

"She'd have to be, to put up with a hell-spawn like you."

"I was right to doubt the truthfulness of your tale. You speak like an ill-bred guttersnipe. Surely all females in the distant future are not as foulmouthed."

Jamie splayed her palms on the tablecloth, leaning toward him as much as the unrelenting boning of her stays would allow. "Women in my time can say any damn thing we please because we are equal to men."

He barked a laugh, his brows climbing nearly to his hairline, and her rage boiled even hotter. Sweat started to pop out on her furrowed forehead as she clenched her jaw so hard she thought her teeth would crack.

"Equal to men? Walking about nearly nude, breaking into houses, and swearing like a low-born stable boy does not mean you are a gentleman's equal."

"Gentleman my ass! You don't know anything about me! And besides, you're forgetting one important thing again. I didn't break into your house, certainly not by choice."

He steepled his fingers, leaning back in his chair like a Wall Street tycoon. "Oh yes. The mysterious bureau deposited you here. So sorry, it must have slipped my mind in the storm of profanity you have spewed since arriving in my home."

She scraped the chair back as hard as she could, wishing the grating noise was breaking bones. His. Particularly that aristocratic nose. "You know what? You don't have to worry about me anymore. I'll find my own way back. Thanks for letting me crash here for the night. I wish I could say it was nice, but…" She shrugged and shook her head. Turning away from him, she marched toward the door.

"Oh, Miss Marten?"

She really didn't want to turn around. She really, really didn't.

With a roll of her eyes, she did it anyway. "What?"

"I have an engagement this evening. If you decide to continue your stay in my home, please do remain indoors. I have no wish to be responsible for whatever havoc you wreak upon London without my supervision."

She narrowed her eyes at him. He'd stood when she did, and as she looked into his face, he had the gall to smile at her. He looked like a movie star, his cleft chin pronounced against his white collar, but he was the most arrogant ass she'd ever met.

"Don't worry. I'll make sure to mind my Ps and Qs. I won't be here to bother you much longer anyway."

She slammed the dining room door shut behind her. It didn't help. If Mrs. Knightsbridge continued to refuse to help her locate Wilhelmina and insisted on trying to make her into Mike's ideal woman, she was going to have to change him into someone that Jamie could spend three minutes with comfortably. Right now, at 120 seconds, she was ready to clock him.

❧

Micah sank back into his chair, not as happy at having bested her verbally as he thought he'd be. He felt, actually, rather disappointed in himself. Bracing his forehead in his palm, he groaned. He'd not intended that. But the letter from his ex-mistress, Collette, that had arrived that morning had eradicated his already thin patience. Miss Marten's quite pointed barbs had shattered the last shreds of his control, causing him to fire back when he should have remained silent. Clearly his talent with the fair sex did not extend to his uninvited houseguest.

"That was a good job, wasn't it, lad?" Micah said to Baron, whose nose was now propped on the earl's knee. "How was it in her bed, then?"

The greyhound said not a word but gave a pointed look to his lordship's plate. With a sigh, Micah laid the porcelain on the floor, so Baron could have at the scraps of his breakfast.

"You spoil that dog, my lord." Mrs. Knightsbridge bustled into the dining room, smiling fondly down at the hound.

"As do you, Mrs. Knightsbridge." Micah stood, rounding the corner of the table to block the house-keeper's path. "Pardon me, but I'd like a moment of your time."

She turned to him, head tilted slightly. "Of course, my lord."

Micah clasped his hands behind his back and stood tall. "I should like to know what you think of Miss Marten."

A slightly nervous smile crossed Mrs. Knightsbridge's face. "Well, my lord, I think she's a wonderful young lady. Quite spirited and beautiful, not at all in the common way."

"Yes. A bit too far out of the common way," Micah said with a bit of sarcasm. "Her tales are a bit fantastical, are they not? Colorful musical objects; traveling through a magic bureau from hundreds of years in the future?"

The housekeeper bit her lip and glanced away. "It is quite a tale. Do you know, I think I hear Cook calling me? Do pardon me, my lord."

In any other household, with any other peer of the realm, a servant would never dismiss herself without leave. But Micah only quirked a smile as he watched the little round woman scurry from the room in the opposite direction from the kitchen. Mrs. Knightsbridge had always been more like a mother to him than a housekeeper, so he said nothing about her odd behavior. In truth, she behaved oddly more often than not.

Baron looked up from the now-clean plate and whined.

"You greedy cur, you have eaten more than your share." Micah ruffled the dog's ears as he rounded the end of the table and placed the plate back on it. He'd think about what Mrs. Knightsbridge had said. Perhaps he owed the uncommon Miss Marten an apology. She was obviously unfamiliar with his home and his time, whether or not it was through a fault of her own. He'd extended her his hospitality, and so far, he'd been a most ungracious host. If she left his home, what would become of her? As a gentleman, he could not, in good conscience, toss a young woman onto the mean streets of London. The thought was insupportable, and he chastised himself as he picked up his letters. One fluttered back to the linen tablecloth.

Grimacing, he picked up the missive from his ex-mistress and laid it atop his other correspondence. On the way from the room, he carelessly tossed the lot on the hall table. His secretary could deal with them when he arrived. Micah wanted nothing more to do with Collette. Her histrionics and frequently outrageous demands on him were done. He only wished he'd known her true nature before taking her as his mistress.

Shaking his head determinedly, he strode into his estate room, shutting the door with a satisfying bang.

Seven

"No. *No way*, Mrs. K. I am *not* his lordship's best chance at love and he sure as hell…um, sorry." Jamie rolled her shoulders, the stays digging into the undersides of her breasts with the movement. "What I mean to say is that I can't stand him. He's a…an apple. A rotten, wormy, grumpy apple. And his countess is in another castle. I don't have any intention of tying myself to him. *Ever.* So you might as well have your sister send me back. Like, today."

The housekeeper smiled at the crystal she was cleaning. "I am sorry, Miss Jamie, but I cannot do that. Now, you must not fret. Wilhelmina is never wrong. You simply must give him a chance. You will see in time."

"Time? In time, I will commit murder. Seriously. Don't you have any way to contact her now? Like a crystal ball or newt's blood or something?"

Mrs. K shook her head.

Jamie slumped her shoulders as she leaned forward in defeat. If Mrs. K wouldn't get her sister the witch to send Jamie home, she had nowhere to go. So much for her grand breakfast exit. "I'm not cut out for this."

"Do not fret, Miss Jamie. We will soon put your

worries to rest. Run along now. I must finish the crystal before we can resume our lessons."

Jamie groaned. "Really? More lessons? Wouldn't it be easier to just kill me now?"

"Shoo." The housekeeper winked at Jamie. "I won't be a moment, and then we will begin lessons in deportment."

"Deportment? I'd like to be deported to America, circa the twenty-first century," Jamie grumbled under her breath as she left the room. She wandered around the first floor aimlessly, not really sure what to do with herself. If she were at home, she'd have logged on an hour ago. She'd be happily questing through Mount Ujlek, racking up badges to turn in for her new helm. She liked that new helm. It was spiky and had some powers that Killaz could really use. It would also match her purple hair nicely. Jamie sighed. It was no use even thinking about what she was missing at home. She was here for the time being, and she'd have to make the best of it.

As she rounded a corner of the hallway, a sheet of parchment caught her notice. It slumped against the baseboard like a bum against a public building. As she stooped to pick it up, she recognized it. *The letter Mike was reading at the table earlier.*

The paper was thick, its texture weird. Unable to resist the impulse to snoop, she unfolded it. Oddly curling handwriting met her gaze, and she had to squint kind of hard to make sense of it.

> *Micah,*
>   *I cannot help but assume that your lack of response bodes ill. Have you not received my missives? It is insupportable that you would continue to ignore me in this ill-bred fashion. I will not remain so patient with you forever.*

Waites tells me that you are to propose soon to Miss Lyons. I must speak with you, dearest Micah, before this event occurs. It would be the gravest of errors on your part to propose to that young lady.

We are meant to be together. I care not a fig for position or wealth or any of that nonsense. But I must have you, my dearest one. If I do not, there is no hope for me. I shall die of a broken heart. The only death I wish is with you, my love. You must visit me as soon as you are able. We shall put this nonsense behind us and be happy as we once were.

I remain yours eternally,
Collette

With a stunned shake of her head, Jamie laid the letter with the others on the hall table. *Wow. Talk about clingy exes.* At least she'd let Logan go gracefully when he flew the coop. This chick needed some serious therapy.

Jamie opened the first door she came to and was pleasantly surprised by the sight that greeted her. A garden with high brick walls and the early blooms of spring surrounded her. She let the door fall shut behind her as she walked down the gravel path into the vibrant-hued sanctuary.

There was a slight nip in the air, and her arms were quickly covered in goose bumps beneath the thin fabric of her borrowed dress. Fortunately, all the layers over her middle kept her core warm. She started to enjoy her little stroll. Buttercups were out in full force, undaunted by the remnants of winter. The whole garden had an air of burgeoning life, a promise of wakefulness that the coming spring would deliver. She took a deep breath and surprised herself by smiling. This wasn't so bad after all. She hadn't really spent much time outside in the last couple of years. Life had been too busy, too hectic, first with Logan, and then with the gnawing depression his absence had left her with.

The path curved past a tree, and a stone bench was nestled there beside the mossy trunk, out of sight of the house. She sat down on it, the cold stone slightly damp. She didn't care. She breathed in the crisp, clean air and enjoyed the scenery around her.

"Lovely, is it not?"

Her calm dissipated like smoke in the breeze, and she whipped her head around at the sound of that voice. Of course, it was Mike. He rounded the bend in the gravel path, his boots crunching on the small stones. So much for her solitary peace. No way could it withstand another verbal boxing match with Mike.

"Don't you have someplace to be?" She didn't bother to hide her weary tone.

He sat on the bench next to her, ignoring her question. "I often come to sit out here. It's very tranquil, quiet. It helps to be alone with one's thoughts sometimes."

"I wouldn't know." She lifted a brow at him pointedly. He looked at the low-hanging branches beside him, examining the tiny green buds. A ball of nerves grew in her chest. Why was he there? He didn't like her, so why was he sitting next to her? There was a good six inches between his leg and hers, so why did it seem like his leg was burning her through the tight linen pants he wore?

"I would often come out here last season, when things were not so pleasant. I took peace in the solitude, the lack of accusing eyes…" He fell silent, leaving her wondering what the hell he was talking about. He then cleared his throat and spoke again. "Miss Marten, I must again apologize to you. I had no intention of being rude to you at the breakfast table, but I did just that. I behaved like a boor. Please do forgive me."

He was unbelievable. She searched his features, looking for the punch line, but all she saw was clarity in his face and in the set of his broad shoulders.

Jamie didn't know what to say. Maybe he had been upset at breakfast by that letter. Maybe she should forgive him. She tried to ignore the fact that he was so close to her and so handsome and looking at her, but her stupid body wouldn't cooperate. Warmth bloomed in the pit of her stomach, and she was suddenly very self-conscious. She tried to tear her eyes away from the strong line of his jaw, the way his hair curled over his ears, the way his nose was a little too shiny, but she couldn't. Her brain was useless.

"Miss Marten?"

She shook her head. "Sorry. I…yeah. Sorry." English had apparently deserted her with the sum total of her good sense.

"You are welcome to stay in my home as long as is needed." The polite smile dissipated as he drew in a deep breath, and his eyes were troubled. "There are many dangers that can befall a female person in the streets of London."

"Thanks," she said lamely. She reached up to tuck her hair behind her ear, but of course, it was still perfectly smooth. The dress. It had to be this getup they'd stuffed her in. She wasn't normally this twitterpated in the presence of a handsome guy. But then again, she thought as she straightened the skirt over her legs, she'd never really spent much time with a gorgeous earl.

"I should apologize too. I haven't been the easiest person to get along with since yesterday. It's hard because I don't know what I've gotten into, you know?" She hadn't really intended to be that honest with him, and it embarrassed her a little. She could feel her cheeks getting hot.

He nodded, not commenting on her blush. "I can imagine, if things are as you insist they are, that this must be incredibly difficult for you. I cannot fathom how a simple bureau could facilitate such a random act of magic, but it seems it must be so." He grinned, staring straight ahead. "That, or I'm as addle-brained as the dowager Duchess of Ware." Mike turned and looked at her, his confusion clear. "Do you still have that small box you brought with you?"

She shifted on the bench, uncomfortable and feeling like a fraud despite the sincerity of her situation. "It's in the Lemon Room."

"The Lemon Room," he repeated, brows drawn down in confusion.

"Yes. The bedroom Mrs. K put me in last night? It looks like lemons." She smiled. "It's really pretty."

"I am happy that it pleases you." He cleared his throat. "What other things are different in my home than in yours? If that little device is any indication, there must be many other such things that I am unfamiliar with."

"You have no idea. I miss my shower, my toilet, my toothbrush, my computer, my car…" She trailed off at the confused look on his face. "Sorry again. It's hard to remember that none of that stuff exists yet. I should probably shut up."

"No," he said, the corner of his mouth curling. A thrill went through her when he reached over and took her hand. "Please. I would like to hear of them."

His fingers were warm and strong, his skin a bit lighter than her own. Why was she letting him hold her hand? And the bigger question was, why wasn't she able to stop him? She looked into his eyes again and realized she really didn't care about answering that question. She had some others to take care of first.

"Well, the first and best thing is the shower. We have pipes that bring water into our houses…"

They sat there together on that chilly stone bench in the garden, and she told him about her life. He held her hand the whole time, no trace of the normal snobbery that seemed to follow him like a black cloud. She relaxed, comfortable to reminisce in the presence of the much-friendlier-than-normal earl. After she described the miracles of modern plumbing and cars and airplanes, they moved on to computers. She thought they were Mike's favorite because his eyes danced with the same gleeful light she'd seen in them yesterday while he was playing with her smartphone.

"So, this web connects the entire world? And messages are sent within seconds? How extraordinary." A light squeeze traveled from his hand to hers as he leaned closer. She swallowed hard, trying to keep her stupid heart from jumping out of her chest. She could almost forget that he made her want to shoot laser beams out of her eyes most of the time. If he kept this up, she might be in trouble.

"It's pretty cool. And you can send more than emails. You can send videos, pictures, all sorts of things. You can buy and sell things, meet people, and even control satellites in space if you've got that kind of access."

He shook his head incredulously. "How limiting and backward this time must be for you. When your life has consisted of speaking with those across the world, how can you be satisfied with being confined to my home?" His thumb traced a light circle on her knuckle.

She swallowed hard, eyes glued to the tempting curve of his lips. "It's not been…so bad…"

Lord help her, she wanted to kiss him again. He was so near now, only inches from her. It wouldn't take much—a quick lean forward, and their lips would be touching. Their mouths would connect, and she could let her tongue trace the fullness of his lower lip…

The scrabbling of claws on gravel should have warned her, but she was a bit too preoccupied with imagining kissing Mike to notice.

"Baron, no!"

Paws landed in her middle, knocking the little bit of oxygen she could breathe with those stays out of her. Overbalanced, she tipped over the back of the bench with a squeak. Her slippers stuck straight up in the air, and she landed solidly on her back in the dirt. The greyhound tangled in her petticoats and began a merciless attack on her face with his tongue.

"Baron," the earl barked in a stern voice. "To me!"

After one last lick, Baron trotted away.

The dirt beneath her was cool and damp. She stared up at the branches of the tree, wondering how in the hell she was going to get up without embarrassing the shit out of herself. It was really too late, though.

"Miss Marten, I do apologize for Baron's exuberance. He is still young, you see, and rather excitable." Mike reached down and scooped her from the ground like she weighed no more than a doll. Her arms wound around his neck as he carried her back around the bench.

It was the adrenaline from the fall that made her heart beat that fast. It was only thankfulness that made her want to kiss Mike even more now than she had moments ago. But as he let her legs descend and her slippered toes touched the gravel, she couldn't convince her arms to release their hold around his neck.

"Are you quite well?" he asked her softly. Concern raised his brows as he looked into her eyes.

"I'm fine," she whispered. *Kiss me*, she begged him in her head. *Come on, Mike, please.*

Two seconds, three, and she thought her subliminal message might have worked. He leaned down ever so slightly, narrowing the gap between them. One heartbeat, two, and she let her eyes start to slide closed. He was going to do it. He was going to kiss her...

And then he stepped away from her, gently breaking her hold on him.

"Please excuse me, Miss Marten." He bowed, and with a command to Baron, they left her, Mike speaking to the dog in a soft voice the whole way.

She stood alone in the path, dress damp and dirty, arms empty and cold, and rejected for the second time in two days. When was she going to learn? Mike had no interest in her. Honestly, when he was being his normal, arrogant, jackass self, she didn't have any interest in him. So why'd she keep trying to kiss him?

She half ran back up the path toward the house. She couldn't get back home fast enough. It was time to fail some lady lessons.

❦

Jamie thought Mrs. Knightsbridge was going to pass out when she saw the state of the dress Jamie wore. The housekeeper's normally cheerful, round face elongated with horror.

"Miss Jamie, whatever have you done?"

Jamie threw her hand up and continued up the stairs.

"It was another accident with that crazy dog. I'm going up to change."

Mrs. K followed Jamie to the Lemon Room, clucking like a ticked-off chicken. She fussed over Jamie, dressing her as if she couldn't fend for herself, and redoing her hair. After checking to make sure the housekeeper's ferocious hairpinning hadn't drawn blood, Jamie followed her back down the stairs into what she called the drawing room.

When Jamie had sat through calculus classes in college, she'd thought nothing could be more boring. Nothing could suck the life out of her more than staring at Professor Clark doodling on the whiteboard with that strange combo of letters and numbers that made absolutely zero sense to her. At least in college she could sit in the back of the class and scribble song lyrics in her notebook.

Jamie was Mrs. Knightsbridge's only student, and "What a Lady Must Do upon Pain of Death or, Worse, Ruination" was apparently the woman's favorite subject.

For three hours, Jamie sat in the drawing room, attempting to embroider and being preached to on the finer points of being a lady. A lady mustn't ever speak to someone to whom she's not been properly introduced. A lady must be modest, soft-spoken, and never ever use the word "shit." A lady must be a spineless, giggling, mindless fluff of femininity that can do needlepoint, sing, and paint with watercolors. An unwed lady mustn't ever appear in public without a chaperone. A lady discovered in a compromising position must immediately wed or join a convent. A lady...

"Please, Mrs. Knightsbridge, can we take a break? I've listened to all the backward, sexist, historical crap I can take for a while."

With a roll of her eyes, the housekeeper nodded. "If you insist, Miss Jamie. I'll leave you to practice your embroidery. We'll resume our lessons at teatime."

Jamie focused on the scrap of fabric in her lap until the door shut behind the housekeeper, then took great pleasure in chucking it across the room. It hit the back of the door and flopped onto the rug like a dead fish.

1816 sucked ass.

Eight

LUNCH WAS TASTY, ESPECIALLY SINCE THERE WAS NO cranky earl to contend with, but afterward, Jamie was bored out of her mind. She prowled around the house for hours, desperately searching for something to keep her occupied. Also, she tried to keep out of Mrs. Knightsbridge's way. She didn't want to risk being sentenced to more embroidery. Talk about a fate worse than death. She'd rather never play a computer game for the rest of her life than pick up that damned needle and fabric again.

She was even desperate enough to try to find Mike, despite the whole greyhoundus smoochus interruptus, but he'd apparently bolted for the afternoon. Typical. The one time he could have been useful, and he was nowhere to be found.

Baron followed Jamie through the house, nails tick-ticking on the wooden floors. He bumped her hand with his nose, and she scratched his ears as she propped against a wall in the upstairs hallway. She made a face at the sour-looking portrait of some crotchety old aristocrat. Did he really have to look that grumpy?

"Pardon me, miss?"

Jamie jumped, putting a hand on her thumping heart. It was a footman, a guy who looked about sixteen. His cheeks held bright pink splotches, which contrasted sharply with his orangey-red hair.

"Yes?"

"Mrs. Knightsbridge sent me to fetch you. It is time for your lessons."

Jamie stared at the boy, horror widening her eyes. "You aren't heartless, are you?" She took a step closer to him. His eyes went wide, and his face paled, making his strawberry-colored cheeks almost neon.

"I beg your pardon, miss?"

"You look like a nice guy. You don't look like a guy who would willingly send a girl into the maw of Mount Doom. I really don't think you want to do this."

"But Mrs. Knightsbridge said—"

"I know what she said." Jamie lowered her voice into a whisper and bent her head, squeezing her eyes shut as hard as she could. It wasn't hard to muster a drop of moisture at the corner of her eye. When she looked back up at the footman, she knew he could see the gleaming wetness.

"Please don't make me." She let a little quiver sneak into her voice. "Please. I just want some time to be free. Just to take a little stroll. Can you tell her you couldn't find me, and then ask Muriel to accompany me on a little walk?"

Jamie felt sort of bad manipulating the young footman like that. After all, he was only doing his job. But seriously, another two hours of Countess 101 would make her permanently brain dead.

The footman nodded reluctantly, worrying his lip with his teeth. "All right, miss."

She smiled at him tremulously. "Thanks. What's your name?"

"George, miss."

"Thank you, George. I'll wait outside for Muriel." As he turned to walk away, she gave him a sad little wave. Poor kid. She hoped it wouldn't get him into trouble. She looked down at the hound by her side.

"Hey, Baron, want to go for a walk?"

Jamie put on a cape kind of thing that she found in the trunk at the foot of her bed, and she used a length of twine she found to make a leash for Baron. He probably had one somewhere, but she didn't want to waste time looking for it. As they stopped at the bottom of the stairs, Mrs. Knightsbridge's voice floated down the hall from the direction of the dining room, questioning George about her whereabouts. Fortunately, Thornton wasn't around, so there was no one to witness their covert exit. Moving as quickly and quietly as they could, she and Baron slipped out the front door and ducked down beside a bush to wait for Muriel.

Much as she hated to admit it, she was kind of having fun. The air had warmed a little since her morning walk in the garden, and it was turning out to be a really nice day. A pair of well-dressed ladies strolled by and gave Jamie an odd look. Playing it casual, Jamie propped against the wall and examined the prickly leaves of the bush she hid beside.

"Baron, I'm not sure if she's coming." Jamie worried the inside of her cheek with her teeth. "Think it would be awful if we took a quick walk through the park alone? It won't take long."

The whip-like tail wagged in answer.

Jamie smiled and stood. "Good enough for me, dog. Let's go."

Baron trotted along at her side as they wound their way down the long lane in the direction that Jamie hoped was the park Muriel had mentioned.

Jamie hummed to herself as they walked, smiling at strangers that they passed. Some of them smiled back, most looked puzzled, and a select few guys actually leered at her. It didn't bother her. She felt fairly confident in her ability to take care of herself. Leah had dragged her to one of those self-defense courses a couple of years ago, and she'd passed with flying colors.

She knew from what Mrs. Knightsbridge had told her that walking around without a chaperone was a huge no-no. Especially since no one knew where she was. But honestly, she'd tried to get Muriel to come with her. It wasn't really her fault it hadn't worked out. Besides, nobody knew she was staying with Micah. She wasn't from this time and place, and she certainly didn't have a future as the Countess of Dunnington, no matter what Mrs. K and her witchy sister thought.

She and Baron crossed the street to the pretty little park. While passing through the arched gates, a man's unfamiliar voice called behind her.

"Ho there, miss!"

She turned and tried to hide her confusion at the pair in front of her.

"Hi," Jamie said with a small smile.

The woman, whose boobs were nearly falling out of her dress, was sitting in an open carriage next to a thin man. He was dressed in the most brightly patterned waistcoat Jamie had ever seen. His companion's mint-green gown matched the leaves on her straw bonnet, contrasting nicely with her honey-colored hair.

"Lovely day, is it not?" the lady called in a sweet voice.

Consternation nipping at her heels, Jamie stopped next to the carriage. Baron tugged at the twine in her hand. Even though she wasn't sure if she should be talking to these people, she didn't want to be rude—although she would enjoy having a conversation with somebody that wasn't a stuck up earl or his sadly misguided housekeeper.

"It is nice," Jamie agreed.

The thin guy looked down his nose at Jamie, the wind buffeting his mousy brown hair around the brim of his hat. "Your intriguing coiffure caught my eye."

Jamie put her hand up to her hair self-consciously. "Um, thanks."

The woman gave a kind smile. "What is your name, dear?"

"I'm Jamie Marten." Jamie stuck her free hand up to the green-garbed woman.

The lady looked more and more amused, but extended a gloved hand to Jamie. Jamie shook it with her bare one.

"Marilyn Munroe," the lady said.

Jamie couldn't help but laugh. "Really? Marilyn... Munroe?"

Her heart-shaped face lost a little of its pleasant expression. "Yes, that is my name."

Jamie composed herself. "I'm sorry, I just know someone else with that name. It's a nice name."

She smiled again, seemingly placated. "I thank you."

At that moment, Jamie saw a carriage go by with a very familiar earl in it. An earl whose face looked like he'd been possessed by the patron saint of Rage. An earl who was probably going to cheerfully strangle Jamie when he caught her. He was sitting next to a golden-haired girl with thin lips, big eyes, and a white hat. It was covered with feathers and cherries. Jamie hated it, and her, on sight. The one thing that made her feel a little better was that he didn't seem to be paying blondie the slightest bit of attention. His head swiveled as they passed, eyes staying trained on Jamie the whole time.

"Well, it was nice meeting you, but I've got to get

going." Jamie craned her neck toward his carriage, trying to figure out which way he was heading so she could bolt in the opposite direction.

Marilyn turned and looked after the carriage that had disappeared into the park. "You are acquainted with Lord Dunnington?"

"Um, only a little. We're not, like, close or anything. Just friends." Jamie stared at the park entrance, petrified that the carriage would emerge and Mike would murder her.

The loudly dressed guy beside Marilyn nudged the woman with his elbow. "Well, at least this mistress shan't cause much of a stir if she drops dead." He laughed loudly, coughing barks that sounded sort of painful.

Jamie stared at the guy. *What is it with these people?* "Why would I drop dead? That's a real asshole thing to say. And excuse me, but no, I am *not* his mistress. I'm not anybody's mistress. I'm an independent woman who can do fine on her own, and your archaic, backward ideas about females completely do not apply to me."

He smirked and shook his head. Addressing Marilyn, he said, "I am quite glad that my own mistress behaves with much more circumspection. Come, my dear. Say good-bye to your simple friend."

Marilyn smiled, her perfect face puzzled. "It was a pleasure to make your acquaintance."

With a sharp command to the horses, the guy flicked the reins, and the couple's carriage disappeared down the street.

"Come on, Baron," Jamie said, scanning the path into the park. No sign of Mike. He'd apparently kept going for his afternoon ride with Miss Pretty-Pretty-Princess. "Let's finish our walk."

Jamie and Baron kept on past the park, since she didn't want to chance running into Mike again. When the shadows grew long and the air started to cool, they turned around.

"All right, dog, time to head home." Jamie patted Baron's silky ears as they walked. He really was a nice dog when he wasn't constantly knocking her down. He probably needed more exercise.

They'd taken so many turns and byways that Jamie wasn't really sure exactly where the house was. She walked back in what she hoped was the right direction, holding Baron's twine tightly. As it got darker, she got more and more worried. What if she couldn't find the way back?

If she asked anyone for directions, they might find out she was staying with Mike. And she didn't want to bring him any more trouble. Damn it, she should have waited for Muriel. She hadn't meant to go this far; she was just trying to avoid Mike's wrath. Why'd she have to be so fracking impulsive?

Her slippers had started to rub blisters on her feet. She stopped for a moment, leaning on a newly lighted post to adjust her borrowed footwear. Propping her ankle on her opposite knee, she pulled off the slipper and examined the raw spot that had appeared beneath her borrowed silk stockings.

"Well, well, wot's this then?"

"Looks ta me like a bit o' muslin waitin' fer a toss."

Jamie looked up as two men approached from across the street. They were both grinning at her, their brownish, rotting teeth proclaiming their lack of dental hygiene. One had a dark beard, and the other shaggy sideburns. The smell of their BO hit her when they were still a good ten feet away.

She shoved the slipper back on her foot and waved a hand in front of her nose. "Jeez, Baron, you'd think they could at least smell each other." She tugged lightly on the twine, and Baron obligingly walked next to her as they continued down the street.

"Oy, where you goin', then?"

Jamie looked back over her shoulder. The men were following her. *Crap.* "I'm going home. Leave me alone."

"Don' worry, sweets, we'll do ya right." Coarse laughter made her spine tingle with fear. "Aye, I've an itch ta scratch, and ye'll do just fine."

She walked faster. "Fuck off, assholes." She didn't turn that time, but she spoke loud enough that she knew they'd hear her.

"Will ya listen to the tongue in her head! Wot a naughty lass she is." Jamie heard the wet sound of spit hitting the cobbles.

"I loike 'em naughty."

Elongating her stride, she rounded the corner. Baron had to trot to keep up. When she looked ahead, she realized she'd made a grave mistake. Instead of the stately homes that she had hoped to see, there were docks spread out in front of her, only a few ships moored there. Damn it, she'd really screwed up this time. She must have wandered miles out of the way. At this late hour, there wasn't a lot of activity, but there were plenty of places a couple of guys could hurt a clueless girl. *Stupid, stupid, stupid.*

"Baron," she whispered to the hound who'd kept pace with her, "I'm going to have to let you go to fight these guys. Please don't get lost, okay? I really like you, and I'd hate for anything bad to happen to you because I got us into this mess. I'm sorry." Fear put a tremble in her voice. She swallowed it and kept moving.

The thudding footsteps behind her were coming

closer, and she searched her surroundings for any sort of weapon she could use against them. When they came after her, they'd probably have no issues using force. She had to be ready to protect herself.

There. A length of metal propped up against a large wooden crate was only about thirty feet away. She would get there, then make a stand. Her hand shook on Baron's leash as she mentally ran through the checklist of targets that she'd gotten in that self-defense class. *Let's see, nose, solar plexus, groin…*

Before she could reach the makeshift weapon, a meaty hand closed heavily on her shoulder. The smelly man with the beard spun her around and pulled her close to him. The stench of him was only surpassed by the disgusting feeling of his fleshy body pressed against her.

"'Ere, lass, give us a kiss." His blotchy red lips pursed as they descended toward her face.

"I'll kiss you, all right," she spat as she rammed her knee upward as hard as she could.

He let her go, coughing and gagging as he cupped his junk. He fell to the ground, moaning.

"Git her, Jacko!" His voice was a hoarse whisper.

Sideburns started toward her, an ugly twist to his mouth. "Ye'll pay for that, lassie."

"No, she won't." The sound of approaching hoof-beats made her glance away from her attacker.

Never in Jamie's life had she thought she'd have a knight in shining armor come rescue her. Well, except maybe for that time that she was questing in the Quailiard Caverns and she was overcome with were-jaguars. Then, a knight in shining silver armor who happened to be doing the same quests rescued her.

Mike wasn't exactly a knight, and his dark, long cloak wasn't exactly shining armor, but when Jamie saw him jump down from the back of his horse and draw a thin blade from his cane to defend her honor against Sideburns, she could honestly feel a swoon coming on. Bloody murder flashed in the earl's eyes as he charged at the two creeps.

"Mike!"

"'Ey, Gordon, it's a toff. Gerrup." Sideburns backed off at the sight of Mike's slender blade trained at his chest and yanked on Beard's arm. Helping his still-sniveling friend to his feet, he dragged him off toward the opposite end of the docks.

When they'd gone, Jamie couldn't help throwing her arms around Mike. He felt as wonderful against her body as Beard had felt horrible. The difference was night and day. "Oh, Mike, thank you. I'm so sorry. I won't ever do that again."

He didn't hug her back, but she didn't care. When she pulled back to look at him, the blood and murder had disappeared, but his eyes were still thundercloud dark in the dim light of the streetlamps.

"You are correct, madam. You won't. How could you be such a fool? Do you know what they would have done to you?" He nearly roared at her by the end of his question, knuckles white as he clenched a fist. "Murder would have been a blessing by the time they were through. Do you have no care at all for your safety?"

She backed off a little, nervous at his vehemence. "I…I'm sorry."

He hung his head, shoulders shuddering as he breathed. Three seconds, four, and he lifted his head and set his jaw. After mounting his horse again, he reached a hand down to her. When she swallowed hard and took it, he pulled her up behind him. Taking Baron's twine, he wrapped the extra length around his gloved hand.

With a soft word to the horse, Mike guided it back the way she'd come. Baron trotted beside them, ears pricked and long whip-like tail wagging.

She held tightly to Mike, the unfamiliar bouncing of the horse uncomfortable. The dress was racked up above her knees, sitting astride as she was. She was so in her head about Mike's reaction that she didn't have a chance to be nervous about the thousand-pound animal plodding along beneath her. As awkward, uncomfortable, and terrifying as the night had been, she couldn't help but enjoy the sensation of Mike's warm, muscular back pressed tightly against her. She let her cheek rest against the black wool of his cloak. She could almost pretend that things were wonderful this way. That she was happy here and that Mike liked her, and…

At that moment, Mike stopped the horse. A footman, thankfully not George, helped her down.

"Escort her back in, please. Inform Mrs. Knightsbridge if she leaves the house unescorted again that there will be dire consequences." Mike's voice was as cold as the Arctic Sea. The ride back home must not have done anything to cool his temper.

The footman bowed and guided her toward the house as if she were a naughty child. Jamie looked over her shoulder at Mike's departing back, her gratitude now tainted. A woman on a white horse approaching Mike caught her eye. There was something dark in her gaze as she looked at Jamie. Ignoring her, Jamie slogged through the door, Baron trotting happily at the footman's heels. She reminded herself of the reasons why she and Mike would never ever ever be together. This episode was only the latest in a growing list of perfect examples.

Fury tightened Micah's hands on the reins as he rode away. How stupid! How utterly thoughtless she'd been to wander toward the docks alone—and after dark! His teeth ached from the clenching of his jaw, and he desperately fought the dark visions that assaulted him as he cantered away. If he'd been just minutes longer, she surely would have been dragged off, never to be seen again. The thought shot ice through his veins, and his heart pounded with anger and something else that he determinedly ignored. He was responsible for her as his guest, that was all. It was merely that and nothing more.

"Dunnington!"

His jaw tightened in vexation. Glancing over his shoulder, he was unsurprised to see the beautiful white horse and its female rider closing in on him. As much as he'd like to gallop away from Collette, he pulled up on the reins instead. It would not do to be so rude to a woman he'd once cared for. Hart tossed his head, snorting.

"Easy," Micah muttered, patting the glossy black neck of his horse.

"Micah, darling, have you not gotten my letters? I've been writing to you for ages now, and you've not replied." The full, pouting red lips and sweet voice would once have tempted him, but no longer.

"My apologies," Micah said simply.

Collette raised her beautifully arched brows at him. "Well, I am here now. Let us forget these silly misunderstandings, shall we?" She smiled at him, fluttering her dusky lashes in an alluring manner.

It would have been alluring if he was still a grieving, lonely man. But Collette had played him false too many times to take him in again so easily. Her last betrayal, telling secrets about his personal life to the highest bidder, was unforgivable. "I beg your pardon, Miss Dubois, but

I am late for an engagement." Micah gave her a shallow bow and clucked to Hart. The gelding snorted and took off as if he was delighted to be distancing himself from the female. Micah couldn't agree more.

As he neared Miss Lyons's home, it was not his ex-mistress that occupied his thoughts but Jamie. Micah tried to put all thoughts of Miss Marten from his mind but to no avail. How frightened yet brave she'd looked as she took on her attackers. How relieved she'd appeared when she caught sight of him. How her breasts had pressed full against his chest when she hugged him in gratitude.

He shifted in the saddle, denying the warmth that bloomed at the thought of her body against his own. He'd enjoyed that too much and would think of it no longer. Miss Felicity Lyons. He'd think of Miss Lyons and their upcoming evening together.

He tried not to notice how quick the warmth in his loins died at the thought.

Nine

MRS. KNIGHTSBRIDGE WRUNG HER HANDS WHEN JAMIE told her the story. It was hard to tell which made the housekeeper more upset: the ruffians who had nearly attacked Jamie or the fact that she'd gone out unescorted, no hat, no gloves, and risked someone finding out that she lived with the earl—not to mention making the acquaintance of a professional paramour.

The only upside was Jamie didn't even have to complain to get a bath brought up to her room.

When she'd been scrubbed and stuffed into another deathtrap, ahem, gown, she was allowed to go down to the dining room for dinner. Mrs. Knightsbridge refused to leave her alone. She wasn't sure if it was because of Mike's threat of "dire consequences" or Mrs. K's own plans for her. The housekeeper used the mealtime as an excuse to teach Jamie about the finer points of dining in company. Apparently Jamie, and everyone else she'd ever known, had been doing it wrong all these years.

There were rules about when and where to sit. How to get food onto her plate. How to pass things. How much and how fast to eat, what to talk about, what to never mention, and even when to get up from the table.

It was enough to give her indigestion. But she listened to it without complaint. She'd been enough trouble for one day.

Jamie was done eating way before Mrs. K was done talking, so they went into the music room to continue the lessons. When the housekeeper asked Jamie about any talents she had, and then discounted the fact that she could tie a cherry stem in a knot with her tongue, Jamie confessed that she could play the piano and sing.

"Well, let's hear it then," Mrs. K said, shooing Jamie toward the piano bench.

Jamie rolled her eyes but sat down. Stretching out her fingers, she wondered what to play. Mrs. K would be expecting something trilling and charming and suitable for polite company. The devil on Jamie's left shoulder whispered that she should play some Lady Gaga, but she ignored it. She was trying to behave, at least a little.

Jamie played the "Moonlight Sonata" first, and then sang a couple of the cleanest things she knew. She figured everyone would like the Beatles, and apparently she was right. Mrs. Knightsbridge beamed when Jamie was done.

"See? I told you. His lordship cannot help but be impressed with your talents. Now if you would only show the same passion for the other areas of study…"

"Mrs. K, I'm sorry, but I'm really tired. Can we call it a night?"

The plump lady smiled at Jamie and nodded. She placed a warm hand on Jamie's cheek. "Of course, dearie. Get some rest. You will see in the morning that things can be quite nice here."

As Jamie ascended the stairs, Muriel chattering happily behind her, she wondered what sort of stuff Mrs. K was smoking. She'd need it to get through the rest of her time here apparently. How much longer could

Wilhelmina go without contacting her sister? Jamie hadn't expected to be here this long, and it was starting to concern her. What if she could never go home? She shook herself, trying to chase the dark worries away as she entered the Lemon Room.

Muriel helped her out of her dress, and after the maid had gone and Jamie pulled the covers up to her chin, there came another scratching at the door.

She sighed and opened her eyes. "What, Baron?"

He was relentless, continuing to whine.

"You're like playing tennis with a brick wall," Jamie muttered as she opened the door. Baron wagged his tail and hopped onto the bed, balling his bony body up in a surprisingly tiny round.

Jamie climbed into bed behind him and stroked his slick fur. He fell asleep nearly instantly. She propped her chin up on her fist and watched the hound's chest expand as he breathed.

She'd come really close to getting into serious trouble today. If Mike hadn't come when he had, she had no doubt that those grubby, smelly men would have done horrible things to her.

I've been treating this like a big joke, she thought as she rubbed Baron's silky ears. *I haven't been taking this seriously and I nearly ended up raped, as well as a potential dockside murder statistic, because of it.*

She flopped onto her back and stared at the ceiling.

This was serious. This was potentially life-threatening, and she was through wasting time. She was going to have a heart-to-heart with Mrs. K in the morning, and if the housekeeper wouldn't help her get home, she'd go looking for Wilhelmina herself. Jamie wasn't cut out for this time. She wasn't cut out for Mike. She needed to get back home, where she knew the rules.

She stared at the ceiling for a very long time, listening to Baron breathe.

❦

Micah sent Thornton to bed as soon as the butler took his coat. It was too damned late for the old man to be waiting up for him, but no matter how the earl admonished him, Thornton refused to retire early.

Looking longingly toward his estate room, Micah sighed and, instead, trudged up the stairs, holding a candle aloft to light the way. What a horrid night. After the debacle with Miss Marten, and then the encounter with Collette, he'd been in a foul mood. Miss Lyons hadn't enjoyed the play, making comments about how *awful* the villain was and how so very *naughty*, and wouldn't he just leave the poor hero alone? That in itself would have been bearable, but she'd also chattered nonstop about that cloth-headed Sir William Knightley, the bloke who'd been courting her before Micah himself. He'd very nearly wished to strangle her, but when he uttered a cross word, she'd burst into tears. He'd taken her home and gone to his club, where he'd lost several hundred pounds in the card rooms. He reached the top of the stairs at last. Wanting nothing more than to retire, when he saw a white-clad form standing in the corridor by his bedchamber, he frowned.

"Go back to bed, Miss Marten."

"Wait," she said, coming closer to him. "I've got a robe on. I need to talk to you."

He sighed heavily and set his candle down beside hers on the small side table outside his door. "Can it not wait until morning?"

She shook her head. "No, it can't."

He gritted his teeth and crossed his arms over his chest. Her knuckles were white as she clutched the neck of her dressing gown closed, her braid lying over her shoulder. He ignored the itch in his fingers, the one that longed to see if her hair was as soft as it looked. "Be quick about it, then."

She blinked several times, tongue darting out to wet her lips. She opened her mouth, blew out a breath, and then closed it, clearly at a complete loss for what to say.

The image of her at the mercy of those ruffians by the docks leapt unbidden to his mind, and he didn't even attempt to stop the words that broke her extended silence. "If you meant to apologize for earlier this evening, please do not. I'm sure you have learned the dangers that can befall a woman unescorted on these streets. I trust you will not be so foolish a second time." His voice dripped with anger.

Her high brows and soft mouth disappeared in an instant, replaced by a mask of outraged temper. Her eyes snapped as she said, "I already told you that I wouldn't. I'm not stupid, you know."

He barked out a laugh. "It is difficult to believe you when you have insisted upon doing foolish things since your arrival, Miss Marten, not the least of which seems to be earning my ire."

His blood heated as she dropped the neck of her dressing gown and it fell open, revealing the soft curve of her breast beneath her night rail. She set her candle next to his and put both hands on her hips, exposing more of her front to his gaze. Her display would have been more alluring had her face not looked so cross. "I wouldn't insist on doing stupid things if I had a blessed clue what was right and what was not here. This place has more rules than a dictator's regime."

"I do apologize if the accommodations are unsatisfactory. Perhaps you would care to end your stay?" She couldn't go. Not now. She'd probably attend the mill at the heath if he wasn't around to prevent it. *Senseless, beautiful wench.*

"You know I can't go anywhere right now." Her frustration was plain in her voice.

"Ah, yes. You must stay near the magic bureau. Well, it appears you will have to make the best of it then." He didn't even attempt to hide his triumphant look.

She glared at him. "You don't believe me at all, do you? You think I'm crazy, a liar, and weird to boot. I don't know why I ever thought I wanted to kiss you." Her chest heaved as she clenched her jaw.

He found the challenge too much to ignore. He stepped toward her, but she didn't back down. Tilting her head back to accommodate his height, she kept her eyes locked with his. The fight in her was very tempting, he had to admit, and he was done fighting the temptation.

After a long moment in which his gaze never broke from hers, a shuddering breath left him. "Jamie"—she trembled sweetly as he said her given name—"for anyone to kiss you, you must remain silent."

When her mouth opened with surprise at his statement, he wasted no time. Closing the gap between them, he kissed her.

Her body was stiff against his, but her lips were as smooth and soft as he'd imagined. He was tender with her, coaxing her submission with gentle movements that asked rather than demanded. As she relaxed against him, he drew her body a bit closer to his, relishing the feel of her soft form through the thin cotton of her night rail. His tongue traced her lower lip, and he nearly groaned when she opened her mouth wider, allowing his tongue to delve inside. The moist heat there fired his blood, arousing him further.

He tasted her deeply, thoroughly, but he wanted

more. His breath mingled with hers, his hands resting on her slim back, but it wasn't enough. But at the slight pressure on her back, she pressed her soft breasts fully against his chest, and he tore his mouth from hers in surprise. Her lips shone softly in the candlelight, and her eyes were dark with passion.

He stepped back, and the cold air rushed into the gap between them. It was not far enough. He could not take her. She was not a courtesan; she was his guest. He could not take advantage of her gratitude. It would be unforgivable. She started to move closer to him, but he stopped her with splayed fingers in the air.

"I... I..." He shook his head, raking his hair back from his forehead. "Forgive me, Miss Marten." Without looking at her or saying another word, Mike grabbed his candle and disappeared into his bedroom. The click of the latch sounded like a gunshot, and he thumped his closed fist against the table by his bed.

He was an ass. A lecherous ass.

She stared at the shut door, wondering what in the holy hell had just happened.

Her bare toes started to go numb in the drafty air of the corridor. When she wrapped her brain around the fact that, yes, Mike had kissed her and, no, he wasn't going to open that door again, she picked up her candle and padded silently back to the Lemon Room.

Baron poked his head up out of the covers when the door squeaked open, but lay back down when he saw it was Jamie. She didn't go to bed. Instead, she grabbed the slippers that rested in front of the fire and stuck them onto her feet. When she left the bedroom this time, she could hear the dog's even breathing once more.

As she passed Mike's bedroom, she stopped for a second. She pressed her ear against the cold wood of the door. No noise inside the room. She shook her head, inwardly berating herself for her continued stupidity.

Maybe Mike's right, she thought as she made her way to the music room. *Maybe you are a fool. Know what? No maybes about it. You're a dumbass, Jamie Marten.*

After checking to make sure she was completely alone, she let the music room door click shut behind her. She set the candle down on the side table and sank down onto the bench.

Her fingers on the piano keys played as soft as a whisper, but the confusion and pain were plain in her song. The house was large enough that no one should hear her faint notes down in the secluded room. Music was her only solace in this strange world, and even at whatever the hell time it was, she had to have some relief from the swirling emotions eating her up inside.

Ten

It wasn't easy to avoid Mike for the next few days, but Jamie was determined. She stayed in her room until she saw him leave the house, hiding behind the curtains like a princess in a tower. Acting like a chickenshit wasn't the best course of action, but she didn't care. She couldn't face him yet. Muriel smuggled books up to the Lemon Room for her, so she wouldn't go bored out of her mind. Jamie started to get a newfound appreciation for Shakespeare. Those plays were as tawdry as any episode of *CSI* she'd ever sat through.

Mrs. Knightsbridge kept up the countess lessons, but Jamie thought the housekeeper knew that her heart wasn't in it. Jamie didn't tell her about the ill-fated kiss in the hallway, but it seemed kind of obvious that something had happened between the earl and his uninvited guest. After a few fruitless sessions of prodding Jamie for information, Mrs. K let it go.

But when it came to the dancing lessons, the diminutive housekeeper was as ferocious as an ogre. She forced Jamie down into the music room, talking her ear off all the while. Without regard to propriety or her fancy duds,

Jamie flopped down on the settee beneath the window while Mrs. K chattered.

"Come now, you must do this. A proper countess must be able to perform the country dances, and it will be acceptable for you to waltz once you are wed…"

"Mrs. K, for the billionth time, there's not going to be any wedding. Mike has zero interest in me. None. He can't stand me, and the feeling is very much mutual."

Jamie had never been the best liar, but she thought she delivered that pretty well. It didn't stop the doubt from creeping over the housekeeper's round face, though. She acted like Jamie hadn't said a word and continued shuffling sheet music.

"As I said, when you are wed, then permission will not be a problem. Ah yes, here is his lordship now."

The thudding footsteps in the hall confirmed her statement. Jamie jumped up from the settee, truly a feat since she was still stuffed into those damn unforgiving stays. "Wait a minute, you didn't say he was going to be involved with this. I can't dance with him. I can't even be in the same room with him without someone attempting murder."

There was an evil sort of twinkle in Mrs. K's eye. "Well, how can you learn to dance without a handsome and capable partner? Your lordship, thank you for attending us."

Mike didn't even look over at Jamie as he entered the room. He looked, well, fricking fantastic in his dove-gray coat and tight fawn pants. His boots were so shiny she thought she could see her face in them if she bent down. Of course, he might kick her in the face if she tried. Jamie sighed inwardly. She'd really fucked everything up, once again.

"Yes, Mrs. Knightsbridge, I understand you needed my assistance?"

The housekeeper nodded happily, her round cheeks bright. "Yes. I will accompany you on the piano if you will be so kind as to guide Miss Jamie in the steps of the cotillion."

The horror on Mike's face would have been funny if it wasn't so damn painful. His eyes flared wide, panic clear in their brown depths.

Am I really that bad? Jamie looked down at the rose-colored muslin dress she wore and smoothed the skirt down self-consciously. These damn petticoats made it look like she had thunder thighs. Fashion back in her time was really more flattering to her figure. Maybe that would help Mike be able to tolerate her more.

"Cotillion? Mrs. Knightsbridge, I cannot—"

"Oh, do not be so modest, your lordship. You are a wonderful dancer."

"That is not the issue. I simply—"

Jamie couldn't take his namby-pamby avoidance of the issue anymore. If he wasn't man enough to come out and say it, then she'd do it for him. "He doesn't want to dance with me, Mrs. K. He doesn't like me."

You could have heard mice whisper in the walls if Mrs. Knightsbridge wasn't such a great housekeeper. Mike and Mrs. K both stared at Jamie like she'd sprouted polka-dotted bat wings. She didn't think it was possible to feel even more uncomfortable, but there Mike was once again, proving her wrong.

"Nonsense, Miss Jamie," Mrs. K sputtered like an ancient engine. Mike continued staring at Jamie. "His lordship thinks very highly of you and will prove it by aiding in your dance lesson." Mrs. K pinned him with a glare that dared him to deny it.

He shook his head slightly, composed his face, and drew himself up taller. "Of course, Miss Marten. I would be delighted to assist." He offered Jamie his hand, and she stared at it, disbelieving.

He doesn't want to do this. Every time they had ever touched, he'd disappeared immediately afterward like his ass was on fire. The only reason he hadn't run this time was because Mrs. K had put his masculinity on the line, and as a "gentleman," he couldn't desert Jamie without looking like a total asshat. Jamie wished Mrs. K hadn't put him on the spot like that. Forcing him to be with Jamie certainly wasn't going to make him like her. But if Jamie ignored him, then she was the bitch, and she'd played that particular role more than enough lately.

Jamie steeled herself and took his offered hand. She wouldn't pay attention to the strong warmth of his skin on hers. She would studiously ignore the fact that her heart fluttered being close to him again. She would not focus on the way her lips tingled, longing to touch his again. She would get through this damn dance lesson without embarrassing herself if it was the last thing she ever did.

"Excellent." Mrs. Knightsbridge settled herself on the piano bench, a satisfied smile on her flushed face. As Mike led Jamie to the center of the room, she imagined creative ways to kill the housekeeper. Slowly. Thoroughly. Perhaps with the use of flesh-eating beetles.

"Now, Miss Marten, have you danced before?" Mike looked over at Jamie as they reached the open area of the room.

"Leah talked me into a belly dancing class one time."

Mike arched a brow at her. "Belly dancing?"

Still holding his hand, Jamie executed a smooth hip circle. Mrs. Knightsbridge gasped with shock.

Mike's other brow leapt to match the first in height, and his throat worked as he swallowed hard. He might have been fighting a grin. "Ah. Yes. Well, that is not exactly, well, hrm."

Jamie couldn't stop the smirk that climbed unbidden to her lips. "Guess that's not what you were going for, huh?"

"Gentlefolk do not dance in that way, no."

She rolled her eyes. "Why am I not surprised?"

Mike cleared his throat and began to instruct Jamie in the steps of the cotillion. It reminded her of a complicated grown-up version of Ring Around the Rosie. Lots of skippy little steps and do-si-do-ing and such. She didn't have the most coordinated feet in the world, but she paid attention, and despite her reluctance, she began to have fun, skipping and hopping and grabbing Mike's hands at appointed intervals.

Mike was a great teacher, once he stopped acting like she had a contagious fatal illness. They paraded through the music room together, Mrs. Knightsbridge accompanying them on the piano. Jamie laughed aloud when she almost tripped over Mike's foot. This was fun, the most fun she'd had since being sucked two hundred years into the past.

As Jamie skipped around Mike, she let her eyes linger on him. The strong breadth of his shoulders, the way his tight pants defined his legs, the now-pleasant twinkle in his eyes—they all drew her toward him. When she skipped too close and tripped over him, it was only a little bit an accident.

"Careful, Miss Marten!" He caught her, his strong arms around her middle. The tinkling tune from the piano stopped abruptly.

"Sorry." Jamie laughed as she looked up into his face. His eyes were still bright with what she hoped was pleasure. Was it her imagination, or did he let his hands linger at her waist?

When Jamie was steady, Mike stepped back, putting distance between them. "Well, you seem to have grasped the basics." He straightened his waistcoat and cleared his throat.

"Yes," Mrs. Knightsbridge called in a bright voice. "Miss Jamie has done very well with the cotillion. Now, I think a waltz." Without missing a beat, she began to play a sweeping song in three-four time.

Jamie stood there and stared at Mike. His face had lost its cheerful expression, and something darker and worried had taken the place of the twinkle in his eyes. He took a faltering half step toward her and stopped.

"You don't have to waltz with me," Jamie whispered to him. She didn't know if he'd hear her over the piano or not. She hoped the disappointment that gripped her chest wasn't obvious on her face. Why wouldn't he want to dance with her? Was she really so horrible?

Jamie looked down at her slippered feet, trying hard to swallow the knot of self-loathing that had taken root in her throat. Maybe if she were different, Mike would want her. Maybe Logan wouldn't have gotten bored with her and left. The only common factor between them was Jamie—and the fact that neither wanted anything to do with her. *God, what the hell is so bad about me?*

A strong, warm hand suddenly took hers. She looked up through eyes that were curiously teary.

"Dance with me."

It wasn't a question; it was a demand from a man that was completely used to having his own way. It didn't bother her. She let him pull her toward him, and suddenly she felt like Baby in *Dirty Dancing*. She was in her dance space, and he was in his, but the way that he looked into her eyes made her feel completely possessed by him.

Her heart sped at the way he guided her. His hand on the small of her back burned her. He led her through the swirling steps—one, two, three, one, two, three—spinning her in dizzying circles. Their eyes were locked, their hands clasped, and as she rested her other palm on his muscled shoulder, she didn't know if she was Jamie Marten, songwriter and self-avowed geek girl from 2012, or Miss Jamie Marten, genteel and refined English miss from 1816.

If she was Miss Marten, and the music room was spinning around her while she was in the arms of a handsome earl, then she might be contemplating the idea of falling head-over-slippers in love with the dashing nobleman.

But if she was Jamie, and the music was winding down and the steps were coming slower, then she should not be imagining anything like that. No matter how delicate and beautiful he made her feel as they twirled like a couple on the top of a music box. No matter how strong his arm felt around her, no matter how her heart beat faster as he pulled her slightly closer to his warmth.

She pulled free from his arms as the last notes floated in the air.

"Thank you for the lesson, Mike."

Without allowing him to respond, she turned and left the room.

❧

"What the devil?" Micah whispered after she disappeared, watching the now-empty doorway as if expecting her to reappear at any moment.

"So sorry, my lord. I'll go and see to her, shall I?" Mrs. Knightsbridge stood, smoothing her skirts as she crossed the floor.

Micah shook himself inwardly and stepped forward. "Wait, please."

The housekeeper stopped at his commanding voice, looking at him expectantly.

With a sigh, he shoved his hair back from his forehead. "Did I behave poorly? To Miss Marten, I mean."

Mrs. Knightsbridge gave a soft smile, her round, pink cheeks and eyes glowing. "No, my dear, I believe you behaved like a gentleman should. I'll soon set her to rights. Do not worry."

With no comment about her informal speech, Micah stepped aside and allowed Mrs. Knightsbridge to leave the room.

He'd forgotten.

While they were dancing that damned waltz, he'd forgotten all the reasons that he should stay far away from Miss Marten. It had felt good, to hold her thus. To guide her in the steps that were obviously unfamiliar to her, to steady her when she stumbled, to look into her smiling, laughing face and marvel at her clear skin, her thin nose, her full lips. To remember how it had felt to kiss her. And to anticipate doing it much more.

Micah slumped into the chair at the corner of the room. Nonsense. It was all a load of utter nonsense. Miss Lyons was his future, not some maid from the future with laughing eyes and no discernable manners.

He stood and strode from the room. Amberson should be there shortly, and he'd put the secretary to arranging the necessary details for his nuptials. It was time to put this bloody absurdity behind him.

❧

Jamie paced through the little garden, Baron trotting at her heels. Her thoughts were swirling faster than she had been in Mike's arms during the last dance. Why was she doing this to herself? She and Mike could never have anything together. He didn't want her there. And she wanted to go home. She hadn't felt clean in days. Her phone's battery was nearly gone. She'd only turned it on for quick sessions of Fruit Ninja to stave off boredom anyway, but that tiny link to the future was almost extinct. She wanted her toothbrush, her shower, and her weekly stash of comics.

She wasn't cut out for this world. She couldn't survive here happily. The walls of the garden seemed to close in on her, and the hairs on the back of her neck prickled, almost like someone was watching her.

"Baron, what do I do?" She flopped down on the stone bench and let the greyhound lean against her as she scratched his ears.

"Miss Jamie, are you well?"

Jamie sighed. Mrs. Knightsbridge was rounding the bend in the path. Jamie should have known the house-keeper wouldn't allow an escape from the nefarious dance lessons without a good explanation.

"Hey, Mrs. K. I'm fine. Just needed some air."

Mrs. K motioned for Jamie to scoot over on the bench, and she did so reluctantly. She wasn't in the mood for a heart-to-heart, but the little woman wasn't going to take no for an answer apparently.

"He's been hurt, you know."

"Who? Mike?" A little thrill of fear shot through Jamie's chest. "What happened? Did he fall or something when I left the room?"

"Oh no, not now, Miss Jamie. Before."

"Oh." Jamie felt stupid for the worried flutter in her heart. "What happened?"

Mrs. K sighed and smoothed her drab brown skirt. "It is a long tale."

Jamie cut her eyes at the housekeeper. "What am I going to say, I don't have time because I'm supposed to meet up for a guild run before my international teleconference? Tell me."

Mrs. K shook her head slightly but complied.

"He had recently inherited the earldom. He took a mistress not long after, a woman named Louisa Maucier. He was young then, not much more than a boy, really, and fancied himself in love with her."

Jamie crossed her arms and made a face. "Sorry, but I really don't understand the whole mistress thing."

Mrs. K looked at her quizzically. "Do men in your time not have needs? Do they all marry before sating their fleshly desires?"

Jamie laughed. "Of course not, it's just that sex isn't, well, you're supposed to care about the person you do it with, unless it's a one-night stand or something. But even then you're not obligated to stay with the person; it's just part of some people's dating life." As the words left her mouth, she realized how hypocritical that sounded. In 2012, casual sex wasn't that big a deal, and she was looking down her nose at Mike for having just that? She sighed. "Sorry. Forget I said that. So, he loved her?"

Mrs. K shook her head and picked at a loose thread on her cuff. "No, not at all. She was very beautiful and very worldly, and she fascinated him. He escorted her to the theatre, to the park, anywhere polite society allowed a gentleman to bring his light o' love. She was affectionate toward him, but any fool could see that it was a matter of business between them. He was infatuated with her charms, but nothing more lasting than that."

The knot of jealousy in her stomach that had started when Mrs. K said that he loved Louisa eased a little at that statement. She nodded to the housekeeper, hoping she'd continue.

"After they had been together for nigh on a year, another courtesan began attempting to attract his lordship's attention. Collette Dubois. She was young, a raven-haired doxy with a vaunted opinion of her own charms. She tried to woo his lordship away from Louisa but was never successful until The Incident."

Baron whuffed, snuggling under Jamie's hand like he'd heard the capital letters too and they worried him. Jamie pulled the greyhound closer. "What incident?"

"The Incident," Mrs. K corrected her pronunciation, "occurred one evening when his lordship escorted Louisa to a dinner party for gentlemen and their paramours. It wasn't a proper dinner party, not in the best sense, as it was given by Sir Arthur Williams for his mistress, Marilyn Munroe."

"Oh, I met her." Mrs. K's jaw dropped as Jamie continued. "The other day, when I went out with Baron. She was in a carriage with a skinny, rude man. They called me over."

The housekeeper looked as if she'd eaten a handful of lemons, but she nodded. "Yes, that was Sir Arthur and his mistress. We have discussed the improprieties of that exchange already, and I trust…"

Jamie stopped her with a wave of her hand. "Yes, I know, it was a bad idea. I'm sorry. What happened?"

"Louisa and his lordship arrived at the party, which was by all accounts a rather raucous event. After his lordship procured a glass of wine for Louisa, she suddenly became violently ill. Her limbs shook, she trembled all over. Within an hour, she was dead.

"Mr. Lionel Waites, Collette Dubois' then protector, accused his lordship of poisoning Louisa's wine.

His lordship denied it, of course. No one should have believed such a wild and baseless accusation, but gossips will talk. Some of the household staff departed after that. None that were worth keeping, of course, but it was quite a surprise when his lordship's valet disappeared with hardly a word. He's not found a suitable replacement and so Thornton has been dressing him for quite a while now, poor man."

Jamie shook her head. Mike was kind of stuck-up, but he wasn't a murderer. There was no way he'd poisoned Louisa. She hoped the valet was stuck scrubbing chamber pots after that.

"His lordship wasn't blamed, but there was an inquiry about the affair. For several months he received a scant handful of invitations. He refused to accept the few his true friends delivered. He kept to the house, not going out into company, unwilling to bring more shame onto the earldom. Soon after he finally began accepting invitations again, Collette broke off her association with Mr. Waites, and began to dally outrageously with his lordship. Eventually, he took her as his mistress."

Mrs. Knightsbridge lost all traces of her normal cheerful expression. She leaned closer as she said, "That Collette was pure poison. Her actions were, at times, most unsettling. It is as if she cares more for coin than a normal creature of her stamp. His lordship became suspicious of her within a month, but he kept the lease on her house for six months after. He didn't want to cause another scandal, you see. He gave her *congé* a fortnight ago, when he decided to begin courting Miss Lyons in earnest. His lordship is almost forty now, and must think of begetting an heir, so this courtship was just the thing to end that damaging association."

Bile rose in Jamie's throat at the thought of Mike

sleeping with that crazy woman, and then marrying that pasty little blond thing she'd seen with him in the carriage. He was supposed to marry blondie and knock her up to get an heir? He didn't love her. He couldn't, not the way Jamie had seen him looking at her as they danced. He'd marry and sleep with a woman only to get her pregnant? What a completely disgusting thought.

Jamie stared down at Baron's back, hoping Mrs. K wouldn't see the way her worries flitted across her face. "Why are you telling me all this?"

The warmth of Mrs. K's voice penetrated the chill in Jamie's heart.

"Because I know you love him."

Eleven

JAMIE JERKED HER HEAD UP, STARING AT MRS. Knightsbridge. She was smiling softly, like a mother would. Jamie's mouth worked silently for a second, as her brain scrambled to catch up with the rest of her.

"Wait, what? I don't love him!"

The soft smile turned into a knowing grin. Mrs. K leaned over and patted her hand reassuringly. "Of course not, Miss Jamie."

"I can't stand him! He's stuck-up and snobbish and obnoxious, and way too handsome for his own good, and smart and funny and…oh my God." Jamie clapped a palm over her open mouth.

Mrs. K nodded and rose to her feet. "I'll leave you to get some more air, dearie. I believe you have some thinking to do."

The gravel crunched under her feet as she rounded the corner of the path and disappeared in the direction of the house. Baron pulled away from Jamie and trotted after the housekeeper, leaving Jamie completely alone in the spring air of the garden.

She stared at a brilliant yellow clump of buttercups nestled against the base of the budding tree. *Love…*

Mike? Could she really be falling in love with Mike? The thought was, well, not as appalling as she'd imagined it would be.

He infuriated her, and she him. She did everything wrong, and she made him crazy. But then, his eyes when they'd danced, the way he'd stopped her tears with his high-handed demand for a waltz. Was it true? Could she love him?

She stood and paced the length of the path in front of the bench.

If she was falling for Mike, so what? He didn't love her, and there was no future for them. He had an earldom to take care of, and she…she had to get back where she belonged. She wasn't cut out for this time and place. She couldn't spend the rest of her life here. *Could I?*

Jamie tilted her head back and looked at the cloud-covered sky. *Mike, me, love, future, past, impossible.* The words tumbled in her head like jeans in a Maytag. She couldn't make sense of all this stuff on her own. Puffing her cheeks out in frustration, she turned on her heel and headed into the house. Mrs. K thought, for some reason, that Jamie and Mike were destined. It was time for Jamie to face the fact that she was beginning to believe the housekeeper, as crazy as that was. Mrs. K had to have some kind of idea as to how she thought this could possibly work. Jamie needed to find her to get some shit figured out.

She wasn't in the kitchen among the busily cooking and scrubbing maids. She wasn't in the dining room polishing silver. She wasn't in the sitting room arranging knickknacks. Jamie had decided to head upstairs to see if Mrs. K was on the upper floor when she heard Mike's voice. It was coming from the room off the main hallway that had always been locked when she tried it. The door was slightly ajar, and she peeked through the crack.

Mike stood by a large desk made of dark wood. Ivory pages were scattered on the surface, and another man spoke in a concerned tone. Mike took a step toward the door, eyes locked on the other man, and Jamie ducked back out of sight.

"Nonsense, Amberson," Mike said. The wood of the desk creaked then. He must have sat on it. "I assure you, the *ton's* gossipmongers have had plenty of new scandals to focus on. Poor Louisa hasn't been in the spotlight for over a year now."

"My lord, it is simply a precaution. Sir Frederick Lyons has had his solicitor poking around, asking questions about your situation, both financial and personal. It would only be natural for Miss Maucier's death to be examined. I am doing my best to protect your interests, but I would be remiss if I did not inform you of his activities."

Mike snorted. "Sir Frederick has no concern for Miss Lyons's safety. He is simply making sure that my pockets are as well lined as they are reputed to be. Since Miss Lyons's match with Lord Kensington did not occur, he's set his sights on me as the next available fish to gut, despite Sir William Knightley's interest. Apparently, the young gentleman's coffers are not so deep."

The strange man's voice was surprised. "Does that anger you, my lord?"

"No," Mike said thoughtfully. "Despite her family's grasping nature, Miss Lyons is of a meek and amiable disposition. She'll do as my countess."

Jamie's stomach knotted painfully, and she swallowed hard to keep the nausea at bay. She pressed her body back against the doorframe hard, listening despite the urge to run.

"Is your mind made up then, my lord?"

"It is. I will propose next week, on Tuesday."

Slamming her eyelids shut, she bit her lip hard. The bitter tang of blood stung her mouth.

"Very good. Shall I send your regrets for the Wentworth masked ball on Monday evening then?"

"No, not at all. Miss Lyons will be away in the country, so I will attend alone."

George, the footman, chose that exact moment to round the corner from the kitchen into her part of the hallway. Jamie whirled around at his thudding footsteps, hand clasped to her racing heart.

"Oh, pardon me, Miss Marten."

She didn't answer him. She didn't want Mike to hear her, to know she'd overheard his plans. She rushed past George and up the stairs. If she wasn't careful, then she was going to do something really dumb and emotional. Like collapse on her bed and cry.

Apparently, her eyes didn't realize that she was being careful, and the tears pricked as she flew down the portrait-lined hallway to the Lemon Room.

Jamie nearly took out Mrs. Knightsbridge when she shoved open the door to her bedroom. Ignoring the housekeeper and her armload of dresses, Jamie flung herself down on the neatly made bed and let the sobs wrack her body.

This is completely idiotic, Jamie told herself as the hot tears soaked her sleeve. She didn't care if Mike proposed to some stupid, spineless woman with no boobs and insipid yellow hair. She didn't care if he married her to have beautiful little Colin Firth–lookalike future earls. She didn't care if he crushed her heart beneath the heel of his way-too-shiny boots by marrying someone with the combined IQ of a paramecium and bubblegum on a stick. *It is completely fine with me*, Jamie thought as snot clogged her nose and her cheeks stung with hot, salty tears.

A gentle hand rubbed her back.

"Go away, Mrs. K," she rasped into the bed covers.

"Miss Jamie, whatever is the matter?" Her soft voice lashed Jamie like a whip. She couldn't take the sympathy; it would break her into a million pieces.

"Nothing. I'm fine." Another wave of tears overtook her, and she sobbed hoarsely, not raising her head.

"I doubt that. Come now. Dry your tears. Tell Wi... me what's the matter."

Despite her misery, Jamie lifted her head and looked at the housekeeper through watery eyes.

She nodded and pulled a handkerchief from her apron pocket. Jamie took the offered square of linen and wiped her wet cheeks, sitting up on the bed.

"Whatever can cause such a strong woman to cry as though her heart would break?" Mrs. Knightsbridge's warm hand rubbed her shoulder comfortingly.

"I'm not strong, Mrs. K. I'm not. I heard Mike tell some guy that he's going to propose to Miss Lyons next week, and I don't know why, but it makes me so miserable." Jamie covered her face with the hanky, trying to stem the fresh flood of tears that threatened to overtake her again.

"Shh, dearie. Don't fret. When did he say the proposal would occur?"

"Tuesday. But I can't stop it, and I shouldn't. I can't live in this time, not happily. And if she's really who he wants, then why should I get in the middle of it?"

Mrs. Knightsbridge's gray eyes glinted with a knowing light. "Why are you so certain that Miss Lyons is who he really wants?"

Jamie refolded the hanky to find a dryer spot. "Why wouldn't she be? She's apparently meek and amiable, two words that no one in their right mind would ever say about me."

"His lordship is a forceful man, a strong man. He needs a woman who will stand up with him, not a wilting flower to be crushed under his bootheel. He will never be happy with less. You, Jamie, you are the sort of woman that he needs."

"Tell him that," Jamie said darkly as she wiped her nose with the square. "He can't stand the sight of me. You saw how he acted when you wanted him to dance with me."

"He reacts badly because he fears his feelings for you. He does not understand. It is up to you to make him see the truth. You are his ideal woman."

Jamie looked over at Mrs. Knightsbridge. Her round face shone with sincerity.

"Why do you care about him so much? Why go to all this trouble to make sure he's with the right person?"

The housekeeper looked down into her lap. Jamie's eyes followed. Mrs. K pulled back the cuff of her sleeve and traced a delicate scar across her wrist. She spoke without lifting her gaze.

"I know the pain of a bad marriage. Micah is like a son to me. I'll not let him suffer as I have suffered."

"Is that…" Jamie's voice trailed off.

Mrs. K shook her head. "Let's not speak of it. For now, we must plan." She jerked the cuff down and rose to her feet with a determined smile.

"Plan what?" Jamie stood, watching Mrs. Knightsbridge pace. The evidence of the woman's pain had shaken Jamie.

"How to convince his lordship that you are the perfect countess, of course. Now, you must listen carefully."

"Wait. I can't convince him of that. I'm pretty sure it's not true. I'm not cut out for this time."

Mrs. K smiled at her. "Jamie, whenever you are, wherever you are, you'll always be perfect for Micah. Now, come. Indulge me."

❦

By the time they were done scheming, Mrs. Knightsbridge almost had Jamie convinced. Like it or not, Jamie cared about Mike. A lot. Maybe even bordering on that other L word that she was terrified to even think. Even if he didn't end up with Jamie, she couldn't let him marry that other woman just to get an heir. The thought was sickening. She had to convince him to marry for love, whether it was her—*gulp*—or someone else.

Mrs. Knightsbridge's plan was deceptively simple. Jamie was to be as near to Mike as possible. Day in and day out. Talk to him, laugh with him, ask him to help her practice dancing, teach her to ride a horse, spend time with him. Give him a chance to see how compatible they were when they weren't fighting about his arrogance or her ignorance of the time she was stuck in.

The housekeeper was convinced, by next week this time, Mike would be head over heels in love with Jamie and forget he ever thought to propose to Miss Lyons. Jamie wasn't sold, but what choice did she have? She couldn't let Mike marry blondie unless he loved her. He deserved to be happy. She didn't know if she could ever live in this time happily, but she owed it to herself and Mike to figure out if there was something possible between them.

By the Wentworth masked ball Monday night, Jamie would have had every opportunity to let the man know how she felt about him and his loveless marriage idea. Mrs. K was going to work on a costume for Jamie to wear, and she'd promised to procure her an invitation to attend the ball. She'd meet Mike there, and if things hadn't worked out between them, it would be their good-bye. Not that he would know that. Mrs. K promised to have Wilhelmina open the portal that Tuesday if

Jamie failed. If she succeeded, well, then that was a whole other barrel of monkeys to be dealt with.

Mrs. Knightsbridge helped Jamie scrub her face, removing all traces of tears. After pinning up her hair, leaving a few curly tendrils dangling by her ears, Mrs. K walked with her downstairs.

"Now remember," she said in a quiet voice, "stay with him. Be patient with him, and all will be well. He is headstrong, but you mustn't let that vex you overly. He will see reason if you stand your ground."

"Here goes nothing," Jamie muttered as Mrs. K left her and she strode purposefully into his office.

He looked up at Jamie from his seat behind the large wooden desk. He was alone in the room now, no sign of Amberson. He paused, his hand still poised on the quill pen that hovered over a half-scribbled sheet of parchment.

Jamie swallowed hard, searching for strength to spend time with him without further compromising her heart. As a smile broke out across his face when he saw her, she felt herself sliding farther into the danger zone.

"Miss Marten." He rose to his feet smoothly. "I trust you are well? You left our lesson rather quickly."

"Yes, I'm fine." She leaned on the bare corner of his desk. "Sorry about that. I had some thinking to do."

He sat back down. "I see." The nib of the pen scratched across the parchment as he resumed his letter.

She moved a little closer. "What are you doing?"

He glanced up at her quickly before dipping the nib in the inkwell. "Writing."

She rolled her eyes. "No shit. What are you writing?"

"A letter. And must you continually use foul language? It is hardly becoming."

Irritation boiled up within her, but she tamped it

down hard as she remembered Mrs. K's words. *Don't let him vex me.* It was a damn sight harder than she realized.

"Sorry."

That simple little word stopped all forward progress on Mike's letter. He looked up at her wide-eyed. "I beg your pardon?"

"I said sorry. As in, I'm sorry for offending you."

Jamie almost laughed aloud at the sight of his strong jaw dropping. She'd truly shocked him. Maybe this would be easier than she thought.

He sputtered as he tried to answer. "Well, I…it is… well, no harm done." Turning back to his letter, he shook his head slightly, as if stunned.

"What are you doing when you're done? Writing, I mean."

"I have no pressing business."

She ran her nail along the smooth edge of the desk. "Do you think, maybe, you could teach me how to ride? A horse, I mean."

He laid his quill pen down flat on the desk. "Whyever would you want to learn to ride?"

She swallowed, her brain scrambling for an answer that wouldn't sound like the complete lie it would probably be. "I had fun the other night, riding. I think I'd like to know how to do it. On my own, I mean. And besides, there are horses back in my time. It might come in handy."

He eyed her warily, and she swallowed. It had been a stupid lie. The only reason she hadn't been petrified of the horse was the leftover fear of her would-be attackers and the fact she was pressed up against Mike's strong, warm back. He'd never believe her. This was a bad idea. She'd have to…

"I would be delighted. You will need to change your

gown, however. Mrs. Knightsbridge should be able to help you locate a riding habit. I shall meet you at the front door when you are suitably attired."

She couldn't stop the relieved grin that spread across her face. She hopped down from the desk. "Thanks, Mike. See you in a few."

She left the office and winked at Mrs. K as she thundered up the stairs. Phase one of the plan was working. Now, she had to get over the idea that she'd be stuck on a huge horse all by herself.

Mrs. Knightsbridge entered the Lemon Room in time to see Jamie yanking the gown over her head.

"Heavens, dearie, slow down. Let me help."

"He's going to teach me to ride. Is there something I can wear? God, I'm so nervous. What if I make a fool of myself again? Crap, I've got a hairpin caught."

Her struggles against the gown and her hair only got her entangled further.

"Still, now. Here." Mrs. K easily detached the pin and finished pulling the gown over Jamie's head. "Now, let me look. The late countess was fond of riding in her younger days. She was a talented horsewoman. Ah, here we are."

She pulled an outfit from the trunk, the vibrant green of a wine bottle. It had a full skirt, with a jacket embroidered with gold and black braids. She fetched a hat from the wardrobe, a tall-looking black thing with ostrich feathers adorning it.

Jamie looked up at the ceiling. "Really? Feathers? Did I do something horrible in a past life?"

"Come now, we mustn't keep his lordship waiting."

Much as Jamie hated to admit it, the riding outfit did look good. The ornamented jacket was tailored, and it fit her like a glove. The skirt was so long that it covered the toes of the dark leather boots that completed the outfit. They were a touch too big for her, though not so much that it would be difficult to walk. When she'd pulled on the tan gloves and Mrs. K had repinned her hair up and placed the hat on top of it, she gaped at the sight of herself in the mirror.

Her normally pale skin glowed. There was a light in her eyes, something approaching excitement. She stood tall, and her figure looked more womanly than it ever had before. Seeing herself this way made her think that Mike might be able to see them as a couple. She looked the part, even if inside she was still Jamie.

"You look a treat, Miss Jamie. Come now. Off you go."

With a quick kiss on her cheek, Mrs. K steered her out of the bedroom and down the hallway. Butterflies beat against the inside of her stomach as she descended the stairs. What was the matter with her?

When she saw Mike standing beside the front door, hands clasped behind his back, the butterflies turned into water buffalos. When he looked at her, brows lowering, eyes hungry, they turned into rampaging African elephants.

"You are looking quite fine, Miss Marten."

"Thank you, my lord."

Her use of his proper title earned her a cryptic look. "Shall we?"

"Let's do," she said grandly, and sailed through the door that was held open by a footman.

Twelve

HER BRAVADO LASTED EXACTLY TWO MINUTES AND sixteen seconds. On the seventeenth second, a stable boy led two horses from their outdoor residence.

"Holy shit," Jamie whispered as one of the beasts was walked directly in front of her. She was eye-to-shoulder with the thing. And Mike expected her to ride this monster. Alone. The other day when Mike had pulled her up behind him had been the first time she'd ever sat on one of them. They always seemed way too strong and big for a single person to handle—especially if that person was Jamie.

"Um, Mike? This is a weird-looking saddle. How does it work?"

"You sit atop it."

She shot daggers at him with her eyes. Was that a smart-ass smirk on his face? She thought it was. There was no mistaking the mischievous curl to his lips.

"Wow. Thanks for the insight there, Batman." She bit her tongue, remembering too late that she was trying to be easy to get along with.

Before she could apologize, Mike had grasped her around the waist and hoisted her atop the beast.

"Oh my gosh. Okay. How about a little warning next time?" She grabbed at the horse's mane to steady herself. It tossed its reddish head and snorted.

"Easy, Belle," Mike crooned to the creature, patting its soft nose. "Easy."

When he'd finished calming her horse, he gave her a couple of pointers, then mounted his own horse. They started a sedate walk toward the park. A groom followed them on another mount several yards back.

Jamie clutched the reins with a white-knuckled grip, holding them the way Mike had shown her. The side-saddle was awkward, and she felt very precarious up there on top of the world. The horse's feet clacked loudly against the cobbles of the street, and she gritted her teeth, willing her body to stay rigidly still.

"Miss Marten, relax. Do not fight the rhythm of Belle's walk. Watch me."

She looked beside her and watched Mike's body as he rode. His body was relaxed, easy, and natural. His lean hips rolled with the horse's movement, almost as if he and the beast were one. She swallowed hard and shifted a little in her saddle.

Belle sidestepped at the sudden shift in weight. Jamie felt her hips start to slide off the left side of the horse. Panicking, she threw her body right to compensate.

"Careful, Miss Marten!" Mike reached out a hand and steadied her before she could slip off the sidesaddle into the street.

Her heart thumped hard. She locked her eyes forward and mentally glued her ass to the polished leather seat. "Sorry," she whispered.

"No harm done. I say, are you quite sure you want to continue?"

She nodded, never looking his way. She didn't want

him to see the embarrassment-slash-terror in her eyes. "I'm sure."

After nearly falling on her ass, she was much more careful. She pretended she was on a quest, and in a very real way, she was—one that would hopefully end with her winning a very distinguished prize.

By the time they'd reached the park, she was starting to get the hang of the rhythm of Belle's walk and the odd sidesaddle. Fortunately, the park wasn't crowded. She'd hate to embarrass Mike in front of a big group of people.

"You are doing quite well, Miss Marten."

Mike's voice startled her, but she was careful to keep steady as she swiveled her head to look at him. "Really?" Her voice came out sort of soft and shaky.

"Yes. For a lady who has never ridden before, you are taking to it quickly. In time, I think you will find you're enjoying yourself."

She smiled at him and looked forward once more to the grassy expanse of the park ahead. "You know what? I think you're on to something. This *is* fun."

He chuckled then, a warm, deep sound that made her suck in her breath. "Simple pleasures, Miss Marten, should never be taken for granted."

"You might be right, your lordship." Her wink at him brought a true grin to his face.

He flicked the reins lightly against the deep black of his horse's neck. As the animal broke into a trot, Mike called back over his shoulder. "Simple pleasures, Miss Marten, like feeling the wind in one's face."

She scowled at his back as the distance between them grew larger. She was really starting to get the hang of this, and he had to go and show her up like that? So not fair. She chewed the inside of her cheek, wondering if it was a stupid idea to coax Belle into catching up with him.

She'd almost made up her mind to nudge her horse's side with her boot and to hell with the consequences when Mike stopped his horse next to an open carriage. His voice carried over the chattering birds, sounding pretty happy to be talking with whoever the old man was. The salt-and-pepper whiskers on the older gentleman were kind of startling. She hadn't decided whether they made him look like a badger or a demented and ancient elf when a woman's voice called behind her.

"Hello there."

Laying the rein across Belle's neck carefully, she was relieved when the horse responded by turning around to let Jamie see who was speaking.

The dark-haired woman gave a tight-lipped smile from her perch atop a snowy white horse. She was wearing a riding dress of deep red, her skirt looking like a splash of blood against the stark white of her mount.

"Hi," Jamie said, smiling back in a confused way.

"It is quite a beautiful day to be enjoying the park, is it not?" The stranger tilted her head at Jamie slightly, a quizzical look on her face.

"Yes, 'tis. Quite." Jamie tried her best to sound authentic, but her "quite" came out sounding like "quoit."

"I do not believe I have made your acquaintance, but it is easy to see by your lack of chaperone that we share a certain, ah, occupation." Her horse tossed its head, and she jerked on the reins rather viciously in response. Jamie winced. She wasn't a horse fan, but that didn't mean she thought they should be mistreated. "Those in our position would do well to band together, do you not think?"

Jamie was pretty sure that she wasn't mistaking the subtle venom in the woman's tone. Her mount apparently agreed with Jamie, its eyes rolling wildly as it stamped one hoof.

"Sorry, but I think you're mistaken. My chaperone is back there, and I should really be getting back to Mi... er, his lordship. Good day," Jamie said with as polite a smile as she could manage, and tried to turn Belle back around. Where the hell was Mike?

"I shall accompany you. I would dearly love to make the acquaintance of your protector," the woman purred as her horse drew alongside Belle.

"No, no, I would hate to bother you. Honestly, I'm not a hooker, erm, mistress. Just a normal woman." Jamie nudged Belle's sides to encourage her to speed it up. She didn't trust this person, and she wanted to get far away from her. Mike was only about fifty yards away.

The black-haired female must have followed Jamie's gaze, and her gasp jerked Jamie's attention over to her. "Whatever are you doing with Lord Dunnington, you common trollop?"

The skin between Jamie's shoulder blades pricked and burned, and she stopped Belle in her tracks as Mike had shown her. When Jamie turned her head, she wasn't at all surprised to see the raven-haired beauty glaring death. Jamie's sense of self-preservation warred with frustration and the need to retaliate. The snark won hands down.

"Listen, if you're going to call me names, you should at least know the one I was born with first. I'm Jamie Marten. And you are?"

The woman drew herself up taller, the vibrant red of her riding dress matching the flame of temper in her cheeks. "I am Collette Dubois, if you must know. I demand that you answer me. Who are you to Lord Dunnington?"

"That's not really polite, you know." Jamie stared straight into her eyes, not backing down a bit. "I'm not sure what kind of mother you had, but even where I'm from, you catch more flies with honey than vinegar. Of course, I don't know that I should expect anything more from somebody who writes horrible, pathetic letters practically begging for the return of her sugar daddy."

Jamie swore she could hear teeth grind together. She hoped in the back of her mind that the woman would bite down hard enough to break one loose. The stranger probably could have put up with the return insults, but when Jamie smiled at her, sweet as pie, that was the straw that broke the hooker's patience.

"You know nothing of me, you damned bitch!"

When time slowed to a crawl and the riding crop in her white-gloved hand rose, then fell toward Belle's hindquarters, Jamie knew that she had no one to blame for this predicament but herself. If she'd kept her damn trap shut and caught up to Mike, then this wouldn't have happened. But she'd let her stupid jealousy over his former lover goad her into this. As the whip cracked against Belle's flank and her shriek cut the air, Jamie had the guilt of her horse's pain as well as the anticipation of her own that would surely be coming very, very soon.

Time restarted with a vengeance as Belle took off running headlong. Jamie grabbed at her long mane, but the smoothness of the saddle made her slip and slide at the violent pace of the horse's gait. Jamie had enough time to hear hoofbeats thundering behind her as Belle rounded a tree and sent her sliding off the slick saddle into the very thick, very hard trunk.

❧

The sound of pounding hooves turned Micah's head from his conversation with Sir Humphrey and stopped his breath all in one go. Belle was bolting away from them, and a terrified Jamie was being jounced atop her back like so much dead weight. Without a word to Sir

Humphrey, Micah whipped Hart into a gallop, trying to catch up to them before Jamie's grip failed. When Belle rounded the curve of the path, she slung her rider into a tree with a sickening crack.

Micah flung himself off Hart's back and dashed to Jamie's side, fear surging through his veins.

"Jamie!" He knelt by her side, somewhat relieved to see her wide eyes looking at him, dazed though they were.

"Mike?" Her voice was thin and confused.

Leaning closer to her, he cupped her cheek with a gloved hand, cursing the fabric barrier. Her eyes fluttered closed, and her forehead furrowed in clear pain. Her jaw tightened, and her body went rigid as a corpse. He panicked.

"Jamie, open your eyes. Look at me, damn it!" He'd probably sounded too demanding, too commanding for her current state, but he could do no less. He needed to see her eyes again, to make sure she was alive. He breathed a silent prayer of thanks when her lids slitted open.

"Stop being so damn bossy," she whispered, pain robbing her of her voice.

"Stay with me." Mike scooped her up and placed her atop his horse, keeping her steady with one hand as he mounted up behind her. He barked a sharp order to the groom to fetch her mount, kicked Hart into a brisk gallop, and headed homeward as quickly as he could, steadying her against his chest.

"Ah," Jamie gasped, grabbing at the back of her head. The bouncing of the horse must have been excruciating for her, but he could waste no time, not knowing how badly she'd been hurt.

"Stay with me," he repeated, one arm drawing her body close to his. He steadied her, and she melted against him, finally relaxing the rigid set of her muscles. It worked. He held her still, absorbing the shocks of Hart's gait through his tensed muscles.

She turned her nose into his jacket, and he tried not to think of how wonderful it felt to hold her close. She was injured, for God's sake. She might even die, and it was all his damned fault for tweaking her nose as he had. She'd probably tried to coax Belle into a trot and spooked the horse somehow. A soft moan emanated from her lips, and he tightened his arm around her and nudged Hart's sides to encourage him to go faster.

While it was only minutes before he reached the townhouse, it felt as if hours passed before he handed her down to Thornton. Tossing Hart's reins to George, he clasped Jamie against his chest once more and dashed up the stairs to her bedchamber.

"It hurts," she whimpered as he laid her on the bed.

"I know, dearling, I know." He gently pulled the pins free of her hair, tossing the feathered hat away. He rolled her onto her side. "Wait here."

He'd rung for Mrs. Knightsbridge, but he did not intend to wait for the housekeeper to arrive. He'd see to her needs until then. He studiously ignored the thumping ache in his chest as he dipped a clean cloth into the basin and wrung it out. It was guilt, guilt for her injuries that were solely his fault. He eased down on the bed behind her, pressing the cloth to the swollen knot at the back of her skull.

"Do not fight it, Jamie. Trust me. The pain will lessen if you relax. Doesn't this cloth feel good?"

"Yes," she whispered. His bare fingers brushed a hair from her forehead. "Don't leave me, Mike."

"I shan't, dear." The endearment fell from his lips unbidden. "I am sorry you fell. I should not have left you."

She smiled at him without opening her eyes. "No, you shouldn't. You're going to owe me for that one."

"Whatever you ask, Miss Marten. A gentleman repays his debts." He'd give her anything she wished, so long as she came through this whole.

A harried Mrs. Knightsbridge bustled into the room, toting a basket clinking full of bottles.

"Oh good heavens, your lordship! Whatever happened to poor Miss Jamie?" Mrs. Knightsbridge pulled potions, herbs, and cloths from her basket and began spreading concoctions out on the dressing table.

"An accident, Mrs. Knightsbridge." Micah did not prevaricate, admitting his guilt full on. "I left her, and her horse spooked and threw her into a tree. She has a swollen area on the back of her head."

"Belle didn't spook," Jamie grated, wincing as she looked at them. "That damn bitch cropped her and made her run."

"What?" Mike took a step toward Jamie, an ominous thunder gathering in his brain.

"She said her name was Collette Dubois. She called me names, and we argued. At the end, she whacked Belle across the ass and nearly killed me."

Collette. Mike yanked on his waistcoat so hard he nearly popped a button.

"Miss Marten, I am deeply sorry for the pain you've suffered this afternoon." He reached a hand to her but stopped before it could caress her soft skin once more. He schooled his face into its proper, emotionless mask. "I will approach the lady in question and demand an apology on your behalf."

Mrs. K painted a foul-smelling mixture into Jamie's hair over the sore spot on her head. Jamie wrinkled her nose and looked up at him, obviously attempting to downplay her discomfort. "Please don't worry about it, Mike. Even if you make her apologize, she won't be sorry. She made it pretty clear that she hates me."

"This was a grievous action. She might have killed you, and I will ensure that she bears full responsibility for her reprehensible behavior. I will leave you to Mrs. Knightsbridge's care." With a sharp bow, he strode from the room, determination and fury warring for the upper hand in his chest.

"Sorry, Mrs. K," Jamie whispered.

"For what, dearie? Running afoul of a miserable, jealous harlot?"

"I screwed things up. How am I supposed to—ouch!"

Mrs. K pressed a poultice against the tender goose egg on the back of Jamie's head. "On the contrary, Miss Jamie, I would say that things are progressing quite well. I am only sorry that Wilhelmina did not warn me of this mean-spirited action before it occurred. I will insist that she be more vigilant in her scrying when next we speak. But did you see his lordship's face when he vowed to make Collette pay?"

He had been kind of pissed. Livid, actually. "You think that's good?"

"That is quite good. He's beginning to realize that he cares for you. Now, lie still. I will fetch you some tea, and in the morning, you will be right as rain and ready to resume your mission."

Thirteen

JAMIE WASN'T QUITE "RIGHT AS RAIN" THE NEXT morning. In fact, it was Wednesday before she was ready to face the world again. Her frequent headaches had been accompanied by bouts of nausea and vomiting. That damn Collette had given her a real-life concussion. She spent Tuesday swinging between wanting to murder the bitch and being really, really grateful that it hadn't been serious enough to kill her. Even a simple injury at this particular point in history could have had fatal consequences, and she wasn't about to shuffle off this mortal coil quite yet.

After helping wash the smelly gunk from her hair that Mrs. K had applied like clockwork for the last thirty-six hours, Muriel dressed Jamie in a pale blue gown that she swore set off Jamie's blue-green eyes to perfection. After the maid pinned up her now-clean hair, Jamie stood in front of the mirror for a good ten minutes, nerving herself to go down to breakfast. She wanted to see Mike, but she was worried about his reaction. He hadn't come back to her room since the accident. Mrs. K kept saying he was concerned, but what if she was only saying that to make Jamie feel better?

What if Collette told him I lied? What if he believes her instead of me? What if he's sitting at the table writing a love note to his Miss Lyons and planning a beautiful late summer wedding? Well, Jamie thought as she smoothed the patterned blue skirt down over her petticoats, *it's time to get it over with*.

As she walked down the stairs, the clatter of toenails on polished wood greeted her. Prancing at the bottom of the stairs with an unmistakable grin on his long face was Baron.

"Hey there, bud!" Jamie dashed the rest of the way down the stairs, so happy to see her long-legged friend. She hadn't felt up to having an audience watch her puke yesterday morning, and she had spent the rest of yesterday afternoon napping, so the poor hound had to find somewhere else to sleep for the last couple of nights. When she reached the bottom of the staircase, she sat down on the lowest step and cuddled the goofy dog. He showered her with long-tongued kisses all over her cheek.

"Ew, Baron, cut it out. Silly mutt." She scratched behind his ears and hugged the long neck close.

"I am glad to see that you have suffered no permanent damage."

The warm voice startled Jamie, and she stopped scratching Baron. Mike had come out of his office, followed by a mousy-looking short man. The stranger nodded to Jamie and disappeared out the front door.

"Yes, thank you." Jamie stood. "Much better now."

"Have you broken your fast? I'd be delighted to accompany you." Mike held a hand out to her, and she took it with a self-conscious smile.

"Thanks."

Mike escorted her down the hallway, Baron

following behind them like a happy-go-lucky grooms-man. Jamie tried not to notice how good Mike's arm felt under her hand.

As they entered the dining room, a delicious smell assailed her nostrils. *Mmm.* She really hadn't realized how hungry she was after the whole ordeal.

Mike slid the chair back for her, and she sat. Wow. This whole gentleman thing was serious. When she and Mike weren't at each other's throats, he really made her feel special. Delicate. Protected in a way that she'd not realized would be so appealing.

As Mike took his own seat, she started loading her plate to distract herself from how good he looked this morning. Midnight-blue pants hugged every muscle of his long legs. A buff-colored waistcoat was framed by a forest green jacket. An ivory cravat, as she'd learned they were called, was knotted expertly at the base of his strong throat. His dark, wavy hair was perfect, the ends long enough to curl over his ears. All in all, she was beginning to believe that modern movie stars had nothing on Micah Axelby.

Jamie took a bite of ham and snuck a piece under the table to the warm chin resting on her knee. Baron gobbled up the treat with delicate greed.

"I trust you are feeling well? You are looking so much better that I assumed so without asking."

"Oh, yes," she said. The concern in his eyes made her stomach flutter a little. "I'm a lot better. I think it was just a mild concussion."

He shook his head at the unfamiliar term.

"A lot of bad headaches. I feel a lot better now. Thank you for taking care of me—after it happened, I mean." She looked down in her lap. Large brown eyes stared up at her, pleading. She snuck Baron another piece of ham.

"It was my fault you were injured," he said seriously. "Had I not teased you, leaving you behind, you would not have faced Collette alone. It was unforgiveable of me, and I beg your pardon." There wasn't a discernable shred of duplicity in either his words or his face.

She wiped her fingers on the cloth napkin, unable to explain the knot of awkwardness that swelled in her throat. "Have you been thinking about that since Monday? Honestly, Mike, it wasn't your fault. I appreciate you taking the time to teach me how to ride. You didn't have to do it, and you were a really good teacher. I just let my mouth overload my a...er, bottom, with Collette. You weren't to blame. I was."

He kept his stare trained on her. "Nonetheless, I beg your forgiveness. I know my own blame in the matter."

She shook her head but agreed. "Okay. If it will make you feel better, you're forgiven for something that really wasn't your fault to begin with."

Some of the darkness left his face, and he nodded solemnly. "I thank you, Miss Marten."

She gave him a half smile and attacked her breakfast. Mike also turned his attention to the steaming plates of goodness in front of him. They ate in silence for a while, but it was a friendly silence. Every third bite Jamie took, she shared a bit with Baron. The hound showed his appreciation by resting his chin on her leg. All in all, it was as comforting a breakfast as she'd had in a long time.

When Jamie sat back, replete, sipping her tea, Mike spoke again.

"I have been unable to locate Miss Dubois, but I assure you that my secretary, Amberson, is awaiting her return most anxiously, with orders to inform me at once. Her protector, Mr. Waites, has apparently whisked her off for a jaunt, presumably into the country."

Jamie set her teacup down on the table, chagrined to see the way her hand shook a little. "I'd like to forget about it and move on, if you don't mind. Can we drop it?"

He tilted his head quizzically. "Am I to understand that you would prefer to leave her unpunished for her crime?"

Jamie twisted the cloth napkin in her lap. Baron sniffed at it eagerly, probably hoping it was stuffed with ham or eggs or toast and jam. "I don't want her to get away with being a bi…um, horrible to me, but I think karma will kick her later on. I'd rather focus on happier things than Collette."

A wry twist to his mouth was answer enough without him speaking. She hurried to change the subject.

"Anyway, are you busy today? I was thinking I'd like to work on a project."

"I have to meet with my solicitor this morning, but I will be free for the afternoon. I will be at your service after luncheon, if you wish."

"That'd be great." She smiled. He returned the expression, and she sighed inwardly. Another afternoon in his company. Now that his days as a bachelor were numbered, these hours were becoming more and more precious to her. She rose to her feet, watched him bow and leave the room. Now she had to figure out what the hell kind of project she could possibly come up with for them to do without any electricity, computers, video games, board games, cars, comics, or anything else she was used to. She had a feeling embroidery wasn't going to cut it.

Mrs. K wasn't really much help. When Jamie cornered her in the kitchen to beg her for ideas, the housekeeper just stared at her. For that matter, the rest of the kitchen staff did too. She should have remembered to ring that stupid bell that called someone into the sitting room, but she hated treating people like trained monkeys. It was only a kitchen, for crying out loud. She was perfectly capable of walking into it and begging the housekeeper for something to do.

"It is quite simple, Miss Jamie. Play the pianoforte. Walk in the park. Sketch a portrait of him. I would suggest going for a brisk ride, but since your last outing ended so badly, perhaps a jaunt in the carriage would be safer."

Mrs. K went back to arguing with cook over what to serve with boiled beef. Apparently, it was really important that cabbage be served alongside it. Jean Philippe was in favor of potatoes and greens. Such a big decision surely couldn't be trusted to a mere cook.

The heat and noise of the kitchen disappeared behind Jamie as she moped her way from the house into the back garden. She dropped onto the bench and stared at the toes of her dark-blue slippers.

If she were back home, she'd take Mike out to the movies or maybe even the mall. He was so fascinated by gadgets that she was sure he'd love the escalators. If they were stuck at home, they'd probably watch some TV, or she could show Mike her game characters. He might even like to make one of his own. *He'd probably be a melee class,* she mused with a smile. *Huge, strong, and completely dominant.* Bossy types usually made great tanks, and Mike was definitely tank material. She probably wouldn't mind healing if Mike were running point for their group.

She shook her head as she rubbed her nails against the stone bench. *Stupid.* Mike would never touch a computer. He'd never drive a car, never listen to an iPod, never know the wonders of a cotton-polyester blend shirt. She was still thinking like a modern woman. Despite the week-plus she'd spent in old London, she still wasn't good at finding ways to kill time enjoyably. She wanted to wow Mike. To show him something he'd never get to see with anyone else in the world. To give him a taste of what it was like to live in her time.

That's it!

Jamie rocketed off the bench and flew into the house. She nearly tripped over a sleeping Baron at the foot of the stairs, but she jumped over him in the nick of time. Getting to her bedroom was the work of a moment, and the door shut behind her with a resounding click.

When Muriel answered the bell, she looked curious. Jamie hadn't ever really rung for the maid before. When Jamie explained the idea, Muriel was horrified, then dubious, then reluctant. But she helped a lot. With her assistance, Jamie changed into her tank top and shorts, and together they transformed a spare room to her exact specifications.

Jamie had to put a robe on to talk to Jean Philippe, the cook. He shook his head, not even stopping his potato peeling when she told him what she wanted him to do for her. He was completely against it. But when Jamie went toe-to-toe with the volatile Frenchman, looking him straight in his nearly black eyes, he had no choice. It probably didn't hurt that she threatened to tell Mrs. Knightsbridge about his boiled beef mutiny. He paused on his potatoes to complete the mission she'd given him. She looked over his shoulder as he worked, giving tips and pointers.

When lunch was in the oven, Jamie bolted back up the stairs with strict instructions for Thornton to send Mike up as soon as the earl arrived. Muriel would bring their lunch up to them when it was done. Jamie sent George out to the nearest pub for the other stuff she needed, and before she knew it, the clock downstairs struck one. Showtime.

Jamie waited nervously by the open door of the spare room, which happened to be located next door to Mike's bedroom. He probably wouldn't like this idea at first. He'd most likely hate it. But she knew, if he gave it a chance, that he would really have fun. And, she thought as she tugged on her shorts, it certainly would be an afternoon that he'd never, ever forget.

The sound of Mike's feet on the stairs made her heart jump into her throat. She tucked her hair behind her ear nervously, the weight of it unfamiliar on her shoulders after so many days of it being tucked into pins atop her head. She hoped he would give her a chance to explain all of this before he judged it. It might be a hard sell for her proper earl.

"Miss Marten?" he called when he reached the top of the stairs. She poked her head out of the doorway.

"Hey, Mike! Come on in. I hope you don't mind, I set us up in here for the afternoon."

He crooked his brows at her but took a step forward. She stopped him with a finger in the air. "Oh, one more thing. No jackets allowed. Or waistcoats. Or cravats. You can keep your boots on, but just a plain old shirt and pants."

Drawing himself up to his full height, Mike gave a doubtful sigh. "Miss Marten, it is hardly proper—"

She stopped him by stepping into the hallway. His eyes bugged at her bare legs. "Don't give me that. I know that my living in your house for the last week and a half hasn't been proper either, but we're both still kicking. Come on. Do this for me? Please? I promise it will make sense soon."

He pursed his lips but disappeared into his room. She hoped he was doing as she'd asked but honestly felt like she might be left standing alone in the hallway for a very long time. Fortunately, she was wrong, and he came out of his room in his form-fitting trousers and shirt, open at the throat. She'd never seen him out of his formal earl-type-wear, and the difference was astounding. He looked even more gorgeous, if such a thing was possible.

"At your service, Miss Marten."

She grinned. "Thanks. Oh, and this afternoon, it's not Miss Marten, and it's not my lord. I'm Jamie"—she pointed to her chest—"and you're Mike." He looked down at the finger she poked into his sternum. "Nothing fancy. Just a couple of friends hanging out. Come on."

She grabbed his hand and pulled him into the room.

"What is all this?"

Muriel and Jamie had done an excellent job of turning the formerly stuffy sitting room into a replica of the twenty-first century. The rose-patterned embroidered settee was covered in a woolen blanket with pillows strewn everywhere. A desk in the corner held a small wooden box, liberated from the kitchen, to represent a computer screen. Jamie had drawn out letters on a piece of paper, and laid it out keyboard-style in front of it. A small book with a string wedged between the pages represented the mouse. Another larger box sat opposite the couch, their makeshift TV. Stacks of cards and books lined a side table, and a sheaf of blank paper lay on the desk chair, with a quill and inkwell at the ready.

"Welcome to my time. Well, as close as I could get it, anyway. Here, let me show you around." She grabbed his hand and dragged him over to the couch. When she flopped down onto it, he didn't follow. He stood beside the covered settee, looking sort of confused and vaguely uncomfortable. She pulled on his arm.

"Sit."

He eased his way down, perching on the very edge

of the couch. Small victory won, she grabbed a tiny
wooden portrait frame that she'd doctored up.

"That's the television. This little thing in my hand is
a remote control. I can change channels and watch different movies and TV shows. They're like plays, but on
that little glass screen."

He smiled. "Like moving portraits?"

"Exactly!" She grinned at him, glad he seemed to be
relaxing. She showed him the computer, the way the
mouse would move a pointer on the screen, the way
websites looked. They'd started talking about comic
books when there was a knock on the open door.

"Miss? I am supposed to say 'pizza delivery'?"

Jamie jumped to her feet and ran to Muriel, clapping
her hands. "*Bravissima, bella*! Yes. That's perfect. Jean
Philippe really outdid himself."

George came into the room after the thin maid and her
large, circular burden, carrying a jug of ale and two glasses.

"Guys, this looks awesome. Thanks. Just set it on the
coffee table and skedaddle."

George turned to Muriel, his freckled face confused.
"Does she always speak in that manner?"

Muriel rolled her eyes and nodded. Relieved of their
deliveries, they both disappeared.

Jamie turned back to Mike with a huge smile.
He was staring at the pizza with brows lifted, mouth
pursed, and head cocked. She couldn't help but laugh
at his quizzical expression.

"What's wrong?"

"What have you done with Jean Philippe? This is not
his usual fare."

"I know. I ordered it special for us. This is a pizza. And
beer, or ale, if you'd rather. This is the kind of food that
we would eat on a date if you were in my time with me."

He lowered one brow. "A date?"

She gulped. "Yeah, that's when friends hang out together." Her nervous smile must have tipped him off because his nod was not all that trusting.

Once she'd explained the bread, tomato sauce, and cheese concept, Mike was less reluctant. When she cut him a slice and demonstrated the proper technique, he actually started to enjoy himself. The beer was way stronger than she was used to, and the alcohol went to her head pretty quickly. They sat next to each other on the couch, closer now than before. After she watched Mike drain his beer, she sighed and let her head rest against his shoulder.

He froze.

She snuggled closer, her insides warm from the beer and her outsides warm from, well, him.

"Miss Marten?"

"Nope," she said, smiling against his arm. "Jamie."

"Jamie," he said, gently pulling away. "This is not…"

She put a finger against his lips. "Sssh. None of that, remember? This isn't 1816, this is the twenty-first century. And in my time, do you know what I'd want you to do?"

"What?" he whispered against her forefinger. Before she could answer, he pressed his lips to her finger, his hand covering hers to keep her trapped against his mouth.

Whatever she'd been planning to say got sucked away in the delicious sensation of Mike's mouth against her fingers. He didn't stop there. He kissed the back of her hand so softly, lips pressing a path up her wrist, against the delicate blue veins when he turned her hand over.

She was frozen in place but burning all over. Her body responded to Mike's kisses, warmth blooming in her breasts, her belly, and lower. His mouth traveled up her arm, soft but strong and insistent.

Was this really happening? Or was she having a post-concussion alcohol-fueled erotic daydream? Only one way to find out.

Shattering the ice prison that her body was encased in, she pulled her arm away from Mike. He looked up at her, brown eyes questioning, but she answered him with her lips pressed against his.

This kiss was even better than the one in the hallway had been. There was none of the soft, sweet touches of lips, questioning teases that let two people get to know each other. This was a willing mutual exploration.

Mike pulled her body against his, lying back on the settee enough to pull her slightly atop him. Their tongues tangled sweetly, tasting each other, wild in their mutual passion. Mike's hands wandered over her back, starting at her bare shoulders, then down, caressing her shoulder blades, down the length of her spine. His warm, strong hands stopped at the curve of her hips, where he pressed against her intimately.

She gasped into his mouth when she felt his hardness pressing into her. She'd have been lying if she said she hadn't wanted this, but she'd not expected it to feel so damn good. Too damn good. So damn good that she knew it was too good to be true.

With a huge sigh, she pulled her mouth from Mike's. For a moment, she let herself stay there, staring at him. His eyes were dark, his lips were full and swollen from their kissing, and his hips still pressed into hers. She wanted him so much. But she didn't want a quick fling with Mike. Anything between them had to be all or nothing because she wouldn't be able to live with herself any other way.

"Thank you," she whispered to him. She pressed another kiss to his lips, this time a chaste, innocent one.

"I should probably go." She didn't miss the wanting gleam in his eyes as she got up and left the room. As much as it killed her, leaving him wanting more was probably the best option. Too bad cold showers hadn't been invented yet.

Fourteen

ON SATURDAY, ONLY THREE DAYS AWAY FROM THE make-or-break night of Mike's (and quite possibly her) life, Jamie had a panic attack.

She'd tried to be as near Mike as possible while attempting to keep her head the last few days. It was so damn hard. Every minute she spent with him made her realize how much time she actually did want to spend with him. Namely, the rest of her life.

They'd taken walks together. He'd showed her how he kept up with his estate books and maintained the day-to-day operations of his many properties. She began to feel sorry for Amberson, the secretary. Poor bastard had never even seen a calculator.

But Saturday afternoon, her carefully constructed emotional barriers came crashing down.

She'd been out in the garden, playing with Baron. She tossed a stick for him, over and over and over, and the young greyhound had tirelessly chased and returned it. Jamie was exhausted way before the dog was. She was pleading with Baron to come inside with her and they'd go beg Jean Philippe for some snacks when Mike came through the door.

"Where are you going?" he asked her, a small smile on his lips.

"I'm pooped. Your dog is a slave driver."

Mike laughed and bent to rub Baron's ears. "Nonsense. He simply knows who is an easy mark. *I* do not allow him to sleep in my bed." Mike winked at her, despite her bugged-out eyes and dropped jaw.

"Well…well…" she sputtered. "You entertain him then if you're so special!"

"If you insist." Another wink from him made her cheeks burn. She leaned up against the door and watched the earl as he proceeded to play with his dog.

A long pole was produced from a small lean-to shed. A string was wrapped around the end of the pole, making it resemble an extra-large fishing rod.

Mike unwound the string and tied his clean white handkerchief to the end of it. Baron jumped up and down, tail wagging and tongue lolling. He obviously knew what this strange setup meant, even if Jamie didn't.

Mike walked to the open area on the left side of the garden, a wide patch of grass bare of other vegetation or shrubbery. Baron's leaps became higher, and she could hear his jaws snapping excitedly.

"Please make sure to keep your distance. Baron can get very, ah, exuberant." Mike smiled at her, and her heart tap-danced.

Mike threw the hanky straight out and began to turn in a circle, swinging the pole with its hanky-baited line. Baron took off after the hanky like a shot, body moving faster than Jamie could have imagined. His lean body curved and bent as he darted in a wide circle around Mike. Mike's broad shoulders flexed as he swung the heavy pole around, eyes alight with joy at the sight of his dog having such fun. The sight of such shared happiness moved something inside Jamie, deep in her chest.

Mike's laughter carried across the lawn to where she stood beside the house, a hand pressed against the swell of her breasts which were pushed up by those damn stays.

She had to face it. She was falling in love with a nineteenth-century earl. And for a twenty-first century girl, that was pretty damn terrifying.

The game lasted less than ten minutes, but at top speed, Baron was plenty exhausted enough to give up. Mike relented, and on the last swing of the pole, let the blue-gray hound catch the hanky.

"What a gentleman," Mike crooned to his dog, untying the line from the hanky. Baron shook it like a dead animal, cheerfully strangling and dirtying the clean linen. "Excellent work, Baron. Good lad."

Mike petted his dog, praising him for such a remarkable performance. The pleasure, pride, and love in Mike's eyes as he looked at Baron were too much for Jamie.

She couldn't watch anymore. Without another word, she waved at Mike and headed to the door of the house.

"Miss Marten?"

She pretended not to hear and ascended the steps to the door.

"Jamie?"

His use of her first name, combined with his boots crunching the gravel of the path behind her, stopped her in her tracks. She turned.

"Are you…" He trailed off. He swallowed hard. His cheeks were drawn, and his eyes had gone dark. He was in the grip of some strong emotion that she really wasn't sure she wanted to identify.

"What?"

He cleared his throat and went on. "I would like

you to have dinner with me this evening. Would you attend me?"

Jamie looked down at the brick steps beneath her slippers. Mike went out almost every night. When she'd asked Mrs. Knightsbridge about where he went so often, the housekeeper made comments about dinner parties, balls, routs, soirees, and numerous other entertainments. What that meant was, they'd only really had breakfast together regularly. The rest of the meals Jamie ate were either alone in the dining room or up in her room with a book.

She couldn't make her answer come out. Her yes was stuck in her throat like a wad of stale pretzels. From her vantage on the second step, she was looking straight into his eyes. He took a step closer, and her arms ached to reach out to him. She could nearly feel the heat rising from his body, both from his exertion and, she hoped, their chemistry.

"Jamie?"

She tore her eyes from him, choosing to focus on Baron's heaving sides instead. The dog was obviously elated with his handkerchief prize. If only things were that simple for her. "Yes. I'll have dinner with you."

He smiled at her then, an expression that sliced straight through the last shield she'd erected in front of her heart.

She walked with him back into the house, and even gave a polite good-bye at the bottom of the stairs. He went into his office, and she went up the stairs to hyper-ventilate in private. When she collapsed on the bed, flat on her back because of those stays, she faced reality.

Jamie loved Micah Alexander Axelby, Earl of Dunnington.

He was a guy that she should never even have met. She loved a guy that she would have to abandon her entire life to be with. Her friends, her house, her computer, her shower. Shower. Running Water. Toothbrushes. Those neat little personal hand-sanitizer bottles.

She threw an arm over her eyes. *What the hell am I supposed to do now?*

Her heart pounded like that for an hour. She was too keyed up to sleep, too jittery to be around anyone, too anxious to focus on any sort of activity. An elephant sat on her chest, one that had nothing to do with the whalebone and lacing compressing her middle.

Eventually, when the logical portion of her brain managed to wrestle the rest of it into submission, she pushed herself off the bed and started pacing in front of the now-dark fireplace. The afternoon sun shone through the open curtains, and she focused on the familiar light that she passed through again and again.

She had some decisions to make. The rhythmic thudding of her slippers against the rug helped her focus her breath. *Calm. Focus, Jamie.*

"Oh God," she said aloud, hands braced against the wooden mantel, head bowed.

Could she do this? Could she lose the person she always thought she was in order to be the perfect countess for the man she loved?

A knock on the door told her she didn't have time to make that decision then. Muriel skipped into the room, thin face alight with joy.

"Mrs. K said I was to help you dress for dinner with his lordship."

Despite her inner turmoil, Jamie had to smile at Muriel's adoption of her nickname for the housekeeper. "Mrs. K, huh?"

Muriel didn't miss a beat as she pulled a peach satin gown from the armoire. She winked at her and said, "Yup. Sure did."

Jamie laughed aloud at that. No matter what the outcome of her time here would ultimately be, at least she'd made a mark on someone.

Muriel didn't comment on Jamie's unusual reticence as she helped her bathe and dress. Normally, Jamie would have complained about the ridiculous amount of underwear, the aggravating nature of stays, and the crazy number of hairpins that were necessary to hold her high-lighted mop off her shoulders. Jamie sat there without a word, watching the way her neck looked longer because of the hairstyle Muriel had chosen. The way her skin glowed against the peach satin. The way her eyes looked strange and frightened, almost like a hunted creature.

"You're lovely, miss." Muriel stepped back after placing the last curl in front of her ear. "A real treat."

"Thank you, Muriel." Jamie stood, completely unsurprised to find her ankles as shaky as Jell-O. She took as deep a calming breath as she could and forced a smile to her lips. Time to go downstairs and face the music—whether it was a symphony or thrashing death metal.

The staircase seemed way too short. The hallway even more so. She was at the door of the dining room hours before she was mentally ready to be. She took a deep breath, gathered her courage, and looked in. Mike wasn't there.

Oh.

She wasn't a fainting flower. She really wasn't one of those people that tear up at greeting-card commercials. But when she saw what she perceived to be Mike standing her up, she was suspiciously ready to cry. The table wasn't even really laid for their dinner yet. Had he changed his mind only moments after speaking to her? Why didn't he let someone know?

"Miss Jamie."

She blinked, shaking her head from the disappointment before turning to George, the footman.

He smiled. "His lordship awaits you in the drawing room."

Oh. Oh!

Could she stop leaping to conclusions for about twenty seconds? It would probably make her life much easier.

She followed the footman to the drawing room and was both relieved and astounded by the sight of the man standing by the window, peering out into the night.

The earl was dressed even nicer than usual, and that was pretty damn nice. He wore all black, save for the crisp white shirt points and snowy cravat at his throat. The stark contrast only served to emphasize broad shoulders that tapered down to his slim hips. The flickering firelight cast delicately dancing shadows on his strong jaw. He was gorgeous. Truly the handsomest man she had ever seen.

Her heart caught in her throat as she drank in the sight of him. Knowing how she felt about him now, how could she continue this way? Choosing to stay with him would be the hardest decision that she'd ever make. But could she honestly say that life in this day and age would make her happy? With or without Mike, she wasn't sure.

"Miss Marten." His voice was warm as he turned to her. "You look splendid."

A wry smile twisted her lips. "Thanks. You don't look so bad yourself."

He laughed, and the deep sound went straight to her belly like a body blow. He crossed to the sideboard and picked up a decanter with reddish-brown alcohol inside. When he asked her to join him for a drink, she didn't hesitate. She crossed the floor toward him, knowing sink or swim, she was all in.

Her hand barely trembled as she accepted the glass he

held out to her. She took a sip, savoring the warmth of the liquor. She tried her best to avoid eye contact. He'd know. If he looked into her eyes, she had no doubt that he would see the way she felt about him.

"Baron seemed to enjoy your sport with him this afternoon." The polite tone of his voice helped her to tamp down some of her nerves. "He enjoys chasing sticks and things." Liquid splashed into another glass as he poured himself a drink.

"Not as much as that greyhound-fishing-pole you rigged up," Jamie said. She took another sip, keeping her gaze locked everywhere but on him. She couldn't trust herself.

"That was an idea of Mrs. Knightsbridge's. I think she's more fond of the hound than she lets on."

"I think we all are. He's a pretty special dog." Jamie toyed nervously with one of the curls dangling by her ear.

"Indeed."

Mike fell silent then, and she chanced a sideways glance at him. He'd been watching her pretty hard. Was he thinking the same thing she was? Was he wondering about her, about the possibility of a future together?

It was fortunate that Thornton chose that exact moment to announce that dinner was ready.

"Permit me to escort you, Miss Marten."

She couldn't say no. She walked alongside him, desperately trying to ignore the feel of his strong arm under her hand.

He seated her, pulling out the chair for her as if she was a gentleman's daughter or some titled personage. She ignored the flutterings of her heart. She had decided nothing, and she wouldn't let that stupid organ rule her head until she did.

She managed to make it through the first three courses

without making a complete fool of herself. Mike was more relaxed than normal, and that eased her nerves somewhat too. By the time dessert was brought in, she was starting to wonder if maybe, just maybe, they might be able to somehow make this work.

She poked at the sweet custard with her spoon. "So, what's the latest gossip in the upper crust?"

He crooked a brow at her and swallowed the bite of custard he'd spooned between those sinful lips. "Gossip?"

"Yeah. What's the newest scandal? Has Lady Folderol been seen without six layers of petticoats? Lord Fiddle-dee-dee got drunk and spilled punch all over Miss Whosit's cleavage?"

"Nothing so interesting, surely," he said with a smile. He took another bite of custard before answering, "No, the latest *on-dit* is of a more serious nature. But gentlemen do not gossip."

Jamie snorted, and he looked at her with a crooked brow. "Don't give me that. Leah's granddad, Pawpaw Milton, is glued to *Entertainment Tonight* every evening at seven sharp. Guys care just as much about gossip as girls do."

He shook his head. "It is not seemly."

"Oh, come on. I don't know any of these people. It's like an imaginary story to me."

With a sigh, he complied.

"Lucas Humphries, the Baron of Easterly, eloped three days ago."

"Oooh," Jamie said, leaning forward slightly. "That is juicy!"

"He eloped with his mistress." The expression on Mike's face stopped her amusement in its tracks. All traces of his former mirth were gone, and in their place was a deep disapproval lurking in the corners of his downturned mouth.

"Okay. So she was his mistress. And he's going to make an honest woman out of her. That's good, right?" Jamie spoke slowly, trying to make sense of the situation, and Mike's super-negative reaction to it.

Mike shook his head vehemently. "It is not that simple. Lord Easterly has left his estate in ruin. He has broken his engagement with Lady Elise, the daughter of the Marquess of Glastonbury. The only reason he was able to keep the creditors at bay before was his impending marriage and the promise of the healthy dowry that would accompany it. Now, the families who depend on him for survival, his servants, the residents of the farms at his country estate, his mother—they are all left destitute because of his selfish actions." The disgust fairly flew from his mouth at the end of his tale. His eyes were dark, his jaw tight, and she almost felt bad for the bowl of custard that bore the brunt of his displeasure.

Jamie looked down at her own dish. "So, is a nobleman not supposed to marry for love? Not ever?" It was the most important question she'd ever asked him, so she couldn't quite get all of the tremble out of her voice.

"With position comes responsibility. Duties to one's house, to one's name. To throw all that away in the name of an emotion? Despicable." He dropped his napkin beside his plate with unnecessary force. "Love will not feed the villager's children. Love will not keep his family clothed and out of the poorhouse. While he is touring the continent with his new bride, the vultures will pick the bones of the barony."

And with those words, Jamie felt her insides crumble. She laid her spoon down with a clink. Wiped her trembling fingers with the cloth napkin. *What the hell do I do now?* she thought, trying desperately to keep her features calm.

"Miss Marten, are you ill?"

She glanced up at him. God, he was so beautiful. But he was as far away as the hero in a historical movie. She had a better chance of being with the real Colin Firth than she did with Micah Axelby, Earl of Dunnington. She swallowed the growing lump in her throat enough to answer.

"No, I'm fine. Just...tired."

She turned her attention to the food. The rest of the meal was tense, quiet. She gave one-word answers to all of Mike's questions, the roiling discomfort in her guts not allowing her to be more effusive. What was the point, anyway? This whole thing had been a waste of time. Mike's duty was more important to him than any relationship she could have had with him.

When the torturous meal was finally done, she scraped her chair back. "Thanks for the great meal, my lord." She bobbed a quick curtsy and turned to go.

He rose quickly, a bewildered look on his handsome features. "Please stay. I had hoped you would agree to play the pianoforte for me after dinner."

Her eyes fluttered closed. "I'm sorry. I can't."

An extended silence opened her eyes again. Mike stared at her, lips pursed in confusion. "I will bid you good evening, then."

"Good evening," she repeated woodenly, and left the room, her infant dream of their relationship lying dead and burnt behind her.

❧

He'd bungled that properly.

Micah lined his fork and knife up beside his plate, brow furrowed in consternation. Whatever had caused Miss Marten to look as though her heart was breaking?

He'd imagined that they would spend a pleasant evening together after they dined. Perhaps even culminating in another kiss or three. Instead, he rose and left the dining room quite alone.

His estate room was cold, the fire banked in anticipation of an evening spent with much more pleasant company. Instead of calling a servant, Micah stoked it himself. The orange flames licking up the sides of the wood reminded him of his damnable failure to treat his houseguest with more care. He'd consumed her bright nature, just like these hungry flames. The softness in her eyes had died as surely as if he'd smothered it with his own two hands. He sat back on his heels, breathing deeply as he searched for clues in the leaping blaze.

Baron Easterly. His elopement. What in that discussion could have possibly caused Jamie hurt? Or was she truly ill and felt poorly enough to cut their evening together quite short? Micah shook his head and stood. It mattered not. The whole damnable charade was insupportable, and he'd been just as blind and stupid as Lucas Humphries.

He splashed brandy into a glass and downed it in one go. Why was he pursuing her? He had duties, for God's sake, duties that were binding and unavoidable. Marking time with Jamie Marten would be the height of folly. It would jeopardize his planned engagement, stir up another bumble-broth within the *ton*, and quite possibly cause his distant relatives more grief. They were already planning his demise quite happily over the Louisa scandal.

No, damn it, he was through. He dashed the glass into the fireplace, the glass shattering and the tiny droplets of liquor causing the angry flames to spark blue. Enough. It was outside of enough.

His duty, his name, those were the important things. Not a strange girl with striped hair and eyes the color of the sea. He strode from the room, demanded his cloak from a surprised but silent Thornton, and went out into the dark London night.

Fifteen

JAMIE BARELY SLEPT THAT NIGHT. SHE SNUGGLED NEXT to Baron, who'd been extremely happy to resume his position as her nighttime bodyguard-slash-hot water-bottle. She kept remembering Mike's face, the disgusted look on it when he'd said, "With position comes responsibility. To throw all that away in the name of an emotion? Despicable."

She turned over.

Despicable. He'd almost spat the word out like it tasted bad.

He'd never defy convention and marry some nobody who knew nothing about his time. He needed the perfect countess—a woman who knew her place, who had money and property and would act like a countess should. Not some jumped-up gamer chick with depression issues and a flighty muse. She was no better than Lord Easterly's mistress in his eyes. And she'd never be, because she was born in the wrong place and time.

She refused to cry. To cry would be to admit to herself that she'd lost something. The truth was she'd never really had anything at all.

A soft knock drew her attention.

"Yeah?"

Mrs. Knightsbridge appeared in the doorway, shutting the door softly behind her. Sitting on the edge of the bed, she brushed a lock of hair from Jamie's forehead.

"I heard your conversation in the dining room. You must believe, dear."

"Believe what? That this is a complete waste of time and no way in hell will Mike ever ditch his responsibilities to be with me?" Jamie tried to smother the telltale waver in her voice, but it wasn't easy.

Mrs. K smiled. "Come time for the ball, he will be professing his love for you." The housekeeper brushed a motherly kiss over Jamie's forehead. "And if I am wrong, Wilhelmina shall open the portal for you the next morning. You've nothing to lose."

Except my stupid heart, Jamie thought as she closed her eyes against the tears.

⤜∾⤏

She'd planned to spend Sunday in Mike's company. After all, it was one of the last times she'd be near him. But instead, Jamie spent the day in the garden with Baron. She'd taken both breakfast and lunch alone in her room, unwilling to run into Mike again. It would be too damn painful. But by the time Muriel had collected the tray with her mostly uneaten lunch still on it, Jamie was going stir crazy.

Baron was more than willing to keep her company as she paced the length of the gravel path down and back again. Eventually, he collapsed in a beam of sunshine, watching her walk. Then he fell asleep, and she was completely alone with her thoughts.

It was simple. She had failed in her attempt to convince Mike to marry for love, whether to her or someone else. Mrs. K would be disappointed, to say the least. There was no reason to even think about going to that stupid ball tomorrow night. She'd probably make a giant ass of herself anyway.

She snorted and kicked a rock across the path. Baron's ears flicked at the sound.

Why had she ever thought that she could pull off something like a huge society ball, anyway? From what Mrs. Knightsbridge had told her, these things were like breeding grounds for the best gossip. If Lady Such-and-such danced too close to someone that wasn't her husband, then the titters would begin. Would she be able to remember all the stupid rules like that? Hardly. She could barely remember not to say "fuck" in front of anyone here.

The sun was setting before she was done with her pacing. Baron eventually tired of her, and she couldn't blame him. She let him in the house when he stood on the back steps and stared at her pitifully. Honestly, other than Mike, Jamie thought she'd miss Baron most of all.

After the door swung shut behind the hound, Jamie sat on the damp brick and held her head in her hands. Mrs. K had promised to have Wilhelmina open the portal in only thirty-six hours or so. She'd go back to her little house. Back to the summer heat. Back to the lonely episode of *Hoarders* that was her life.

The creaking of the door at her back startled Jamie, and she whirled. Fortunately, it was only Muriel.

"Miss Marten, Mrs. Knightsbridge wanted me to fetch you. It's time for your fitting."

Jamie looked up at the thin-faced girl. "Fitting?"

Muriel beamed and nodded, white mobcap flopping. "For your ball gown, miss. She's told me how you're going to the masquerade."

Jamie looked back down to where her knuckles where white against the rusty-colored brick. "Yeah."

"Come, Miss Marten." Muriel reached down and grabbed her hand, pulling Jamie after her. "You must see the beautiful gown she has made for you! You shall be the toast of the ball."

Jamie couldn't break the maid's heart by telling her she wouldn't be going, so she allowed the maid to drag her through the house and up the stairs to the Lemon Room, where Mrs. Knightsbridge was placing the finishing touches on a gown that would never see the ball at all.

When Jamie walked into the room, Mrs. K immediately hustled her out of her green muslin gown. "Come, Muriel, help me. Miss Jamie, lift your arms."

They snatched the gown over her head and immediately replaced it with what looked like silk lifted straight from a fairy tale. It was silver, light as gossamer, and it hugged her curves like a BMW 645 on a mountain road.

"Wow," Jamie breathed, staring at herself in the mirror. She was...beautiful. She looked like a princess. The wide neckline showed off the curve of her collarbone, making it look delicate. Mrs. K brought her a mask and placed it gently over her eyes. It only covered half her face, the wide eye-slits making it easy to see through.

"There," Mrs. K breathed. "You are lovely."

Jamie couldn't drag her stare away from that woman in the mirror. The silver made the highlights in her hair look brighter, her skin glow with health and life, and her eyes shine with possibilities.

A deep sigh broke her gaze, and she looked at the two people staring into the mirror beside her.

Muriel's face was bright, her smile so big Jamie thought her face would break. Mrs. K stood on her other side, tears brimming in the woman's clear gray eyes. She swallowed, a watery smile breaking across her face.

"You shall be the most beautiful lady at the ball." Muriel sighed happily. "You will have your pick of any gentleman you could wish for!"

Except for one, Jamie thought, her heart breaking as she turned away from the mirror. *The only one I want.*

❧

In the end, Jamie couldn't crush Mrs. K and Muriel by refusing to go to the ball. They'd worked so hard to make her ready for it. Mrs. K on the gown, which she'd apparently been working on every spare second for the past week, and Muriel when it came to dressing Jamie for the event itself. When they were done with her, she barely recognized herself. The hairdo, which Muriel had proudly informed Jamie was "a la Grecque" or something, was an intricate twist of curls and braids. It made her look a foot and a half taller, slender, and so willowy that she thought runway models would envy her back home. Well, if runway models had nearly C-cup breasts. And hips that were curvier. And carried a healthy body weight. So maybe not so much like a runway model. Still, more beautiful than she'd ever been in her life.

Mike, fortunately, had already departed by the time Jamie made her way down the staircase, feeling like the world's fakest Cinderella.

She was bundled into a carriage and waved off with nothing but Mrs. K, a wink, and a prayer.

Mrs. K smiled at her from across the carriage. Even though it was a masked ball, no lady of quality would be there without a chaperone, she'd told Jamie. Once they arrived at the ball, Mrs. K would disappear, leaving Jamie and Mike to have the most awkward public good-bye ever. Jamie sighed. She wished, as the carriage bounced its way along the dark streets of London, that someone would reassure her that this wasn't the stupidest idea in the world.

If she was Cinderella, then she could have her prince, or earl in this case, and it wouldn't matter that she was a servant in her wicked stepmother's house. But since she wasn't, and Jamie Marten was in this carriage watching the moonlit streets go by, then this was another chance for Mike to understand how completely wrong she was for his world.

As they descended the carriage to the brick walkway in front of the huge home, Jamie made a decision.

"Mrs. K?"

"Yes, dear?" The older woman was almost pretty in a simple gown made of dark-blue fabric. Her silvery mask obscured most of her face. No one would recognize her as a servant, Jamie was fairly certain. She must have conjured up the gowns for the both of them because no way could she have purchased them on a servant's wages.

"Can you have Wilhelmina send me home as soon as we get back?" Jamie's voice came out a little shaky. She wouldn't even tell Mike she was going. She'd find him in this crowd somehow and grab a memory that would have to last her for the rest of her life.

Mrs. K shook her head. "Let's not worry about that right now, dearie. Come. You've a ball to attend."

The music and laughter was carried on the night air through the open doorways. Jamie's nerves sped her heart, and she contemplated running straight back the way she'd come. But when she turned, the carriage had already rounded the corner to make way for more arriving guests. Mrs. K grabbed Jamie firmly by the elbow and steered her down the walk. Jamie sighed. The sooner she went into this ballroom filled with the cream of the English crop, the sooner she could beat feet for 2012.

"Now." Mrs. K dug through her tiny purse—she'd called it a reticule—and produced a thick sheet of paper with gilt edging. "We'll need this to gain entry."

Jamie gulped and took the sheet of paper. She hadn't really thought about getting into the damn party. She'd figured it would be like a frat party back in her days as a college student. Show up, grab a beer, and find someone she could hold a conversation with. Usually, it was some lonely looking smart boy in the corner. Lucky her, the last time she'd done that the lonely guy had been Logan.

This shindig, however, was nothing like that. A puffy-looking guy in a powdered wig with a warm brown coat and tails stood guard at the doorway. Mrs. K pulled Jamie aside, and they watched the couple that had gotten out of the carriage behind them. The gentleman handed an invitation to the servant, and he waved them in with a bow.

"Go," the housekeeper whispered, nudging Jamie on.

Swallowing hard, Jamie approached the man.

"Good evening," he said with a bow.

Jamie nodded, graciously she hoped, and handed the invitation over. Mrs. K was nearly bouncing with excitement.

"My apologies, miss, but this invitation is for the Granfield ball, two weeks hence." The servant's tone was condescending. "Are you known to the Baroness Wentworth?"

Frantically looking over at Mrs. K, Jamie gulped.

The housekeeper sputtered. "Oh dear, I must have brought the wrong invitation. How silly of me." She went into titters, thwapping the man on the arm with her fan. He winced.

Jamie rolled her eyes.

"Please, don't let my poor daughter miss the event because of a silly mistake."

The servant started to shake his head. Just then, lighted lanterns over to the east side of the ballroom caught Jamie's eye.

"Pardon us, sir. I need a word with my mother." Pulling Mrs. K aside, Jamie whispered, "There's a path to a garden. There has to be a back door into this place. Come on, let's use it."

They waited for a gentleman with a pointy-nosed mask to make his way to the entrance before slipping off into the cover of night. The night air had deposited early dew on the lawn, and Jamie hoisted her skirt high to keep the hem from dragging. She and Mrs. K tiptoed as quick as they could through the darkness, making a beeline for the lighted path.

They made it without incident. Smoothing her skirt, Jamie took stock of her appearance. Hem still mud free, white gloves still bright and clean, mask on straight, hair still "Greek" to her. Mrs. K placed a warm hand on her shoulder. "Miss Jamie, we must go inside."

Ascending the steps to the balcony, her housekeeper chaperone behind her, Jamie kept her senses on alert. As she drew closer to the open doors to the ballroom, a problem occurred to her that she hadn't even considered before. A problem that would quite possibly mean that she couldn't even say good-bye to Mike tonight. Disappointment gripped her, and she wondered if it was worth it to even try.

"What is wrong, my dear?"

Jamie swallowed the knot in her throat. "There are masks everywhere. On everybody."

Mrs. K laughed. "Of course, my dear. This is a masked ball."

"But how will I ever find Mike?" She leaned against the marble railing of the balcony, halfway hidden behind a potted tree, dejection soaking her thoroughly.

There were tons of men there. They were dressed in all shades, ranging from severe black and white to the color of regurgitated Skittles. Masks covered whole faces on some, three-quarters on others.

Mrs. K snapped her fan open. "I shall locate him. Wait here." Sailing off like the mother ship, Mrs. K marched determinedly into the ballroom, long skirt swishing. Jamie couldn't help but shake her head at the housekeeper's fancy dress and unfailing faith. Better Mrs. K than her, though. From what Jamie had heard, tabloid reporters were kittens when it came to gossip compared to the women of the British *ton*.

She stood there, chewing her lip, digging the toe of her slipper into the ground, when the nervous, high laughter of a woman interrupted her internal soliloquy.

"Sir, you should not beg me so. It's unbecoming, and I've no need for new company."

"But, Marilyn, you must know how I feel for you. How I long to bask in the sunshine of your love…"

Blecch.

Jamie peeked around her tree to see a couple walking briskly up the garden path toward the house. Well, the woman was walking briskly anyway. What Jamie assumed was a besotted swain trotted after her, not stopping his stream of ridiculously bad poetry. Jamie had written better love-struck crap than that when she was only seven years old. J. T. Keibler never knew what he'd missed.

As they came closer, Jamie examined the woman as unobtrusively as she could. The beauty was dressed all in white, gold braids and borders edging the skirt of her gown. Her honey-brown hair was done up in more gold, chains, and braids decorating the mass of curls. Her heart-shaped face was covered by a small mask over her eyes, the slits edged in gold paint.

Wait a minute. That guy said Marilyn, didn't he?

Before they could reach the steps of the balcony, the guy, who apparently was as stupid and cruel as he was bad at poetry, decided he wasn't going to take no for an answer. Grabbing her arm, he twisted it high behind her back, eliciting a cry of pain from her.

"You bedamned tease, you'll deny me no further." He started to drag her back into the garden, away from the lantern-lit path. His hand clapped across her mouth, muffling her terrified cries.

Oh the hell you will, Jamie thought, and yanked up her skirt for a full-on run. She didn't give a shit what year it was; she wasn't going to stand by while a woman got attacked.

Sixteen

IGNORING THE BUSHES THAT GRABBED AT HER SILVER skirt, Jamie followed the sounds of the struggle. He couldn't go very fast with Marilyn fighting like she was, brave woman. Jamie tried to be as quick and quiet as possible, realizing that surprise was the best way for her to overcome this quite possibly inebriated dumbass. He had a height and weight advantage against Marilyn and Jamie, but if she could get the jump on him, they'd get her away safe. She hoped.

He dragged Marilyn behind a large old oak tree, the secluded area lit only by the soft glow of the moon overhead. Throwing her against the trunk, he pressed his lips roughly against hers.

She thrashed against him, kicking and scratching wildly. He spread his legs, using one of his to pry hers apart. *Bingo. My chance.*

Jamie darted behind him, not daring to breathe. In a move worthy of a professional wrestling low blow, she dropped to her knees and punched upward as hard as she could. He barely made a squeak before dropping to the ground, coughing painfully.

Marilyn kicked at his face, but he caught the heel

of her golden slipper with the hand not cupping his privates. She screamed, falling back against the tree as he pulled her off-balance.

"You bitch," he rasped in a thin voice, rising into an awkwardly off-center crouch. "For that you shall suffer."

"Leave her alone," Jamie shrieked as she belted him in the ear as hard as she could. Her blow upset his already precarious balance, and he fell sideways onto an exposed root, head cracking loudly against the wood. Marilyn yanked up her skirts and ran back toward the house. After kicking the douchebag in the kidneys to make sure he wouldn't give chase, Jamie followed.

Once they were back on the lantern-lit path, Marilyn turned to Jamie with a sob. She threw her arms around Jamie.

"Oh, thank you, thank you so much. I don't know who you are or how you knew I needed help, but without you, Mr. Collins surely would have…"

"Shh, Marilyn, it's okay," Jamie murmured as she rubbed her back with a still-tingling palm. Jamie was shaking too, if she was being honest with herself. Her own encounter with attackers hadn't been all that long ago, after all, and she wasn't sure that the sick feeling of terror would ever leave her fully.

"How did you know my name?" Marilyn pulled back, lifting her delicate mask enough to wipe her tears away.

Jamie glanced over her shoulder. She sure as hell didn't want to wait around for the drunken asshole, but she might miss Mrs. K if she went inside. Opting to take her chances with the rabid *ton* instead of the wannabe rapist, she hoped the woman wouldn't mind lending her a hand.

Jamie left out the part about being from two hundred years in the future. She didn't figure Marilyn would buy the truth. Jamie told her that she'd fallen in love with the wrong man and that there was no working it out. She needed to find him to say good-bye. Marilyn agreed to help her immediately, as if it was the most natural thing in the world. It seemed that love was something that a mistress could understand better than a titled and landed gentleman. Men. *Go figure.*

Apparently, as Marilyn told Jamie, masquerade balls were sort of the free-for-all of the *ton*. Normally rigid rules were relaxed, braver members of the less-than-virtuous frequently found their way there, and it was sort of a game to figure out who was who. Mrs. Knightsbridge had certainly brought Jamie to the only society event that she could make it out of unscathed—if she was careful enough.

After Marilyn helped Jamie brush the dirt from her skirt and Jamie knocked the stray bits of bark from Marilyn's, they were ready to navigate the ballroom. Marilyn had spied a few men earlier that might be the earl and was going to take Jamie along in order to find out for sure. Once she'd made a positive ID, Jamie would lure him out to the balcony and share one last conversation with the most maddening, bright, and wonderful man she'd ever met. It would have to be enough because there was no hope for more between them.

The noise inside was more than Jamie had been prepared for. Parties in her day were loud, crazy, screaming things full of throbbing bass and repressed cube-dwellers. She'd been expecting some nice string music and quiet chitchat. Boy, was she wrong.

She was almost there on the music, but the orchestra was having to saw hell bent for leather on their violins and cellos to be heard above the myriad conversations and gales of laughter from the raucous attendees. It was almost like home, but without the beer kegs and the strung-out stoners in the corner.

"Close to me now," Marilyn reminded Jamie, as she skirted the edge of the dance floor. Jamie walked as close to Marilyn as her full skirt would allow. Jamie smiled at those who smiled at her, ignored the interested looks and downright ogles, and kept her heart as still as she dared. Mike was in there somewhere.

The first one Marilyn had seen was dancing with a lady dressed as a peacock. The brilliant blue-green of her gown and mask contrasted sharply with his lavender coat. *Ew.* Jamie didn't have the heart to tell Marilyn that she was sure Mike would never be caught dead in a coat that color. It wasn't his style.

When the orchestra finished their song and the partners bowed to each other, Marilyn hustled Jamie across the floor. The gentleman was speaking to an elderly lady in a rose gown and pink mask. Arm in arm, Marilyn and Jamie passed close behind him, and Jamie strained to hear what he was saying.

"...quite a crush, by all accounts," he was saying in a nasal tone.

The older woman nodded her agreement. "Yes, Lady Wentworth must be quite beside herself. I say, Sir Andrew, have you seen Lord Somerset? I had so hoped he would dance with my eldest, Lydia…"

Marilyn looked at Jamie with a tilt of her head. Jamie shook hers in response. *Not him.*

They continued past the couple, and Jamie kept searching the crowd for a glimpse of those broad shoulders. The dark hair that curled around his collar. Those eyes that reminded her of Mexican hot chocolate. Rich, sinful, with the right amount of belly-warming spice.

The next man was in the card room: a gentlemen-only

space that gave them a place to smoke, drink, and gamble away from the pestering presence of matchmaking women.

Jamie pressed her masked face to the crack of the open door. The men had discarded their own masks in the comfort and privacy of the room, so she was able to quickly see that Mike wasn't among them. She was sort of hoping he'd be in there. At least there he couldn't be dancing with some other girl. *Jamie, you are a jealous idiot.*

With two of Marilyn's ideas down and the hour growing late, the two decided to split up to find the final gentleman.

"He was speaking with the hostess last I saw him," Marilyn told Jamie in the quiet of the hallway outside the card room. "Dressed all in black with a deep red mask. He was the height of Lord Dunnington, as I recollect."

"Thank you, Marilyn. I really appreciate this."

She smiled at Jamie a little sadly. "I believe that my debt to you goes farther than helping you locate a gentleman in a crowded ballroom. I shall take the right side. You search the left."

Jamie nodded, gave her a quick hug, and wandered off in search of Mike.

Jamie hadn't exactly realized how much safety Marilyn's presence had lent her until she wandered through the ballroom on her own. She should probably have waited outside for Mrs. K. Men that had only leered before felt confident enough to proposition her and let their hands casually brush against her body. When she'd stomped the third man's toe, some of them started to get the message and gave her a wide berth. The lessons continued until she'd made a complete circle around the perimeter of the large room.

She flopped down on a bench beside a potted palm. No sign of the man in black with a red mask. No conversation about the dashing Lord Dunnington. Where the hell was Mike? He'd said he would be here. Had Mrs. K already found him? Were they looking for her?

But more important, what if she didn't get the chance to say good-bye?

Her heart locked in the iron grip of desperate sadness, she stood. She couldn't do this to herself forever. It hurt too goddamn much.

When she made it back around to the balcony doors without sight of him, she slipped outside. The cool night air blessed her cheek, and she tilted her head up to the moon.

"Your protector is inside. You should go to him."

Jamie froze. That was Mike's voice, coming from the ground beneath the balcony.

"Micah, my darling, it was only a foolish misunderstanding. A woman in my position must have security, you know. If you were to renew our acquaintance, then I would have no need for Mr. Waites. Please, do say that you want me as I do you, for we both know that it is true."

Jamie nearly blew her cover when the silence extended for a long moment, fearing that Mike was kissing Collette, but then his voice stopped Jamie from running toward them.

"Collette, there was no misunderstanding. I have no wish to renew our acquaintance. I have not forgotten your betrayal. I merely sought you out to inform you that your actions very nearly gravely wounded a young woman in my care. It will not be tolerated a second time. Now, I must take my leave."

"In your care? You cannot mean that the trollop lives with you?"

Jamie crept closer to the voices, keeping herself hidden

behind another potted palm. Thankfully, the Wentworths had spared no expense on their patio plantings.

Mike lost some of his cool. "She is in my care, and I will not tolerate another attempt to harm her."

Collette lost some of the sugary sweetness in her voice. "Have you forgotten so quickly the last time you flouted Society's dictums? You were ostracized, treated as a pariah. I held you close, ignoring the others who said I'd meet the same fate as your former mistress. Does my sacrifice and love count for nothing? You let this baseborn trollop abide in your home when I was never allowed to darken the door?"

"Your comfort, madam, was short-lived and selfishly done. I regret that I allowed myself the dubious pleasure of your company then. Louisa…" He trailed off, and a lump came into Jamie's throat at the subtle, ragged note in his voice. "Louisa was special to me, and in my grief at her death, I formed an assignation with you. It was a mistake, one that I have paid dearly for and has since been rectified. My relationship with Miss Marten is of no concern to you."

"Can you not see that I was desperate?" Collette's voice was thin with anger. "I had not a farthing to call my own, nothing that you did not provide. What you see as my betrayal was merely a business matter. You must know that letting such a creature live with you will cause a scandal the likes of which you'd never survive. In any case, she cannot please you the way I do." When she composed herself again and groomed her voice into that bedroom purr, Jamie snapped. As she strode down the balcony steps she heard Collette say, "Micah, that baseborn whore will never…"

Jamie snatched a handful of raven-dark hair and yanked Collette away from Mike. The black-haired hussy had been pressing herself up against him like a *Hustler* girl on a pole. Collette flailed her hands, shrieking bloody murder as Jamie slung her to the ground. Jamie bent down to yell into Collette's blue-masked face.

"So, I'm a whore? Really. You don't know anything about me!"

"Let me go, you Bedlamite!" Collette tried to slap her, but Jamie grabbed an arm and twisted it down into the dirt first.

"Not until we get some things straight," Jamie snarled, and plopped down on the woman's chest. Jamie pinned her arms down with her knees. Collette cried out, thrashing her legs, but Jamie had her good. Jamie grabbed Collette's chin and forced her to look into her eyes.

"You listen to me, and you listen good." Mike's hand closed gently on her shoulder, but Jamie shrugged it off without looking back at him. "Mike doesn't want anything to do with you. Not last week, not now, not a month from now. You sold him out, and he doesn't owe you a damn thing."

Collette pursed her lips to spit at Jamie. She dodged it in time, not acknowledging Mike as he moved to stand beside the two women, blocking the view from the balcony.

"Oh, that was so not smart. Mike is a good man, a great man. He's brilliant and gorgeous and way too good for either of us, to be honest. He's trying to court someone who won't give him a flaming case of syph." Jamie pressed Collette harder into the dirt as the woman squirmed. "If you know what's good for you, then you'll back the hell off and let him have his life, okay? That's what I'm doing, and I love the guy! So get the hell out."

Collette glared at Jamie but nodded. Probably because she couldn't breathe with Jamie sitting on her.

"Good."

Jamie stood quickly, moving away from the courtesan before she could grab for Jamie. Collette stood, trying ineffectively to wipe the damp streaks of dirt from the back of her skirt. Glaring at Jamie, she spoke instead to Mike, whose masked face was devoid of emotion.

"If this is the type of woman you prefer, then by all means, Micah, tup your whore. But you'll regret it in the end." With a longing look at Mike and a glare at Jamie, she snarled, "If you do not leave his house immediately, I shall see that you pay for this. Society's bad opinion will mean naught in comparison to what I will see done to you. I do not make idle threats. You have been warned." She limped away toward the front of the dark lawn.

Anger boiled inside Jamie as her chest heaved. She watched Collette go, wishing she'd slugged the bitch instead of sitting on top of her and threatening. It wasn't even close to what she deserved. Too bad electric chairs hadn't been invented yet. *Man, this time is turning me into a bloodthirsty wench.*

A quiet clearing of Mike's throat reminded Jamie that she wasn't alone. Her anger dissipated instantly, hot shame taking its place. So much for not embarrassing Mike. So much for making a beautiful memory to last the rest of her life. Now when she looked back on this night, she'd probably remember the giant lecture that Mike was sure to give her.

Time to face the music. She turned, her breath catching in her throat. Mike had removed his dark red mask and was staring at her with the strangest expression on his face. It wasn't the anger she'd been expecting. Instead, his brows were slightly lifted, his mouth was soft, and his eyes were curiously tender.

Jamie froze. Mike pulled her to the darkened corner beside the balcony, dropping his mask to the ground. Her heart pounded harder with every inch she drew closer, beating like a hummingbird's wings when he stood close enough to touch.

He reached out and removed her mask, lowering it gently from her face. She felt oddly naked when it was gone. There was nothing hiding her from Mike. She'd screamed in his ex-mistress's face that she loved him. She hadn't really planned to reveal that tidbit of info at all, let alone at max volume while pummeling a professional paramour. What would he think of her now? Was he angry, despite the gentle way his palm cupped her cheek? Why was he leaning closer to her?

"Jamie," he whispered softly, then kissed her.

Seventeen

Jamie barely registered the soft thump as her mask hit the earth. Mike pulled her close against him, and she melted, completely boneless. Her arms wound around him, delighting in the feel of his lean muscles beneath his tailored coat.

His tongue traced the line of her lips, teasing her. She parted her lips for him. His tongue entered her mouth, and she moaned. She let him possess her, his mouth, his hands, whatever he wanted. She didn't want to deny him anything.

While he explored her mouth, his hands ran down her back, cupping her ass. He brought her hips into sharp contact with his own, and she nearly cried out at the feeling of him against her lower belly. She cursed the thick layers of clothing that separated them. Heat grew low in her loins, a burning tingle that drove her to grind her hips against his.

He tore his lips from hers and gently guided her under the shadowed edge of the balcony. Before she could completely register their surroundings, he started kissing his way down the bare column of her throat. His teeth grazed the pulse that beat there, and she dug her fingers into his shoulders. *God, his mouth.*

He nibbled at her collarbone, and she threw her head back to give him better access. Her hips were moving now, silently begging for the hard heat that pressed against her.

When his lips traveled downward, to the soft mounds of flesh that rose above her dress's neckline, she thought she'd die. Mike's mouth was on her breasts. He tasted her skin, running his tongue down her cleavage, as low as the dress would allow. His hand moved upward, cupping her breast, thumbing the hard peak through the silky silver material.

"Mike," she whispered hoarsely, hitching her leg up against his hip. She tangled her hand in his hair, trying to keep him close to her. "Oh God, Mike…"

Her breath exited her lungs in a squeak when his hand delved into her bodice, lifting her left breast free of the material. Under the soft light of the moon, her nipple looked dark, its usual rosy color muted. Mike pulled back, his gaze captivated by the sight of his hand on her flesh.

"So beautiful," he said, his voice almost a growl. Jamie shivered with anticipation. He flicked her nipple gently with a finger, the peaked point hardening further at his touch. It was so tight now, it was almost painful.

"I want to taste you," he said, bending his head low. His breath blew against the point of her erect nipple as he spoke. "I want to put my mouth on you, Jamie. May I?"

Holy shit. In answer, she pulled his head down farther, eliminating the last inch that separated his lips from her breast.

She couldn't stop the soft cry that escaped her when his mouth captured the aching tip of her breast. He sucked, licked, tasted, nipped, and almost drove her to the brink of insanity with his talented tongue. Her knees went liquid, and only the desperate clinging of her hands on his shoulders kept her upright.

He pressed a soft kiss to the hardened bud and lifted his head. He reached for the right side, fingers running along the neckline of her gown, gently dipping past the fabric to free her other breast, when loud voices suddenly sounded from the balcony. A burst of laughter came, and footsteps thumped just above their heads.

With a deep sigh that sounded suspiciously like regret, he helped her fix the front of her dress. He grabbed both their masks from the damp ground and then took her hand.

"Where are we going?" she whispered as he started walking toward the front of the house.

"Home," he said over his shoulder, causing a little flip in her heart. "We must speak privately."

After locating Mrs. K and sending the other carriage back home, Mike helped them into the shiny black conveyance with the Dunnington crest on the side. Jamie looked over her shoulder to the side of the manor house, and she could have sworn that she saw a woman's pale face with dark curls surrounding it, watching from the veranda. Before Jamie could be certain of who it was, the face disappeared behind a column. She ignored the shiver that went down her spine and enjoyed Mike's oddly comforting proximity. He sat next to her, cradling her hand, staring into her eyes. Neither of them said a word. With Mrs. K right there, Jamie didn't know what to say. Anything she could think of immediately got lost in the delicious feeling of his thumb rubbing against her knuckles.

The bumpy ride was over with too quickly. He helped her down from the carriage and escorted her through the door that Thornton held open for them.

"That will be all, Thornton. You may retire for the evening." Mike dismissed the butler curtly. The old man's face registered zero surprise at the order.

"Yes, my lord." After a quick bow, the elderly gentleman disappeared down the hall, followed by a beaming Mrs. K. Before Jamie could make a comment about the high-handed way he'd gotten rid of Thornton, Mike shuffled her into the front sitting room, closing the door behind them.

Her mouth dropped open in surprise, but Mike only used that to his advantage as well. He kissed her wildly, both hands cupping her face, his tongue exploring her mouth.

She took advantage of their privacy and let her hands run underneath his jacket, her fingers tingling at the warmth of his body. She let them trail lower, settling on his hips. He pushed them into her, and she moaned softly at the thought of his erection again. *Too many damn clothes…*

As if he read her mind, he stopped kissing her long enough to turn her around. Cursing the long row of buttons at her back, he dealt with them rather quickly. She tried not to imagine how much practice he'd had.

"Jamie," he said roughly as he revealed the stays and petticoats beneath her dress. "You are so lovely."

He kissed the nape of her neck, his breath gently blowing the small curls at her hairline. She leaned back into him, feeling suddenly beautiful and desirable. He pushed the shoulders of her gown down, and she pulled her arms through the short sleeves, letting the bodice fall. His hands wandered upward, reaching in front to lift her breasts free of her stays. Their only cover now was her thin shift.

Her breath hissed out slowly as he palmed her flesh,

then softly rolled the nipples between his strong fingers. She pressed her ass back into him, wanting to be closer to him. She could never be close enough to Mike.

"Your body feels so exquisite," he said, his breath blowing hot against the skin of her shoulder. "You have bewitched me."

She laughed a little at that, twisting her hips slightly. "Well, thanks, but I've never been great at that nose wiggle. I'd prefer to think that we're really compatible."

With a sigh, he let his hands fall away from her breasts. He stepped backward, and a chill went through her, one that was only partway due to the loss of his body heat.

"What's wrong?" She turned, trying to fight the urge to cross her arms in front of her breasts.

His brows were drawn in consternation but that look in his eyes warmed her blood again. Whatever he was thinking now, he still wanted her.

"I am sorry, Miss Marten. I should not have taken such liberties with your person." He stepped closer, lifting her bodice to help her put it back on. She grabbed his hand, stopping him.

"Wait just a minute, sir. That was mutual, consensual, and downright delicious. No apologies for that. Well, except maybe for stopping it."

He sighed heavily, closing his eyes. His voice was rough when he spoke again.

"You do not know what you say. It would mean ruination."

She shook her head, one corner of her mouth crooking up. "Mike, I'm not from here. I can't be 'ruined.'"

His eyes turned dark as he grabbed both her arms. "You are here now, Jamie. And whatever force has brought you here has not seen fit to take you back, has it?"

She looked down, unwilling to let him see the guilt on

her face. She hadn't told him about Mrs. Knightsbridge's plan or her powerful relative. He didn't know that she was still there because of him.

He placed a finger beneath her chin, raising it so she was forced to look into his eyes.

"I would treat you with care. Is that difficult to fathom? That I would care enough for you to treat you with respect?"

"You…" She trailed off, biting her lip. After swallowing hard, she continued, "You care for me?"

When he didn't answer right away, she got worried. Maybe she shouldn't have asked him. Maybe she was pushing him too fast. Maybe she was delusional and imagined that this had happened.

After four heartbeats, he spoke.

"I care for you deeply. As deeply as I've cared for anyone."

"Even Louisa?"

He winced a little at the mention of her name, and Jamie felt like a bitch for bringing up the ghost from his past.

"Louisa was my first lover. I was quite taken with her. When she died—" He shook his head, jaw tight. "When she died, I blamed myself."

"But it wasn't your fault," Jamie said quickly, putting a hand on his arm to soothe him. "It sounded like she had a seizure or something. You couldn't have done that."

His eyes flew wide and he stared at her. Whoops. Guess she should have remembered that she wasn't supposed to know anything about that.

"Mrs. Knightsbridge told me. She was trying to help me understand why you're so grumpy all the time."

He gave her a long look, and she started to squirm. "Here. Let's sit down and talk for a minute."

Jamie turned her back to him and shoved her arms back through the sleeves of her gown. If they were going to have serious conversations, she wanted to be more clothed. Without the buttons fastened behind her, she had to press a hand to the neck of her dress to keep it upright. Small price to pay for being covered during this conversation.

She sat next to Mike, being careful to keep her bodice in place.

He kept his eyes locked on her face when he said, "You said you love me."

Caught. Skewered like a frog on a pole. Hand in the cookie jar. Red-handed, come 'n' get her.

"Yes," she said, looking into her lap. "I really think I do."

A finger beneath her chin lifted it, forcing her to meet his gaze. "Do not be ashamed of it, Jamie," he whispered. "Love is a wondrous thing."

"Not when it's impossible." Her voice broke. She stood to put some distance between them, shoving the sleeve of her gown back up to her shoulder as it fell. "You said it yourself. Noblemen can't marry for love. And I'm not willing to stand by while you marry some other woman because she's got the right pedigree to be a countess." She stood by the fireplace, keeping her back to Mike.

Big, warm hands cupped her upper arms, and it was all she could do to stop herself from leaning back into him.

"I was planning to propose to Miss Lyons tomorrow."

"I know."

Her admission silenced him for a few moments. When he spoke again, he stepped even closer, cradling her body in the heat of his own.

"I will postpone that. I cannot plan nuptials with another woman, not now. Not until things are more settled between us if it comes to that."

She let her eyes flutter closed, hoping he couldn't tell exactly how relieved she was. When he pulled her back, closer to him, she didn't resist.

The soft kiss he laid on her neck gave her shivers.

"It is late. Permit me to escort you to your room."

She tried not to let it show how much that statement disappointed her. Keeping her bodice up with one hand, she slipped the other through the crook in Mike's arm when he offered. They ascended the stairs together, and she tried to tell herself it was a good thing that they were going to be sleeping in separate beds. They were still from opposite ends of the timeline. Not a damn thing was different than it had been three hours ago. Well, except for the fact that Mike now knew she loved him. She should still probably disappear in the morning...

When they reached her bedroom, Mike pulled her into his arms. Lowering his head, he kissed her thoroughly, passionately. Their lips and tongues melded together. She savored the kiss, letting herself fall into the swirls of desire that capsized her brain.

"Good night, Jamie," he whispered when he lifted his head. He pressed a kiss against her forehead. "We will speak more tomorrow."

She nodded numbly and entered her bedroom. When the door shut softly behind her, she slumped against it.

What the bloody hell do I do now?

❧

He stood with his palm pressed against her bedchamber door. *What the bloody hell do I do now?*

She'd appeared from nowhere, attacking Collette like an avenging angel coated in spun-silver. She'd handled her with no help from him, proving that she was no wilting flower or simpering miss. She'd stated, rather loudly, that she loved him. Their encounter beneath the balcony, her soft flesh against his skin, the way her breasts had looked in the dim moonlight, dusky nipple puckered, ready for his lips…He could enter her chamber right this moment, help her out of that gown, see all of her lying there, naked to his gaze, arms up, inviting him with a smile…

His palm slid down the door, and he stepped backward. He was undone. He was, quite simply, undone.

He entered his bedchamber and began removing his evening clothes slowly, methodically, trying to make sense of the tightness in his chest and the heat in his blood. When he was nude, he turned and caught sight of his form in the bureau's mirror.

He was a man. Only a man. And when Jamie had said she loved him, something inside his brain had turned, shifting his entire world. He'd been as unable to stop touching her as he'd been to transport himself to her time. Her body had drawn his as if magnetized.

With a groan, he stroked his length. She was so beautiful. Her body was exquisite, and the feelings she roused in him…

He dropped his hand. He'd not spill his seed in his hand like a callow youth. Defiling the thought of her in such a way was not the mark of a gentleman.

Stretching atop his bedcovers, he stared at the ceiling, wondering what the morrow would bring. His definite plans suddenly seemed diffuse as a cloud. It was a long time before sleep claimed him, and even then, he did not rest.

Eighteen

MURIEL DIDN'T COMMENT ON THE FACT THAT JAMIE'S buttons were already undone when the maid came up to help her dress for bed. Muriel had to know something was up though, even if Mrs. K hadn't spilled the beans. Jamie hadn't grown any extra arms to help do it herself, after all.

It wasn't until later, when Jamie was curled up next to Baron in bed, that she realized Mike hadn't said he loved her too.

She sat upright, staring at the flickering light in the fireplace. He hadn't said he loved her. Did he? Or was he being polite by postponing his engagement to Felicity until he could prove to her that they'd never work out? If that was his game, then why'd he kiss her?

Ugh. She flopped back onto her pillows, causing Baron to raise his head in alarm. Why were things so damn complicated?

Well, one thing was certain. She couldn't leave now. She had to find out if Mike loved her too, if he was changing his mind about that whole can't-marry-for-love thing. If Mrs. K kept her promise and had Wilhelmina reopen the portal, she wouldn't go through it, not yet. Mrs. K would probably be over the moon about the whole thing anyway. Meddling busybody of a matchmaker.

Baron got tired of her tossing and turning. She let him out when he sat at the door and whined. She didn't blame him. She wouldn't want to be with her confused and sleepless self either if she had a choice.

When the sun finally came up, she got cleaned up and dressed as well as she could on her own. She couldn't wait for Muriel. She had to get out of this room. The lemon-yellow walls were crushing her. She needed room to breathe, to think, to make some decisions. A plan of action, a way to tear down Mike's defenses and see how he really felt about her. She needed a strategy.

You don't run into a big fight, spells blazing, after all, she thought as she trotted quickly down the stairs. *You send in your tank first. Someone to draw the enemy's fire, their focus. That way the rest of your party can chip away at the boss's defenses without being slaughtered so quickly.*

She had a fairly good idea of exactly who her tank would be. He was strong, sweet, and, above all, Mike was crazy about him.

Jamie found Baron in the kitchen, begging Jean Philippe for scraps.

She lured the hound into Mike's office with a small chunk of ham. She fed him tiny bits at a time, trying to keep him calm and quiet. If this was going to work, then Baron would have to be okay staying in here with her and Mike while they talked. If her tank walked, she was done for.

Fortunately, Mike rose early too. Jamie heard him talking to the butler as he walked down the hallway. He stopped at his open office door and looked at her curiously.

"Hey," she said, smiling. Baron, bless his bony little heart, trotted right up to Mike for attention. Mike's face broke into a smile as he rubbed the hound's silky ears.

"Hello there, good lad." Mike looked at her without stopping his petting. "Good morning, Miss Marten. I trust you slept well?"

"Yeah, it was okay." She'd slept well at some point in her life, and he hadn't been specific about which night. "I wanted to talk to you, if you've got time."

He stood, pursed his lips, and nodded. She sat in the chair across from his desk.

"Last night," she began, then her throat closed off. She coughed to clear it, bit her lip, and continued, "Last night, you might have heard me tell Collette that I... that I..." Damn frogs. Always lodged in her throat at the worst possible moment.

Baron picked that moment to trot away from his master, disappearing into the hallway. "You are such a crap tank, Baron," she muttered under her breath.

"I beg your pardon?" Mike said in a confused voice.

"No, that was my brain. In my head. Not for out loud." She wanted to smack herself in the forehead to shake the thoughts loose. "Let me start again."

Mike crossed the room and took the seat next to her. She wasn't sure if she preferred that to him sitting behind that giant desk or not.

"Please, continue, Miss Marten."

She nodded, glad that his tone was patient and kind. She didn't know if she'd be able to take proud asshole Mike this morning or not.

"Last night, I told Collette that I loved you."

The words came out rushed and squished together. She could almost smell her own terror in the air. She continued quickly, deathly afraid she would lose her cool.

"I was wondering if you had any idea how you felt about me in return. I'm not asking if you love me, because we haven't known each other all that long, and I've done tons of stupid things that you should probably hate me for, but since I'm living here and you postponed your engagement for me, well, not really for me but because of me, anyway, I was wondering if you maybe felt something for me?"

Jamie squeezed her eyes shut, wishing a hole would open in the floor and swallow her up.

When long seconds went by with no reply, she peeked through one slitted lid at Mike.

He stared at her, his lips barely parted. Was that shock? Surprise? Was he wondering how to let her down gently?

"Just say something," she blurted out.

"Miss Marten." He stopped, cleared his throat. "Jamie."

When he gently took her hand, she stopped breathing and opened her eyes. He shook his head, his forehead furrowed slightly.

"Jamie, I do not know what to say. There is much, much that I would say, but I have not the words. You have…"

He trailed off. Her heart stuttered. "I have what?"

"You have made me think…differently. The truths that I have held as sacred for years are now being called into question. I do not know…I do not know."

"You don't know what?" She slapped her hand down on the desk. "Spit it out, for chrissakes!"

He let out a confused chuckle. "I do not know anything anymore. Louisa…I thought I loved Louisa. She was very special to me. When she became ill…I swore that I would never feel that way about a woman again." His eyes became desperate, his shoulders tense. "But since I have known you, as maddening, irreverent, and outspoken as you are, I have realized I did not love Louisa as I had thought I did. Last night, beneath the balcony…" He trailed off again. She bit her lip when he continued, "I cannot be without you, Jamie."

"So," she drew the word out. "Where does that leave us?"

He shook his head again, clasping her hand tightly. "I do not know."

"Well." She looked down at their twined fingers. "Why don't we try to find out?"

He sighed. "There is much to consider. The earldom, my responsibilities, the duties to my name…"

She waved her free hand in the air. "Mike, listen. Let's forget about all the reasons we shouldn't be doing this for a while, okay? Let's just be." She reached up and pushed a wayward curl from his forehead. His hair was so soft, almost baby fine.

He let his eyelids slide closed. Feeling slightly bolder at his unspoken acceptance, she trailed her palm down his cheek. It was smooth with the feel of a fresh shave. She traced the cleft in his chin with a finger, smiling to herself when she touched the lace at his throat.

"Jamie," he whispered, slitting his eyes barely open. He leaned toward her, and she met him halfway.

When their lips met this time, it was new, delicious, and different. There was none of the surprise that the rest of their kisses had carried. This one was quieter, sweeter, and somehow more passionate for its expectedness.

When he leaned back, severing their contact, she sighed.

"Time. We will give this time, if you are amenable." He wasn't smiling, but he didn't look pissed either. His eyes were soft, and his mouth was a straight line.

"I think we can do that," she said slowly.

"Good." He stood and paced agitatedly in front of the

fireplace. He looked like there were fire ants crawling under his skin.

After watching him for a few seconds, she stood. He clearly needed some time alone to think some things through.

"I'll leave you alone," she said quietly, and turned to go. A warm hand on her arm stopped her.

"Jamie." His voice was pained, and his eyes were troubled. "I…"

She smiled at him, putting her hand against his cheek. "It's okay, Mike, really. I understand. Take your time. I'll be here."

A small half smile crept over his face, and this time when she turned to go, he didn't stop her.

She passed Baron in the hallway. The big gray dog was gnawing on a hambone he'd evidently suckered out of Jean Philippe.

"Traitor," she hissed at the dog, but without any real venom. She didn't blame him. If she could have run away from that awkward conversation, she would have too.

She found herself heading into the music room, sinking down onto the bench, and allowing her troubled fingers to find a tune.

So Mike cared for her. Not loved. Cared for. Deeply cared for, but not loved. What did that mean for them? For her?

Time. Give it time, Jamie.

As luck would have it, she ran into Mrs. Knightsbridge in the hallway outside of the Lemon Room. The housekeeper took one look at Jamie's face and hustled her into the privacy of the yellow bedchamber.

"Good heavens, dearie, whatever is the matter?" Mrs. K set her armload of linens down beside Jamie's prone body where she lay flopped on the bed.

"Okay. Say there's this woman. And she's in love with the complete wrong guy. The guy is interested in her, but they're completely wrong for each other in every single way. And then, the guy's ex-girlfriend finds out something about the woman and the guy that might kill whatever chance they might have had at a relationship that was probably doomed in the first place. What would that woman do?"

Mrs. K's face was one great big giant question mark.

Jamie sat up with a sigh. "I love Mike. He said he 'cares deeply'"—she made air quotes—"for me. At the ball last night, he might have let slip that I was living here. Collette said that if I didn't move out she'd make me pay. It sounded like she'd tell all of society about it."

"Mercy," Mrs. K whispered. Her round face went Clorox white.

"Yeah." Jamie tried to swallow the knot growing in her throat. "What do I do?"

After a moment or two of stunned silence, the house-keeper started pacing by the trunk at the end of her bed. "Well, Miss Jamie, there is but one thing to do."

"What's that? Go forward in time, grab Drew Barrymore, and tell her to take over for me?"

The housekeeper didn't even bother to acknowl-edge her smart-assedness. She turned to Jamie, drew herself up to her full height of five feet one inch, and looked straight into Jamie's eyes as she said, "You must seduce him."

Nineteen

STUNNED SILENCE WAS ALL JAMIE COULD MUSTER FOR several long moments. She stared at Mrs. K, trying to see the punch line, but the woman seemed to be completely serious. Out of all the things that Jamie had ever thought she'd hear coming out of Mrs. K's mouth, seduction was definitely not on the list.

"What the hell are you talking about?"

Mrs. K sat next to Jamie, and her voice took on a motherly tone. "Miss Jamie, you must understand. This is for his lordship's own well-being. Without our intervention, he will never discover the wonders of true love. If you seduce him, then he will do the right thing, the only honorable thing, and wed you. Now, I trust you are a virgin?"

"Wait just a fricking minute!" Jamie rocketed to her feet. "I am not going to force Mike into bed or into a relationship with me. I wouldn't be any better than that bitch Collette if I did that."

Mrs. K, bless her heart, had the sense to look a little ashamed. "I can understand your reluctance. But what are we to do otherwise?"

Jamie crossed her arms over her bodice and chewed

her lip thoughtfully. Mrs. K was right. This wasn't an easy problem to solve. How could she help Mike make up his mind about her? And what the hell would they do if he decided that he loved her back? She certainly didn't want to spend the rest of her life without a shower, that was for certain.

"I really don't know. Maybe we should lay low for a while, give it more time," Jamie said to the housekeeper. She looked up at Jamie like she'd stolen her favorite sewing needles. "Seriously. I'll stick around here, and hopefully Collette won't make good on her threat. Mike needs some time to figure some things out. And honestly, I do too."

Mrs. K shook her head. "So be it." She gathered up her armload of linen and turned to leave. "I do not agree with your method, Miss Jamie. I must, in all fairness, tell you that I intend to forward his lordship's progress by whatever means necessary."

Jamie sank down on the bed, flopping against the cream-colored pillows. "Be my guest, Mrs. K. If you can help him make up his mind about stuff, then I can get home sooner."

Jamie realized, as Mrs. K let the door softly click shut behind her, that was probably about the dumbest thing she ever could have done. Jamie had basically handed a relationship junkie a loaded syringe.

When Muriel came upstairs to dress Jamie for dinner, she figured out that the loaded syringe on the loose was the least of her worries.

Jamie pegged the thin girl with an open-mouthed stare.

"What do you mean Mike's here for dinner? He's only eaten dinner with me once in the whole time I've been here! What would make him stay here tonight?"

Muriel shook her head and held out a cream-colored

silk gown for Jamie to put on. "Mrs. K didn't see fit to let me know, miss. She said to make sure you were looking your finest. Now, please, allow me to do up the buttons."

Shaking her head incredulously, Jamie turned and allowed Muriel to work. *Man.* When Mrs. K made up her mind about something, she really went balls to the wall. It was sort of inspiring, actually. If she believed in Jamie and Mike that strongly, maybe there was something worth chasing after all.

Muriel finished up Jamie's buttons and seated her by the dressing table so the maid could do her hair. Jamie watched her in the mirror as she worked. Tonight, she'd settled on piling the hair in loose curls around the crown of Jamie's head, leaving a few tendrils to curl temptingly down the length of her neck.

Muriel produced a small glass vial from her apron and removed the stopper. With a gentle finger, she applied a tiny amount of the substance to the nape of Jamie's neck, her wrists, and behind her ears.

"What's that?"

"It's tincture of roses, miss. It will make you smell like a beautiful garden. His lordship won't be able to resist."

Jamie rolled her eyes and turned to face the maid. "Mur, does everybody in this house know about Mike's and my, um, interest in each other?"

At her nod, Jamie wished she could melt into the floor. Jean Philippe, the kitchen maids, Thornton, George the footman, even the stableboys knew she had a crush on the earl? Oh Lord. This was worse than the time she'd accidentally put her sweatpants on inside-out before going to the gym. That had been the end of her brief foray into physical fitness. No less embarrassing than this particular moment, though. Too bad she couldn't borrow a disappearance spell from Wilhelmina.

When Muriel left her, Jamie had a couple of minutes before dinnertime. She made her way down the hallway. Before she could reach the staircase, she stopped at the open door of Mike's room.

A faint squeak drew her attention.

Gingerly, she poked her head through the door. The bedclothes were rumpled, and a large, bony body was curled up in the center of them. Baron's yawn had apparently been what she'd heard because he smacked his lips a couple of times, gave her a look, and went back to sleep.

She started to back out of the room, but then the bureau in the corner caught her eye.

Had Mrs. K talked to Wilhelmina again? Or was the portal to her time still open?

Drawn by curiosity, she made her way across the dimly lit room to the tall bureau. The mirrors glinted in the dying rays of the sun that shone weakly through the window. She stood before the mahogany wood, arguing with herself.

Should she test the mirror? What if the portal was open, and it sucked her through? Could she take that chance? She'd never be able to return again if she did.

But what could it hurt, just to see?

Her hand lifted slowly, almost of its own volition. She watched her trembling fingers as they moved closer to the glass. Closer. Only a couple of inches away. In another heartbeat, she'd be touching the glass. Would it be solid, or would it pull her through again?

A high-pitched whine broke her trance. She whirled around. Baron had sat up on the bed, large eyes worried.

She crossed over to the hound, sat beside him on the bed, and hugged the hot, bony body.

"It's okay, boy," she said, her voice shaking slightly. "I'm not going anywhere. Not yet."

As if satisfied with her promise, he gave her a gentle kiss on the nose before lying back down.

With a sigh, she stood and knocked blue-gray hairs from her silk gown. She didn't look at the bureau again as she left the room. That had been a stupid thing to do.

When she got to the sitting room, only Thornton, the butler, was there. He smiled when he saw her and ladled a pink concoction from a cut-crystal bowl into a glass. Handing it to her, he said, "Miss Marten. His lordship will be down momentarily. In the interim, he asks that you have a drink of his special punch. An old Axelby family recipe."

Jamie wasn't fooled by the old man's innocent smile for one second. Pegging him with her best bullshit-detector stare, she said, "Yeah, right. Mrs. Knightsbridge made this punch, didn't she?"

The butler drew himself upright, looking offended. "Not at all, Miss Marten. I believe that Mrs. Knightsbridge has had the evening off. His lordship prepared this and bade me give it you when you arrived."

The old man was staring her straight in the eye. His body was stiff, not moving a bit. It was hard to tell if he was standing that way because he was offended at her question, lying, or because he was a starched-up old butler. After a few seconds, when he didn't move, break his gaze, or collapse in tears, Jamie sighed.

"Okay." She took the glass he offered. If anyone was going to slip her a mickey, it wasn't going to be sweet old Thornton.

He smiled and bowed. "Please enjoy, Miss Marten."

"I'm sure I will." She couldn't help smiling back. When he left the room, she took a suspicious sniff of the glass. It smelled like lemons, sugar, and some kind of liquor.

"Bottoms up," she muttered, and took a swig.

It was like an electric lemonade with rosemary, mint, and some fucking killer gin. THIS was a cocktail. The Axelbys apparently knew their way around a bar.

"*Slainté*," she toasted the closed door behind Thornton, and downed the rest of the drink. Wow. Talk about liquid courage.

By the time Mike entered the room, she was pleasantly warm inside. She was working on her fourth drink, and the tips of her fingers were going a little, well, numb.

"Heya, Mikey!" She tossed back the rest of her cocktail and set the glass down on the table beside her with a solid thunk. Gosh, Mike had probably had a little too much Axelby punch too. He wasn't walking too straight. He weaved back and forth as he crossed the room toward her. She giggled at the sight.

"Good evening, Miss Marten." His eyes were bright as he sat beside her on the settee. She tried to check his pupils to see if they were dilated, but his head wobbled around too much for her to see clearly.

"Nice of you to have me for dinner. Whoops. Invite me to dinner, anyway. Or have dinner with me. Whatever."

Her loss of the English language didn't seem to bother Mike. "My pleasure. Shall we go in?"

"I'd love to."

Well, she would have loved to if that damn cocktail hadn't put gin where her kneecaps should be. Her first two attempts to rise failed miserably. Fortunately, Mike seemed to be a bit more sober than she was. He helped her to her feet, steadying her when she would have pitched forward too far.

"Thanks, Mikey." She grinned. Impulsively, she threw her arms around him, pressing her face into his black evening jacket. "God, you smell good. Did you use some of Mur's rose tincture too?"

Mike's laugh rumbled through her cheek, and she snuggled against the soft vibrations. "Jamie, dearling, I do believe you are foxed."

She yanked back, nearly giving herself whiplash in the process. "No! Well, maybe." She checked her fingers, tapping them against each other. Nothing. She dug her middle fingernail into her thumb. Bupkes. She bit her thumb. No pain. *Oh shit.*

"Yeah, I might be drunk. Sorry." She looked up at him, her forehead wrinkling as she frowned.

"Whatever have you been imbibing?"

She swatted at him, missing the arm she'd been aiming for completely. "It's all your fault. Thornton told me about the punch. Family recipe, huh? That shit's dangerous."

Mike shook his head at her. "You are talking nonsense now. Best to get you to bed."

A mischievous grin spread across her face, and she draped her arms around Mike's neck. "Was that your plan? Get me into bed? You didn't need to get me drunk to do that."

She pressed her lips against his then. She wasn't sure if his mouth had been open because he was about to say something else, or if he was really into the idea of kissing her. At that point, she really didn't give a shit. Her libido had been working overtime since she'd figured out how she felt about Mike, and this alcohol-hazed make-out session was just what the hormones ordered.

Mike's arms wrapped around her, his hands resting lightly on her hips. He responded to the bold forays of her tongue with passion. She moaned deep in her throat at the feeling of his tongue tasting the depths of her mouth. God, he was such an incredible kisser.

Feeling even bolder, she rubbed along his back, down

to his ass. She pulled the firm muscles closer to her, craving the hard heat that she knew was between them. There was a good reason she despised these damn petticoats, and by gum, she was going to feel him tonight.

When he pulled his mouth from hers, she took advantage of the opportunity. She pressed her lips along his smooth jaw, kissing her way down to the cleft in his chin, then fumbling with the buttons of his waistcoat.

"Jamie," he hissed in a whisper. "Whatever are you doing?"

"Getting you naked," she said to his chest. "What's up with these damn buttons?"

He grabbed her hands, stilling them. "No. You mustn't…"

"Don't keep telling me what to do!" She blew up at him, her frustrated lust and drunk brain obliterating whatever filter she had left. "You've been wanting me for a while. I want you too. You know I love you, so what's keeping us from doing what people do?"

Mike looked at her for the longest time without saying a word. Her insides grew cold.

"Forget it." She pulled free from his grasp and turned to head out of the room, doing her damnedest to keep from wobbling.

"Jamie, wait."

She ignored him, focusing instead on trying to finish her exit without walking into anything. It was damn difficult, considering the floor kept moving on her.

"Jamie!"

She'd thought she'd been moving pretty quickly, but Mike caught her anyway. She tried not to notice how good his body felt pressed against the length of her back.

"What?"

His lips pressed to the column of her neck, giving her

shivers. She tilted her head, lost in the sensation of his light, nipping kisses against the sensitive skin.

"I will accompany you to your room, if you wish. Only give me a moment." His breath blew against her neck as he spoke.

"Okay," she breathed.

He led her to the doorjamb, placing her hand on it to keep her steady. She closed her eyes while he was gone. Were they really going to do this?

"Jamie?"

She fluttered her eyes open. Wow, that was fast. "Hey," she breathed, smiling like an idiot.

She let out a squeak as Mike scooped her up into his arms. "This may be safer than allowing you to walk up the stairs."

"Probably." She giggled and wrapped her arms around his neck as they ascended to the second floor. He was so strong. He made her feel light and delicate and all womanly and stuff. God, he was handsome.

When they reached her bedroom, he let her down to stand on her own.

"Are we, I mean, do you want to come inside? Get comfortable?" Suddenly awkward, she wasn't sure what to do next.

He shook his head with a sad smile, his hand hot against the small of her back. "It would be wrong of me to take advantage of you in this way. You are foxed. A gentleman cannot…"

"Fuck the gentleman," she growled, and kissed him again.

He pulled away this time, not giving in to her demands.

Hot shame took the place of the bubbling lust in her belly. She looked down at the floor, eyes curiously filled with tears.

"Sorry," she whispered. She turned to go into her

bedroom, but her foot caught on her long skirt and she fell against him.

"Careful," he said quietly, helping her regain her footing. She shrugged free of his gentle grip.

"I'm fine. Go off to your mistress or whatever. I'll be gone tomorrow."

When she would have shut the door in his face, he stopped her. His body was tense, face dark as he said, "You will do no such thing, Jamie Marten. Call Muriel. Once you have changed into your nightclothes, I will meet you in my bedchamber."

Twenty

MIKE HAD TO SHUT THE DOOR FOR HER. JAMIE WAS TOO stunned to do it for herself.

His words had the effect of an ice-cold shower on her brain—still fuzzy but a helluva lot clearer than it had been before. Holy shit. Were they really going to do this?

Jamie yanked on the bell cord a little harder than necessary. Muriel entered the room only moments later at a dead run.

"Whatever is wrong, miss? Are you ill?"

"Yes. No. Not ill. Tipsy. Well, drunk. Seriously. Not kidding. And sorry. Can you help me change?"

Muriel's pale-blue eyes went round at Jamie's response, but she came forward and started undoing the buttons anyway. Jamie caught sight of Muriel's face in the mirror and guilt gnawed at her when the maid pulled the pins from her hair. Muriel had done such a great job on it, and she hadn't even given Mike a chance to look at it before she got shitfaced.

Once Muriel had loosened all the layers enough so Jamie could take over, Jamie shooed her from the room. Muriel didn't need to see the last-minute cleansing session.

Jamie had had her daily bath, but she hadn't felt clean

enough in weeks. She used the chilly water in the basin and a clean cloth, trying her best to scrub any lingering offensive odors away. She didn't wash away Muriel's special perfume though. She liked it.

She'd contemplated having Mrs. K borrow Mike's razor so she could shave her legs, but once she'd learned it was a straight razor, she'd given up. Knowing her luck, she'd go all Sweeney Todd on herself accidentally.

Jamie stood naked in front of the mirror, turning this way and that, nerves chomping at her confidence and draining the comforting haze of alcohol away.

She'd put on a little weight since she'd been there. Jean Philippe definitely cooked better than she was used to. Her hair looked good, a tumble of soft curls down her back, but her highlights had started growing out a bit. Dark roots showed at her crown.

Her legs weren't smooth and hairless as she liked them to be. The first thing she was going to do when she got back home was invest in some laser hair removal. She grimaced as she realized she wasn't beautiful like Collette was. The black-haired beauty probably looked like a perfect porn star when she was naked. Jamie sighed in disappointment and turned away from the mirror. Either Mike would be interested or not. He'd want her or not. He'd love her or not. And there wasn't a damn thing she could do to influence any of those decisions.

She slipped the nightgown over her head, pulled on a robe, fluffed out her hair, practiced an alluring smile, and headed out of her bedroom to Mike's chamber. *Here goes nothing. Or everything. Whichever.*

Her soft knock on Mike's door was met by his voice calling, "Enter."

She laughed nervously as she opened the door. "You sound like Captain Picard when you say that."

"Who?" He crooked a brow at her and rose from his seat by the fireplace. He'd removed his jacket, waistcoat, boots, and cravat. He looked much more comfortable in his stockinged feet, shirt, and breeches. There was no sign of the hound who'd been snoozing on the bed before dinner.

Jamie shook her head. "Nobody." She walked over to him, trying her best to control the rampaging circus poodles in her stomach.

"Please, have a seat." He gestured to the chair next to him.

"Okay."

She sat. He sat. They stared at each other. He cleared his throat. She tucked a curl behind her ear.

He smiled. "Allow me to pour you a drink."

Her jaw dropped, and she couldn't stop the snort of laughter that escaped her as he cracked up.

"You…you cretin! That's not funny!"

He wiped his eyes. "My apologies, Miss Marten. It seemed to help lighten the mood, however."

She poked at his shoulder. "Yeah, it did that. But I think I'm going to stay away from the Axelby punch from now on if that's okay. Where'd you get that recipe, anyway?"

He cocked his head to the side, not unlike Baron did when he heard an odd noise. "Axelby punch?"

"Yeah, the pink stuff I was drinking. Thornton told me you made it for me. Or was that a secret that I blew?"

Mike's forehead furrowed. "No, it is not. To my knowledge, no one in my family has ever had a punch recipe. Pink, did you say? Mrs. Knightsbridge used to be fond of a sort of punch that was that color, as I recall."

She narrowed her eyes at the bedroom door. "Ooh, that Mrs. K is crafty. She put the butler up to doing her dirty work. Well played, adversary, well played."

"What?"

Jamie shook her head at Mike. "Don't worry about it. I'll talk to Mrs. K tomorrow."

He leaned forward, cupping her cheek softly. "I should not want you in this way. You are not a Cyprian; you are a lady. I should wed you before lying with you."

She closed her eyes against the tiny flutter of hope that took root in her heart. Back home, that might have meant he loved her. But in this time? No. It wasn't a declaration of anything other than that he was a gentleman. But if she wanted to discover his true feelings, then she'd have to ride this thing out.

"I'm not a lady," she said, raising her hand to cover his. She squeezed it gently, enjoying the feel of his long, lean fingers. "I'm just me. And you're just you. That's all we have to think about right now."

He closed the rest of the distance between them, pressing his lips to hers. The distance from her chair to his proved too far for either of them, and she was eager to stand when he pulled her against him. He shoved the robe from her shoulders, and the fabric pooled at her feet.

The single layer of her cotton nightgown was so much thinner than the dress and petticoats had been. Mike's erection pressed plainly against her belly, burning hot against her. Her hips twisted against his as they kissed.

She wasn't sure who maneuvered who to the bed, but she was thrilled to be lying on it. The heady feeling of Mike's kisses and the alcohol still fogging her brain made it tough to keep on standing.

Mike's body pressed her down into the softness of his bed, their mouths tangling wildly together. His tongue traced the line of her teeth, and his hands roamed her body hungrily.

"Jamie," he rasped when he lifted his head. "If you are not sure about this, then I need to know immediately. I am only a man. I cannot…"

"Shut up and kiss me," she said, pulling his head down to her. *I've always wanted to say that.* She smiled to herself as they got lost again in their kiss.

Their mouths, hands, arms, bodies tangled there on the sheets. Her fingers had gained enough feeling back in them that the buttons on his shirt presented less challenge than before. She managed to get three of them undone before popping the rest as she pulled the shirt free of his shoulders.

He ran his hand up her bare leg, beneath her nightgown. She shuddered at the feel of her hands on his shoulders, of his hand on her thigh, of the wet heat gathering at her core. She arched her back, pressing her breasts against him. The barrier of her nightgown irritated her. She wanted her bare breasts against his chest. She wanted to feel his naked body against hers. She wanted him, all of him.

He knelt between her legs as he shoved his shirt free from his arms. She let her eyes linger on the sight of his lean, strong body. His abdomen was lined with just the right amount of hair dusted across his pecs, thickening in a line that disappeared below his trousers. His broad shoulders trembled, a light sheen of sweat coating them. Backing off the bed, he stood, fingers poised at the waist of his trousers.

"Last chance, Jamie." His voice was rough with passion. "If you do not stop me now, then I will not be able to."

She smiled at him. Rising onto her knees, she lifted the nightgown over her head.

The breath that blew from him at the sight of her nude body was ego candy, pure and simple. His nostrils flared, his eyes went wide, and a hungry look crossed his face.

"I don't want you to stop."

He unfastened his trousers, all the while keeping his eyes trained on her. She leaned back, feeling womanly, sexy, and as desirable as she'd ever felt. When he pulled the tight black pants down, revealing his fully erect shaft, she blew out a breath of her own.

"You are incredible, Mike. Really incredible."

He removed the trousers, leaving them in a heap on the wooden floor. He stood in front of her naked, erect, and completely unashamed. She felt a rush of heat to her core, wetness pooling in her center for him. She'd never been so aroused at the sight of a man before.

Mike came closer, standing at the edge of the bed.

"You are staring at me."

She didn't look away from that delicious object between his legs. "Yes, I am."

He grew harder under her gaze. *Oh Lord.*

Her legs rubbed together in an unconscious bid for relief. Her body was tuned tighter than a guitar string.

He didn't keep her waiting for long. When she held her arms out to him, he knelt on the bed, covering her body with his own.

She'd liked kissing Mike before. With layers and layers of clothes between them, it had nearly ignited her bloomers. But this, as their naked bodies were pressed flush one against the other, this almost made her die on the spot with want.

His hardness pressed against her belly, so hot she thought he'd burn her. Her hands roved the muscled planes of his back, down to his ass, up his lean hips, to his shoulders, and back again. His lips took possession of hers, lips, teeth, and tongue all engaged in pleasuring her.

Her nipples, harder than they'd ever been, pressed against the soft hair on his chest, the tickling sensation beyond erotic to her fevered brain.

Mike rolled them so that Jamie was lying atop him. She lifted her head, lips swollen and tingling from their kiss. With a wicked smile, she straddled him.

"Ah!" A surprised moan escaped her at the feel of the slick head of his shaft rubbing against her wet heat. She ground her hips against him, savoring the feeling.

"Careful there," Mike groaned, his fingers digging into her hips. "I'll not last long that way."

She leaned forward, her hair making a curtain around them. Pressing her lips to his neck, she kissed her way down it like he'd done to her. He tasted so good.

The strong lines of his collarbone, the firm muscles of his pecs, the flat masculine nipples—they all got her attention. She ran her hands all over his body, every place she could reach. He felt so good, his skin smooth, hot, and firm. When she reached behind her body, between his legs to cup him, his hips pushed upward, harder against her. She thought she'd die as his erection ground against her clit.

"Jamie," he rasped.

She fondled him gently, the smooth, slightly cool skin feeling so good to her palm. She was so focused on the hand that was occupied with caressing him that his touch on her breasts took her by surprise.

He captured them both, hands firm but gentle upon her flesh. He flicked both hardened nipples with his thumbs, pinching and rolling them slightly as she moaned.

With regret, she released him and leaned forward to press her hands against Mike's chest.

"What are you doing to me?" she cried softly, clamping her thighs tightly against his hips.

"Only what you asked for," he said, then wrapped an arm around her shoulders to pull her down to him.

It wasn't her mouth he was after this time though.

Bracing her hands on either side of his neck, she supported her body while he positioned her breast above his mouth. He pulled her down, close enough to suck on the tight bud.

His lips played her, teasing, taunting, flicking the sensitive flesh. Her hands fisted in the bedclothes as she fought for control. Her belly was burning, deep down, low, and his skin against the sensitive damp of her core was driving her crazy. His erection pulsed against her sensitive flesh, his mouth went from breast to breast in a ploy designed simply to drive her insane, she was sure. Another few minutes of this and she would burn up in complete and total frustrated lust.

"Please," she begged, twisting the sheets in her grip as Mike bit her nipple. "Please, I want you so badly."

"What do you want?" He blew a breath against the sensitive, wet skin of her breast.

"I want you inside me," she whispered close to his ear.

His hand rubbed down her body, his fingers dipping into the wet sheath between her thighs. A finger parted the folds, and her body responded, welcoming him. His fingers moved within her, wrenching a gasp from deep in her throat. She was ready. She was beyond ready.

He didn't wait to be invited a second time.

He rolled them over again, covering her body with his own. Her legs were still open, and he was poised at the entrance to her body. When she glanced down between them, she saw the dark heat of him, slick from where he'd been pressed against her core.

"Please," she begged again, lifting her hips to him. "Please, I need you."

His hips pushed forward, the head of him barely breaching her. Her nails dug into his shoulders as she fought for control. Her body had turned into a mindless organism, focused on one thing alone. That thing was Mike and the incredible pleasure he was giving her.

He slid forward slowly, so gently, taking his time. He stretched her softly, her body's wetness accommodating him with ease. A centimeter at a time, it seemed, he came deeper into her.

It was too much. She couldn't wait anymore.

With an upward thrust of her hips, he came high and deep into her. She gasped with pleasure, her inner walls pulsing around his thick erection. Her body seemed to grab onto him, not wanting to let him go. She let her arms follow suit, winding around his back.

He groaned against her neck, a rumbling shudder that pulsed into her.

"Don't stop," she said, pushing her hips up again. "It feels so good…"

She had to give it to the man. When a woman told him what felt good, he went for it with gusto.

He started a rhythm, slowly at first, groaning when he nearly left her body to come sliding home once more. He increased his rhythm gradually, looking into her eyes, kissing her, rubbing his hands anywhere and everywhere he could get to.

"Mike," she panted, opening her hips wider. "Oh God, please."

She was burning up. She was on fire. The slick motion of their bodies together, the sweat on both of them, the friction of his chest against her painfully hard nipples—all of it. She was going to explode, and there wasn't a damn thing she could do to stop it.

Her hips strained against his, her body aching for that

peak. He drove deeper into her, higher, their bodies crashing against each other wildly. He got even harder inside her, his shaft thickening, lengthening, filling her deeper and more thoroughly than she ever had been filled before.

Cries ripped from her throat as he pounded into her. She tried to muffle them by biting against his shoulder, but it was too much. He buried his face in her neck, reached beneath her to cup her ass, and thrust his hard length inside her to the hilt.

She exploded.

Bits of her consciousness flew everywhere as her body shuddered, nails digging into his back, pelvis thrusting up against him. She shook all over, her movements becoming uneven, uncontrolled as she crested the wave of pleasure Mike had given her. She throbbed all over, the beat concentrated in the juncture of her thighs, her body rippling around his erection. He held her for a moment when she collapsed. He was still achingly hard inside her.

Jamie let out a mewl of sadness as he pulled out of her. He rose to his knees, fisting his slick, wet erection as his dark eyes looked down on her.

"So beautiful," he groaned. Three strokes, four, and his breath stilled as he spilled himself on her stomach.

She smiled a little as he collapsed on the bed beside her.

Even in bed, such a gentleman. She laughed to herself before snuggling against his shoulder and falling asleep.

Micah stared at the ceiling. A sleeping Jamie was tucked beneath his arm, her head pillowed on his chest. Tangles of blond-streaked hair covered his shoulder. Satiety, content, and sheer panic warred in his brain.

He'd done it. He'd taken her to his bed. She'd been

no virgin, of that he was sure, but it mattered not. He'd surrendered to his baser whims, and for that he must do the honorable thing.

She sighed and hitched a leg over his knees. He couldn't stop the smile that climbed unbidden to his lips. Would it be a burden to take her to wife? He thought not.

Tenderly, he brushed a lock of hair back from her cheek. She was incredible. Clever, strong, tenderhearted, beautiful, bull-headed, and completely insufferable, but so wonderful that she made his teeth ache. He'd never felt this way about a woman before.

Careful not to wake her, he extracted his arm from beneath her head. She rolled onto her back with a soft mewl and fell silent. Her lovely breasts rose and fell evenly with her sleeping breaths.

Micah stood at the foot of the bed and looked down on her. Even now, he grew hard again thinking of her soft curves pressed against him. He shook his head and slipped into his dressing gown. She would need time. He dipped a cloth in the basin of water and gently sat beside her. He'd wash his seed from her and cover her to keep her warm. He'd take care of her now, and she'd want for nothing for the rest of her life. The thought was oddly pleasing to him.

Despite the care he'd taken to warm the cloth, her eyes fluttered open when he gently wiped her belly.

"I am sorry," he whispered. "I did not mean to wake you." When her skin was pink and clean, he rose and put the cloth back beside the basin.

"It's okay," she said, yawning. He smiled at the sight of her crawling, nude, up to the head of his bed to snuggle against his pillows. She breathed in deeply and relaxed with a happy sigh.

Unable to resist the lure of her soft flesh, he sat on

the edge of the bed and caressed her hip gently, lovingly. "Are you awake, dearling? I must speak with you."

"Seriously? You give me the best, most incredible, most mind-blowingest sex of my life and you want to have a long, in-depth discussion afterward?" She peeked at him with one eye over the pillow.

He crooked a brow and curled his lip at her. "Mind-blowingest?"

"It's an expression." She buried her face in his pillow. "C'mon, Mikey, let's talk tomorrow."

Using both hands, he rubbed her derriere gently, massaging the rounded muscles. His blood heated at the feel of her soft skin. Her sigh was muffled by the goose-down pillow. "Okay, you win." She rolled over and looked up at him, the cross resignation on her face looking patently adorable. Sitting up, she scooted closer to him, letting her fingers play on the vee of skin that was exposed by his dressing gown. "What's on your mind?"

He took a deep breath, suddenly unsure of himself. "We must discuss our future."

"Future?" Her voice was wary.

Micah nodded, stilling her shaking hand by taking it in his own. "You must not worry that I will insult you by casting you aside. I will do the honorable thing."

She shook her head, forehead furrowed. "What do you mean, honorable?"

"As I have lain with you, the only proper thing to do is to wed…"

"Wait, wait, wait," Jamie said, pulling her hand from his. "You would marry me just because it's proper? That's what I've been trying to prevent you from doing all along, you stubborn, overly noble man!" She shoved off the bed, pacing alongside it, seemingly completely unaware of her nudity. The curls of her hair swished across her bare back, and her nipples were peaked in the chill of the room.

Mike sat on the edge of the bed, perplexed. This was not going at all as he'd imagined. "What do you mean, trying to prevent?"

She turned to him, hands propped on her bare hips. "You were going to propose to Miss Lyons. Today, in fact. You didn't love her, you were just going to do it because of society, because of your position, and numerous other reasons that don't matter at all." She ticked off the points on her fingers. "She wouldn't make you happy. She is all wrong for you. I had to show you that. And now that you've realized you and I have something amazing, something way deeper than society, position, wealth, and all that crap, the reason you're going to propose to me is to protect my nonexistent reputation?" She shook her head vehemently, eyes snapping in anger. "No. Not happening."

She walked past him, not paying the slightest bit of attention to his gaping mouth or shocked expression. Scooping up her nightgown, she swam through the layers, attempting to pull it over her head.

"Jamie." He stood when he finally found his voice. If not for the gravity of the situation, he'd have been amused that she was being drowned in her own night rail. He helped her pull the uncooperative garment on. "Please, wait for a moment."

"Why? So you can convince me that my fragile reputation is critically wounded by our having had sex? Not buying it. Sorry." She pulled free of his grasp, heading over to the puddle of her robe in front of the fireplace.

"No," he said, raking a hand through his hair. "So I can tell you that I love you, damn it!"

She stopped, half stooped, frozen. Had he really said

that aloud? He must have because she was standing slowly, her eyes wide as she looked at him. "You...love me?"

Did he? He'd told Louisa that he loved her, and he'd not felt a quarter of what he now felt for Jamie. If this was not love, then what was? Did a stronger feeling exist than what he now held for her? It couldn't. Not on this earth.

He nodded, sure that his internal consternation was bleeding out all over his features. "Yes, I do. Despite everything. I have tried to deny it, to ignore it, but I am helpless against it. I love you, Jamie Marten. I love your beautiful body, your brilliant mind, and even your foul mouth. It makes no sense. I have tried long and hard to convince myself of the contrary, but I cannot. I would have you as my countess. Will you wed me?"

Twenty-One

OH, SHIT.

Had Mike really said that he loved her? What did she do now?

First things first.

She threw her arms around him, holding him close. Emotions swamped her—happiness, terror, excitement, fear. "Oh, Mike, I love you too."

He kissed her again, their lips tangling passionately. She let his tongue possess her mouth, opening for him when he probed at her lips. She held his shoulders as he loved her, lips and hands roving where they would. She tried to shut down her buzzing brain, but it kept shouting things like *home, Leah, cars, showers, computers, sundresses*, over and over again.

Shut up! she screamed at herself when Mike's hands wandered to her breasts again.

That did it. Pleasure overrode the worries, and a rush of heat flooded her limbs.

Her nightgown pulled off much easier than it had gone on—probably because she let Mike do it.

After several minutes of moaning, touching, and kissing, they collapsed on the bed. Mike pulled her body over his. Something inside her had unlocked his confession. She wanted him even more than she had earlier that night. He loved her. She loved him. And she wanted to give him every little piece of her to prove that.

"I want to enter you this way," he groaned, palming her breasts. "I want to watch you."

"You're the earl," she said with a deliciously wicked smile. She rubbed her wet heat against his shaft, reveling in the growly moans that ripped from his chest. She was so wet, so ready for him, that she decided not to delay either of them pleasure any longer.

She rose up slightly, reaching between their bodies to palm his hardness. A gasp wrenched from him at the touch of her hand on his length.

"Like that?" she asked, rubbing the slick head against her.

"Oh, yes," he hissed, hips twisting beneath her.

"Want more?" She gripped him harder, rubbing the tip against the tingling nub of flesh at the apex of her thighs.

"Yes." He grabbed her hips, positioning the opening of her body against his erection.

"Okay," she said, impaling herself on his length.

Both of them gasped then, the intense feeling of the depth surprising them both. He was even deeper inside her now than he'd been before.

Bracing her hands on his chest, her hair fell forward as she began a slow, steady rhythm atop him. He was so hot, so hard inside her. She swiveled her hips a little, heightening the sensations.

"Yes." Mike's stare was intense as he looked into her eyes. "Don't stop."

Jamie sat up, cupping her breasts as she quickened the pace of her movements. Watching his face for clues, she pinched and rolled her nipples. *He seems to like that*, she mused as his hips bucked hard beneath her, wrenching a moan from her lips. *Honestly, I like that too.*

Faster she rode him, harder, her breasts bouncing when she released them to grip the strong thighs at her back. He reached upward to grip them, squeezing so softly, then harder when she cried out for more.

"Ah, Mike," she cried, the rhythm driving her hard. "Touch me, please."

She didn't have to explain further, bless his heart. He let his hand rub from her breast down to the wet nub that screamed out for him.

His thumb caressed it, soft at first, then harder as she panted out, "More!"

The pleasure racked higher within her, her belly burning with lustful heat. He filled her so deep. He was so thick, so hard, and hot with lust for her. She clamped her hips harder around him, pumping fast, straining for that peak.

"I'm going to come," she cried when the pleasure reached its zenith. "Oh God, Mike!"

Jamie couldn't stop the scream that wrenched from her when he pressed hard against her clit. That was it for her. She crested the wave of pleasure, her movements frantic against him, body shuddering inside and out. *What have you done to me, my lord?*

She collapsed on his chest, her breathing ragged.

"Jamie," Mike rasped against her ear, hips still pumping slowly against her, "I cannot wait much longer."

He was right. He was growing harder within her, body rigid as he tried to control his thrusts. She tried to lift her head, but pleasure had wrung every last ounce of strength from her body.

"Don't wait," she whispered against his neck.

"Are you sure?" His voice was almost frantic as he struggled with his desire.

"Yes." She pressed a kiss to his shoulder.

His hands grasped her hips, fingers digging into the soft flesh there. She held onto his shoulders, her body still thrumming with the last vestiges of her orgasm.

Three thrusts, four, and his own orgasm overcame him. She nearly came again at the erotic feeling. His movements slowed, his legs stretching out beneath her as he finished.

"I love you, Jamie," he whispered, pressing gentle kisses on her mouth.

"I love you too, Mike." She smiled, happier than she'd ever been before.

He rolled them to their sides, still cradling her close. She snuggled against his strong chest as he pulled the covers over them, happy to be there with the man she loved.

Jamie woke hours later when the fireplace was nothing but embers and weak rays of dawn were reaching through the windows. Mike's arms were still wrapped around her, and her inner legs were sticky from their lovemaking.

Her brain finally opened the channel of communication she'd shut down last night.

Oh yes, Jamie. Glad you finally joined us. The rest of your brain was just thinking WHAT THE FUCK HAVE YOU DONE? You've had unprotected sex with a guy that LIVES TWO HUNDRED YEARS IN THE PAST! For this particular gem in your otherwise stellar record, you receive an impossible decision, a broken heart, and a pregnancy scare. Excellent work, moron!

Oh shit. Her brain was right. That had been an incredibly huge mistake.

Mike blew out a sigh behind her, his breath tickling the curls at her cheek.

Wrapped there in his arms, she couldn't regret it. She wouldn't. She'd never felt as connected to anyone as she had to Mike last night, and as she moved closer to him, she tried to cover her worries with that feeling.

So, what are you going to do? Give up your house, your shower, your friends, your entire life to be a countess in a society that will probably shun you?

For Mike, she thought as she turned over to stare into his now-open eyes, *I think I might.*

He smiled at her sleepily. "Good morning, dearling."

"Morning." She snuggled into his chest, loving the way his arms pulled her closer. "I like it when you call me dearling."

He laughed softly. "I hope to call you that for quite a while."

She gave a tight-lipped smile. "Me too."

He squeezed her for a moment, then released her when she pulled away to sit up. She shoved a long hank of hair back over her shoulder.

"You did not answer me last night." He propped up on one elbow, looking at her.

"Answer what?" She turned to him, picking at tangles in her hair.

"When I asked you to wed me. You did not give me an answer."

"Oh." Jamie looked at him. Decision time. She had to say something; the worried set to his forehead told her that much. If she stayed, then both society and Collette Dubois would be out to get her in a very real way. If she left, then paralyzing heartbreak was almost certain. A flash of thought cut through her confusion.

"Okay. Why don't we say this: Yes. Conditionally."

He pursed his lips, eyebrows lowered. "Meaning?"

"One, I need to see if I can fit in here. I mean, besides

you and me. If I'm going to be living here for the rest of my life, I need to see if I can find things to make me happy other than you. If you are the only thing that makes me happy here, then that's putting unfair pressure on you, and I don't want to do that." She held up a second finger.

"Two, I don't want to run to a Vegas-style wedding chapel to do this. I want to be engaged for a while, to make sure we can live together happily. I'm pretty sure divorce in this time is way harder than it is in 2012, and I don't want either of us to have to go through that because we rushed things." She reached out and took both his hands in hers, reassured at the way his touch grounded her.

"Three, I love you, Micah Alexander Axelby. It has nothing to do with the fact that you're an earl or that you've got buckets of money or anything like that. I love you, the man. I want the same from you—respect, mutual admiration, and partnership. That's what marriage means to me, and if you're in it for any other reasons, it's a no. Think you can agree to all that?"

His expression had changed from consternation, to distaste, to calm in the space of one minute. After a long while, he nodded.

"I agree to your terms, Miss Marten."

She smiled. "Good." She brushed a quick kiss across his lips. "Now, I'd better get back to my room before the whole house knows I didn't sleep there last night. See you at breakfast?"

He nodded, pulling her close for another kiss, this one lingering, soft, and sensual.

"Mmm," she said as she pulled back. "We'd better stop that, or I won't make it back to my room."

He winked at her as she hopped from the bed to put

her clothes back on. "I intend to spend much more time doing that in the near future."

She knotted the robe at her waist. "Be my guest, your lordship." She bobbed him a mock curtsy and left the room, almost skipping with the lightness of her gleeful heart.

Her levity ground to a quick halt when she got to her bedroom and saw Muriel and Mrs. K conferring in whispers at the foot of her still-neatly-made bed. Jamie stopped dead when they locked eyes with her.

Oh, crap.

"Morning, ladies!" Jamie chirped, doing her best to appear bright-eyed, bushy-tailed, and completely chaste. "Thought I would get up early today. How are you guys?"

Muriel hid a giggle behind her thin hands. Mrs. Knightsbridge raised her brows. "If you were sleeping here last night, then why did Muriel fetch me when you were not in your bed at two of the clock when Baron roused her to allow him entrance to your room? And why did we hear, ahem, some telling sounds from his lordship's bedchamber?"

Jamie's ears, cheeks, and neck burned bright red. She'd been discovered.

"Well, it's your fault." Jamie pointed at Mrs. K. "You're the one that talked Thornton into lying for you about that damn pink punch. You intentionally got me drunk!"

Muriel squeaked, looking rapidly from the housekeeper to Jamie and back again.

"I did nothing of the sort." Mrs. Knightsbridge fidgeted with her apron as she replied, avoiding Jamie's accusing stare by looking at the floor.

"You did too. You're lying, and not very well at that."

"Well, I did tell you I would do whatever I deemed necessary."

Check and mate. "Fine." Jamie stalked into the room, pushing the door shut behind her. "You won. Congrats. Can I have a bath now?"

Mrs. K smiled victoriously. "I think, under the circumstances, that can be arranged. Muriel, please go inform the footmen. I will assist Miss Marten."

Muriel's face fell as she realized she wasn't going to be in on the hot new gossip. She bobbed a disappointed curtsy and left the room. Jamie guessed this was the most excitement the poor girl ever really got. A real live scandal in her own house? How much more thrilling could it get for a teenaged maid? Jamie made up her mind to make it up to Muriel later.

"Now," Mrs. Knightsbridge said, smiling a knowing smile, "I trust you were successful in your efforts?"

Jamie shook her head vehemently. "I wasn't successful because I didn't set out to *do* anything. I had a few too many, and Mike escorted me up here, and after I changed, well, stuff happened." It was honestly worse than having to confess to her sixth grade teacher that she'd started her period for the first time. The awkward knot of embarrassment swelled in her throat.

Mrs. K's smile turned into a full-out grin.

"There. See? Are you not glad that I did not open the portal and send you back yesterday?"

Twenty-Two

"YOU."

Mrs. Knightsbridge's face went paler than a fish belly. Jamie crossed the room toward her, finger pointed accusingly.

"It was you the whole time, wasn't it? There is no sister at all!" Jamie stopped just in front of the housekeeper, pointer finger shaking as she vented her frustration.

Mrs. K looked down, red leeching into her blanched cheeks. "Yes. It was me."

"All those times you told me Wilhelmina was in hiding for her safety, that she wouldn't send me back, that was really just a cover so you could keep me here to do what you wanted. And what *kills* me is, it worked." Jamie threw up her hands as she walked to the window. "Now, I'm in love with the guy, I've done the deed with him, and I've agreed to marry him, and it's all because you tricked me into having to stay here!"

Mrs. K's delighted cry whirled Jamie around. The housekeeper clapped her hands and beamed. "Oh, Miss Jamie, how wonderful! I'll see to it that his lordship procures a special license so you may be wed immediately. I believe St. George's should do for the ceremony…"

"Wait just one minute, *Wilhelmina*." Mrs. K winced at

her emphatic use of her given name but didn't lose the triumphant look while Jamie continued. "I am not going to run out and marry him tomorrow. We've agreed on some conditions. A long engagement, for starters. And I've got to make sure I can be happy here even without Mike. I don't know much about proper society, but since this is all your fault, you're going to help me learn, got it?"

The beam toned down to a bright smile. "But, Miss Jamie, that's what we've been doing all along. I shall be happy to continue showing you the ways of polite society."

Jamie sighed and dropped down on the bed. "Okay. But you need to promise me something right here, right now."

Her face was dead serious as she pegged Mrs. K with a dark stare. "No more lies. No more manipulation. I want to know that I can trust you. If I ask you to open that portal again, you won't deny me, no matter what. Understood?"

The housekeeper nodded solemnly. "I do apologize for my duplicity. It was not meant to cause you pain, I promise you that. It was a necessary precaution, one that I regret has caused you harm."

Jamie nodded slowly. "I understand."

A knock sounded on the door at that moment. Mrs. K crossed the room to open it.

Two footmen, one of them George, struggled in with the copper tub. It was filled with steaming buckets of water within another ten minutes. It seemed some witch may have foreseen the need for the water to be heating much earlier than she'd let on.

Mrs. K smiled. "I shall send Muriel to you in a few moments. In the meantime, please relax. I know you have some things to ponder."

That was an understatement. Jamie thanked the housekeeper for the bath and watched as the diminutive woman left the room.

The hot water soothed muscles that were sore from her night's exercises. Jamie reclined into the warm curve of copper against her back, watching the fire dancing in the grate. Was Mike thinking about the same things she was at that moment? Was he wondering how they could ever pull that off? Was he remembering the way their bodies had fit together so well last night?

"Stop that," Jamie hissed to her stomach as a curl of warmth grew there. She wasn't normally ruled by her libido, and she didn't intend to start.

She grabbed the soap Mrs. K had set alongside the tub and got to scrubbing. As the water cooled, her trepidation grew. How could she possibly marry a man from two hundred years in the past? How could she survive in a time where women were regarded as vessels for men's pleasure and the propagation of the species? How could she honestly hope to make Mike happy when she couldn't even manage to remember all of the stupid rules that guided this society? She'd embarrass him. He'd start to hate her—exactly like Logan had when he'd claimed she wasn't the woman he'd fallen for. She tried to wash all the uncertainty, worry, and fear away, but it would take something much stronger than the lavender-scented suds to do that. She dipped beneath the surface of the water and massaged her scalp with the soap.

C'mon, Jamie, she said to herself. *Where's the good feeling? Where's the everything-is-right-with-the-world calm that goes along with getting clean?*

Her toes went pruny and her fingers were raisins before she realized it wasn't coming.

❧

Muriel was full of chatter when she came in to help Jamie rinse her hair and dress. The one-word answers and lack of ebullience didn't deter Muriel either. She kept up a long stream of talk as she brushed out Jamie's hair, laced up her stays, and selected a gown for her to wear.

"After all," Muriel said as she pulled her last set of petticoats on over Jamie's head, "it is not every day that an earl weds a lady with no connections or family."

"Muriel, we kind of want to keep it secret right now, okay?" Jamie felt bad asking. Muriel was clearly swept away by the romantic idea, and she didn't want to hurt the girl's feelings, but honestly, the situation wasn't feeling that wonderful to Jamie yet. There were still way too many variables for her to be as ecstatic as Muriel was.

"Oh," Muriel said. Her face fell as she brought the pale pink gown to Jamie. "I am sorry, miss."

"No, it's okay." Jamie took the dress. "We've got to get some things settled first, that's all. I promise you, you will be the first person to know when it's time to shout it from the rooftops."

That seemed to placate her. "Thank you, miss." She smiled and helped Jamie into the gown.

Jamie sat in front of the mirror, as she did every day, and waited as Muriel put pins in her hair. As she watched the thin hands expertly separate and twist strands of hair, fixing them securely to the crown of her head, she was impressed with Muriel's talent. The maid really was great at what she did.

"Hey, Muriel, you'd probably make a lot of money doing hair in my time."

Muriel paused, three pins hanging from her mouth. "Really?" she slurred around them.

"Yeah. You'd have to learn some of the modern

tools, blow dryers, flat irons, that kind of thing. And hair coloring. You'd need to learn that. But honestly, I think you'd pick it up, no problem. You're really good at it."

A surprised grin crossed her face. She nearly lost the two pins still hanging from her lips. "Thank you, Miss Jamie!"

Jamie winced a little when the maid's excitement nearly cost her a patch of scalp. It was worth it to make Muriel feel good. Someone should be happy today, and Jamie wasn't sure if she could put her worries aside enough for it to be her.

Jamie ended up being late to breakfast because of her prolonged soak. She hoped Mike was still there. She wanted to see him, despite her worries and concerns. Maybe he could help her put them to rest.

As luck would have it, she passed him on his way out of the dining room.

"Hey," Jamie said breathlessly. "Sorry I'm late. I needed a bath."

His smile was tender as he looked down into her eyes. "Good morning, Miss Marten. I trust you slept well?" His brow quirked slightly.

She rolled her eyes with a wry grin. "Yeah. Great, thanks for asking."

He clasped his hands behind him, and a ripple of want went through her at the way his tailored coat fit his muscular form. "I must meet with my solicitor this morning. Would you care to ride out with me this afternoon? It is a fair day, and I thought a ride in my phaeton would be quite the thing."

She smiled. "Sounds great to me."

Mike glanced around surreptitiously and then brushed a kiss across her lips. He lifted his head, and with a smile said, "Until later, my love."

Her pulse fluttered like crazy as he walked away. She didn't even pretend not to check him out as he left. What a man. What the hell was she going to do with him?

Baron stuck with her while she ate breakfast. She felt guilty about abandoning the dog last night. She wasn't sure where he'd ended up sleeping after he woke Muriel, but since he made a point to stay with Jamie every night, she was pretty sure it wasn't as comfy as her bed was. She gave him extra ham to make up for it. She thought he forgave her.

Jamie walked in the garden with the hound after breakfast, still trying to wrap her brain around things. She tried to think of herself as Jamie Axelby, Countess of Dunnington, but it didn't work. When she'd dreamed of marrying Logan, she'd always thought she'd hyphenate. Jamie Marten-Camp had a ring to it. Then again, Jamie Marten-Axelby sounded nice. But there was no way she could get away with hyphenating her name in this time. Women's lib was still way off in the future. She'd have to have Mike's permission to do anything. No one would do business with her; no one would take her seriously on her own merits. She couldn't write music and get paid for it. She wasn't worth as much as a person here as she had been at home.

What a lowering thought. She'd never been someone with huge self-esteem anyway, but the thought of needing a man's permission if she wanted to set up a bank account really hit her hard.

She flopped down onto her bench, trying to slouch, but the damn stays wouldn't let her. She sighed instead.

"Baron, this is really tough." The dog licked her hand, trying to find any remnants of breakfast. "It's easy for you, isn't it? Doesn't bother you where you are or who's there, as long as you've got a warm bed, lots of food, and cuddles, huh?"

She ruffled his ears.

What was stopping her? Honestly? She had told Mike she was going to give this a shot, and dammit, that was exactly what she was going to do. They deserved a chance to be together.

"Thanks, dog." She stood and marched purposefully back into the house. She needed to dress for their ride, and she wanted to look her best. Better go ahead and get started. Mike would be back in only a couple of hours, the perfect amount of time to dress to impress society. She hoped.

Mrs. K joined Muriel in dressing Jamie to the nines for her carriage outing with Mike. The housekeeper produced a lilac carriage dress, high-necked with a pointed collar and a lilac ribbon-belt. Muriel piled Jamie's hair atop her head again, arranging curls to spill temptingly around her face. They perched a white chip-straw hat on top of the curls, pinning it securely atop her head. Mrs. K wrapped a darker purple shawl around her shoulders, tiny tassels dangling from the corners.

"There." Mrs. K stepped back to admire their handiwork. "No one shall fault your appearance."

Jamie took as deep a breath as she could. No wonder women were always passing out in the olden days. They couldn't breathe in these damn deathtraps. Just when she thought she'd gotten used to them, Muriel would cinch them just a little bit tighter. "But what if I do something wrong while I'm out there and somebody sees me? I don't want Mike's reputation to suffer because of me."

"It is simple, Miss Jamie." Jamie replayed Mrs. K's words as she descended the stairs to meet Mike, whose face had lit up charmingly at the sight of her. "Be polite. Do not speak with anyone to whom you are not acquainted. Let his lordship guide you. He will not lead you astray."

"Miss Marten." He held a hand out to Jamie, and she put her gloved one in his. "You are looking quite fine."

"You are as well, my lord," she said with a bashful smile. "Thank you for taking me riding."

"It is my pleasure." He pulled her hand through the crook of his arm and led her out the front door to his waiting phaeton.

The gleaming black carriage had a beautiful brown leather seat, which Mike handed her up to. It was surprisingly comfortable, and she was much happier to sit behind the horses than on them. The beasts stamped their feet as Mike climbed in beside her.

"Are you ready?" he asked her with a grin.

"Let's go, chief. Wagons roll!" Jamie pointed ahead with a laugh as Mike flicked the reins and they were off.

She was grateful for the thick purple shawl that coordinated with her outfit so well. The early spring wind was a little chilly atop the high carriage. She wished she could cuddle closer to Mike, enjoying some of his body heat, but she wasn't willing to embarrass him. She was testing herself to see if she could do this the right way. So far, so cold, so good.

The horses' hooves clattered against the cobbled streets as they made their way to the park. Mike nodded to a few gentlemen on horseback but, fortunately, didn't stop to talk. Jamie breathed a little easier when the phaeton turned into the park's entrance. There were fewer people around to worry about embarrassing herself in front of.

"Are you enjoying the air?" Mike asked.

She nodded. "Yeah, it's a little chilly, but it's good

to get out of the house. And the company is pretty nice too." She winked at him, and he chuckled.

"I must agree. Very pleasant company indeed."

A second or two passed as they rounded a corner in the path. Jamie realized that she didn't know as much about her earl as she should.

"We haven't really talked about family, you know. Do you have any?"

His face darkened slightly. "My mother and father have both passed on. I have no siblings. There are some distant cousins on my father's side, one of which is my heir. They reside near the Scottish border."

"I'm sorry," she said, running her fingers along the embroidered edge of her shawl. "My parents are both dead too."

Mike looked at her. "We seem to be more alike than not, Miss Marten."

Jamie nodded, a half smile on her face. "Guess so, my lord."

After that, they fell into a companionable silence, the only noise the horses' hooves on the gravel pathways. Jamie scooted a tiny bit closer to Mike, hoping she was still far enough away for polite society. Honestly, she wanted nothing more than to snuggle up under his arm, pressing her cheek against his chest. She sighed inwardly and pulled the purple shawl tighter around her shoulders. It would have to be enough for here and now. She could do this. It wasn't that bad, honestly. She just had to mind her manners and everything would be fine.

They rode for quite a while. When they rounded a bend, deep in the park, Jamie spied a hound being walked by a uniformed footman. The dog was the same dark gray-blue as Baron but with a splash of white across its nose.

"Hey, Mike, that dog looks a lot like Baron, don't you think?"

Mike's jaw tightened as he took in the sight of the footman yanking on the dog's lead. Jamie winced in sympathy herself.

"That is the Duke of Granville's footman. If I'm not mistaken, that's the same chap that dumped Baron and his siblings in the river."

"What?" She turned to Mike, horror freezing her blood.

Mike nodded, turning the carriage down a side path to avoid the man with the dog. "I saw it happen. It was over a year ago, in January. I found out later that the man was not supposed to breed that particular pair, as another stud was to be used, and was trying to cover his mistake by disposing of the pups. He pitched a wicker basket into the icy waters of the Thames. I tried to stop him, but he was too far away to hear my shouts. I ran to the river as he walked away. I plunged into the icy water myself and grabbed the basket. Three of the pups inside had already drowned. I put the two remaining in my waistcoat and rode as fast as I could for my townhouse. The female pup expired before I could get them home. Baron was very weak, but he survived the ordeal. Mrs. Knightsbridge was an invaluable help, devising a way to help the pup nurse. Between the two of us, we saved him."

"Oh my God," Jamie said, a palm covering her gaping mouth. "That is so awful."

Mike nodded. "That was only weeks after Louisa's death. In many ways, I think Baron helped me to heal. He is a very special hound."

Blast and damn propriety. Mike was hurting, and she needed to comfort him. She reached over and squeezed his hand softly. "He is, and he's incredibly lucky to have you. It's easy to see that he's crazy about you."

Mike smiled at her. "The feeling is returned." He laughed as he pulled the reins back, stopping the horses. "Do you think it is foolish to love a man who cares so deeply for an animal?"

Jamie shook her head. "Not at all."

A shrill female voice cut between them like a two-handed sword.

"What is the meaning of this?"

"Ah, for chrissakes," Jamie muttered, looking over her shoulder. Collette was riding up behind them, her burgundy riding habit looking like spilled wine against her horse's white flanks. "Here we go again."

"Miss Dubois," Mike called in a stern, deep voice. "We are having a private conversation. Please take yourself elsewhere."

"I will do nothing of the sort." She brought her horse up to her side of the carriage, eyes snapping at Jamie. "You were to leave Dunnington alone. Why are you still here?"

"Maybe because I couldn't give a crap about your opinion?" Jamie said, opening her eyes wide and smiling with tight lips.

Collette gasped.

Jamie rolled her eyes. *Seriously? Is she really expecting me to hop down and trot away when the bitch snaps her fingers?*

"Micah, you will not let her speak to me in this coarse manner. Silence her immediately."

Mike shook his head. "I will not. You are not wanted here, so Miss Marten can express her displeasure in whatever manner she sees fit."

Jamie turned back to Mike and smiled at him. "Thanks."

He nodded.

"This is an outrage, Micah. I cannot allow this to go on. I will inform Mr. Waites about your disgusting paramour living in your home. He'll make sure that all of society knows before the week is out. You will no longer be invited to anything. Almack's will shun you for good. The prince himself will censure you. It will be a scandal that even your lofty position will not save you from, not so tidily shoved under the rug as your last *contretemps* was." She lowered her voice, fluttering dark lashes at him. "It can all be quite simply avoided, dearest one. I have no wish to harm you; I only wish to free you from this damaging association. Now, are you sure you wish to throw me over for this harlot?"

Jamie hadn't seen Mike really lose his temper since that night he'd saved her from Beard and Sideburns. He made up for that when he roared at Collette.

"If you insult my intended bride once more, I shall not be responsible for my actions. Mind your tongue, for what is mine, I keep." His knuckles turned white where he gripped the reins. The force of his yell must have startled the horses, for they stomped nervously, rocking the phaeton wheels back and forth.

Collette stared at Jamie, disgust plain in her wrinkled nose and gaping mouth.

"Intended…bride?"

Twenty-Three

A FEW DAYS AGO, GEORGE HAD STRUGGLED WITH A load of coals down the hallway. Jamie had jumped up from her seat on the piano bench to help him, but they'd spilled all over the rug before she could get there. He'd propped his hands on his hips, scowled at the mess, and said, "Well, that's torn it."

The expression seemed particularly apt there too. Collette's face was the perfect picture of shocked dismay. "You cannot…Micah, it is not…You must…"

"Good day, Miss Dubois." Mike flicked the reins and the horses obediently started walking.

Jamie glanced over her shoulder. Collette still sat there atop her white mount, mouth working.

"I'm guessing you didn't mean to do that," Jamie said to Mike when they'd put some distance between them and his former lover.

"No, I did not," he sighed. "It was not well done of me. Well, now or later, we shall weather the storm of gossip."

A heavy weight settled in her chest. "I don't want to cause you problems, you know."

He nodded, clucking to the horses to speed them up on the road. "I know."

Jamie rubbed her gloved fingers together in consternation. She couldn't stand the thought of Mike being hurt by society the way he had when Louisa had died. "If it would be better for you, I could go. Back, I mean."

Mike's sharp command to the horses stopped them in the center of the street. A hoarse shout behind them cursed them for stopping.

"That is not acceptable," Mike said, his voice as high and mighty as she'd ever heard it. "You will not leave me."

His possessive attitude was flattering, but the autocratic manner was not. She reached out and laid her hand atop his where it clenched the reins.

"Hey. Listen. I'm not going to make any decisions like that without your input. But remember the partnership part of our agreement? That means both of us get equal say, okay? The whole lord-of-the-manor bit isn't going to fly with me. Got it?"

He opened his mouth to argue, but she arched a brow at him, refusing to back down. With an angry sigh and flick of the reins, he agreed. "Very well. But you must promise to speak with me before doing anything so rash."

"I can agree to that."

The phaeton rolled to a stop in front of Mike's house, and a footman assisted Jamie as she descended. With a polite bow, Mike said he'd see her at dinner and disappeared into his office.

Muriel followed Jamie up the stairs to help her change. You'd think without sewing machines, people wouldn't want to change clothes so many times in a day, but apparently not. Jamie had kind of gotten used to the frequent costume changes. They did make her feel kind of pretty and girly, after all. Tonight, Muriel put her in a scarlet-red gown, daring and lovely. She couldn't wait to see what Mike thought of it.

Jamie was heading toward the stairs when Thornton's voice floated up from the foyer. "My lord, a missive has arrived from Sir Frederick Lyons."

Jamie hustled down the stairs. Mike stood by the front door, his jaw tightening as he read the letter.

"What does it say?" Jamie crossed her arms over her middle nervously. Without a word, Mike handed her the letter.

> Lord Dunnington,
>
> I have received a report from Mr. Waites of a quite serious and alarming nature. It is rumored that you are not only harboring an unwed woman of no reputation in your very home, but that you have offered marriage to this same person. As you have been squiring my Felicity about, we have been led to believe that you intended to propose marriage.
>
> Do know, sir, that if these tales prove true, I will have no recourse but to swiftly inform my many acquaintances how you have used my family so abominably. I pray, for your sake, that these rumors are false.
>
> Sir Frederick Lyons

The letter fluttered from her fingers as she stared at Mike in bewilderment. As a footman retrieved the paper, Mike offered a stunned Jamie his arm and escorted her into the sitting room.

"Have a seat, dearling." Mike crossed over to the sideboard and poured himself a drink. When he offered Jamie one, she shook her head vehemently. She'd had enough alcohol to last her a while, thanks.

"What are we going to do?" she asked Mike when he sat down beside her.

He took a sip of his drink before replying, "If Mr. Waites is spreading Collette's venom for her, then the tale will have reached throughout the *ton* by noon tomorrow. There is naught we can do to stop it."

"Great. Absolutely wonderful." *On second thought...* She took a tiny sip of Mike's drink. *Ugh. Brandy.* She coughed, her eyes watering.

"Are you all right?" Mike took the glass that she shoved back at him.

She nodded, hand gripping her throat. "Yeah, I'm fine," she wheezed.

Mike rolled his eyes and thwacked her on the back.

"Sorry," she said when she had her breath back. "I'm better now." She took a deep breath before continuing. "What will this mean for you? I mean, I know it's bad, right? Exactly how bad could it get?"

The dark, stony look on his face was all the answer she needed, but he went on anyway. "It will not be pleasant. I worry not so much for myself but for you. The stares and whispers are not unfamiliar to me, after Louisa's strange death, but you should not be exposed to their waspish ways."

"How can we stop them? I don't want to deal with them any more than you do, but I don't see how—"

"I must hide you," Mike said. He tossed back the rest of his brandy and set the glass back on the side table. "I will send you to my country home. You will be safe there, and I can weather the storm of gossip here alone. Once the worst has passed, I shall meet you there, and we can wed. When that has happened, the wagging tongues will soon find other targets." He came back to the couch, grasping both her hands as he sat beside her. "I will not let anyone harm you again, Jamie."

The knot in her throat nearly cut off her air. "I

appreciate that, I really do, but remember what you agreed to? How can I ever figure out if I fit in here if you have to hide me from everybody you know?" He was gorgeous, he was proud, and he would be hers if they could figure this shit out.

"It is only temporary, dearling. Once this scandal blows over, they will come to love you as I do."

He leaned forward, taking her lips in a gentle kiss. His mouth tasted of brandy, much sweeter than it had been in the glass. The kiss went to her head in an instant, and she was lost. He pulled her close, pressing his chest against her breasts. She clutched at his shoulders as his tongue plundered her.

Too soon, he lifted his head.

"We will plan for your departure on the morrow. Until then, we must not miss dinner a second time in a row or Jean Philippe will leave us. Permit me to escort you, Miss Marten."

She was glad to have Mike's arm to hold on to as he led her into the dining room. He steadied her, but even his touch couldn't completely calm her fears.

❧

After a delicious dinner, they went into the music room. Mike sat beside Jamie on the piano bench.

"Play for me," he said, smiling as he kissed the tips of her fingers.

"What do you want to hear?" Her voice shook a little. She had only had a little wine with dinner, but the feel of his nearness was way more intoxicating than alcohol could ever hope to be.

"Something you have written. I want to hear your talent."

She scratched her nails against the ivory keys nervously. "Okay."

What to play? She'd been writing music since she was a tiny girl. It took her hours to get through piano practice because she'd never play what the teacher had assigned; she always wanted to make up her own stuff. There were more compositions floating through her head than she could remember.

When she thought of the perfect song, she smiled.

"This one is for Mike."

The song started with soft, tinkly high notes that she had to lean across him to play. She took advantage of the contact, letting her breast brush against his arm. As she came down the scale, the minor key twisting a poignant knife in her heart, she let her eyes slide closed and pictured Mike as the music poured from deep within her.

The first time she'd seen him, with that haughty look on his face. The way he smiled at the phone while playing that game. The breadth of his strong shoulders framed by his perfectly tailored clothes. The way he laughed at Baron's antics. The tenderness in his eyes when he'd entered her body. The crescendo ripped through her fingers like ocean waves crashing. This was her man. This was her earl. And she had to be with him, no matter what sort of problems they'd face along the way.

The song ended with a repeat of the high notes. Mike closed the tiny gap between their bodies, pressing kisses to her neck as she struck the last keys.

"That was beautiful," he whispered against her skin. He lifted the curls from her ear, nibbling on the soft shell. Tremors rippled through her at the contact.

He turned her body so he was sitting behind her, straddling the piano bench. His hands came around to cup her breasts as he kissed his way down her neck, to the shoulder that was left bare by the wide-necked dress.

Her nipples tightened to a near-aching state as he

fondled them, rolling the tight buds through the silk of her dress. She pressed her ass back against him, reveling in the feeling of his erection pulsing against her.

He released her breasts, leaning down to feel his way beneath the hem of her skirt. His hand was hot on her leg through the silk stockings.

"Mike," she whispered, "I'm wearing an awful lot of clothes to be doing this, you know."

"Shame, that," he whispered back. "I can assist, if you would like…"

She shook her head, standing quickly. "Everyone already knows we were together last night, and I'd like to kind of keep things quiet right now, if you know what I mean. I don't want everyone thinking that you're a debaucher, and I'm a loose woman."

He sighed, and she almost caved at the sight of the pathetically pitiful set to his mouth. Baron had nothing on Mike when he was disappointed.

"If you insist."

She pecked a quick kiss on his lips. "Give me ten minutes. I'll change and meet you in your room."

Muriel was all agog over the letter from Sir Frederick. The discussion cooled Jamie's blood, and by the time she was dressed in her nightgown and Muriel had gone, she wasn't sure if she should go to Mike. Yes, she wanted him, and he wanted her, but with the way Collette was spreading her tales, should she be more careful?

Jamie sighed, pulled on her robe, and padded down the hall to Mike's room. This was his world, so she'd have to let him make that decision. He'd promised not to let anyone harm her. She trusted him enough to let him take care of her.

Her knock on the door was answered nearly instantly. Mike pulled her straight into his arms, kissing her madly.

All her worries burned up in the heat of his passion. It was a huge relief to let herself go, to enjoy the feel of his body against hers.

His hands were everywhere, her back, her breasts, her ass. He seemed as desperate to forget their troubles as she was. She wrapped her arms around his neck to stay upright.

He scooped an arm behind her knees, picked her up, and deposited her softly on the bed. He ran his hands beneath her gown, up her thighs, and she shuddered.

"Take off your robe." He grasped her foot, kissing her ankle, then her calf. She unknotted the robe, pulling her arms through the sleeves.

Mike pushed the nightgown up to her waist, baring her body to his gaze. His eyes went dark with lust when he looked at her nude body.

"Open for me," he whispered, hands rubbing her thighs.

She bit her lip and parted her knees slowly. He sucked a breath in through his teeth. "God, Jamie, you are so lovely."

He started to reach forward, to touch her, but she stopped him. "Wait. Take your robe off."

His hands went obediently to the knot at his waist, but he stopped. "I am unclothed underneath. If I am to remove my robe, you must remove your gown."

She quirked a smile at him. "Tit for tat. I like that. Fine. On the count of three. One, two, three." She pulled the nightgown over her head and tossed it aside.

Mike still stood with his hands poised on the knot of his robe.

"You shit!" Jamie laughed. "You were supposed to do it at the same time!"

"I lied," he sighed without budging his gaze from her now-naked breasts.

She grabbed a pillow from the head of the bed and covered herself with it. "Okay, now your turn. You can't see anything else until I see what I came in here for."

He laughed, a sound that warmed her all over. God, she loved to make him laugh.

"If you insist, Miss Marten."

He went agonizingly slowly, unraveling the knot one long tail at a time. He used one hand to keep the front of the robe closed. She didn't want to spoil his striptease by pointing out that she could plainly see his erection standing proud beneath the velvet. It would have spoiled the entertainment. And as he turned, dropping the robe to the floor, she was glad she hadn't said anything.

"Wow."

She reached out, unable to stop herself from rubbing her hands down his back, to his slim hips, over his ass, and down those finely muscled legs. He was built, her Mike, that was for sure.

He laughed and turned back to her. From her vantage point on the bed, she was face to head with a very interesting portion of his anatomy.

"Hello," she said, addressing his member. "We've met before, but I don't know that we've been properly introduced." She pointed at her chest. "I am Jamie"—she touched the rounded tip—"and you are delicious."

Mike's chuckles disappeared when she took him in her mouth.

She gripped the base of his shaft with one hand and ran her mouth up and down his length. His ragged breath and gentle moan encouraged her to continue.

"Jamie," he said hoarsely. "You do not have to…"

She pulled her mouth from him long enough to speak. "Mike? Shut up. Enjoying myself here."

She wrapped her lips around him again, closed her eyes, and savored the feel of him in her mouth.

Only a minute later, he pulled away from her. Her "what's wrong?" was cut off by him pushing her back onto the bed.

"I want to taste you in return, Jamie." Mike crawled up between her spread legs. Her already throbbing core grew even hotter as his breath blew against the damp folds. "May I?"

She nodded.

His tongue in her mouth had been magic. His tongue on her breasts had been incredible. But when he pressed that same tongue against that tiny nub that screamed out for him she thought she'd lose her ever-lovin' mind.

"Mike," she gasped, hands tangling in his dark hair. "Oh God, don't stop."

He licked his way from top to bottom, suckling her, nipping gently, caressing her with his mouth. If she'd been wearing her stays, she would definitely have passed out because all available blood in her body was rushing downstairs to greet him.

She couldn't take it. If he stayed there much longer, she'd never last.

She pulled at his shoulders, and he lifted his head.

"I want you inside me." She held her arms out to him.

He rose on his arms, positioning his body above hers. He probed at the entrance to her body. "Are you ready?"

"Yes," she said, rubbing her hands along his back. "Please, Mike."

He slid into her gently, his hardness filling her, stretching her inner walls. She moaned, lifting her hips to meet his.

His hips snaked against hers, a sensuous rhythm that stole her consciousness, burning it away in a haze of passion. The motion rubbed against her most sensitive areas, heightening her pleasure immeasurably.

She cried out as he quickened his pace. "Oh God, please don't stop."

His movements were frantic against her as his body plundered hers. She met each of his thrusts, bringing him deeper, farther into her body. With one hand, he cupped her breast, and with the other, he gripped her ass. Her hands clenched his hips, desperately trying to bring him farther into her.

When sweat covered their bodies and his erection pulsed hot and hard into her, she screamed with pleasure, hiding her face in his shoulder to cover the sound. Hot jets of passion flowed onto her stomach as he pulled out at the last second. She was momentarily disappointed to be robbed of the delicious feeling, but only for a second. It had been the smart thing to do, after all.

Mike pressed soft kisses against her cheek, her brow, her lips, and then rose to clean her up again. He was so gentle, his hands moving smoothly as he cared for her. She relaxed and enjoyed feeling like a princess.

"Thank you," she whispered when he crawled back into bed next to her.

"For what?" he whispered back, pulling her into his arms.

"For being you."

He dropped a kiss on her nose and they both went to sleep.

Despite the beautiful feeling of sleeping in his arms, tension and worry overtook her. She had dark dreams that night.

Twenty-Four

A RAUCOUS HORDE OF LADIES AND GENTLEMEN, HEADED by Miss Lyons, chased Jamie through the pitch darkness of the Wentworths' garden. Their angry cries ripped through her heart like jagged arrows. Her slippers were made for dancing, not running through the woods. She couldn't outrun them for long.

She yelled Mike's name as she ran, begging him for help, but he didn't answer. There wasn't a friendly face anywhere that she could see. Bushes and brambles tore at her beautiful gown, slowing her even further. She chanced a look over her shoulder. They were gaining on her, Miss Lyons's eyes glowing red like a demon's.

Jamie's breath came in burning gasps as she rounded a huge oak. She stopped short. A huge stone wall extended for miles in either direction. She jumped, digging her nails into the smooth stone. The ledges weren't large enough to give her purchase. She couldn't climb it in jeans, much less this frilly gown. She whirled, pressing her back against the cold stone barrier. She watched, helpless, as they came for her.

As they ran closer, shrieking in evil joy, they began to disappear, one by one. By the time the red-eyed Felicity was within ten feet of Jamie, she was the only pursuer left. Felicity stopped her headlong sprint, smiled with her too-thin lips, and sauntered to Jamie, walking hips first, like a slutty supermodel.

"Leave me alone," Jamie yelled, cold tears tracking down her cheeks. She tried to leap at Felicity, to attack her, but her body was frozen with fear. "I didn't do anything to you."

"Oh, but you did," Felicity purred, her golden curls turning the jet-black of an oil slick. Her figure became fuller, her lips grew into a sensual pout, and then Collette Dubois was cupping Jamie's chin, eyes still burning like hellfire.

Collette put her head against Jamie's cheek, and whispered, soft as a kiss, "You took what's mine. Now you will pay."

Jamie woke with a gasp, sitting bolt upright in Mike's bed. He grunted softly in his sleep but didn't wake fully. Weak fingers of dawn poked through the glass of the window. A shiver that had nothing to do with her nudity raced down her spine. *I'd better get back to my room.*

Swiftly and silently, she dressed. With a last longing look at Mike, she shut the door softly behind her.

⁕

The quiet knock on his bedchamber door barely roused Micah. He imagined that he dreamt it and reached to his side to touch Jamie. She wasn't there. A second knock, louder than the first, pried his eyes open.

"Enter," he called, pulling the sheet up to his naked chest.

"My lord," George, the footman, said from the crack in the door. "A messenger has come from His Grace, the Duke of Wellington."

"The Duke of Wellington," Micah said disbelievingly. "At this hour?"

"His Grace has requested your presence this morning, at nine of the clock. What shall I say to the messenger?"

Micah rubbed a hand through his hair, curling his lip in confusion. "Of course, I will attend His Grace promptly."

"Yes, my lord." George dipped his head and shut the door softly.

So much for a leisurely morning spent planning for Jamie's departure to the country. They would need to postpone her journey until the morrow at the earliest. The Iron Duke, so famous for routing the Corsican upstart Napoleon, was not the sort of person one could ignore.

As Micah hastily went through his daily ablutions, he found it hard to keep his mind on business matters. Glimpses of Jamie kept flitting through his mind. It was enough to drive a man daft, and Micah quelled the small smile that was pasted on his lips at the thought of his intended bride. Remembering the threats that hung over them both did much to temper his pleasure.

The door to his bedchamber swung softly shut behind him as he descended to break his fast, determined to keep his brain fresh on business matters this morn. He'd attend to His Grace and then make arrangements to send his love to the country. The pleasure, and there would be much, would come later.

❦

Jamie beat Muriel to the Lemon Room by a good half hour. Jamie had just drifted into an exhausted sleep when the thin maid woke her. She held a steaming cup of chocolate.

"Morning, miss," she trilled, setting the cup on the bedside table. "Isn't it a lovely day?"

Jamie stretched as she sat up and yawned. Leaning

forward on the bed, she looked out the window. Overcast. "Yup. Gorgeous."

"You must hurry if you wish to see his lordship this morning." Muriel scooted over to the wardrobe, pulling out a pale-yellow gown. "I heard Mr. Thornton say that the earl must meet with the Duke of Wellington at nine of the clock."

So much for a day with my guy, she thought as she threw back the covers. Not even time for a bath. Just great. Mike better not send her off to his country house without spending some time talking to her about it first. She needed to know that this wasn't a life sentence before she agreed to it.

A quick scrub in the basin later, she was dressed and on her way to meet her earl for breakfast. She hadn't taken that long to get ready, but Mike was pulling on his gloves at the door while Thornton held his greatcoat.

"Hey," Jamie said as she walked down the last few steps into the foyer. "Are you leaving?"

"My apologies, Miss Marten," Mike said, his frown wrinkling his forehead. "I have been called away by His Grace."

"Oh. Okay." She ran her fingernail across the banister as she looked at Mike, consternation furrowing her brow.

"I shall be back for dinner. We can discuss your journey to my country house then. I apologize for the delay, but I mustn't keep His Grace waiting."

Jamie wanted to give him a good-bye kiss or hug him or even squeeze his gloved hand briefly. She was feeling so weird after those creepy dreams. But none of that was allowed. Mrs. K said that even married couples didn't touch each other in the presence of other people. So, instead, she gripped the banister hard, and said, "Be safe."

She bit her lip as he put on his hat.

"Until this evening, Miss Marten." He held a hand out to her. She took it, and he pressed his lips to her knuckles so softly.

"Bye." She didn't let her voice tremble.

He walked out the door into the now-drizzly morning.

Breakfast with Baron was lonely. Jamie let the dog have most of her ham and half of her eggs too. She wasn't hungry. She was bored. She had no friends, other than Muriel and Mrs. K, who were both busy with their daily duties. She tried to beg Thornton to play cards with her, but the old butler was scandalized by the thought. George went mute when she tried to talk to him, only answering in nods and shakes of his head. One of the other maids shooed her out of the music room for its weekly cleaning session.

She paced down the length of the hallway, the rain keeping her from her usual thinking spot in the garden. Baron curled up by the front door, watching her.

She'd read everything of interest in the house three times. She was crap at embroidery and had no need to ever get better. She tried to teach Baron to howl after she said the word "ThunderCats," but he lost interest and wandered into the kitchen. Typical male.

She flopped onto the settee and watched the raindrops roll down the glass of the window. Propping a cheek on her hand, she sighed. She really felt useless. She couldn't go out and get a job, making friends there was something you apparently needed a college degree in societal relations for, and no one would even let her clean. She was stumped. Locked in a frozen computer screen, nowhere to go. And tomorrow she'd be dumped in a house that was even more lonely than this one. It was a hard pill to swallow.

When a knock came at the door, she nearly ran out to answer it herself, desperate for a new face to break the monotony. Just in time, she remembered Mrs. K's warning: no one else must know she was living there. Period. At the moment, all society had was rumors from a jealous ex-lover, and the last thing they needed was cold hard evidence. Besides, with her luck, it'd probably turn out to be Collette. After that dream, she didn't want to see her again if she could help it.

She hid behind the doorway and tried to listen, but the visitor's voice was too quiet for her to decipher.

When the door shut, she went out into the hall, looking carefully to make sure there was no stranger there. "Hey, Thornton, who was that?"

"It was a shop boy." Thornton turned to Jamie, a ribbon-wrapped box in his hands. "He said that his lordship had sent this package for you, Miss Marten."

She smiled like a teenage girl who's heard that her crush likes her back. *Mike sent me a present?* She bit her lip and skipped over to Thornton. "Really? It's for me?"

The old man smiled fondly down at her as he handed her the package. "That is what the boy said, miss."

She clasped the beribboned box to her chest. "Thanks."

She flew into the sitting room, fingers picking at the knot before she'd even sat down. What had he gotten her? A book to keep her from going crazy with boredom? Jewelry because, well, they were engaged? Or maybe he'd talked to somebody about making her a toothbrush. Oooh, she'd murder for a toothbrush.

When the lavender ribbon finally melted apart, and she got the lid off the box, she realized it was none of those things.

It was candy.

They looked sort of like she'd imagined Turkish

Delights would look. Like the White Witch gave to Edmond in the Narnia books. Little gumdroppy mounds of crystal sugarcoated color.

She smiled down at the box. She wasn't a huge fan of candy, but since Mike had given them to her, she'd try one.

Reaching into the box, she picked one with a light dusting of powdered sugar. She sniffed it. A light citrus scent clung to the sweet. She parted her lips and delicately bit down into it. A strange mix of sweet and bitter filled her mouth.

"No!" Mrs. Knightsbridge flung open the door to the sitting room and flew across the room to Jamie. She knocked the rest of the candy from Jamie's hand back into the box. "Spit it out, spit it out!"

Jamie spit the half-chewed bite into her hand. "What the hell is wrong?"

Mrs. K yanked the box from her lap and grabbed her arm. "That one too. Drop it in the box, quickly."

Jamie did as she asked, completely confused. "Okay, mind telling me what the problem is?"

"We do not have time to lose." Mrs. K grabbed her by the upper arm and dragged her toward the kitchen. "You have been poisoned."

Twenty-Five

"What?" Jamie cried.

Mrs. K did not hesitate as she dragged Jamie from the room. "Collette has poisoned you. Come quickly!"

Fear sped Jamie's heart and she followed the housekeeper as fast as she could. Mrs. K shoved the beribboned box at one of the kitchen maids.

"Here. Do not touch any of the sweets. They have been poisoned. Take that box as far away as you can and discard it."

The maid's face was as terrified as Jamie was sure hers was, but the young girl took off out the kitchen door at a dead run.

"Jean Philippe, I need soap, hot water, clean cloths. Quickly. Miss Marten's life is in danger. Muriel, go and fetch her robe. Clara, bring the wooden box from beneath my bed. Now!"

The housekeeper sat Jamie down on a wooden stool and plunged their hands into the steamy bowl of water Jean Philippe set on the table in front of them. With a soapy stiff-bristled brush, she scrubbed at Jamie's right hand, the one that had held the sweet Jamie thought Mike had sent her.

"How do you know?" Jamie asked through a terror-thickened throat. "How did you know to stop me?"

Mrs. K dipped their hands in the basin and started brushing again. The bristles scraped at Jamie's skin, stinging with the strong soap. "My scrying bowl. The same one I saw you in. Collette. Louisa. The wine, the candy, the same violent shaking. It will happen again. I can only pray that we have caught it in time. Clara, set the box beside me, please."

Jamie's chest tightened, and she had trouble breathing. "Collette...poisoned me?"

Mrs. K nodded without looking up from her desperate task. "Jean Philippe, fresh water, now. Where is that robe, Muriel?"

After Jean Philippe delivered another bowl of hot water, he was banished from the kitchen. Jamie's beautiful yellow gown was cut from her body and thrown straight into the fire, in case any stray particles of the poison had found their way into the folds of fabric. Muriel removed Jamie's stays and petticoats, and dressed her in the nightgown. Muriel braided Jamie's hair as Mrs. K scrubbed her hands and arms until the flesh was bright red and raw.

For the first few moments, Jamie was too terrified to move. She let them work on her, obeying when they told her to move, to sit, to bend, whatever they asked.

But then the skin of her face tightened. The taste of pennies and metal filled her mouth. She couldn't sit anymore. She had to walk. To breathe. To run away. To shake off these small bugs crawling inside her skin. She had to get *out*.

"I...I'm sorry...Mrs. K...I can't sit." Jamie pulled away from Mrs. K as the housekeeper dried her arms. She needed to go. To move. Something.

She paced through the kitchen. Wringing her hands, she ignored the stares and worried voices of the maids around her. She was as juiced as she'd ever felt. More so than if she'd drunk a dozen Red Bulls. The room almost vibrated around her.

"Miss Jamie, drink this." Mrs. K held out a small brown vial.

Jamie reached for it, but her hands trembled too much to grip the glass. Mrs. K held her head gently in the crook of an elbow and poured a dark brown liquid into her mouth. Jamie coughed but swallowed the woody-tasting brew.

"Now come. We must get you to your room." Mrs. K laid a gentle arm around Jamie's shoulders. Her head wobbled, almost like one of those little dashboard Chihuahuas, knocking against Mrs. K's arm over and over. She couldn't keep it still, no matter how hard she tried.

Flashes of light fringed her vision, and her heart ran faster than Baron after a handkerchief. Tears streamed out of the corners of her eyes as Muriel and Mrs. K helped her up the stairs. Her toes dragged on the carpet of the stairs, vibrating alien beings that no longer had any connection to her brain.

They reached the landing after a million years, but her legs gave out in front of Mike's room. She collapsed to the cold wood, knocking the back of her head against the hall table.

"*Thornton, George*! We need your aid, *quickly*!" Mrs. K's voice sounded shrilly, sort of far away.

Jamie's heels drummed against the wooden floor. She tried to grab them, to stop them, but her hands were shaking too hard. Ice cold. Her limbs were freezing, but sweat broke out all over her body. Her teeth chattered.

A shock of pain skewered her chest, arching her back in agony.

This is it.

I'm going to die.

She didn't have to choose between a future with Mike or a future at home.

I have no future at all.

Several sets of hands picked her up. She wished she could have seen how they held her. She was flopping worse than a newly caught fish. But she couldn't stop, no matter how hard she tried. Even after they laid her in her bed.

Jamie didn't know how long she lay there, shivering, trembling, and shaking all over. Muriel and Mrs. K stayed right there with her. Mrs. K put cool cloths on her brow when her fever spiked higher.

The flashes didn't stop. Whenever she moved her head, which was a lot because of the way her back continued to arch, another beam of light would skewer her. The pains in her chest continued, over and over and over again. She wondered how long it would take for this poison to kill her. She wished she could pass out and miss it. She was afraid. She didn't want to die. Tears leaked from the corners of her eyes as she fought the poison's grip. It was too hard. She wasn't going to be able to beat it. She'd die here in this Lemon Room, without the love of her life anywhere near.

"Mike," she whispered hoarsely through the agonizing pain gripping her chest. "Mike."

"Please, Jamie, oh please stay with us." Mrs. K's face was streaked with tears as she cupped Jamie's trembling cheek.

❧

Never in Micah's life had he been such a slave to his own fear.

When the footman burst into His Grace's estate room, all the gentlemen in it had stared at such a sudden intrusion. But Micah had leapt to his feet and followed George without so much as a by-your-leave to his host. Damn the consequences, for the look on the boy's face could mean but one thing—his Jamie was in danger.

George caught him up on the wild ride back to the town home in Micah's phaeton. When the words "poison" and "tremors" met the earl's ears, cold terror closed his throat. He should never have left her. He whipped his horses into a gallop, tooling them expertly down the twining streets of Town.

After Micah pulled his team to a stop, he threw the reins to a surprised George and leapt to the ground, not stopping as he bolted into the house. Taking the steps two at a time, he hit the landing in a dead run. He rounded the corner of the hallway and skidded to a stop in the doorway of Jamie's beloved Lemon Room.

Her limbs flopped and flailed, despite the restraining hands of both Muriel and Mrs. Knightsbridge. Her eyes rolled wildly, almost like an animal out of its mind with fear and pain. Anguished moans poured from her, and tears tracked down her reddened cheeks.

Micah slammed his lids closed and staggered backward. No. Not again. Not to Jamie.

"My lord," Mrs. Knightsbridge called desperately. "Please. She's called for you."

The prison of his panic could not keep him from his love. Opening his eyes, he set his jaw and marched determinedly to her bedside. Muriel backed away in tearful deference, and he took the maid's place at Jamie's side.

"Jamie," he said, ashamed at the naked pain in his voice. "Jamie, can you hear me?"

"Mike?" She focused on him for a moment, her head bobbing and trembling as she fought the poison.

"Yes, dearling, I am here. What has happened to you?" He laid his hand on her cheek, helping to steady her against the raging storm in her blood. Her teeth clacked together as her body fought. She didn't answer him.

"Mrs. Knightsbridge, what can we do?" He had to keep himself composed. He could not afford to fall apart. Jamie needed strength, and by God he would give it to her.

"We've done all we can, my lord." Mrs. Knightsbridge's voice was clear, though her face was also tracked with tears. "Just be here with her, in case…"

"No." He leapt to his feet, not releasing Jamie's hand. His glare nearly skewered the housekeeper in half. "Do not invite tragedy here. She will survive. I refuse to accept any alternative. Is that clear?" She had to survive. He could not be responsible for the death of another woman, most especially the only woman he'd ever truly loved. And by leaving her, he was just as culpable as if he'd poured the poison down her throat himself.

"Yes, my lord." The housekeeper turned away, busying herself with clean cloths and potions on the small table by the window.

"Mike?" Jamie's voice was so faint he barely knew it was her.

He dropped to his knees by her bedside. "Yes, dearling."

Her tremors worsened, and he fought them as best he could without bruising her, holding her shoulders lightly against the covers. "I…I…"

"Shh, love," he said past the bitter lump in his throat. "Rest now. You can tell me when you feel better."

With a sigh, she closed her eyes, and her body went limp under his hands.

His anguished cry echoed from the yellow walls she'd loved so. "Jamie!"

Twenty-Six

WHEN JAMIE WOKE UP, SHE WASN'T DEAD. THAT KIND
of surprised her, so she blinked twice. *Nope. Still here.* She
sat up and peered around. The Lemon Room, looking
messier than she'd ever seen it, surrounded her. Basins,
cloths, bottles of medicine, teacups, glasses, and clothing
were scattered throughout the room. It almost made her
feel at home—like, back in her time home.

She threw back the covers and swung her feet over
the edge of the bed. Her body responded normally. Her
jaw was sore, and her nerves jittery, but other than a
weird desire to take up jogging, she was back to fighting
form. Whatever Collette had used had apparently not
panned out like she'd planned.

Even thinking the name of that bitch sent a cold shock
down Jamie's spine. *Collette.* She'd tried to kill Jamie
twice now. The first time might have been an accident, but poisoning her? That was pure premeditation.
Collette had it out for her, there was no denying that.
If not for Mrs. Knightsbridge's scrying bowl keeping a
check on that psychopath, Jamie would be dead by now.
Considering she'd only ingested a tiny amount of the
poison, and the pain she'd gone through, without the

housekeeper's intervention she'd be pushing up tulips. *Wait, those are from Holland, aren't they? Lavender. Pushing up lavender. That sounds suitably English.*

Jamie padded across the cream carpeting, avoiding a mound of white cloths, and headed for her old pal the chamber pot. While she was behind the screen, the hinges on the bedroom door squeaked.

"Be right out," she called. She yanked her nightgown back down, rounded the screen, and headed for the basin to wash her hands. Mike stood by the foot of her bed, face pale and drawn. She half smiled at him, but he didn't speak until she'd dried her fingers on a soft white towel.

"Jamie." His strained voice brought her head around. "I cannot tell you the depth of my regret."

Jamie shook her head, confusion wrinkling her forehead as she closed the gap between them. "Regret? Why…"

He stepped past her, ignoring her outstretched hand. "I have been unable thus far to discover the source of the poisoned sweets. I have hired a Bow Street Runner to assist in the search. I cannot imagine the anger you must feel for my failure. I will discover who sent them. I promise you…"

"But I know who sent them," Jamie blurted, wondering why he didn't.

He shook his head as he leaned against the mantel. His knuckles were white as he gripped it. "I know what you are thinking. Collette did threaten you, but she cannot have been responsible. She was with her protector all day yesterday. They were seen together."

Jamie shook her head, sinking down on the edge of her bed as her knees went curiously weak. "That can't be. There's proof it was her! Mrs.…"

Jamie trailed off as Mike turned to face her. She didn't know why her throat suddenly closed off, but the lack of air gave her a second to collect her wits. *Mrs. Knightsbridge. A witch. Her nervousness about anyone finding out about it.* As much as Jamie wanted Collette to pay for what she'd nearly done, Mrs. K had saved Jamie's life. It wasn't her secret to tell.

"I know it was Collette. I can't tell you how I know, but you have to trust me."

"What proof is there? Why can you not tell me?"

Jamie looked down at her toes as anxiety twisted her lungs into pretzels. "I just…can't."

After a moment of strained silence, Mike straightened his waistcoat. "Collette is being watched, but since you refuse to tell me the truth about your suspicions, I cannot be certain. I need to ask you a very important question."

His stare speared her, and she took a shuddering breath.

"Do you yet know how to go back to your home?"

She wasn't sure what made her hesitate to tell him the truth. This was Mike. Her earl. The best man she'd ever met, mule-headedness notwithstanding. He loved her. She'd probably hurt him by refusing to tell him about Mrs. K. She couldn't hurt him more by lying to him now.

She nodded slowly.

He closed his lids and tipped his chin skyward. She watched his Adam's apple bob up and down above the white froth of lace at his throat.

"I must ask, for your own safety, that you return there." His deep voice was as serious as his eyes were when they opened.

She stopped breathing. Swallowed hard. An odd prickle started in her eyes as she asked, "Will you be coming with me?"

She anticipated the shake of his head before it even happened. He hesitated, but the answer, when it came, was definite. "No."

Tiny cracks ran through her heart, spiderwebbing the battered organ. "Oh."

He took a faltering step toward her but stopped just shy. His voice was strong as he said, "I have failed you. I nearly caused your death."

She jumped to her feet, indignant that he'd even suggest it. "No, you didn't…"

He stopped her with a palm in the air. "I did. I should have anticipated the threat. I did not, and you almost paid with your life. It is unforgivable."

"No," she whispered, anxiety clogging her throat. "No, it wasn't your fault."

"Don't you see, Jamie?" His voice lowered, roughening. "Seeing you the way I saw Louisa has broken me. I cannot face it again."

"But it wasn't your fault," she said, closing the gap between them, grabbing his hands. They were ice cold. "It wasn't you at all."

He stepped back, pain clear on his face. "A man who cannot keep you safe is a man who does not deserve you."

He crossed to the door.

"Mike, please," she said through her tears. Her voice came out strained, pitiful. "Let's talk about it."

He didn't turn to face her as he turned the knob to leave. So softly she couldn't really believe that she heard it, he said, "There is nothing that can be done. I have failed you. Please, be safe upon your return journey. Good-bye, Miss Marten."

He closed the door behind him, the click of the latch finishing the crack in her heart.

She stared at the back of the door, wondering what in the hell she was supposed to do now. She sank down on the edge of the bed and let the tears fall.

It was only a few minutes later when a timid knock sounded.

"Miss Jamie? Are you well?" Mrs. Knightsbridge's voice floated through the door.

"Not really," she said, turning as she dashed the moisture on her cheeks away. "But come in anyway."

Jamie flopped onto her back as the door shut behind the housekeeper. She started picking up the mess in the room, not commenting on the evidence of Jamie's recent crying jag.

When Jamie was sure her throat had relaxed enough to sound more normal, she spoke. "Mrs. K?"

"Yes?"

Jamie turned her head toward the housekeeper. "What would happen if Mike found out you were a witch?"

Mrs. K paused midstoop, abandoning the basin she'd been about to pick up. She stood and faced Jamie, looking older and more careworn than Jamie had ever seen her. She walked to the bed, sitting softly beside Jamie.

"Micah is like a son to me," she said, looking down at her hands. "For a man in his position to employ a witch? It would be unthinkable."

"So, it's not that someone would throw you in jail or kill you, but you don't want to disappoint Mike." Jamie sat up, pinning the housekeeper with a look of complete desperation. She had to tell the truth. It was Jamie's only shot.

"People still fear the old ways. His lordship has suffered enough without having to bear the shame of a housekeeper that dabbles in witchcraft."

Jamie swung her legs off the opposite side of the bed, staring at the wall. "So, we can't prove that Collette tried to kill me because you don't want Mike disappointed in you. He's broken our engagement and told me to go home because he can't keep me safe from whoever's trying to kill me. He has no proof it's Collette because the one with the proof is scared to give it to him."

Jamie stood and rounded the end of the bed. She stared at the old woman, hoping the pain and confusion that boiled inside her was plain in her eyes.

"If you cared about him the way you say you do, then you'd tell the truth. I love him, and I really think he loves me too. But how am I supposed to figure this out now? You are my only shot at happiness with him, and you won't say a damn word."

Mrs. K didn't reply, only shook her head sadly.

Jamie slammed the flat of her hand against the wall, anger and pain overwhelming her control. "You are the whole reason I'm here! You didn't give a shit about what you took me from, how this little vacation would affect my life, or anything! You claimed you were thinking about him, but what were you really doing, Wilhelmina? Were you thinking about him or about yourself?" Jamie stepped over to her, her voice lowering to a harsh whisper. "Well, congratulations. I'm in love. He's in love. And now we're both fucked because you can't tell the goddamn truth."

Mrs. Knightsbridge's cheeks were wet with tears when she got up and left the room. Jamie didn't apologize.

Jamie spent the rest of the day in the garden with Baron. She tossed sticks for him, but he gave up chasing them when she started dropping them right in front of her feet. She didn't have the energy to hurl them across the yard anymore. She didn't have the energy to fight anymore. She wanted things to go back to the way they were before Collette had poisoned her. Back to believing that she and Mike could somehow surmount the odds against them. She saw the obstacles way too clearly now. She didn't like that.

As she slumped against a tree trunk, watching Baron wallow in a patch of sunlight, she thought about doing what Mike had asked her—asking Mrs. Knightsbridge to open the portal, stepping through it, and going back to her lonely existence in her own time. Tears stung her eyes at the thought, and she slammed her lids shut. No. She couldn't. She'd stay here and fight for it. For them. He loved her, she loved him, and they were worth fighting for. Maybe he'd discover it was Collette on his own, and she wouldn't have to depend on the housekeeper. Either way, Jamie had to tell him she'd made a decision and hope that he respected it. It wouldn't be easy to convince him, but she had no other choice if she wanted to keep him.

When the sun fell low in the cloudy sky, Jamie made her way in from the chilly yard. Mike still wasn't back home. She guessed he was out trying to do detective work to figure out what Jamie already knew. Collette was a psychotic bitch who'd killed Louisa and tried to kill Jamie to have the earl—and his money—for herself. Jamie shook her head as she stomped her way up the stairs. *If Mrs. K would…No. She won't.* Jamie would have to do this on her own, without any help from the housekeeper. Jamie shut the bedroom door behind her and rang for Muriel.

The maid helped Jamie dress for dinner, the little maid quieter than usual. Jamie wondered if Mrs. K told her they'd argued. Probably not, as not even Muriel was aware of the housekeeper's other nature. Jamie was sure her nervousness didn't help anything. Her one-word answers to Muriel's questions made it clear she was preoccupied.

Muriel dressed Jamie in the most daring outfit she'd ever put her in—a midnight-blue dress, its wide neckline plunging low, revealing almost as much cleavage as she'd seen in the ballroom a few nights ago. Muriel pinned jewels in the curls she mounded high on Jamie's head and laid a beautiful necklace around her throat. The deep color made Jamie's skin and hair highlights glow.

"Thank you," Jamie said as she pulled on her gloves and stepped to the bedroom door.

"You look beautiful, miss."

Jamie descended the stairs in hopes that her earl would be home for dinner. Thornton gave her a glass of wine when she reached the sitting room, and she sipped it nervously for half an hour. No Mike.

George escorted her into the dining room, seating her in her normal place. There was a setting for Mike, but he didn't show.

The lamb was delicious, and she didn't want to hurt Jean Philippe's feelings, but she couldn't eat more than a few bites. She was too nervous. Where was he? What was he doing, thinking, who was he with? Why wouldn't he come home and let her talk to him?

After poking at her food for a solid hour, Jamie finally gave up and went to the music room. She sank down on the bench, rested her fingers on the keys, and waited.

Nothing.

She rubbed against the ivory, the unique, smooth texture rippling against her fingers, but the music stayed silent inside her. She pressed a few keys, but they came out discordant, wrong. She shook her head, trying to clear it. Where was her muse?

"You should have gone."

Jamie stood, stumbling over the end of the bench. *Mike.* He stood in the doorway, only the white of his shirt contrasting with the deep black of his waistcoat, jacket, and pants. He looked so severe, his cheeks drawn and eyes almost as black as his coat.

Jamie marshaled her courage and loosed the torpedoes. "I'm not going back."

He took a step toward her. "You must."

"No, I mustn't. We love each other. We can beat this thing together, but if I go back, that's it. I think we deserve another chance, so I'm not going anywhere." Jamie lifted her chin, trying to look determined.

He closed his eyes, and his head fell. Half a dozen heartbeats went by before he said anything.

"Is there nothing I can say to change your mind?"

She shook her head, willing her fluttering pulse to even out.

He opened his eyes. His solemn expression seemed to pierce her through. "If you are to stay with me, then I will do what I deem necessary."

A little ray of hope lit her dark and anxious heart. "I can stay, really?"

He straightened his jacket and looked down on her. That look...that autocratic, forbidding, austere look. He hadn't used that look on her since, well, since the first days she'd been there.

"I must go and inform the staff of your decision, and their new duties because of it. I bid you good evening."

His curt bow was followed by a nod, and he turned to go.

"Mike, what does that mean? Wait, come back. Let's talk about this."

He paused in the doorway, not turning back. "I will do what is required to keep you safe."

And he left.

Twenty-Seven

JAMIE SAT IN THE MUSIC ROOM FOR TWO HOURS AFTER Mike left. She didn't play a note. She stared at the wall, wishing she could make sense of everything. Of anything, really. He hadn't fought her decision to stay, but his reaction to it had been so odd. Maybe he needed more time.

It seemed like time was only adding to their problems, though. With every passing day, she was more in love with him, and things were more impossible than ever. What a crap situation this had turned out to be. Nothing was right in her world. Everything was skewed, tilted, just off enough to make things impossible.

When she stood, her legs were numb from sitting so still. As her circulation returned, the angry pins and needles stabbed her with every step she took, and she was forced to go slowly. Muted voices rumbled inside Mike's office, but the door was shut tight. She couldn't make out what was being said, but Thornton wasn't at his usual post.

Jamie climbed the stairs laboriously, clutching at the banister for support. Muriel was waiting for her in the Lemon bedchamber, and as the maid helped her remove the midnight gown, Jamie couldn't help wondering if she'd won or lost that battle.

Either way, she thought as she snuggled in bed next to a bony gray dog, *I'm here. And I'm not leaving Mike without a fight.*

<hr/>

Mike didn't show up to breakfast the next morning. Jamie hadn't expected him, honestly, but it was hard not to be disappointed that he was avoiding her so much. She wasn't really hungry, so she decided to take Baron out for a walk instead of staring at a plate full of food. It wasn't until she'd grabbed Baron's leash and tried to exit the front door with the dog that she figured out why Mike was avoiding her.

"My apologies, Miss Marten, but I cannot allow you to leave the house today." Thornton's voice was kind but firm as he blocked her way to the exit. "George will take the hound for his walk."

"What do you mean, I can't leave the house?" Jamie stared at the old butler as the red-headed footman came forward and took the strip of leather from her nerveless hand.

"His lordship's orders. I am sorry, miss." Thornton stared at her, his salt-and-pepper eyebrows high in sympathy.

George's face was pale but his movements sure as he slipped the lead onto Baron. The footman and the dog disappeared out the front door, Baron's whip-like tail wagging faster as he trotted out into the sunshine. The door shut softly behind them, leaving Jamie alone with the butler in the dimly lit entryway.

She looked down at the toes of her slippers. "Guess I'll go walk in the garden, then."

Thornton stopped her as she turned. "Miss?"

"Yeah?"

"You are not to leave the house."

Her jaw dropped. "I can't even go out into the garden?"

He shook his head slowly.

Frustration simmered in her chest as she stomped away from Thornton. She had to leave before she shot the messenger. It certainly wasn't Thornton's fault that his master was an overprotective dictator.

Jamie, he loves you. Somebody tried to poison you a couple of days ago. He's trying to keep you safe.

Shut up, logical side. I have no time for you.

Jamie flopped down on the settee in the parlor and stared at the ceiling. *Lord, I thought I'd been bored out of my skull before. What the heck do I do now?*

The day passed more slowly than any previous day ever had. Jamie tried to bribe Muriel into sneaking her out the servants' entrance. She just wanted to get some fresh air. The maid agreed but chickened out when Mrs. K began loudly singing as she swept the back stairs. Jamie opened her bedroom window and poked her head out, but the garden was too far down to jump. She'd probably break a leg if she tried it.

Jamie sat in her bedroom, chair scooted as close to the window as she could get it. She propped her chin in her hands on the windowsill and sighed as bluebirds hopped from branch to branch in the garden tree. Since her phone was completely dead now, there was nothing to distract her at all. Her thoughts turned to her real-life adventure game, which could be deadly if she didn't stay on her toes.

Collette couldn't know she was still alive. Her poison had worked for Louisa, and there was no reason she should suspect a different outcome for Jamie. Jamie would have to make sure to keep Collette in the

dark. Any other attempts on Jamie's life would probably convince Mike he had to force her to go back
home. She'd evaded his wishes this time, but she had
a feeling it wouldn't be a regular occurrence. He was
too used to getting his way. *Smug, entitled, beautiful,
wonderful man.*

Jamie killed time staring outside and chucking some
hazelnuts out the window to the squirrels. She almost
beaned one upside the head with a nut. *Whoops.*

She still wasn't hungry, but she was so excited when
lunchtime rolled around to have something to do that
she could barely stand it.

When she got into the dining room, Mike was seated
at his usual place. Two plates full of food were set in front
of him, and two glasses were full beside them. He held a
fork, and another lay beside one of his plates.

Jamie walked to her usual spot, confusion wrinkling
her forehead as she sat at the empty space. Where her
place setting usually was, empty tablecloth gleamed at
her. What a way to diet.

"Are you extra hungry? If you're a growing boy, you
can certainly have some of mine, but it's polite to ask
before you steal someone's food."

Mike shook his head, not even acknowledging her
lame attempt at humor. He continued cutting into a
piece of beef on one of the plates. He took a bite, chewing thoroughly before swallowing. His mouth worked,
almost looking like he was tasting it thoughtfully.

"Is everything okay? Should I come back later?"

He swallowed and wiped his mouth before replying.
"One moment."

She watched as he finished sampling a bite of everything on the plate, making the same thoughtful tasting
face after each bite. He took a healthy swig of the wine

in one of the glasses, swished it around in his mouth, then nodded.

He stood, lifting the plate and glass he'd been eating and drinking from, and brought them over to her place. He set the plate in front of her, and the glass at her right hand.

"There. It has all been tasted. I have suffered no ill effects, so you needn't be concerned with tainted food or wine."

She stared down at the plate in front of her, trying to process what had just happened. Mike went back to his own plate and began cutting his meat.

Jamie picked up her fork, but the metal was strangely cold to the touch. She put it back down again, rubbing her palm against her skirt. She looked over to Mike, who was now eating like nothing had happened.

"What was that all about?"

He swallowed the bite he'd been chewing and looked at his plate as he spoke. "Since you refused to return to your own time where you are safe, I am taking measures to protect you. Any further attempts to poison you will fail, as you will not consume anything that has not been first tasted by another."

Bitter, leaden worry filled her stomach like rocks. "So if someone poisons my food, it's not a problem because you'll drop dead instead of me. Is that what you're saying?"

Mike crooked a brow at her as he sipped his wine but didn't say anything.

"Sorry, but that isn't really okay with me. Oddly enough, the last few days haven't made me stop loving you. If someone tries to poison me again but gets you instead, I'd be worse off than if I'd died in the first place."

He leaned forward, jaw tight and eyes intense. "I asked you to return. You refused. This is my home, and if you wish to stay here with me, then I will do what is necessary to keep you safe."

Jamie stared at him for a long time. Her brain and her heart couldn't agree on what to feel. On one hand, Mike's caring and consideration made her feel priceless, loved, cherished. On the other, his autocratic, high-handed manner and refusal to see her as an equal felt about as great as sandpaper on a sunburn.

She looked down at the plate that he'd set in front of her. If she ate, then she'd be showing him her approval of his actions. If she didn't, then she'd be throwing his protection in his face. Talk about damned one way or the other.

She shook her head and breathed heavily. The truth. She had to tell him. They couldn't go on this way, not without her wanting to strangle him with his high-handed attitude. Closing her eyes, she said, "We need to talk."

"There is nothing to discuss."

"No, Mike, there's a lot to discuss. I know that things are different here, but where I come from, men and women in a romantic relationship are partners. Equals. I know you think you're doing the right thing, but you're making me feel like a child who can't take care of herself."

"What would you have me do, Miss Marten? Shall I stand by and watch you waltz into harm's way with naught but your wits to save you?" The rough edge in his voice pulled her eyes open.

"We need to talk about these things. We need to come to decisions about what to do together. You can't make up rules for me without discussing them with me first. Tell me the truth about what you're feeling, what's going on, and we can decide what to do together. If Collette tries something else, then we'll…"

"The truth, Miss Marten. What an interesting idea. Perhaps you'd care to enlighten me about a truth of your own. Perhaps the proof of your certainty that Collette Dubois is responsible for your most recent brush with death?"

She couldn't say a word, and the anger and pain that crossed Mike's face nearly crushed her. *Damn it, Mrs. K. You have no clue what you're doing to us.*

"I see." He slid his chair back and laid his napkin beside his still mostly full plate. "Enjoy your meal, Miss Marten."

He left the dining room without another word.

When he'd gone, she looked down at the plate in front of her. A neat, square segment was cut from the meat. The potato had the marks of fork-tines in it. Everything on her plate bore tiny reminders of Mike's love, even if it had manifested in an overbearing kind of way.

With a heavy heart, and a head chock full o' confusion, she proceeded to eat the meal that Mike had placed in front of her.

⤔

Two more days went by in the same way. Mike barely spoke to Jamie, and when he did, he grilled her more on her certainty of Collette's guilt. Jamie begged Mrs. Knightsbridge to tell the truth, but she refused over and over again. Mike didn't kiss her, and he definitely didn't invite her to his bedchamber after dark. She prowled the house like a caged tiger in the zoo, with a growl and a temper to match. Everyone avoided her with the exception of old Thornton. Jamie thought he kind of liked having someone to argue with.

Jamie sat in the music room, but the notes wouldn't come. She stared at the pages of a book she'd already read, but her eyes couldn't focus on the words in front of her. She tried to remember how to make chocolate chip cookies, but Jean Philippe kicked her out of his kitchen when she caught an apron on fire.

She was stir crazy in the worst way, and by the third day, she had decided that she'd almost rather be killed than spend another hour cooped up in that house.

"Baron, this is crazy," Jamie told the greyhound. He was curled up on the foot of her bed, cheek puffing out with his breaths as he slept. *Even the dog ignores me.*

She talked to him anyway.

"I've got to get out. Just for a walk. I learned my lesson last time, and I'll stick close to the house, but I've got to get some air. It's for my sanity. I'll sneak out and nobody will ever know. You can keep a secret, right, boy?"

Baron yawned and stretched, long bony legs hanging off the edge of the bed.

"I'll take that as a yes." Jamie patted his head before walking away from him.

She pulled a cloak on over the plain blue gown that Muriel had dressed her in only an hour ago, plunked on a bonnet, and left the snoozing greyhound in her bedroom. Listening carefully, she waited at the top of the servants' stairs. Low voices mumbled far away.

She tiptoed on the edges of the stairs, breathing as lightly as she could. Her heart thumped like crazy, and adrenaline thrummed through her body. Her slippers were silent and she moved fast, conquering the stairs before more than a few seconds passed.

She paused, flattening her back against the wall before the door to the kitchen. It stood open, and the voices that she'd heard before were much clearer now. Jean Philippe was going over the night's menu with the kitchen staff.

"The mutton will be hashed, and the vegetables must

be roasted. I will require some wine for the *jus*, and the onions and potatoes must be peeled promptly."

She chanced a peek around the corner.

The big chef stood in the center of the crowded room, his large hands gesturing fluently as he spoke. The kitchen maids were all clustered around him like so many mobcap-wearing grapes. Their attention was completely trained on the chef. No one even glanced in her direction.

Hey, good luck for once! Jamie ducked past the doorway quick as a bunny and was out the door and down the alley in a flash.

The sun shone fiercely, and the day was almost too warm for the cloak she'd put on, but she couldn't have cared less. She was out, and she was free, and she was going to enjoy it, come hell or high water.

It was sort of early in the day for most of society to be out and about, and she was glad for that. There was less chance of running into anyone who would possibly try to kill her. She'd walk for fifteen minutes or so and sneak back in through the back door of the house before anyone noticed she was gone. Piece of cake.

She hummed to herself as she went along, feeling more relaxed than she had in almost a week. Out there in the sunshine, she could almost pretend that things were normal, that she and Mike were good, and nobody was trying to kill her, and they were happy. She wished Baron was with her, but sneaking out with a big grey-hound might have been a wee bit obvious.

Most of the people around at that time of the morning were servants, tradesmen, and people who looked like they worked for a living. They hustled along the cobbled streets, not really even glancing in her direction. She loosed the frogs of the cloak and removed it with a relieved sigh. Bundling the thick blue wool over her arm, she rounded the corner of the street.

She was careful this time, making sure to keep track of every turn and step she made. She never strayed too far from the house. After all, she wasn't interested in actually getting killed—only getting some air.

The sun rose higher in the sky, and a nagging worry wormed its way through her calm relaxed mood.

You shouldn't have left the house, Jamie, her subconscious admonished. *Mike will be so hurt. He's trying to keep you safe, and you ignore him this way? He'll never forgive you for betraying his trust like this.*

She shook her head, trying to keep the doubts at bay, but they whispered insistently, stealing the peace that her walk had restored to her.

She turned and headed back the way she'd come.

She'd been really vigilant about her route this time, and it was much easier to find her way back home. She hurried, worried now that her absence would be discovered. She didn't want to hurt Mike, not at all. It was so hard to convince him that she wanted to be his partner. This little stunt would probably ruin any chance she had of convincing him of that if he found out about it.

Jamie was within about six homes of Mike's when a dark-haired woman caught her eye.

She was standing in front of an open window on the second floor of a beautiful house. The panes were open, curtains fluttering in the slight breeze. Her red lips formed a word, but Jamie was too far away to hear what it was. It looked like "you."

Terror soaked Jamie's limbs. She slung her cloak over her shoulders, yanked her bonnet down farther on her head, and hustled as quickly as she could for home.

What a complete disaster. Not only had she snuck

out of the house like a troubled teen, she'd been seen by the one person on earth that would like for her to die a horrible, painful death. How much of an idiot could she be? Maybe Mike was right, and she wasn't smart enough to be treated like an equal. Lord knows she'd acted like a complete idiot, running out in broad daylight when she was supposed to be hiding.

She stepped on a loose stone and rolled her ankle over, twisting it with a gasp. Her momentum pitched her forward. The sharp report of gunfire echoed in her ears as she fell.

Twenty-Eight

JAMIE HAD ALWAYS HAD A PRETTY VIVID IMAGINATION. Since she was an only child, her playmates were the cartoon and movie heroes of her time, swashbuckling characters from the funny pages. When the villain caught up to them and the hero was cut down by gunfire, the Amazonian princess and Jamie were the only ones who could save the galaxy. They were both grievously wounded but fought bravely, and they always eventually saved the day.

As Jamie hit the ground hard, it was a lot easier to focus on the distant past than the painful present. Back there, she was safe and comfortable. Here, she was lying facedown on the rough, hard cobblestone street. There, a serious injury would be completely healed when her mom kissed it all better. Here, agony screamed through her arm, a supernova of pain with its vibrant center in her upper biceps. There, the evil would always be defeated by bedtime. Here, if she couldn't shake off the pain and shock of the idea that she'd really, truly been shot, Collette was sure to come down there and finish the job.

Lying prone on a stone sidewalk is actually not a bad place to take stock of injuries if you can get past the incredible discomfort of it. Her arm, of course, was screaming with red-hot streaks of agony, making it hard to focus on her other problems. Her shortness of breath was almost certainly due to fear and shock. Other than a tingling ache in the ankle that she'd rolled, she was surprisingly okay.

"Up, Jamie," she said aloud, the sound of her own voice oddly comforting. "Time to haul ass."

She struggled to her feet as fast as she could, gripping her injured arm tightly with her opposite hand. Hot blood filled her palm, a slow, seeping drip that was almost comforting.

No spurts. That's good. Should mean she didn't nick an artery.

Once Jamie stood, she didn't wait for the world to stop swaying; she sprinted for Mike's house, not looking back. Another pop sounded, kicking up shards of rock only feet from her. She didn't slow down even though the ache in her ankle got stronger with every step. Her slippered feet pounded against the stones of the street as she kept that tall, stately town home in her sights. *Please let me be out of Collette's range, please.*

When she rounded the corner and hobbled into the alley toward the servants' entrance, the sound of rapid footsteps reached her ears. She came face to face with Mrs. Knightsbridge only seconds later.

"Watched any interesting water-bowl TV lately?" Jamie asked, looking pointedly at the blood seeping out from between her fingers.

Mrs. K shook her head and led Jamie into the house.

❧

Jamie sat on a stool in her bedroom, wearing only her corset, petticoats, shift, and bloomers. She winced as Mrs. K tended to the wound on her arm.

"*Ouch*. Careful, that arm is still attached. Well, it was before you got to it."

"You were very fortunate, Miss Jamie. The bullet only grazed your arm. Had you not fallen when you did, it would be a very different outcome."

"That's me," Jamie said glumly, hissing in a breath when Mrs. K applied some more of her mystical healing goop to her wound. "Luckiest bitch alive."

Mrs. K wound strips of clean cotton around her arm, knotting the ends to keep it in place. "There. I shall change the dressing after your bath."

Jamie nodded, examining the white bandage on her arm. It was harder now to speak to Mrs. K than it had ever been before. She'd liked the housekeeper, and more than that, she'd trusted her. But now, when her refusal to tell the truth had nearly cost Jamie her life again, she was less inclined to be so forgiving. Mrs. K started packing her healing supplies back into the large wooden box, and as Jamie watched her, she couldn't help asking.

"Do you think maybe now you can tell Mike the truth about Collette?"

Her hands slowed as they placed a small jar of fluid back into its place in the box. She cleared her throat, and her fingers trembled as they reached for the lid of the case.

"I have told his lordship that I believe she is responsible."

"Did you mention that you had actually witnessed it?"

The box's latch squeaked as she fastened it. She smoothed her already immaculate brown and gray hair, eyes darting back and forth.

The dull throb in Jamie's arm shortened her already tried patience. "That's a no."

Mrs. K lifted the case, not looking back at Jamie. "I must help Jean Philippe prepare the dining room for the evening meal."

Jamie stared at the woman's back, uncertain of what to say for several moments. It was only when Mrs. K stepped out of the room and the door was swinging shut that Jamie spoke.

"It's his happiness or yours, Wilhelmina."

The oak paused, then continued on its way until the latch clicked softly.

❧

Mrs. K apparently didn't tell any of the other servants about Jamie sneaking out or about her injuries. Muriel asked about the white bandage on Jamie's arm as she helped her dress for dinner, but Jamie told the maid that she'd tripped and hit her arm on the piano. Muriel dressed Jamie in a rose-colored silk gown with sort of puffed, long sleeves that concealed the bandage completely.

Muriel piled Jamie's hair on top of her head, taking extra care with it tonight for some reason. Maybe it was because Jamie looked so pale and worried. Jamie knew she could use the extra help that Muriel's clever hairdressing hands could achieve. She placed a delicate chain around Jamie's throat, the combination of the silver and the deep neckline of the gown making her neck look lean and long. Her cheeks were pale, the circles beneath her eyes plain. She turned from the mirror in disgust. Even Muriel's considerable talent couldn't erase the strain the last week had placed on her face.

Every night before, Jamie had wanted Mike to come to dinner. Tonight, as she slowly descended the staircase, favoring her bum ankle and listening hard for the sound of her earl's voice, she hoped he'd be somewhere else. She'd have to lie to him about going out today and what had happened. The truth would hurt him too much.

She hated to deceive him but confessing her near-fatal stupidity was even more impossible to face.

She thought she was home free when Mike wasn't in the sitting room, but when Thornton announced dinner, Mike closed the office door behind him and joined her in the hallway.

"Thought you weren't coming," she said to him softly. She tried her damnedest to keep her stride even, equal, completely normal. It was nearly impossible, pain ricocheting up her leg with every step.

He took her hand and drew it through the crook of his arm. "My apologies, Miss Marten. I did not mean to give that impression." His deep voice was so polite that it eased her tense nerves, but only a little.

Mike pulled out her chair for her, and as she rounded it to sit down, her ankle gave out. She gave a small gasp of pain, stumbling to right herself.

"Are you well?"

She nodded and gratefully collapsed onto the chair he still held for her. "Oh yeah, I'm fine. Sorry about that. Twisted my ankle earlier today. Guess I'm just a klutz." Her laugh came out high-pitched and nervous. She could have kicked herself if she was that limber—and if she had two working feet.

Jamie didn't look up at Mike as he went to his own place at the table.

Each plate of food that was set in front of her had small bites removed. Jamie shook her head but didn't complain. She knew it wouldn't do any good.

The mutton and roast vegetables were really good, and Mike kept the conversation light, happy even. Her tension began to melt away, and she laughed at Mike's tales of dowagers and debutantes. He smiled often, the dimple in his chin deepening and his eyes twinkling

when he looked at her. It wasn't until the plates were cleared away that his speech turned more serious.

"I want to apologize, Jamie."

She gave him a confused half smile. "For what?"

He looked down at his hands, which were clasped together on the table. The snow-white linen of the table-cloth made the small hairs on his hands look darker, contouring the strong lines. "For making you feel less than you are. For treating you as if you have no sense, no thought for your own safety. I only sought to protect you, but in doing so I have made you unhappy. Can you forgive me?"

Oh no. She'd been shot all over again, but this time the word-bullet had found its mark straight through her stupid lies and into the middle of her heart.

Play it cool, Jamie. No blood, no foul. Well, only your blood, and it's secret blood, and he doesn't have to know about it.

"Hey, don't beat yourself up about it," she said brightly. Her arm throbbed in time with her thumping heart, that organ seeming to scream *liar* with every beat. "It's fine. You were doing what you thought was right. I don't blame you for that at all."

Mike rose to his feet, his face a perfect picture of tranquility and love. He came over to her and touched her shoulder lightly before pulling her chair out to let her stand.

When she did, he leaned forward, and his warm breath blew on the bare column of her neck. "I have missed you, dearling. Will you come to me tonight?"

The air in the room turned to methane. Swirling green clouds of putrescence that robbed her of the ability to think. She nodded, screwed a smile on her face, and let Mike escort her to the foot of the stairs.

"I have some matters to attend to, but I will meet you shortly, my love."

He brushed a kiss across her numb lips and disappeared back into his office.

The stairs were steeper than she remembered. Of course, it could have been the huge load of guilt that she was carrying that made them seem that way.

The funny thing about brains is that they never freaking shut up. Not when you take off your rose-colored silk gown, not when you remove your petticoats, your stays, your shift, your bloomers. Not when you adjust the bandage over your bullet wound to pull on your night rail. Not when you brush out your curls in front of the flickering fire, and not even when you sneak down the hall to your fiancé's bedroom. The whole time, the brain is yelling things like *How could you lie straight to his face?* and *Do you honestly think he's not going to notice that big white bandage?* And her personal favorite, *Silly gamer, earls aren't for geek girls. This whole shebang is about to come crashing down, and it's all your fault, Jamie Kennedy Marten. Put that in your kazoo and blow it.*

He wasn't in his bedroom yet when she opened the door. Whew. Maybe she had a chance. She limped as fast as she dared over to the bed and scooted down underneath the covers. She lay on her back, turned her head to the side, and pretended to be asleep. Just in time, too. Only seconds later, the door squeaked open.

For several moments, the sounds of soft steps and rustling clothes were the only noise in the room. She began to wonder if he really bought that she was asleep. As desperately as she wanted to avoid confessing her stupidity to him, she desperately wanted him that much more. She was so torqued up and anxious that she wished he'd do something. The stress must have made her wiggle more than she should have because he softly brushed a lock of hair from her cheek.

She couldn't stop herself from pressing her face closer to his hand. She wanted to be close to him. There had been so much fear, so much anger and strain between them for the past few days that no matter what, she was ready to be with him. Fuck the bandage and the truth. Fuck going home, fuck Collette, and fuck Mrs. K's secrets. She wanted him. Micah. Right now.

When he bent his head down to her and took her lips in a soft kiss, she didn't hesitate. She opened her mouth to him, tracing the line of his lips with her tongue. He matched her strokes with his own, and their mouths mated deeply. He pressed his body down atop hers, and when her hands rubbed up his arms and down his back, she realized that the rustling of his clothes had been to remove them all. He was nude as he lay on top of her, and even through the thick blankets and her nightgown, his erection was obvious.

She groaned softly as he kissed her, getting lost in the feeling of his body against her hands. His smooth, lean muscles made her palms tingle, and his kisses made her throb down low in her belly. One of his hands cupped the back of her neck, and the other rubbed the line of her shoulder beneath the nightgown, caressing it gently before drifting down to cover her breast. She arched her back, her hips twisting in supplication.

He lifted his head and stared down at her, the flickering firelight making dancing shadows across his strong jaw.

He rolled off her and pulled back the covers. His hands delved beneath the hem of her night rail, rubbing up the length of her legs. She shivered as his strong palms traveled up to her thighs, rucking the gown up to her waist.

"You are so lovely," he said as he splayed his fingers

over her hips. He looked over her body like he'd never seen it before. "I cannot tell you how looking upon you makes me feel."

She smiled and reached for the hem that lay across her belly. Moving the fabric higher on her body, she revealed her breasts to him. His low groan sent a wave of heat between her thighs.

"Probably about as good as looking at you makes me feel," she said, leaving the gown bunched up across her collarbone. She cupped her breasts, rubbing the taut points with her thumbs. Her tongue darted out to wet her lips. His eyes darkened at the sight of her breasts being offered to him like a sacrifice.

"I want you," she whispered.

His hands rubbed up her hips, to her waist, her rib cage, and finally to cover her hands where they touched her breasts. His palms dragged over the turgid points of her nipples, sending bolts of sensation straight to her core.

He parted her legs with a knee, then knelt between them, groaning aloud as the gates of her body met his gaze. Releasing her breasts, he rose, palming his thick erection as he looked on the most intimate part of her.

"You are so, so lovely," he said again. She pushed up on her arms to kiss him, and her nightgown fell back to her waist.

He reached for it, drawing it upward, but she stopped him when he moved to remove it altogether.

"It's kind of chilly in here," she lied, hoping he wouldn't question her.

He paused, still holding the hem of her gown. A line appeared on his brow. "Are you certain? I assure you, I will keep you warm."

She shook her head. "It's fine. I promise."

And with that lie, she drew his head down to her to kiss him again.

She poured everything into that kiss. The pleasure he'd given her so far, the fear she'd been hiding even from herself, the guilt at the lies she'd told him, everything. He responded with every bit of fervor she'd given him.

His hands were everywhere—her back, her legs, her breasts, her ass. When he came in contact with her bandaged arm, she gasped, but she covered it quickly with a moan. She didn't think he noticed.

He rubbed a hand down her belly, through the damp curls at the apex of her thighs, slipping a finger between the slick folds. Another rush of moisture greeted his touch, easing the way for his finger to dip into the well of her body.

She gripped his shoulders, clutching at him, trying to bring him closer, farther, deeper into her.

"Please," she moaned when his finger set up a rhythm within her. Her hips echoed his movements, wanting more. He added a second finger, stretching her sheath. Her hands left his shoulders, rubbing through the dusting of hair that coated the strong pecs, the lean abs, down to the nest of hair at his groin where his erection stood hot and hard and waiting to enter her.

She held his length with both hands, reveling in the velvet heat. He felt so good, so damn good to her. His two fingers didn't stop their tortuous rhythm, so she mimicked it with soft strokes of her own around his length.

"Dearling, it is too much," Mike rasped. Jamie looked up at his face, and his eyes were nearly begging.

"Then don't wait," she said, and brought the silky head of him toward her aching passage.

He removed his fingers, but she barely had time to

register the loss before he plunged his length into her. His shaft filled her, stretched her farther than his fingers ever could. Her body's moisture coated him, easing his way, making his smooth strokes deep within her move like liquid silk.

His body pressed her down, a welcome weight across her breasts and between her thighs. He buried his face in her neck and drove his shaft in hard, making her cry out at the sensation. He felt so good, so hard, so deep within her.

He kept his strokes slow at first, smooth, measured, and even. Small gasps escaped her with every plunge as his body came into contact with her aching clit. That tiny bundle of nerves was calling for him, teased and taunted by the unhurried strokes.

"Mike," she moaned as she rubbed down his back to cup his ass with both hands. "More."

He quickened his pace for three strokes, drawing small cries from her, and then returned to that torturous, even pace. Her clit was throbbing, aching in ways that it never had before. Frustrated, she tried to reach a hand between them to rub it, but he didn't lift his hips to give her access.

"Please," she begged, hips thrusting upward as hard as they could. Her body wouldn't be denied. It wanted what it wanted, and it wanted Mike worse than it had anything ever before.

"Please what, dearling?"

"Please fuck me," she yelled, way past caring. "Oh God, Mike, just fuck me!"

He took her mouth in another soul-searing kiss, and his hips took up the rhythm that her body had been begging for so hard. Each thrust brought him deeper than she'd ever thought he'd go, and she could no more stop

the cries that ripped from her throat than she could stop
the orgasm that was bearing down on her.

His hips drove into her, grinding against her clit,
wrenching sensation and response from her body with
every stroke. She rose to meet every thrust, her shrill
cries seeming to come from that aching place between
her thighs where he was in complete control of her.

And then, when she thought she couldn't possibly feel
any more pleasure, he reached between their bodies and
rubbed at that tiny bud that seemed to call him master.

She screamed, her back arching as the waves of
pleasure wrenched through her. Her body shivered and
pulsed around his thick length, the heat of him searing
her from deep within. She shuddered as her cries quieted,
wrung out from the exquisite feeling.

"Jamie," he groaned as he pulled out of her body. He
palmed his shaft, and only a moment later, hot jets of his
pleasure landed on her thigh and her belly, some landing
on the hem of her nightgown. Their breaths came heavy
and ragged in the sudden, thick silence of the room.

He pressed a soft, sweet kiss on her lips, and then left
her alone on the bed. Only seconds later, he returned
with a cloth, damp from the water in the basin. He
cleaned her skin gently, as softly as if she was delicate
porcelain. She smiled. Mike would probably always be
overprotective, but she was beginning to love it.

"I am sorry, dearling," he said as he finished. "Your
night rail has been soiled." He lifted the now-damp hem
again. "Let me remove it, and you can wear my robe if
you are still chilled."

"No, it's fine," she said, trying to bat his hands away.
"It's not that bad."

Mike furrowed his brow, concern written plain as day
across his face. "Jamie? Is something wrong?"

She shook her head vehemently. "No, no, every-thing's great! Really. Just fine. Nothing to worry about at all."

She stared at him and prayed. He shook his head slowly.

"Jamie, please remove your nightgown, or tell me why you will not."

She closed her eyes. No way out. She couldn't look him in the eye and say she'd fallen and cut her arm. She couldn't lie to him anymore.

Jamie lifted the hem of her gown and winced as she pulled it over her head.

Twenty-Nine

MICAH'S EYES LOCKED ON THE WHITE BANDAGE instantly, the thread of doubt that circled his throat suddenly turning to a noose made of certainty. "Jamie? Are you injured?"

She took a deep breath before answering. "Yeah. I'm sorry, but I need to tell you the truth. I snuck out of the house earlier today."

Her words sliced through his heart. She'd lied. He'd done everything in his power to protect her, to keep her safe. She'd not trusted him to care for her and had taken her life into her own hands. His head dropped and his shoulders rounded in utter, complete defeat. He had no words.

"I'm sorry," she whispered in his silence, tears springing to her eyes. "I didn't mean to hurt you. I wanted to get some air and I didn't think…"

"You didn't think," he said when she trailed off. "That is it, is it not?"

She bit her lip as the tears streamed down her cheeks. "I'm sorry."

"Tell me the rest, Miss Marten. Why are you bandaged?" His voice turned cold. It was his last defense, and he clung to the autocratic hauteur that had shielded him so well in the past, trying desperately to ignore the pain in her eyes.

"I saw a woman through the window several houses down. I think it was Collette. I hurried down the street, trying to get home, but I twisted my ankle and fell. I heard a gunshot, and it brushed by my arm. I ran home right after. I'm so, so sorry, Micah." She collapsed into sobs, covering her face with her hands.

He didn't say anything while she cried. He couldn't. To comfort her would break him totally. He'd loved her, offered her everything that was his to give. She'd thrown it all back in his face and flirted with her own death while doing so. He was not enough for her. He'd failed, and now, he would do what he must to keep her safe.

When her sobs had turned to gulping breaths and sniffles, he stood, numb. Walking over to the bureau that had brought her into his life in the first place, he pulled open a drawer. From its depths, he pulled a dressing gown and then crossed the carpet once more. When the velvet fabric was laid in a pile next to her, he turned his back and walked away. He spoke without looking at her. It was the only way he could do what must be done now.

"I must end our engagement, Miss Marten. Please return to your home on the morrow. Even if you decide to remain, we will not wed."

"What?" Her voice was thin with pain.

He did not turn to her. He closed his eyes, trying to keep the vision of her away. It was too tempting. "I cannot marry you. That is my final word on the matter."

She said nothing behind him. He did not move, did not breathe. Just kept his stance wide, his hands clasped behind his bare back to keep them from trembling. Strong. He had to stay immobile, not show any

THE GEEK GIRL AND THE SCANDALOUS EARL 293

weakness. She'd fight him if he showed the least vulnerability. And if she did, she'd die. It was that simple. Someone, be it Collette or someone else, was attempting to kill her. Despite his best efforts, he'd been unable to locate the source of the threat for certain. The runner that tailed Collette had sworn she'd not been the source of the poisoned sweets. If Micah allowed Jamie to stay, he'd bury her as surely as he'd seen Louisa buried. He could not bear that. Better to let her go to her home and never see her again than to see her dead.

There came the rustling of fabric and soft footsteps crossing the floor. Out of the corner of his eye, he could see her tear-stained face looking up at him. "I know you have no reason to trust me," she said, her voice thick and strained, "but I am sorry. Do you think you can ever forgive me?"

He didn't move, keeping his gaze locked on the wall in front of him. "A man that cannot keep you safe is a man that does not deserve you."

"But wait," she said, laying her hand on his arm. "You love me. Please, just wait."

He did look at her then and made no effort to hide the pain on his face. She stepped backward, eyes widening.

"There is nothing to wait for," he said.

❧

When Jamie opened her eyes the next morning, it was with total certainty that she'd completely destroyed any chance she had of a happily ever after with her earl. She'd shattered Mike's already tenuous trust in her, let Collette Dubois know her rival was still alive and well, and bought herself a one-way pass back to Depressionland circa 2012.

Baron hadn't even come to sleep with her last night.

As she carefully stretched, favoring both her injured arm and sore ankle, she couldn't help but think she deserved to be alone. She'd lied straight to the face of the man that she loved more than she'd ever loved anyone. She was doomed to be alone because she was a frackin' idiot.

Muriel's timid knock couldn't have come at a better time.

"Hey, Mur," Jamie called as she opened the door, overjoyed to see someone that she hadn't completely ostracized with her idiocy. "Good morning."

Her overly bright smile must have confused Muriel.

"Hello, miss," Muriel said warily, placing the tray of chocolate on the side table. She headed over to the wardrobe and busied herself selecting a gown for Jamie.

"So, how's things with you? Good?"

Muriel's smile came with a furrowed brow as she brought over a sage green gown. "I am quite well, thank you."

Jamie fell silent after that, feeling kind of foolish. She let Muriel help her dress without another word. She didn't belong here. She was more fish out of water than she was proper English miss. She didn't fit in here at all. It was probably better if she gave up and went home.

She stared down at her suddenly watery lap while Muriel put the finishing touches on her hair.

"Miss?"

Jamie sniffed and blinked quickly, hoping the moisture would disappear. "Yeah?"

Muriel came around from behind her and sank gingerly down on the chair across from Jamie. The maid fidgeted with the pleats of her skirt, pale eyes wide as she blurted, "How do you know if you are in love?"

Jamie bit her lip. *Of all the questions. Of all the days to ask me that.*

"I'm probably the last person in the world you should be asking that question," she said, trying and failing to meet Muriel's gaze.

"No, Miss Jamie, you're the right one. There is a fellow, and I've fancied him for so long, and I think he fancies me too, only I do not know what love feels like."

Jamie held her temples with one hand, wrapping the other arm around her middle. "Does he make your heart run races around you?"

"Yes," Muriel whispered.

"Does he make you feel like somebody hit you straight in the guts, knocking your oxygen supply into next week?"

"He does."

"Can you think of anything else in the world but how it would be to hold hands with him for the rest of your life?"

"I want to be with him forever." The maid's emphatic reply came straight from the depths of her, all the way from her toes.

Jamie looked up then, toying with the green dress's lace collar at her throat.

"Then it's love."

❧

Talking with Muriel had lifted Jamie up a little. Her doldrums were still there, but a sense of determination had bullied them a bit farther down on her attention scale. She wasn't ready to lie down and die quite yet. She and Mike had something incredible, something worth fighting for. She couldn't let her earl go so easily.

He wasn't in his bedroom, and he wasn't in his office. He wasn't in the sitting room, and he wasn't in the dining room. Jamie was about to bribe George to run outside and check the garden for her when she heard the soft notes emanating from the music room.

She walked slowly, almost afraid of what she'd see. As she drew closer, the tune became clearer. The sweet tune, so lilting, faltering, its tempo only a quarter of what it had been originally, filled her heart with bittersweet remembrance. The song she'd written for Mike. She'd know it anywhere.

The doorknob was ice-cold as she wrapped her fingers around it, turning it slowly. The song stopped abruptly as the door swung open.

"Sorry," she said, her eyes greedily drinking in the sight of him. "I didn't mean to interrupt."

He'd rocketed to his feet as soon as she came into view, and his curt bow was his only answer.

She'd never felt so awkward in her life. Not the first time she'd danced with a boy, not the first time she'd thrown up at a piano recital, not even the first time she'd grouped up with unknown gamers, strangers after her own heart, to run a quest and ran them straight into the opposite faction's home city. She walked toward him, wishing he'd say something, anything, even if it were to yell at her. She couldn't tell what he was thinking, even a little. His face was as blank as a dark computer screen.

But when she drew closer to the bench, he said, "Pardon me." Then, with another shallow bow, he walked out of the room.

Once her frozen, stupid brain got going again, she followed him down the hallway, calling his name, but he wouldn't stop. He went straight out the front door without even acknowledging her.

Thornton closed the door behind the earl, giving Jamie a sympathetic smile.

"He'll come around, miss."

She nodded to the butler and went up the stairs. She didn't want Thornton to see her cry.

❧

Jamie thought about talking to Mrs. Knightsbridge, but she decided against it. The clandestine witch was too focused on her own well-being to give a shit about Jamie's situation.

Jamie tied knots in embroidery thread, petted Baron endlessly, and turned her problems over and over and over in her head. No matter how often she thought about them, what angle she attacked them from, what imaginary scenario she played out, nothing ever got any better. It was shit. Shit plus shit equals shit, and her life at the moment was a shit sandwich with shit sauce. Gross. But sadly correct.

About an hour after she skipped lunch, a knock came on her bedroom door.

"Come in," she called, not bothering to get up. Baron poked his head up, saw Muriel, and flopped back down beside Jamie so she could continue her constant ear scratching.

"A letter has come for you, Miss Jamie," Muriel said, handing Jamie an off-white folded paper.

Jamie was scared to take it from her. What if it was from Collette and it was another threat on her life? What if it was a good-bye letter from Mike? Her hand trembled as she took it from the maid, and Jamie waited for her to leave the room before she broke the dot of red wax that kept the note sealed.

> *My dearest Miss Marten,*
> *I am writing to invite you to visit with me tomorrow*
> *morning. I should like to further our acquaintance.*

*Do accept, please. We shall become the best of friends,
almost as sisters. Also, I have some information about
his lordship's former mistress, Louisa Maucier, that
may be of interest to you.*

Yours most fondly,
Marilyn Munroe

Jamie shook her head slightly as she refolded the note.
That was really odd. She hadn't told Marilyn that she
was living in Mike's house, had she? Maybe she had at
the ball when she explained about her and Mike being in
love. But she hadn't seen Marilyn since then, so how did
the woman know Jamie hadn't said good-bye to Mike
like she'd planned?

Jamie tossed the letter onto the nightstand and
resumed her greyhound scratching. She wasn't going, so
it didn't really matter if it didn't add up. By then, she'd
have crashed and burned with Mike again, probably for
the last time ever.

Being a failure sucked so hard.

❧

Jamie dressed so carefully for dinner that night. She knew
that it was probably the last chance she'd ever have to convince Mike that she wasn't a complete waste of space. She
loved him so much, and her aching chest made it hard to
breathe as she helped Muriel pick out something to wear.

Way at the back of the small wardrobe hung a white
silk gown, its square neckline edged with beautiful lace.
Small puffed sleeves accentuated the otherwise simple
bodice, and the skirt fell straight from the high waist,
snug beneath the bustline.

"It's perfect," Jamie breathed, trailing a finger down
the slinky fabric of the skirt.

"You will look so beautiful." Muriel smiled.

Getting dressed with Muriel's help was so familiar now. Jamie wasn't ashamed of her body anymore. Muriel had seen it every day for so long that it wasn't even an issue. Jamie didn't have to be told when to hold her breath so the maid could tie the laces of her stays. She didn't have to double-check which layer went where. It was second nature. It was as normal to Jamie now as throwing on a bra and panties had been back home.

Home.

Where the hell is that, anyway? Jamie wondered as she sat and Muriel began deftly twisting her hair into an ornate style. *Is it the century I live in? The country? The state? The house I bought with my own credit? Or is it here, in a country and time that was completely alien to me for so long?*

Jamie didn't know anymore.

When Muriel was done, Jamie stood, turned, and hugged the maid close.

"Thank you," she said against her white mobcap.

"For what, miss?" Muriel's thin arms wrapped around Jamie, hugging her back.

"For everything. Just thanks."

Muriel didn't say a word and let Jamie stay there as long as she needed.

Micah stared at the piece of foolscap laid out on his desk. His pen was poised above it, and the three words he'd written at the top froze his brain in place.

Dear Miss Lyons,

He slammed the quill down and scraped the chair back. Pacing in front of the fireplace did nothing to calm his anxiety. Would he be able to do this? It would be the only way to prove to Jamie that she needn't stay any longer. It was the only way to prove his lie that he loved her no longer. And that was the only way he could save her life.

Setting his jaw, he rounded the desk once more. Crumpling his first attempt, he started again.

My dearest Miss Lyons,

❦

Jamie sat in the empty dining room for almost three hours. Staring at the untouched place setting for Mike didn't make things any easier. She imagined everything she would have said. Everything she should apologize for, make amends for, promise to never do again. Anything, as long as he gave her another chance to make things work between them.

But it was impossible to apologize to an empty chair and have it mean something.

❦

Micah had thought that by finishing the note to Miss Lyons, he'd feel better. He was wrong. Walking quickly and quietly, he left his estate room and gave the letter to Thornton, with instructions to have it delivered right away. As he ascended the stairs to his bedchamber, the feeling in his gut was akin to the first time he'd gone to Gentleman Jackson's salon to learn to fight. He'd come away bruised and aching for a week. This was much worse than that. He dressed in eveningwear once he reached his bedchamber, knotting his cravat in a careless, hopeless tangle. He would meet Felicity in the morning, propose marriage, and that would be the end of it. He hoped that Jamie would leave before then, but he knew, as he pulled on his greatcoat and headed out into the night, he would be forced to break her heart once more. It was easier to break her heart than it would be to see her die.

❧

Another two hours went by as Jamie sat at the piano. She played Mike's song over and over, hoping it would reach him, wherever he was, whatever he was doing. Was he thinking of her? Was he wondering about her like she was wondering about him? It wasn't fair for her to expect him to be there, not when she'd hurt him so badly. She'd have to give him time.

Jamie closed her eyes, played his song, and wished with everything in her that he were there to hear it.

❧

At White's, Micah sat in the corner, nursing another brandy. The last gentleman to speak to him had received a curt nod, nothing more, and so the rest of the jovial crowd had learned to keep its distance from the brooding earl. Micah swirled the liquor around in his glass. Was she gone? He hoped she was. He did not want to face her after she'd learned what he'd done. Proposing to another woman would break her heart irrevocably, he knew it for certain. But it was the only way.

Draining his drink, he beckoned to the waiting footman for another. It would be a long night, and he had no intention of spending it sober.

❧

It was after midnight when Jamie gave up and headed upstairs for bed. The beautiful white gown went back into the wardrobe, unseen by the man that she'd worn it for. She paced the hallways, her nightgown billowing behind her like a ghost's shroud. She felt kind of like a ghost—achy, empty, and so alone that it hurt.

When the clock downstairs bonged three in the morning, she admitted to herself what she'd really known all along—Mike had no intention of coming home, not tonight. She headed to her bedroom, her sore ankle even more painful from the hours of fruitless wandering she'd done.

She climbed into bed, and Baron snuggled against her, but it wasn't the same. She missed her earl, and her stupid heart wouldn't beat right again until he came back and things were right between them. If they ever could be.

Jamie barely slept a wink. In the dim firelight, she watched Baron's sides rise and fall with his breaths. Time wasn't her friend when it kept her and Mike apart. *But tomorrow's another day,* her heart whispered. *You can try again tomorrow.*

Fat chance, her brain snorted. *You've lost him forever, you selfish bitch. Good job.*

❧

When Muriel came in to wake Jamie the next morning, her thin face was even paler than usual. She set Jamie's chocolate down on the bedside table without saying a word and went straight over to the wardrobe without looking toward the bed.

"Mur?" Jamie called, sitting up. "What is it?"

The maid pulled out a taupe-colored gown, the most drab thing that Jamie had ever seen her select. Muriel's bottom lip quivered as she brushed the fabric out, hanging the dress on the door of the wardrobe.

"Muriel?" Jamie got out of bed and crossed the room to her side, really worried now. "Is something wrong?"

Muriel shook her head quickly. Too quickly for it to be the truth. She busied herself in the basket of hair ribbons, holding up different colors against the brownish fabric.

"Hey, you can talk to me. What's up?"

The maid let out a shuddering breath before turning to Jamie and blurting out, "His lordship has proposed to Miss Lyons!"

With those words, Jamie's whole world shifted.

Mike had proposed to another woman? Her Mike? The one who'd said he loved her and wanted her to marry him? He was going to marry someone else? He'd promised her. He'd proposed to her. He'd asked her to be his countess, and now that pale, blond, annoying girl was going to marry him instead?

He'd taken it back. He'd said he was calling off the engagement, and he'd done it in the most irrevocable way that he could.

By proposing to another woman.

There is nothing to wait for.

Her throat closed off, her eyes burned, and nausea boiled in her gut.

She tried to contain it, she really did. She paced in front of the fireplace, desperately trying to ignore the brokenhearted sobs of the teenaged maid behind her.

It was too much. She had to get out of there. She had to get some air.

"Muriel, help me throw something on quick, please. I need to get out of here for a little while."

With eyes filled with tears, Muriel nodded. Jamie couldn't look at her again. She was barely hanging on to her own.

Baron seemed to know something was really wrong

with Jamie. He stuck right with her as she threw on her clothes with Muriel's help, and even walked with her down the stairs. She grabbed the leash that Thornton held out to her with knowing eyes, and she and the hound walked out the front door.

The sunny day seemed to mock the sludge-like depression that had overtaken her chest. Every breath was like a fresh knife in her poor bruised and battered heart. Baron stayed close to her side, not even chasing a bird that landed in front of them on the walk. She ignored people's happy laughter and chatter as the elegantly dressed strangers rode their horses and carriages down the street.

It was the same. Logan, Mike, it was the same. Things were great, wonderful, perfect, and then Jamie wanted more and they got lost. Big time. Granted, Logan and Mike couldn't be more different. Logan hadn't wanted the house and picket fence that Jamie had been planning. But Mike knew her. The *real* her. He didn't seem to have any problem with the thought of matrimony. And he'd proposed to her, said he loved her. She'd thought they wanted the same things. So why did they fall apart?

Baron pulled a little on the leash, whining slightly. "Calm down, boy," Jamie said, petting his ears. "It's okay."

He pulled harder, whines growing louder. "What is it?" She knelt beside him, hugging the long neck. "What's wrong?"

She scratched his silky ears, looking up in the direction his long nose pointed in.

Collette.

Her heart froze solid as she took in the white horse, the feathered cap, and the look of complete rage on the woman's face. The note from Marilyn. She'd forgotten. It hadn't been from her friend; it had been from a psychotic, jealous bitch with no qualms about murder. Jamie was in serious, serious danger.

"Baron," she whispered, backing up slowly, "we've gotta go."

Jamie turned, keeping a tight hold on the hound's leash. She didn't have a weapon with her, and the look on Collette's face was proof enough that she was completely prepared to succeed today where her previous plans had failed. If Jamie didn't get out of there fast, she was as good as dead.

Jamie quickened her pace. Baron had to break into a trot to keep up. She was within sight of the house. Only a few more yards, and they'd be safe. The street that had been lined with people five minutes earlier was curiously empty now.

The hoofbeats came behind them fast. She barely had time to turn around before the big white horse was upon them. The animal's chest crashed into her shoulder. It threw her down, yanking Baron's leather lead out of her hand. Gasping, she curled up instinctively. Flashing hooves passed perilously close to her head.

It was over almost faster than it began, the big white horse wheeling around for another pass.

"Oy!" She heard someone shout. "What have you done?"

The white horse disappeared down the street, frantic footsteps chasing after it.

It took several seconds for her brain to process the greyhound's cries of pain.

"Baron!" Jamie screamed, scrambling over to him.

The skin of his back leg was shredded, almost peeled back like an orange. His leg had to be broken. Blood was everywhere, splattering his beautiful blue-gray coat. His eyes were frantic, wild with agony. He tried to get up, his paws scrambling on the blood-slicked cobbles, but the pain was too much for him, and he fell back to the cold stones. Tears streamed down her cheeks as she held his head in her lap.

"No, Baron, baby, relax. It's okay. You're going to be okay," she sobbed, trying to keep him calm.

Think, Jamie! Think!

This backward time didn't have a damn thing that could help him. The only person with any kind of medical ability she knew was Mrs. Knightsbridge, but unless the witch had a spell for healing broken bones and restoring lost blood, that was a bust. With the way the normally quiet hound cried out, she knew he was in excruciating pain. He needed a vet or he'd almost certainly die. In an instant, she knew exactly where she could find help for her friend.

As gently as she could, she slid her arms beneath him. He yelped in agony as his injured leg was jostled.

"I'm so sorry, baby, just hang on," she said, panic and tears clogging her throat.

The dog had to weigh seventy pounds, but fear and adrenaline made her strong. She carried him back to the house as fast as she could, screaming at the top of her lungs for Mrs. Knightsbridge.

Thornton threw open the door, his face going pale at the sight of Jamie and the injured dog. She pushed past the butler, carrying a still-howling Baron up the stairs.

"Wilhelmina!" Jamie yelled through her tears. "Get up here and open this damn portal right now!"

Mrs. K ran up the stairs behind her. Jamie turned, still clutching Baron's body against her. He'd gone limp from the pain.

"You need to open it *now*," Jamie screamed at Mrs. Knightsbridge. "I have to get him to a vet. That bitch Collette broke his goddamn leg!"

Mrs. K nodded, tears streaming down her own face. She petted Baron's side gently, then stooped to the floor beside the bureau. Jamie stood in front of it as the witch muttered in an odd-sounding language.

Seconds later, the gold around the edges glinted. *It's time.*

Jamie let Mrs. K hold Baron as she climbed through the mirror feet first. When Jamie reached back for the hound, the housekeeper stopped her.

"I cannot open the portal this way again for quite a while. The fabric of time is too worn here. But when I can, I will send Micah to you," she whispered.

"He doesn't want me anymore," Jamie replied. She took Baron's limp weight and slid out of the mirror into a screaming-hot storage building.

Thirty

THE TRUCK WAS STILL PARKED IN FRONT OF THE OPEN storage building. The keys still dangled from the switch. Jamie laid Baron on the seat beside her as gently as she could, tied a clean towel around his back leg to slow the bleeding, threw the truck in drive, and hightailed it for the nearest vet clinic.

She watched him out of the corner of her eye the whole way. His ribs moved shallowly, breaths blowing ragged in the quiet of the truck's cab. "Stay with me, boy," she murmured, turning as quickly as she could without slinging both of them off the bench seat. The clinic was only five minutes away, but it felt like five years before she parked crookedly in the handicapped space and cut the engine. Baron lifted his head as she opened the passenger door to pick him up again. He whined pitifully, pawing at her hand.

"Hold on, baby, please hold on." Her voice was ragged with emotion.

An elderly couple walked out the door of the clinic as Jamie struggled up the walk with Baron cradled in her arms. The sight of her tearstained face and the bloody, injured hound in her arms galvanized them into action.

"Bobby, hold this door for her! Now!" The gray-haired woman flew into the clinic, and Jamie nodded gratefully at the man holding the door for her.

"Get somebody out here now! This dog is hurt bad!" The elderly woman banged on the desk as Jamie rounded the corner with Baron. The receptionist took one wide-eyed look at her and ran to the back of the clinic.

The techs inside didn't even look twice at Jamie's odd dress and hat; they just put Baron on a stretcher and took him straight back. Jamie collapsed on a sea-green pleather cushion and sobbed her broken heart out, rubbing at the bloodstains on her dress ineffectually. The elderly couple patted her on the shoulder reassuringly and left her with the clinic staff.

A receptionist brought Jamie a box of tissues. "Here," she said, rubbing her back. "He'll be okay. We've got some of the best doctors in the state here. You've got to believe."

Jamie nodded, holding the tissue up to her face. She couldn't lose Baron. She'd already lost Mike; she couldn't lose that silly dog too. She loved him, almost as much as she loved the guy that had saved him from certain death in the first place.

"Can you answer some questions for me, hon?" The redheaded receptionist's voice was kind but direct. She had a job to do, and hysterics wouldn't help a damn thing, especially not the hound who was in pain in the back of the clinic.

"Yeah, whatever you need," Jamie said through her tears, trying to get it together.

"What's your dog's name?"

Jamie started to tell the receptionist that he wasn't her dog, but then she realized that Mike had been dead for probably a hundred and fifty years or more at that point.

She couldn't explain what the sudden spurt of tears was about, but the receptionist rubbed her back until she could speak again.

"Baron," Jamie whispered. "His name is Baron."

"Okay. Baron. And he's a greyhound, right? How old is he?"

"About a year," Jamie said, trying like hell not to think of the man who'd told her that.

"And how was he injured?" The redheaded woman didn't look up at Jamie as she continued to write on her little green clipboard.

Come on, Jamie. Tell as much of the truth as you can without getting thrown into a loony bin. She swallowed hard and mentally thanked Leah for her SCA days.

"We were at a Renaissance Faire, and a horse from the jousting section got loose and took off. It knocked us both down, and it must have stepped on his leg or something."

"Wow, that must have been scary."

"You have no idea." Jamie laughed a little hysterically and wiped her nose with the wad of damp tissues.

"Okay, let me get this info to Dr. Vann. We'll let you know something soon, okay?" The receptionist gave Jamie a reassuring smile and a pat on the shoulder.

Jamie glanced at her clipboard as she turned it to walk away. According to the time she'd written at the top of the sheet, three hours had passed in this time since Jamie had been gone. Mrs. K apparently hadn't been that exact in her time-portation calibrating. It didn't matter though; at least, it wouldn't if Baron made it out of this okay.

Jamie paced through the waiting room, desperate to hear something. Other people came and went with their animals. Several of them gave her curious glances. She ignored them all, walking and crying and even praying. He had to be okay. He just had to be.

A full hour later, a tech escorted her into an examination room for the doctor to talk to her. When the vet came in, he propped two X-rays on the lighted box on the wall. Jamie hoped he was competent. He looked like he didn't need to shave yet.

"Hey, Jamie, I'm Doctor Vann. We've been working with Baron. He's pretty lucky."

"Really?" Jamie said, tears welling again. "Is he going to be okay?"

"He should make a full recovery. We were worried about the possibility of a fracture, but it looks like a really bad skin injury. It occurred with a horse, you say?"

She nodded.

"It seems like either a nail or part of the horse's shoe caught on his skin as it passed over him. Since these guys have such thin skin, it just kind of peels back. Looks horrible, bloody as all get-out, but with some stitches, it should heal okay. He lost a lot of blood, though. You must have had to come a ways to get here."

"You have no idea," Jamie said, shaking her head.

"We gave him a transfusion, and he's being treated with some antibiotics. He's really lucky. If that horse had stepped on him instead of knocking him down, it might be a very different story. We'll keep him overnight, finish up the stitching, but as long as we can avoid infection, he should make a full recovery."

Jamie hugged the too-young doctor and sobbed into the shoulder of his white lab coat. "Thank you so much. You don't know how much that dog means to me."

He patted her back and let her cry for a second, then pulled back.

"He's awake. Would you like to see him before you go home? We're giving him IV fluids and some pain medication right now."

She nodded. "I'd like that."

Their steps echoed on the concrete flooring as she followed the vet to a room in the back. Several shiny metal kennels lined the walls, most of them with IV bags and tubing hanging from the doors. Dr. Vann knelt by one of the largest ones and opened the gate.

Jamie crawled up to Baron and rubbed his silky head.

"Hey, bud. Are you getting some good drugs there?" Her throat welled again. "You stay strong for me. I need you. I'll be here first thing in the morning to see you, okay?"

He licked her hand softly.

"I love you, you stupid dog," Jamie sobbed. After dropping a kiss on his nose, she stood, wiping her tears with her sodden tissues. "Thanks, Doc. I'll be back tomorrow."

He nodded and had one of the techs show her out.

Jamie left her home number at the front desk. Her smartphone was still in 1816. She'd probably never see it again.

She got back in the truck and headed back to the storage building, wondering how the hell she was going to explain any of this to Pawpaw Milton; how in the hell she was going to sleep tonight, worrying about Baron; and how the hell she was going to live without Mike.

Pawpaw was at the storage building when Jamie got back. His wiry, gray-bearded jaw dropped at the sight of her bloodstained taupe walking dress.

"What in the hell has been going on here? What are you wearing, girl?"

Jamie shook her head at him. "It's a long story. You wouldn't believe me even if I told you." She pointed at the back corner of the storage building. "How much for that bureau?"

"What in the world do you want that for? That thing is two hundred years old."

She sighed and raked stray pieces of hair behind her ear. "I know. Chippendale. 1816. I need it. How much?"

Pawpaw argued with her for a long time, but she refused to take no for an answer. Eventually, he gave in and sold her the bureau on a payment plan. She didn't even raise her eyebrows at the price. She'd have to either sell some more music soon or take a job at a fast-food joint to afford it. She didn't know antique furniture could cost so much, but she couldn't stand the thought of someone else having the bureau that Mrs. Knightsbridge had brought her through to meet Mike. She knew he'd never come. Even if he would give up on the earldom, he'd made a promise to Miss Lyons now. Engagements weren't usually broken as quickly as theirs had been. Besides, she'd nearly gotten his dog killed and then taken his beloved hound away from him forever. Mike was sure to hate her now, and honestly, she sort of felt like he deserved to. *I kind of hate me too.*

Pawpaw arranged to have some guys help him deliver the bureau later that afternoon. Jamie thanked him, then headed on home to change and clear out a space for it.

Where the hell was she going to put a giant piece of antique furniture, anyway? It didn't matter. It was staying with her for the rest of her life. The rest of her lonely, godforsaken, miserable life.

It took forever to shed the layers of her clothing without Muriel's help. She ended up ripping buttons on the back of her bloodstained dress. The corset was much the same. Petticoats with red-brown spotted blood pooled on her deep-gray tiles. The bloomers that she'd hated so much looked ridiculous on top of them.

Jamie stood naked in front of her bathroom mirror and removed the brown-feathered cap. She pulled out hairpins and let the mess fall where it would.

There.

My name is Jamie.

Whoever the hell that is.

She didn't enjoy the shower she took. She cried through the whole thing. Shaving her legs, her underarms, applying deodorant, using the hair dryer—all of it made her even more depressed.

When she came downstairs to answer the knock, she was finishing a crying binge. Leah took one look at her and hustled her into the kitchen for a private conversation while Pawpaw Milton and his movers positioned the bureau next to her computer.

"What the hell happened to you, James? Pawpaw said you took his truck and you came back dressed in some kind of fancy old getup?"

Jamie looked at the ceiling. "That's not the half of it."

Leah sat down, giving her the "spill the beans or I will kill you" eye.

Jamie sighed and sat at the table beside her best friend. She never said a word during Jamie's long story; she just let her get it all out. When the movers were done, Leah said a quick word to Pawpaw, and the men left quietly out the front door without talking to her. When Jamie resumed sobbing, Leah grabbed a roll of paper towels and handed her a wad. Jamie finished the story, right up to rushing Baron to the vet, and Leah nodded.

"So, now's probably the part where you tell me I'm completely insane, right?" Jamie sniffed as she wiped her eyes.

Leah shook her head. "Nope. But I am going to call you a dumbass."

Jamie's jaw dropped. "What?"

"You had a Colin Firth–lookalike earl interested in you, and you didn't drag him back here with you? What the fuck?"

"I tried, but he wouldn't listen to me…"

"You should have made him."

Jamie rolled her eyes. "I tried. He was sure that he'd failed me, and no matter what I said, he wouldn't listen. Besides, he doesn't love me anymore." She tried to stifle more tears, but they kept right on coming. *My tear factory: powered by Energizer.*

Leah's palms splatted down on the table. "I don't believe that for a second. So, your lady is a witch, and she knows you're both in love, right?"

Jamie nodded, wiping her dripping nose.

"We'll have to keep watch on that big old piece of furniture then. Hopefully your housekeeper witch will confess the truth, shove him through the mirror into your living room, and everything will be good from there."

Jamie hugged Leah close, breathing in the familiar vanilla and coconut smell of her. "Thank you," she whispered.

"Hey, don't cry. You'd do the same for me. Now, come on." Leah's chair scraped back and she grabbed Jamie's arm. "Let's clear out this living room so Mike doesn't think he's landed in the city dump."

With the help of the best friend in the world, Jamie cleaned out her living room. She even threw a blanket over that ugly-ass couch Logan had picked out, to make it look more like the living room she'd set up for her and Mike's first date. They did laundry, threw out garbage, and put all Jamie's comics and magazines in the spare bedroom. At nearly eleven, Leah took off, after a promise to stay at Jamie's house in the morning, just in case Mike showed up while she was with Baron at the vet.

Jamie cleaned up the kitchen when Leah had gone. Jamie didn't even recognize most of the junk that she had accumulated. It was awful, gross. And so cold. She turned the A/C off completely and opened the windows to let the summer-night breeze in. She felt nearly naked in her shorts and T-shirt, but she kept on cleaning. Mind-numbing chores were the only thing she could stomach at that point.

At two in the morning, she heard a noise coming from the living room. Her heart leapt into her throat, and she ran to see what it was.

There was nobody and nothing in her now-clean living room. Her computer had received a new IM from Kurt. She'd missed tonight's dungeon run.

Jamie shook her head and walked away without replying.

By six o'clock that morning, the kitchen was clean, her bathroom was spotless, and the garbage man was going to be cursing her name for years to come. The vet clinic would open at seven, so she hightailed it upstairs to get ready.

She reached into the shower to turn it on, but she stopped before her fingers touched the metal knob. Instead, she grabbed a washcloth and a bar of soap from the bowl of seashell-shaped "guest soaps" that had previously been only for show. She ran some water in the tub, which had rarely ever been used. She stepped into the bath, closed her eyes, and wished she was in a tiny copper tub in a lemon dream of a bedroom, readying herself for a phaeton ride in the park with her love.

She missed her earl so much.

❧

Jamie walked into the vet clinic, waiting while a couple passed by with a long-haired tortoiseshell cat. When they'd gone, she talked to the receptionist.

"Hey, I'm Jamie Marten. I'm here to see Baron?"

The woman wrinkled her forehead, typing on her computer. "Marten…Marten…and you said the dog's name is Baron?"

Jamie nodded, nerves clogging her throat.

"Hm. Having a hard time finding you in here. I'm kind of new here, so it's probably just me. Hold on…Sheila?"

A whispered conference at the other end of the counter gave Jamie the shakes. Was Baron okay? Had his injuries been more severe than Dr. Vann thought?

A green-scrub-wearing vet tech came through the doors of the back room. "Miss Marten? You can follow me."

Her smile reassured Jamie somewhat, and she followed the tech through to the back of the clinic.

"Baron!" Jamie knelt by the cage the girl had swung open. His back leg was a swath of white bandages, and he had one of those giant lampshade cones around his neck.

"He did fine, but he keeps chewing at the bandages."

Jamie laughed, rubbing the long nose as he thumped his tail against the side of the metal crate. "It's a good look for you, bud." He licked her hand, and she could swear she felt it all the way down in her heart.

Jamie leaned down, touching his cold nose to her warm one. "I love you, stupid dog."

He lapped her right on the lips, and she sputtered, laughing. "Guess I deserved that."

Dr. Vann met with Jamie, explained the different medicines she was to give Baron for the next couple of weeks, and after paying a bill that made her Visa wince, they headed back home to meet Leah. Jamie knew Mike wouldn't be showing up, but she couldn't bear the thought of leaving the bureau alone, just in case.

Leah met them at the door, shaking her flame-colored hair at Jamie.

"Not a peep. Sorry, lady. If you need to go anywhere else, let me know, and I'll stay here with it, okay?"

"Thanks, Leah."

She gave Jamie a quick hug, patted Baron, and left.

Jamie spent the rest of that day sitting on the floor next to Baron's giant pile of blankets, rubbing his ears and staring at the bureau. Every now and then, she'd stand up and press her palm against the glass, hoping it would give. Nope. Cold, solid mirror every time.

She gave up and ate dinner, then resumed her vigil.

Her computer dinged again, but she didn't even touch it. It wasn't important to her anymore. She couldn't enjoy herself in a fantasyland when reality was kicking her ass.

She slept on the couch that night, facing Mike's bureau the whole time.

Thirty-One

HE'D PLANNED TO SPEND THE REST OF THE DAY MAKING social calls, visiting his solicitors' offices, and perhaps purchasing a shiny bauble for his new fiancée. Instead, Micah moped around the park, remembering riding through it with Jamie. How she'd laughed with him, how she'd kissed him, how she'd shared her life with him in little glimpses over the past month. He'd seen her only hours ago, in the music room, but the gaping hole in his life was there just the same.

There was no peace to be found in the park, especially once the *ton* began riding there, making use of the unusually fine weather to see and be seen. Word of his engagement to Miss Lyons was already spreading, despite that it hadn't been announced in the *Gazette* yet, and he accepted congratulations from several well-meaning couples before he bolted for home. Surely Jamie knew by now. He'd made sure to loudly announce his intentions to Thornton with Muriel in earshot. The maid would have told Jamie quickly, of that he was quite sure.

When Micah mounted the steps of the townhouse, heart heavy and feet leaden, the frantic shouts within were the only thing that could pierce his malaise.

"What do you mean by that, Thornton? Come out, say what you're implying!"

"They went upstairs with you, and then they were gone. I may be old, Mrs. Knightsbridge, but I am not daft. What have you done with the young lady and Baron?"

"You daft old tosser, I have told you, I have not done a thing with Miss Jamie nor the dog!"

"You must have. I demand that you confess!"

"I shall not!"

"*Silence*," Micah roared as he came through the door. The housekeeper and the butler, who had been facing off in the foyer, fell silent. "Whatever has happened?"

Thornton stepped toward Mrs. Knightsbridge, who brandished a candelabrum to ward the old butler off. Micah stepped between them before motioning to the butler to speak.

"My lord, Miss Marten came running into your home with Baron in her arms. The hound was gravely injured. She dashed up the stairs, and Mrs. Knightsbridge"—Thornton gestured at the housekeeper accusingly—"followed her. For several moments there were loud voices, and then silence. Moments later, Mrs. Knightsbridge came down the stairs alone. She has done something with the maid and the dog, your lordship, but she refuses to confess as to what."

Micah turned to his housekeeper. She'd set the candelabrum down and stood with her hands fisted by her sides. Brownish-red streaks of blood marred her apron.

"He is right up to a point. Yes, Miss Marten and Baron have gone. She will take care of him, my lord, you needn't worry for that."

"Your, your apron," Micah choked. "Is that…"

Mrs. Knightsbridge moved toward him and grasped the hand that shakily pointed at her apron. "Do not worry, my lord. I promise that all will be well. Come now. Sit in your estate room, and Thornton will bring you some tea, won't you, Thornton?" Mrs. Knightsbridge eyed the butler meaningfully as she steered the numb earl forward.

They'd made it as far as the doorway when Micah's brain returned to him. "Wait," he said, digging in his heels and turning to Mrs. Knightsbridge. "Thornton is right. What has happened? I want the truth."

"They are both safe, Micah." The old woman seemed to stand tall, much taller than Micah himself was. "Trust me. I shan't say another word about it."

He started to protest, but he blinked, and she was gone.

The night of his betrothal ball was clear and lovely, the early summer breeze bearing scents of rose and jasmine. Micah had done all he was expected to do. He'd appeared at his betrothed's side when requested, danced the requisite number of dances, and generally done as he was bidden. *Like a trained dog,* he mused as he relinquished Felicity's arm to Lord Geraldton for a dance. Of course, Baron hadn't obeyed him as well since Jamie had been in residence.

The thought twisted his heart with poignant memory, and he excused himself from his hostess's side to get some air. The crush of the ball attendees faded behind him as he slipped onto the balcony.

Gripping the railing, he looked up into the night. Was the sky the same where she was? Were the stars just as bright? Whispers of cloud still there? Did she think of him now that he'd broken her heart?

A rustle in the bushes below startled him from his reverie.

"Hello?" he said into the blackness. "Show yourself."

Soft steps sounded on the marble, and his housekeeper

appeared. Mrs. Knightsbridge, dressed in a long black cloak with a hood over her graying hair, revealing just enough of the round face for him to be sure it was her, beckoned to him. He glanced over his shoulder. The laughing, gay throng was still dancing merrily, without a care in the world. No one looked his way. The betrothal toast was set to occur at midnight, just moments away. But Mrs. Knightsbridge must have a reason to be there, and he would discover it.

He crossed the balcony to her. When he started to speak, to ask her what she was about, she shushed him with a finger in the air. He watched in awe as she drew a gleaming silver bowl from beneath her cloak. She set it there, on the top step of the balcony. Drawing a flask from its strap on her belt, she dripped silvery, clear water into the bowl. The shine was almost painful, and he turned his head away.

"Watch," she whispered.

Strange words met his ears as he turned back to where she knelt by the bowl. A sharp scent filled his nostrils as she spoke and waved her hands over the bowl. Not unpleasant, it reminded him of lemons and a deep-green lawn. Her voice never changed in pitch or volume, but the intensity of the words toward the end punched him in his gut. He rocked back on his heels, an odd sweat breaking out on his brow. He'd had enough. He'd demand that she stop this odd behavior, stop whatever she was doing that caused his discomfiture…

Before he could say another word, Jamie appeared in the bowl.

Micah dropped to his knees, his gaze locked on the one woman he'd ever loved. Within the shining sides of the bowl, his beautiful, odd girl was wearing a drab taupe gown, cheeks streaked with tears. She held Baron's leather lead. She knelt by his side, then turned as they were run down by a white horse.

"Collette," Micah growled low in his chest. The damned bitch. The runner had sworn Collette had nothing to do with the attacks on Jamie's life. Micah gritted his teeth and dug his hands into the marble on either side of the bowl. He should have known that Collette would seduce his spy.

Jamie wasted no time. Micah watched as she scooped up the injured hound and ran back to his home. He watched as his housekeeper followed her into his bed-chamber. He lost his breath when he saw her disappear with Baron through the mirror.

"You," Micah said, looking into Mrs. Knightsbridge's eyes for the first time. "You."

She nodded but pointed to the bowl once more.

It was Collette again. She was paying a thin, cruel-looking man with silver from her ample bosom. The man gave her a wink and a nod, and then he disappeared. When he returned, he was sprinkling a fine powder into some beautiful glasses. In Sir Frederick Lyons' home. A footman was carrying those glasses to Sir Frederick. They were for Micah and Felicity. The toast of their betrothal.

Micah's voice was dismayed as he asked, "Is that occurring now?"

Mrs. Knightsbridge nodded. "You must go and stop it. Then return to see me. I will set things right." She leaned forward and pressed a kiss to Micah's suddenly cold cheek. "Go."

He entered the ballroom at a dead run.

Thirty-Two

THE NEXT THREE MONTHS WENT THE SAME WAY FOR Jamie. Leah popped in to keep watch and mind Baron while Jamie went grocery shopping, but even that stopped after two months. The sweltering summer gave way to brisk fall. Baron's stitches came out, and he lost the lampshade. He ran around her backyard, chasing squirrels and the odd rabbit. He acted happy.

Jamie still waited, afraid to leave that stupid bureau alone.

She wrote music, all of it depressing, horrible crap. Nobody bought it. Her bills mounted higher. She was going to lose the house soon. She let her subscription to the game lapse. She wasn't interested in playing anymore. She wasn't interested in anything but Baron, and the love she'd lost nearly two hundred years ago. She didn't blame Leah for not coming around much. She couldn't stand to be around herself either.

Jamie sat on the floor, rubbing Baron's ears one September night, staring at the bureau and talking to the hound while he licked her bare foot.

"Did I screw this whole thing up, do you think? Should I have done something different? How could I have convinced him that it wasn't his fault, Baron?

Should I have ratted out Mrs. K? I should have, shouldn't I?"

Baron didn't say a word, just continued nibbling at her toes.

"Cut it out, that tickles. Anyway, if I wasn't such a stupid, girly, emotional wreck, then we wouldn't have gone out walking and you wouldn't have gotten hurt. I'm really sorry for that, I hope you know."

A gentle lick on her hand made her smile.

"You're the best dog ever. If your daddy were here, he'd say the same thing. Mike loved you more than anything in this world, you know." Jamie ruffled his ears, wishing the endless tears would freaking stop.

"Except for you, my Jamie. I love Baron more than anything except for you."

Her heart turned into an anatomically correct still-life at the sound of that voice. She kept her eyes locked on Baron, afraid to turn her head. She was sure she wouldn't see anything. There would be nothing there but a ridiculously expensive piece of antique furniture that she had no chance of completely paying for before she hit Social Security age.

"Jamie?"

When he said her name again, she swallowed hard and turned her head without opening her eyes.

"Is it you, Mike? Or do I need to start taking antipsychotics?"

"I am not sure what you mean by that, but it is me. And I love you."

When Jamie opened her eyes, her heart restarted with a vengeance. Mike stood there, in the flesh, his perfectly tailored tan jacket molding against his shoulders, his cravat perfect, and his boots so shiny they gleamed like the mirror he'd apparently traveled through to get to her.

"Mike!" she screamed, and threw herself into his arms, sobbing like a baby. "Oh my God, I'm so glad, I can't believe, it was an awful misunderstanding, all of it, and I never expected, and then Baron, but he's going to be okay, and I can't believe you're here and I missed you and I love you and mmmmmph!"

Mike shut her up by kissing her senseless. Several passionate moments later, a wiggling, bony body wedged its way between them, bringing them back to the present, which happened to be the present she was used to. Only this time, her stunning earl was in it too.

"Baron, lad." Mike kneeled beside his dog, his beautiful eyes glinting suspiciously as the hound attacked his face with a long pink tongue. "What have you done? Mrs. Knightsbridge told me you had been hurt, but you are looking well enough, are you not?" He rubbed the silky ears and let the hound kiss his cheeks.

Jamie smiled so hard she thought her face would break, hiccupping through her tears.

The doorbell rang.

"Hey, don't move," she said to Mike, hugging his shoulders hard as he knelt by the dog. "I'll be right back."

Leah stood at the door with pizza and some DVDs. "Hey, thought you might be hungry. Feel like a movie?"

Jamie grinned like an idiot. "Leah, he's here."

Her eyes went wide as dinner plates. "Here? The earl? Now?"

Jamie nodded, biting her lip to keep from squealing.

"Move over. I need to kick his ass for letting you get hurt."

"Don't you dare! I'll call you tomorrow." Jamie shoved the door shut. Leah banged on it.

"Jamie? Jamie! Open this door!"

Jamie yanked open the door, grabbed the pizza, and slammed it again. "Thanks. Talk to you tomorrow."

"You owe me twelve bucks!"

She walked away, grinning like an idiot.

When she rounded the corner, her heart stopped. The living room was empty.

"Mike?" she called, dropping the pizza onto the coffee table. "Mike?" She ran over to the bureau, tapping on the glass. Solid. "Mike, where are you?"

"I am here, dearling. I am sorry. Baron walked into this room, and I followed to see...oof!" His breath exited in a whoosh as Jamie threw herself at his middle, arms wrapping tightly around him. They stood in the doorway between the kitchen and living room, Baron leaning against both of their legs.

"Sorry," she said to his jacket buttons. "I was afraid you'd left me."

He held her tight. "Never, my love. Never again."

She pulled back enough to look up at his face.

"What made you come here? Don't get me wrong, I'm beyond thrilled that you're here, but I thought you couldn't leave. What happened?"

He sighed and shoved a dark hank of hair from his forehead. "It is a long tale."

She looked up at him with a crooked brow. "I got nothing but time."

They curled up on her couch together like they'd done almost two hundred years earlier, with a pizza and two beers in front of them. After commenting on how different pizza was in this time compared to Jean Philippe's prototype, Mike set down his beer, held her hands, and told her the whole story. He finished by telling her about Collette's man poisoning the champagne for Felicity.

Jamie clapped her hand over her mouth. "Oh my God, is she…"

He rubbed her shoulders, chafing the suddenly goose-bumped skin. "She is fine. I warned her in plenty of time."

"Oh good," she said, feeling guilty that she'd ever wished ill on the stupid blond girl. Nobody deserved that kind of pain.

"Collette was confronted about her crimes. She proved to be quite mad, I'm afraid."

Jamie had always thought she was sort of a peace-loving girl, but she couldn't pretend to be upset that Collette was going to get her just desserts. "What happened?"

He gave a not-quite-guilty smile. "She was shipped to Australia with a number of other convicts."

"I guess I shouldn't wish they hanged her, huh?"

He shook his head. "Those ships are not very nice, I'm afraid."

"Good. I hope rats gnawed her to death…" She trailed off, her thoughts intruding into what should have been a perfect homecoming. She cleared her throat. She had to ask him.

"Mike, it's been months since I've seen you. How much time passed back there for you?"

He looked away and worry sprouted wings to beat against her stomach's inner walls. Had it been longer for him? Even years? She searched his face for new wrinkles, his hair for stray threads of gray.

"It was June of the year of our Lord…" He trailed off, cupping her cheek and looking deep into her eyes. She took a shuddering breath before he continued, "1816."

She expelled the breath in a rush and walloped him gently on the arm. He winced good-naturedly.

"You jerk. You shouldn't have worried me like that." She pressed a quick kiss to his lips.

"You are right, my love. My apologies." He smiled at her but then looked more serious. "I did what I must to protect you, to keep you safe, but I despised myself for the lies I told you."

"When did you lie to me?"

"I let you believe I no longer loved you."

Jamie rested her head on his shoulder. "You did a shit job. I knew you loved me."

He lifted her chin to look into her eyes. "You did?"

She nodded, lifting and kissing his fingers. "Yeah. If not for Baron, I'd have probably stayed to piss you off more."

He chuckled deeply. "Well, despite my failure, I intended to deceive you for your own safety."

He stood up to remove his jacket, and she let her eyes take in the body she'd missed so much over the past few months. He stretched his neck as he loosened his cravat, laying the wrinkled length of white cloth over his coat. He removed his waistcoat and sank back down on the couch next to her, looking as relaxed as she'd ever seen him. She tucked her knees up, wrapping her arms around them as she stared at him. *He's here. He's really, really here with me.*

"So what happened with Mrs. K? I know she was really worried about telling you the truth."

He looked down, a shadow suddenly falling over his eyes. "She is well."

"Are you sure?"

He nodded, leaning closer to her. Her tongue darted out to wet her lips as her body responded to his nearness.

His hand slid to the nape of her neck, drawing her close to him.

"Jamie," he whispered, before taking her lips with a kiss. His touch was as familiar as it was intoxicating. She reveled in the sensations, winding her arms around his neck, rubbing the firm muscles of his shoulders which flexed as he stood and scooped her into his arms.

"Where is your bedchamber?" he asked between kisses.

"Upstairs." She gasped as he passionately attacked her neck with lips and tongue.

He reluctantly allowed her to stand on her own, and she wasted no time grabbing his hand and leading him up the stairs to her bedroom.

They fell together on the bed, clothes being discarded like dandelion tufts in the wind. When they were naked together, she sighed in both relief and delicious feeling.

Mike stopped kissing her breasts to ask, "What is it, dearling?"

Jamie ran her fingers through his dark hair and smiled down at him. Her earl. Her love. "My heart is so full right now."

He smiled and rose on his knees to kiss her lips again. His tongue plundered her, passionately plumbing her depths, and her belly curled and warmed in response. She rubbed her bare leg against his, moaning softly when she hitched it on his hip and brought his erection into contact with her hot, damp core.

"Oh, Jamie love, you feel incredible." Mike fondled her breast, rubbing his way down her belly with one hand, dipping a finger between her damp folds. She cried out as he flicked the hard, tingling nub of her clit. She pressed her hips against his hand, seeking his filling, hard heat.

"Don't make me wait, please," she begged, pressing soft, nipping kisses against his strong collarbone. She ran her fingers through the light dusting of hair on his chest, delighting in the feel of the pebbled, masculine nipples against her palms. He tilted his head back, baring his strong neck to her as her kisses moved higher. She could not stop her hands from traveling lower, gripping his velvet heat at the base. His groan of pleasure wrenched her, her body screaming out for completion that only he could give.

She brought the slick, damp, silken tip of his manhood close to her, rubbing it against her folds. "Please," she begged again. "It's been too damn long."

He had mercy on her. On both of them. When she brought the head of him to the entrance of her body, he wasted no time thrusting home.

Their gasping breaths mingled as their bodies moved, straining against one another for that mutual peak. He looked into her eyes as he moved, passion mixed with tenderness and love. He grew hotter and harder within her, her body pulsing and welcoming him with each of his thrusts. She wrapped her legs around his hips, bringing him deeper into her. He took her hands, twining their fingers together as he pressed them into the pillow beside her head.

Their movements quickened, their breathing grew ragged, and soft moans became frantic cries. When her hips twisted wildly against him and she started cresting the wave of her orgasm, he took her cries into his mouth, releasing his own pleasure deep within her body. He kissed her when it was over, whispering soft words of love, tenderly brushing strands of hair from her forehead.

She fell asleep with their bodies still connected, hugging him to her tightly.

He woke her later as he moved beside her to draw a blanket over them, shielding her skin from the cool air in the room. She yawned and snuggled close to his side.

So," she said, drawing circles in the tufts of springy hair on his chest, "are you staying?"

"If you'll have me."

"Really?" She sat bolt upright, happiness shooting through her like a rocket, eliminating any trace of drowsiness. "You're going to stay here, in my time?"

He smiled. "The *ton* believe that I have run off to the colonies. I quite successfully spread a rumor that my coffers were empty as the result of a wager gone awry. Felicity cried off, as I knew she would. Her father is much too greedy to have accepted a son-in-law with no coin." He drew a lazy circle on her wrist. "My heir is already making plans to step into my suddenly vacant place. Also, I would like to experience the things you have told me of—the computers and cars and things. I have not come empty-handed," he said, a trace of the old autocratic pride tingeing his voice. He reached off the edge of the bed and shook his jacket. A curious jingling noise filled the air. "I have brought the Axelby family jewels and some other precious stones. My countess shall want for nothing."

"Well, that's a relief," she said teasingly. "I wouldn't want you if you weren't filthy rich." She winked so he'd know she was kidding.

He brushed a soft kiss on her lips with a smile. "Also"—he reached off the edge of the bed once more—"there is the small matter of a marriage to attend to."

In his palm lay a gold ring with a huge ruby mounted in the center. "Holy shit," she whispered.

"Miss Marten," he said in his earl voice, the one that was proud, haughty, and a little bit unsure at the very back, "would you do me the very great honor of becoming my bride?"

She thought about waiting. She thought about letting him stew for an hour or two, maybe taking a week or so to think about it…

"*Yes,*" she squealed and threw her arms around his neck. He laughed, squeezing her back. He lifted her and reached for her hand, pushing the ring on her third finger.

"Oh, and there was one more matter," he said, reaching over the edge of the bed again. She barely looked over at him, so enamored was she of the enormous ruby he'd put on her finger.

"This device does not work anymore." He held her smartphone out to her, tapping the dark screen with a petulant expression on his face. "How am I to play with the Angry Birds?"

Jamie laughed so hard; then she kissed him. Her earl, her Mike, her love.

Perfect for her no matter when.

Acknowledgments

The thanks I feel is almost as hard to put into words as the whole book was, but here goes!

Thanks to my wonderful husband, Scotty, who's never left my side. You are my superhero.

Thanks to Dawn Evans, my very first beta reader and one of my best friends. Your faith in me and encouragement kept me going through some of my darkest hours.

Thanks to Heather Mosley-Beers, my partner in romance-novel-pilfering-from-Mom. Without our shared love for love stories, none of this would have happened.

To my mom, for having those books, and to my dad, who didn't complain too much when we read them.

To my BFF Stephanie Brna, who still wants to run through the woods. Love you a lot.

To my lovely coworkers, who continually yell at me to "write faster!"

To the girls of the long-lost CRITS crew, Carissa Elg, Kara Malinczak, and most especially Kendall Grey. Our paths diverged, but without your support, I might have laid down the pen and not tried again. Much love to you all.

To Carrie Jackson, who's helped me grow tremendously as a writer.

To the fabulous ladies of the Heart of Carolina chapter of the RWA. Your support, friendship, and knowledge has been such a help and comfort.

To my sister-from-a-past-life Denise Tompkins. I love you like WHOA, and your genius continues to astound me. To the careers, baby!

To my wonderful agents Fran Black and Jennifer Mishler of Literary Counsel. You took a chance on me, and I am forever grateful. Here's to you!

To Leah Hultenschmidt, my incredible, encouraging editor, and her fantastic crew. You helped me take this book from the rough and turn it into something I'm incredibly proud of. My eternal gratitude goes to you!

About the Author

Gina Lamm, a wisecracking, marshmallow-addicted, dancing geek, loves nothing more than penning funny, emotional tales of love, lust, and entertaining mishaps. Married to a real-life superhero, she lives with her beloved family in rural North Carolina, surrounded by tobacco farms, possums, and the occasional hurricane. When not writing, you can usually find her fishing or playing World of Warcraft. Badly. Visit her online at www.ginalamm.net anytime.

Geek Girls Don't Date Dukes

Gina Lamm

She's aiming to catch a duke.

Leah Ramsey has always loved historical romance novels and dressing in period costumes. So when she has a chance to experience the history for herself, she jumps at it—figuring it can't be too hard to catch the eye of a duke. After all, it happens all the time in her novels.

But sometimes a girl can do even better…

Avery Russell, valet and prize pugilist, reluctantly helps Leah gain a position in the Duke of Granville's household… as a maid. Domestic servitude wasn't exactly what she had in mind, but she's determined to win her happily ever after. Even if the hero isn't exactly who she's expecting…

For more Gina Lamm, visit:

www.sourcebooks.com

Waltz with a Stranger

Pamela Sherwood

One dance would change her life forever...

Aurelia wasn't hiding exactly. She just needed to get out of the crush of the ballroom—away from the people staring at her scar, pitying her limp. She was still quite enjoying the music from the conservatory. And then a complete stranger—dashing, debonair, kind—asked her to waltz. In the strength of his arms, she felt she could do anything. But both would be leaving London soon...

When they meet again a year later, everything has changed. She's no longer a timid mouse. And he's now a titled gentleman—with a fiancée. Is the magic of one stolen moment, one undeniable connection enough to overcome a scandal that would set Society ablaze and tear their families apart?

For more Pamela Sherwood, visit:

www.sourcebooks.com

Waking Up with a Rake

Connie Mason and Mia Marlowe

❧

The fate of England's monarchy is in the hands of three notorious rakes.

To prevent three royal dukes from marrying their way onto the throne, heroic, selfless agents for the crown will be dispatched...to seduce the dukes' intended brides. These wickedly debauched rakes will rumple sheets and cause a scandal. But they just might fall into their own trap...

After he's blamed for a botched assignment during the war, former cavalry officer Rhys Warrick turns his back on "honor." He spends his nights in brothels doing his best to live down to the expectations of his disapproving family. But one last mission could restore the reputation he's so thoroughly sullied. All he has to do is seduce and ruin Miss Olivia Symon and his military record will be cleared. For a man with Rhys's reputation, ravishing the delectably innocent miss should be easy. But Olivia's honesty and bold curiosity stir more than Rhys's desire. Suddenly the heart he thought he left on the battlefield is about to surrender...

❧

For more Connie Mason and Mia Marlow, visit

www.sourcebooks.com

The Wicked Wedding of Miss Ellie Vyne

by Jayne Fresina

❦

When a notorious bachelor seduces a scandalous lady, it can only end in a wicked wedding.

By night Ellie Vyne fleeces unsuspecting aristocrats as the dashing Count de Bonneville. By day she avoids her sisters' matchmaking attempts and dreams up inventive insults to hurl at her childhood nemesis, the arrogant, far-too-handsome-for-his-own-good James Hartley.

James finally has a lead on the villainous, thieving count, tracking him to a shady inn. He bursts in on none other than "that Vyne woman"...in a shocking state of dishabille. Convinced she is the count's mistress, James decides it's best to keep his enemies close. Very close. Seducing Ellie will be the perfect bait...

❦

Praise for *The Most Improper Miss Sophie Valentine*:

"Ms. Fresina delivers a scintillating debut! Her sharply drawn characters and witty prose are as addictive as chocolate!" —Mia Marlowe, author of *Touch of a Rogue*

For more Jayne Fresina, visit:

www.sourcebooks.com

New York Times and *USA Today* bestselling author

Lady Eve's Indiscretion

Grace Burrowes

❧

Lady Eve's got the perfect plan.

Pretty, petite Evie Windham has been more indiscreet than her parents, the Duke and Duchess of Moreland, suspect. Fearing that a wedding night would reveal her past, she's running out of excuses to dodge adoring swains. Lucas Denning, the newly titled Marquis of Deene, has reasons of his own for avoiding marriage. So Evie and Deene strike a deal, each agreeing to be the other's decoy. At this rate matrimony could be avoided indefinitely... until the two are caught in a steamy kiss that no one was supposed to see.

❧

Praise for *Lady Maggie's Secret Scandal*:

"A tantalizing, delectably sexy story that is one of the best yet from an author on the way to the top." —*Library Journal* Starred Review

"A delight...Strikingly unique characters with realistic emotions and exciting antics." —*RT Book Reviews*

For more Grace Burrowes, visit:

www.sourcebooks.com

Once Again a Bride

Jane Ashford

———— ✖ ————

She couldn't be more alone

Widowhood has freed Charlotte Wylde from a demoralizing and miserable marriage. But when her husband's intriguing nephew and heir arrives to take over the estate, Charlotte discovers she's unsafe in her own home…

He could be her only hope…or her next victim

Alec Wylde was shocked by his uncle's untimely death, and even more shocked to encounter his uncle's beautiful young widow. Now clouds of suspicion are gathering, and charges of murder hover over Charlotte's head.

Alec and Charlotte's initial distrust of each other intensifies as they uncover devastating family secrets, and hovering underneath it all is a mutual attraction that could lead them to disaster…

———— ✖ ————

Readers and reviewers are charmed by Jane Ashford:

"Charm, intrigue, humor, and just the right touch of danger." —RT Book Reviews

For more Jane Ashford, visit:

www.sourcebooks.com

National bestselling author

If You Give a Rake a Ruby

Shana Galen

Her mysterious past is the best revenge...

Fallon, the Marchioness of Mystery, is a celebrated courtesan with her finger on the pulse of high society. She's adored by men, hated by their wives. No one knows anything about her past, and she plans to keep it that way.

Only he can offer her a dazzling future...

Warrick Fitzhugh will do anything to protect his compatriots in the Foreign Office, including seduce Fallon, who he thinks can lead him to the deadliest crime lord in London. He knows he's putting his life on the line...

To Warrick's shock, Fallon is not who he thinks she is, and the secrets she's keeping are exactly what make her his heart's desire...

Praise for *When You Give a Duke a Diamond*:

"A lighthearted yet poignant, humorous yet touching, love story—with original characters who delight and enough sizzle to add heat to a delicious read." —*RT Book Reviews*, 4½ stars

For more Shana Galen, visit:

www.sourcebooks.com